BISCUIT & GRACE

Peony Brown

Exit 26 Publishing

ABOUT THE AUTHOR

Dear Readers,

In the intricate tapestry of life, there are threads that, once woven, forever alter the fabric of our existence. Such was my experience as a co-worker alongside a remarkable individual who illuminated my path with the profound wisdom of love and its boundless expressions. For years, we shared the mundane routines of daily work and the more profound, unspoken lessons that only a kindred spirit can impart.

With her unwavering dedication to her family, this extraordinary colleague showcased an authentic embodiment of love's true essence. Her actions spoke louder than words, revealing a patient, kind, and enduring love. Through her, I witnessed the transformative power of love—not the roman-

ticized version often depicted in literature and media, but a steadfast, selfless, and all-encompassing love.

As I navigated my journey, her influence became a cornerstone, shaping my understanding and appreciation of love's pivotal role in our lives. This revelation spurred the creation of this novel, a heartfelt endeavor to encapsulate the lessons learned and the beauty observed. Hopefully, this will resonate with readers, touching hearts and souls and as a gentle reminder of the paramount importance of love.

We often overlook love's simple yet profound impact in our fast-paced world. My colleague's life was a testament to the fact that love, in its purest form, can heal, inspire, and connect us on a profoundly human level. Her legacy of love became the catalyst for my writing, infusing each page with the warmth and authenticity I experienced firsthand.

As you delve into this book, I invite you to open your heart and allow the story and insights to wash over you. May you find inspiration in love's triumphs and challenges, and may it ignite a renewed commitment to embracing love in all its forms. Let us cherish the moments, the people, and the relationships that enrich our lives, and let us never forget that love is the essence of our being.

With heartfelt gratitude,
Peony Brown

P.S.

The wisdom that comes with age reveals a great truth: Grace is not a competition. It is a precious gift bestowed upon us so that we may freely share it with others and spread love in this world. Like a seed planted in fertile soil, grace has the power to grow and flourish when nurtured by kindness and compassion.

In this life journey, we can cultivate grace and bestow it upon those around us. As we give generously, we also receive abundantly—for grace knows no limits, only endless possibilities for love and growth. Let us cherish this beautiful gift and spread its light to all those we encounter on our path.

To the many families who have touched my heart and demonstrated love in its purest form—to you, I dedicate this book. Your acts of kindness, your unwavering support, and the boundless love you share with those around you have been a beacon of hope and inspiration.

Love begins with a single gesture in its most contagious and rewarding state: loving just one person and extending them grace. This grace binds us together in a world where none of us are perfect, and our perspectives often diverge. It allows us to embrace our differences and find common ground in our humanity.

This story is for everyone on their journey to discover the profound impact of loving their neighbor. May we all find the courage to give love a chance, to forgive generously, and to cherish the connections that make our lives richer.

With deepest gratitude and hope,

Peony Brown

CONTENTS

CHAPTER 1

The morning sun gently peeked through the curtains, creating a warm and inviting ambiance in the Steele household. In the kitchen, Rose Steele stood at the stove with her eyes closed, a serene smile adorning her face as she softly sang the hymn "Amazing Grace." The warm, buttery smell of pancakes and sizzling bacon filled the air, mingling with the sweet sound of Rose's voice.

With expert precision, she skillfully flipped pancakes, tended to sizzling bacon, and flawlessly scrambled eggs. Rose's voice, like a melody, filled every corner of the kitchen with a sense of peace and joy. Suddenly, two young voices interrupted her song. "Grandma!" Junior and Ryder burst into the kitchen, their faces flushed with excitement and anticipation for the delicious breakfast before them, their hearts filled with the tranquility and happiness that Rose's singing always brought.

"Patience is a virtue, my darlings," Rose said in her honey-like voice. She knew her grandchildren were always eager for her home-cooked meals, but she also saw it as an opportunity to impart life lessons. Junior couldn't resist the tantalizing aroma wafting through the air and sneakily reached for a piece of bacon when he thought his grandmother wasn't looking. But even with her back turned, Rose's keen intuition caught the mischief in his eyes. "I see you, Junior," she called out gently without missing a beat in her song. The boy grinned sheepishly, popping the stolen treat into his mouth with a satisfied crunch, a mischievous act that added a playful touch to the warmth and love in the kitchen.

"Your singing is so beautiful, Grandma," Ryder said, her admiration for Rose's voice shining through in her tone. It was a truth they all held dear; Rose's voice had a divine quality that could make angels weep, was a powerful force that strengthened their family bond, and her grandchildren never tired of hearing her sing. "Thank you, sweetheart," Rose replied, giving her granddaughter a tender smile. "Now, let's say grace." As they bowed their heads and prayed together, Junior was strongly affected by the strong faith that held their family together. When the prayer ended, he was inspired to try and mimic his grandmother's singing voice, a small but significant act that showed the profound influence of family values and traditions.

Junior's voice rang out, off-key but earnest, as he attempted to sing "Amazing Grace." The family couldn't help but exchange amused glances, but they all appreciated his effort. "Keep practicing, Junior," Rose encouraged, her eyes twinkling affectionately. "Your voice will come in time." As they gathered around the breakfast table, the love and warmth that permeated the Steele household were almost tangible. The comforting scents of the freshly prepared breakfast filled the air, adding to the cozy atmosphere. This family knew the value of faith, hard work, and each other – and it made every day feel like a blessing.

The golden rays of sunlight started to pour through the wide bedroom window, casting a warm glow over the rumpled sheets and scattered clothes strewn across the floor. There stood a handsome, dark-skinned black man looking outside in a state of reflection. The calm and collected atmosphere of Grandmother Rose's home starkly contrasted with the aftermath whirlwind of activity inside Calvin and Lena Steele's bedroom. "Hand me my tie, will you, baby?" Calvin called out as he deftly buttoned up his shirt, his fingers moving with practiced ease.

He saw himself in the mirror, noting the faint smile lines formed over the years - a testament to a life full of love and laughter shared with his beloved wife. "Here," Lena replied breathlessly, tossing the tie over to him while she struggled to get into her stockings without causing any snags on the delicate fabric. "I can't believe we slept in like this." Calvin couldn't help but grin as he fondly recalled their rare evening alone, a much-needed respite from the chaos of raising their animated children. As he fastened his tie, he felt a surge of gratitude for the amazing woman standing by his side, who somehow managed to balance everything with grace and still be there for their children whenever they needed her. The room smelled faintly of perfume and cologne, a reminder of their intimate moments in this private space.

Pausing momentarily, Calvin crossed the room, took Lena's hands, and pulled her close, their embrace filled with love and warmth as they basked in the peaceful morning. They shared a sweet kiss, lost in each other's eyes, a reminder of the unbreakable bond and unwavering faith that has guided them through life's challenges. "Lord knows last night was just what we needed," Calvin whispered, his forehead pressed against hers. "But we have to get going to church. Mama Rose would be upset if we were late." Lena nodded, her gaze drifting to their family photo on the dresser.

The smiling faces of their children, Junior and Ryder, constantly reminded them of the love and hope that filled their home. "I know," she said as they released each other and stepped back. Calvin's mischievous grin appeared as he tied his necktie. "Can't blame us for enjoying ourselves last night." The sun's rays have started to illuminate the steam coming from both of their souls, warming their bedroom once again and illuminating the remnants of their romantic evening. "It truly was special," Lena blushed but couldn't hide her happiness as she fastened her necklace. "Now, let's not keep God waiting. I'm looking forward to the day ahead," she smiled.

"Right, right," Calvin nodded in agreement, taking a moment to give himself a quick once-over in the mirror before striding towards the door. Lena followed suit, smoothing out the fabric of her dress and ensuring it fell just right over her curves. As they finished dressing, they thought of some warm, mouth-watering waffles and imagined the scent wafting into the room, pulling them both from their thoughts and into a state of hunger. The familiar aroma stirred memories of lazy Sunday mornings spent with family and friends, enjoying homemade breakfast delights around the table.

They exchanged knowing glances, each feeling excitement and longing for what usually awaited them downstairs - delicious waffles and quality time with loved ones. However, they felt a duty, and their commitment to their faith and family was beckoning them. "We better hurry," Lena said softly. Her love for Jesus and her family meant more to her than the simple domestic scene that sometimes awaited them below. "I'm coming, my dear," Calvin replied with determination shining in his eyes. They descended the stairs with purpose, each step bringing them closer to the heart of their home, where the scent of waffles would typically be. It was a simple reminder of the life they had built together - one filled with love, resilience, grace, and unwavering devotion to one another and their Lord.

Calvin's hands, strong and sure, quickly popped two frozen waffles into the toaster and grabbed two plates. With unwavering determination, he couldn't deny his wife the pleasure of Sunday waffles after such a beautiful night together. The warm golden smell of melted butter filled the kitchen as he slathered it on the waffles, its richness seeping into every crevice. Lena added a syrup drizzle, its sweet aroma mingling with the comforting scent of breakfast. As they quickly prepared their meal, a sense of urgency hung in the air, matching the rapid beating of Lena's heart. "Lord, help us make it on time," Lena prayed silently, her fingers gripping the counter's edge. "Alright, let's go," she urged, grabbing her purse and leading Calvin toward the door. He nodded in agreement, understanding the importance of being punctual.

"Right behind you, baby," he replied dutifully, following her lead. They paused momentarily at the doorway, taking in the familiar sights of their 1970s middle-class home on the west side of Chicago. Panning over the vibrant wallpaper adorned the walls depicted scenes from nature, while the furniture exuded comfort and nostalgia from their grandparents, who passed down through generations. Family photos beamed proudly from the fireplace mantel, reminding them of the love and faith that anchored their lives together. "Sometimes I wish we could just slow down," Lena murmured wistfully, her gaze lingering on the sunlit living room. "Stay here with the kids, not worry about anything else." "Me too," Calvin admitted with a sigh, his eyes reflecting the same longing. "But we've got our duties, and this is one of 'em." He reached for her hand, giving it a reassuring squeeze. Lena smiled at him gratefully, feeling grateful for this man who stood by her side through thick and thin. "You're right," she said softly, drawing strength from his touch and determination to face whatever responsibilities lay ahead.

Calvin nodded, his eyes following hers to the open doors of their children's bedrooms. The unmade beds and scattered toys spoke of the familiar chaos and love that filled their home daily. He sighed, feeling a pang of guilt for not being there when their children woke up this morning. "Guess we oughta make it up to them later, huh?" he mused, rubbing his chin thoughtfully. His mind raced with ideas of how to make it up to their children and continue strengthening their family bond. The weight of his responsibilities as a father settled heavily on his shoulders, but he knew their love was strong enough to withstand the occasional absence. "Definitely," Lena agreed, her eyes softening at the thought of her children's laughter and excitement filling the house once more. "I miss them."

She allowed herself a moment to bask in the warmth of her love for her family, letting it shine through the shadows of guilt that threatened to creep in. "Hey," Calvin said, reaching to retake her hand. "We're doing our best, you know? And I think that counts for something." Lena turned to him, her grateful smile lighting up the room and pushing away any lingering doubts or guilt. "You're right," she said, squeezing his hand in return. With renewed determination and a reminder of their love for each other and their family, the couple continued towards the door, their thoughts now filled with plans to spend quality time with their children after church.

Lena reluctantly snapped out of her daydream with a gentle sigh and took one last loving glance around their cozy home. Before entering the crisp morning sunlight, she wanted to commit every detail to memory. The air was cool and refreshing, still carrying the faint chill of night on its breath. As they descended the front steps, hand-in-hand, their shoes crunched softly against the gravel path that led to their dependable car. Above them, a symphony of bird song erupted from the lush canopy of leaves, filling the tranquil air with their harmonious melodies. "It's truly a breathtaking day," Lena whispered, tilting her face toward the vibrant blue sky. Calvin nodded in agreement, his gaze drifting up to the delicate white clouds that floated lazily overhead like cotton candy in a sea of azure.

A smile spreads across Calvin's face as the morning sun peeks through the clouds. It had felt like an eternity since they had seen its warm rays, the seemingly endless stretch of rainy days taking its toll on their spirits. The memory of driving his bus through the city streets, windshield wipers working tirelessly against the relentless downpour, flashed through his mind. "Definitely," Lena agreed, pulling her soft cardigan tighter around her shoulders to ward off the lingering chill in the air. "I just hope the weather holds up."

The possibility of spending a leisurely afternoon with their children was a welcome reprieve from the cloud of guilt that hung over them, and she silently prayed that nothing would spoil their plans. "Should be fine," Calvin reassured her with a gentle hand squeeze. "Besides, even if it does rain, we can always make the best of it. You know how much the kids love splashing in puddles." A small smile tugged at Lena's lips as she imagined Junior and Ryder, their two young children, giggling and shrieking as they leaped gleefully from one muddy pool to the next.

As they approached their car, Calvin held open the passenger door for Lena and gently closed it behind her. The smooth click of the door echoed in the quiet morning air. Then he circled to the driver's side, sliding into the seat with practiced ease. "Ready?" he asked, glancing over at Lena as he started the engine. She nodded, her hands clasped tightly in her lap, her eyes fixed on their destination ahead. With a gentle press of his foot, Calvin shifted the car into drive, and they began to move, leaving behind the guilt of the morning while holding on to the lingering memories of last night. They rolled down familiar streets lined with brick buildings and colorful murals, passing by neighbors' houses and small businesses that had become part of their West Side Chicago neighborhood.

As Calvin and Lena walked toward the church, their minds were still preoccupied with the thoughts of last night and the children. The weight of responsibility was lifted from their shoulders briefly, allowing them to savor this rare moment of peace and tranquility. The children were away at Grandmother Rose's house, leaving the couple to explore each other and the city independently. Hand in hand, they strolled through the crisp Sunday morning air, admiring the grandeur of Chicago's West Side.

The historic brick buildings towered above them, their age adding character to the bustling city streets. "Did you see how excited the kids were?" Calvin mused, his chest swelling with pride as he recalled their children's eager anticipation to be away from home overnight. "I swear, we missed them, but I wonder if they even miss us?" His words hung in the air, mingling with the distant sounds of traffic and laughter from nearby storefronts. Despite their doubts, Calvin and Lena continued their peaceful stroll, grateful for this stolen moment together amidst the whirlwind of parenthood and city life.

Lena let out a soft, melodic laugh that filled the air with warmth and light. Her hand squeezed his gently, sending waves of reassurance through him. "Oh, honey, they're just growing up." Calvin couldn't help but smile at her words. She always had a way of putting things in perspective. "Look on the bright side," she continued, "we had some time to ourselves for once." The simple joy of their conversation washed over him, grounding him in the present moment.

As they approached the church, its towering presence came into view, covered in a blanket of vibrant ivy. The cool morning air carried birds chirping and the sounds from other churches in the distance. Soon enough, the grand entrance loomed before them, adorned with intricate carvings and stained-glass windows. "Morning, Brother Calvin!" an elderly man dressed in a crisp suit greeted them warmly, extending his arm for a hearty handshake. "Sister Lena! Good to see you!" His voice boomed with genuine affection as he welcomed them into the place of worship.

"Good morning, Brother James," Lena smiled warmly, embracing the man briefly. As they entered the church, the couple embraced greetings with a flurry of welcome from their fellow members. The air inside had the scents of old wood and incense, and the quiet creaks of the pews echoed through the space. The stained-glass windows bathed everything in a soft, ethereal light, casting vibrant colors across the walls and floor. "Calvin, Lena, good morning!" The Pastor's booming voice rang out from across the room, his genuine happiness radiating towards them.

"Seeing the entire Steele family attending our service is always a pleasure." "Good morning, Pastor," Calvin replied, returning his smile. "Wouldn't miss it for the world." Lena leaned in close to her husband as they approached their usual seats. "Calvin, we completely forgot about cooking for today's church dinner," she whispered urgently. His eyes widened at the sudden realization, and he muttered, "Ah, shoot." They had been so caught up in their night alone together that they had forgotten their church community duties. Glancing around at the expectant faces of their fellow congregants, Calvin knew they would have to find a way to make it up to them.

The warmth of Lena's hand enveloped Calvin's like a gentle embrace, grounding him amid their shared unease. He could feel the weight of responsibility settling on his shoulders like it did every time he navigated his bus through the chaotic streets of Chicago. "Maybe we can brainstorm during the long sermon," Lena suggested with a hopeful smile, her eyes darting toward the Pastor as he continued greeting other congregation members. She was a woman who always found solutions, even in the face of seemingly impossible situations. It was one of the many reasons why Calvin loved her so deeply. "Y'know what, that ain't a bad idea," Calvin nodded, feeling a spark of hope.

The gears in his mind started turning, searching for a solution to their predicament. "I could slip out and buy a few buckets of chicken." Lena's eyes lit up at the suggestion, her laughter bubbling beneath the surface. Their fellow church members would never suspect that the savory fried chicken wasn't homemade, and it would save them from disappointing everyone with an empty table at the church dinner. They both stifled a chuckle at the thought of escaping from the tedious sermon for a noble cause. "Alright," Lena said with a mischievous twinkle in her eye as she gently rubbed Calvin's backside. The familiar touch sent a reassuring tingle up his spine, reminding him they were together. "Let's see how it goes."

The somber notes of the organ filled the sanctuary, signaling the start of the service. Calvin's heart raced as he offered a silent prayer for guidance. Though he was dedicated to his faith, sitting through the lengthy sermon felt like a heavy burden compared to the urgent need to provide food for their community. He wondered if God would understand the motivations behind his potential absence from the pew today. The thought of Rose, their matriarch and staunch believer, sitting on the same row made him hesitate. She had instilled in them the importance of attending church, and he didn't want to disappoint her.

But with each passing minute, Calvin's mind wandered to the empty bellies and hungry faces waiting for their weekly meal at the church's soup kitchen. "God works in mysterious ways," Lena whispered, reassuringly squeezing his hand. Her touch brought him back to reality, her intuition always in tune with his thoughts. He knew he had to balance his faith with today's pressing task - providing sustenance for their church family. As Pastor Johnson launched his sermon, Calvin offered one last glance towards Lena, who nodded encouragingly, giving him the strength he needed to fulfill his duties as a faithful follower and a provider for his community.

Junior and Ryder slid into their familiar spot beside Calvin and Lena, the worn wooden pews of the small church creaking softly beneath them. The air inside was oh so familiar, thick with the scent of old hymnals and lemon-scented polish, a delightful combination that filled the hearts of the Steele family every Sunday morning. Rays of sunlight filtered through stained glass windows, casting colorful patterns on the polished floors and illuminating the rows of bowed heads. "Mom, Dad! We missed you last night!" Junior exclaimed, his eyes shining like polished marbles.

His parents smiled warmly at him as they exchanged greetings, their voices mingling with the soft murmur of prayers from nearby worshippers. "We missed you too," Calvin replied, affectionately ruffling Junior's hair before turning to Lena and taking her hand in his own. A sudden silence fell as the preacher stepped up to the pulpit, causing Calvin to glance at Lena for assurance on the timing of their departure. Her fingers fiddled nervously with the delicate lace trim of her dress, but her eyes were steady and unwavering. She gestured towards the exit with a subtle nod, urging him to fetch the fried chicken before it was too late. Junior, never one to let a conversation die, eagerly launched into a detailed whispering account of their Sunday school lesson.

Calvin gently placed a finger to his lips, silencing his son with a warm smile. "You can tell me all about it while we run a quick errand, okay?" "But why are we leaving during the sermon?" Junior asked, his brow furrowed in confusion. Junior felt his father's actions went against everything he had taught about respecting and listening to the preacher's words. "Trust me, son," Calvin assured him, leading Junior towards the door with a firm hand on his shoulder. "It's important."

As they slipped out of the church, the muted sounds of the organ filled the air, lending a sense of urgency to their mission. Junior's mind raced with questions, but he remained quiet as they made their way to the car. "Alright," Calvin said once they were safely inside, "Tell me everything you learned in Sunday school today." Junior's face lit up again, his earlier confusion momentarily forgotten as he eagerly recounted the day's lesson, knowing his father would listen with genuine interest and guidance. Junior couldn't help but feel a sense of peace and contentment, knowing he was at his father's side in church and life.

The low hum of the car engine melded harmoniously with the distant sound of church bells, creating a soothing melody that filled the streets of their west side Chicago neighborhood. As Calvin deftly maneuvered the vehicle through the familiar streets, the warm light filtering through the car windows cast a golden glow on Junior's face. The sunlight danced across his features, illuminating the earnestness in his eyes as he eagerly continued his account of the morning's events. "Anyway, Dad," Junior said, his voice brimming with excitement, "Grandma Rose made breakfast this morning, and you wouldn't believe how delicious it was! She even made her famous biscuits from scratch that I made into a sandwich with the bacon."

Calvin couldn't help but smile at his son's enthusiasm, knowing that these simple moments spent with family were what truly mattered in life. As they drove along, the houses and storefronts lining the streets seemed to take on a more vibrant hue, as if imbued with the warmth and affection coursing through the Steele family. "Sounds like you all had a wonderful time at Grandma's house," Calvin mused, glancing at Junior with pride in his eyes.

He couldn't help but feel a pang in his chest at his son's words, knowing that these moments were fleeting and it was up to them to cherish them as tightly as possible. It was a lesson he had learned early on from his mother, who had always stressed the importance of cherishing and holding onto the love and connections that bound them together. "Son," Calvin said softly, gently squeezing Junior's shoulder, "always remember that family is our most important thing. The love we share, the memories we make – those are what will carry us through the tough times." As Junior nodded solemnly, taking his father's words to heart, Calvin couldn't help but feel grateful for the life they had built together as a strong and loving family.

CHAPTER 2

Back at church, Ryder leaned closer to her mother, Lena, a mischievous glint in her eyes as she recounted her younger brother's morning antics. Her lips curled into a smile as she thought about the chaos that ensued when Junior had cleaned out Grandmother Rose's supply of bacon that morning. Lena's laughter lines deepened around her eyes as she glanced over at Rose, who sat beside them. Just thinking about the warm aroma of bacon filled the air, making Ryder's stomach growl in anticipation. "Wow, he must've been starving," Lena chuckled. "Can't blame him,"

Rose joined in, adjusting her church hat and casting a shadow on her face. "He's growing so fast." She paused, then added with a sly smile, "Plus, I may have sprinkled some brown sugar on it. You know how he loves sweet things." The memory of the savory-sweet combination made Ryder's mouth water. She recalled how Junior practically devoured his plateful of bacon earlier that morning. "That brown sugar just took it to another level," she mused, her stomach rumbling in agreement. "Junior even beat me to finishing his portion." The warmth of the church community made the shared laughter and love even more palpable, making everyone feel included and part of the family.

"Your brother always had an insatiable appetite," Lena said, a fond smile playing on her lips as she gently ran her fingers over the pages of her well-worn Bible. Still thinking about the smell of freshly cooked bacon lingered in her mind, causing Ryder's stomach to grumble with hunger. "Can't blame him," she admitted with a chuckle. She couldn't help but wonder if her brother was also dreaming about that heavenly breakfast. "It was delicious." "Grandma knows best," Rose said with pride, winking at Ryder. "The secret to a good meal is love – and just the right amount of seasoning."

Ryder's smile turned thoughtful as she thought about her aspirations. "Maybe I should learn from you, Grandma," she mused, her eyes shining with determination. "I

want to make people happy with my cooking, too."
"Anytime, dear," Rose replied warmly, gently squeezing
Ryder's hand. "I'll teach you everything I know." Gratitude and love swelled in Ryder's heart for the strong
women surrounding her – her grandmother and mother – who were like guiding stars, lighting up her path.
She knew she could achieve anything she wanted with
their unwavering support and guidance.

Calvin's eyes wandered to his son, Junior, who sat
beside him in the front seat. The boy's eyelids fluttered
closed every few moments, but each time they did, a
wide grin spread across his face. Calvin couldn't help
but marvel at the innocence and wonder radiating from
his young son. What secrets and dreams danced behind
those closed eyelids? "Brown sugar bacon," Junior murmured, his words barely audible above the humming
of the car engine. Calvin chuckled, feeling a rush of
warmth at the mention of their breakfast at Grandma Rose's earlier that morning. The memory of sweet,
crispy bacon still lingered on his tongue. "Sure was
something, huh?" he asked, glancing at his son with an
affectionate grin. "How much of that bacon did you put
away, anyway?" "Until Grandma said it was time to go,"
Junior replied with a sheepish grin, his eyes opening to
meet his father's gaze.

Calvin couldn't help but admire how quickly his little boy grew up – and how much food it seemed to take to fuel that growth. "Growing boys need their strength," Calvin said with a nod, reaching over to tousle Junior's hair playfully, causing his son to swat his hand away with a laugh. "Just remember, there's more to life than good food. You gotta feed your soul, too." "Like going to church and helping out in the community?" Junior asked, his brow furrowing as he considered his father's words. "Exactly," Calvin affirmed, feeling a swell of pride in his chest as he saw the understanding dawning in his son's eyes. "Grandma Rose has been teaching you about Jesus, and I want you to hold onto those lessons.

They'll guide you through life's ups and downs." Junior nodded thoughtfully, the playful grin on his face fading into a more serious expression as he took in his father's sage advice. Calvin knew that, although Junior still had much to learn, his son would grow up to be a strong, kind-hearted man who could face life's challenges with grace and resilience – one day at a time.

As they pulled into a coveted spot in front of their favorite local chicken joint, Calvin couldn't help but feel a sense of comfort and familiarity. Junior's eyes lit up as he looked through the window at the familiar tables and chairs, his mouth watering at the thought of their delicious meals. The scent of seasoned fried chicken drifted out onto the street, tempting passersby with its savory aroma. "Man, I love this place," Junior exclaimed excitedly, unbuckling his seatbelt and practically bouncing. "I never thought I'd be cool with slipping out of church for some chicken, but since we're taking it back for dinner, I guess it's all right." Calvin chuckled at his son's enthusiasm, grateful he wasn't upset about their impromptu detour.

"Listen, your mom and I didn't get a chance to cook for the church dinner last night," he admitted sheepishly, rubbing the back of his neck. "So, we're going to buy some chicken instead. And what better choice than this place?" Junior grinned and said, "Amen," before eagerly opening the car door and stepping onto the sidewalk. As they entered the restaurant, the warm and inviting atmosphere enveloped them, along with the tantalizing smells of crispy fried chicken and comforting side dishes. Calvin couldn't wait to indulge in his favorite meal from their go-to spot, knowing that it would always be a special treat for him, his family, and all the church members.

With each step into the cozy restaurant, Calvin couldn't help but feel a sense of warmth and familiarity. He glanced over at his son, Junior, who eagerly took in the sights and smells of the mouth-watering food behind the counter. The tantalizing aroma of spices and herbs filled the air, causing his stomach to grumble in hunger. At that moment, he felt a surge of gratitude for Junior's ability to find joy in life's simple pleasures - something Calvin had always tried to instill in his children.

Calvin spoke up as they neared the counter, reminding them of their family values. "Remember, though," he said, "we can enjoy good food, but we should never forget to nourish our souls too. That's why we go to church and help our community." Junior nodded, a smile spreading across his face as he recalled the countless Sunday school lessons with his Grandmother Rose. "About Jesus and taking care of others?" he asked enthusiastically.

Before Calvin could respond, the plump cashier greeted them with her kind face and tight curls framing her cheeks. "Well, hello there, Mr. Steele!" she exclaimed with genuine delight. "What brings you here on this beautiful Sunday morning?" Calvin felt a blush creep up his neck as he stumbled over his words under the weight of his family's expectations and role as a father and husband. "Uh, well," he began, "we needed chicken for tonight's church dinner. We didn't have time to cook last night." The cashier smiled knowingly, her eyes crinkling at the corners. "Ah, I see. The kids must have been with their grandmother," she said with a playful wink, causing Calvin to fidget with embarrassment.

As they waited for their order, Junior furrowed his brow in curiosity. "What does that have to do with anything?" he questioned, looking between his father and the cashier. Calvin chuckled, placing a hand on Junior's shoulder. "Absolutely nothing, son." Their laughter filled the small restaurant, bringing a sense of ease to everyone around them. As Calvin received their order - several bags filled with golden-brown deliciousness - he couldn't help but appreciate the community surrounding them. "Here you go, Mr. Steele," the cashier said with a smile, handing over their food and a few extra biscuits for the family.

As Calvin's heart swelled with gratitude, he turned to Junior and said, "Thank you." The warmth in his voice put a bright glimmer in Junior's eyes. They left the cozy restaurant, arms laden with bags of fried chicken that filled the air with a mouth-watering aroma. The crisp morning air brushed against their cheeks as they returned to their car. "Let's hurry back to church," Junior exclaimed, his grin returning as he surveyed their delicious bounty. "I bet everyone will be ecstatic when we show up with this!" Calvin nodded in agreement, his determination renewed by the joy on his son's face.

Despite taking an unexpected detour from the church's pews, which was his original plan, they were still fulfill-ing their commitment to their church community – and, more importantly, to each other. As they walked back to the car, Calvin couldn't help but feel a sense of reassurance – no matter their challenges, their unwavering faith and love for one another would see them through. "Right behind you, Dad," Junior said proudly, mirroring his father's smile. With this thought in mind, they drove towards the church, where the community eagerly awaited their return.

The congregation gathered in their vibrant 1970s attire in the dimly lit church basement. The women wore colorful maxi dresses adorned with floral patterns and wide-brimmed hats perched atop their heads. Meanwhile, the men donned patterned button-up shirts tucked into tailored slacks. Laughter reverberated off the peeling, faded wallpaper that lined the room's walls. "Look at everyone! They're so happy to be here, Junior," Calvin whispered, his voice laced with pride as he carried buckets of crispy fried chicken into the bustling room.

The scent of savory spices filled the air, mingling with the aroma of other homemade dishes spread across several tables. The joy on their faces was a testament to the love and appreciation they felt for the community. "Sure looks like it, Dad," Junior replied, unable to suppress his grin as he saw the lively gathering. Amidst the warm chatter and joyful atmosphere, he couldn't help but feel a sense of belonging. "Ah, there's your grandmother," Calvin said, nodding towards Rose, who was engrossed in conversation with a group of ladies from the church choir. Her infectious laughter rang clear and bright, harmonizing with the clinking of silverware and chairs scraping against the linoleum floor.

"Let's get this food on the table before she notices we're back," Calvin suggested, urging Junior forward. Together, they set down the buckets among a plethora of home-cooked dishes. Junior's mouth watered at the sight of tender collard greens, golden cornbread, and bubbling macaroni and cheese. "Calvin! Junior!" Lena called out with a wave at her husband, along with Ryder. "Come join us!" "Where have you two been?" Ryder asked teasingly, her eyes narrowing as she studied the buckets of chicken. "Uh, we just had to run a quick errand," Calvin explained while shooting Junior a warning glare. "Ah, I see," Ryder said knowingly, a playful smile tugging at her lips. "Well, your secret's safe with me." "Thanks, sis," Junior whispered, grateful for her understanding.

Amidst the lively chatter and clinking of silverware, the church Pastor stepped up to the microphone, tapping it gently to capture everyone's attention. The room gradually quieted as he began to speak, his voice resonating with warmth and sincerity that echoed throughout the walls.

"Brothers and sisters," he began, his eyes scanning the sea of smiling faces before him. "Thank you all for coming together today to share this special meal." Junior could feel the love and gratitude from the Pastor's words, enveloping him in a warm embrace. He looked around at the familiar faces of his family, friends, and fellow church members who had become like an extended family over the years.

They had each other's backs through thick and thin, which Junior cherished deeply. "We are truly blessed to have such a loving and supportive community," the Pastor continued, his voice ringing sincerely. As everyone closed their eyes in prayer, Junior felt a sense of peace wash over him. He bowed his head in gratitude for the delicious food before them and the unbreakable bond of love and fellowship that held them together. In that moment, surrounded by those he held dear, Junior knew there was no place he'd rather be than here with his beloved community, united by their unwavering faith.

The words "truly blessed" hung in the air as Junior closed his eyes in prayer, enveloped in the love and warmth of this faithful community. The rhythmic clink of silverware against plates and the low murmur of conversations filled the room, accompanied by the delightful scents of fried chicken and sweet potato pie. He could feel the vibrations of laughter and stories resonating through the space, a comforting embrace that made him feel welcomed and truly at home. Suddenly, a loud voice, starkly contrasting the peaceful ambiance, broke through the tranquility from the church basement entrance.

Calvin's long-time friend and fellow bus driver, Biscuit, strolled in with a wide grin. He scanned the room before heading straight for the food table, his eyes lighting up at seeing the feast before him. "Hey there, Calvin!" he exclaimed cheerfully. "Looks like you've found your way to God's house after all," Calvin said with a playful smirk. Biscuit chuckled and piled his plate high with golden-brown chicken and a generous helping of collard greens. "You know it, my man," he replied between bites. "And the good Lord has blessed us with some mighty fine grub today."

As he watched his friend enjoy his meal, Calvin couldn't help but think about the power of belief and how it can bring people together unexpectedly. Despite not attending the earlier service, Biscuit had found his way to this gathering, a powerful testament to the unifying force of faith. He was now sharing in this particular moment with them.

Calvin playfully scolded Biscuit as he reached for a piece of chicken from the overflowing plate in his hand. "Come on, Biscuit, this chicken is for those who were here to worship today," he scolded, a hint of amusement tugging at the corners of his lips. Biscuit shot him a sly grin and balanced his overloaded plate with one hand. "Well, Calvin, I reckon you believe enough for the both of us, don't you?" he retorted, mischief glinting in his eyes. Calvin couldn't help but think of his son – nicknamed "Junior" – as he watched Biscuit jokingly tease him. Despite their differences and paths in life, they were all part of this close-knit community brought together by love, loyalty, and faith in something greater than themselves.

With a chuckle and a shake of his head, Calvin gave in to Biscuit's request to enjoy the meal without attending the service. But he made a mental note to remind him to join them next time, knowing that deep down, Biscuit was just as much a believer as anyone else in his way.

As Biscuit weaved through the crowded church to find a seat, Calvin couldn't help but feel a sense of warmth and familiarity in the air. These people were more than just neighbors or acquaintances—they were family. And despite any differences or disagreements they may have had, they were all united in their shared beliefs and love for each other.

As the congregation settled in for the meal and Biscuit laughed and joked with those around him, Calvin couldn't help but feel grateful for this tight-knit community he was lucky to call his church home. He closed his eyes and let their voices wash over him, comforted by their presence and reminded again of the power of faith and family.

CHAPTER 3

The neon lights of Sal's Bar flickered in the darkness, casting an eerie glow on the deserted streets. Biscuit pushed open the creaky door, and he immediately felt the nostalgia. As he stepped inside, the smell of fried food and stale beer hit him like a wave. His stomach rumbled in protest, still content from the church potluck earlier that evening. The dimly lit room greeted him, its sparsely populated tables casting ominous shadows against the worn wooden floor. "Sunday night," he thought with a wry smile, taking in the thin crowd. "Always a quiet one."

As Biscuit sauntered up to the bar, his boots thudded on the ground in rhythmic taps, reminiscent of the blues music that often filled the air on busier nights. The familiar scent of cigarette smoke hung heavy in the air, mixed with notes of musk and sweat from the handful of patrons scattered throughout the bar. "Evenin', Sal," Biscuit called out to the Bartender, who nodded in recognition without looking up from polishing a glass. "Same as always?" Sal asked, his gravelly voice carrying across the near-empty room. "Make it a double, my man," Biscuit replied, rubbing his hands together in anticipation. He sat at the worn wooden bar and sighed, feeling at home in this grimy little establishment.

Biscuit's eyes wandered to the far corner, where the sounds of unbridled joy bounced off the walls. A small group of stunning women adorned with vibrant, flowing dresses perched on stools like colorful birds of paradise, their positive energy radiating effortlessly. The sight brought a familiar warmth to Biscuit, akin to the feeling of taking that first sip of smooth bourbon on a fantastic summer night. "Evening, ladies," he greeted with a winning smile, sliding effortlessly into an empty seat beside them. "Ain't it a lovely night?" One of the women returned his grin, her eyes lighting up like twinkling stars in the dimly lit room.

Biscuit couldn't help but catch his breath at the sight of her broad and genuine smile – it was enough to make his heart skip one beat but two. "The name's Biscuit," he introduced himself, extending a hand in greeting. "I drive the city bus, you know. Been doin' it for years." "Pleasure to meet you, Biscuit," the woman replied with a firm handshake. "I'm Veronica. And this is my sister, Denise, and our dear friend, Lisa." "Charmed," Biscuit responded with a playful tip of an imaginary hat. "So tell me, what brings such lovely ladies out on a quiet night like this?"

Veronica took a small sip of her brightly-colored cocktail. Her lips pursed in satisfaction. "Girl's night out," she explained with a grin. "We needed some time away from the daily grind, you know?" Biscuit nodded understandingly, his mind drifting back to his busy day filled with mundane tasks and responsibilities. But now, surrounded by the soft glow of dim lights and the low hum of chatter, he felt a sense of release. It was a sharp contrast to the lively church potluck he had attended earlier, but somehow, this dark bar felt just as warm and welcoming. "Here's to new friends," he proposed, raising his glass in a toast.

The women eagerly followed suit, their glasses clinking together in a chorus of camaraderie. "Cheers," they chorused, each sipping their respective drinks. As the evening progressed, Biscuit felt closer to the women's group. Their laughter bubbled over and echoed through the bar, their stories weaving a tapestry of adventure and excitement. He felt completely at ease and connected with those around him for once. Could this be it? A chance for something real? His heart swelled with hope as he settled into the rhythm of the night, grateful for this unexpected moment of joy and companionship.

Biscuit's gaze swept over the women, capturing every detail of their alluring features. The soft smiles that curved their lips and the sparkling eyes that shone like stars against the dark backdrop of the bar enticed him. His heart raced with anticipation, a mix of excitement and uncertainty as he pondered his next move. Each of the three ladies – Veronica, Denise, and Lisa – held their unique allure, and Biscuit was captivated by them all. "Guess what I'm thinkin'?" he said, spreading a mischievous grin. "It's time for some good old-fashioned dessert tonight." Denise, the one with long, silky hair cascading down her shoulders, arched an eyebrow and replied with a hint of amusement in her voice, "I don't know why you're sayin' that when you come in here smellin' like sweet potato pie." "Ah, well," Biscuit chuckled, leaning closer to her and lowering his voice to a whisper, "that would be because you're smellin' my thoughts of you on my plate." He winked playfully, hoping to charm her with his smooth words and lighten the mood. The air around them seemed to hum with electricity as they bantered back and forth, drawing closer to each other with every word exchanged. At that moment, Biscuit knew he was where he wanted to be.

His eyes stayed fixed on her face, tracing the path of her lips as they curved into a small smile. A faint blush tinged her cheeks, adding to her already captivating beauty. Had he gone too far with his teasing? The thought nagged at the back of his mind, but the warmth and laughter from the group kept it at bay. They seemed genuinely amused by his antics; for once, he felt like he belonged. It was a refreshing change for a man whose last relationship had been with someone he could only describe as unstable. "Smooth talker, huh?" Denise teased, her eyes twinkling with amusement. Biscuit couldn't help but grin in response, feigning innocence. "Just callin' it like I see it." He took a long swig of his beer, relishing the cold, bitter liquid as it slid down his throat. Despite appearing calm, his mind raced, analyzing every word and gesture from himself and Denise. He searched for any hint of reciprocation, hoping that this time, he wouldn't end up chasing after another woman who didn't honestly care for him. Tonight was different - he could feel it in the air - and he was determined to make the most of it.

Biscuit breathed a deep sigh of relief, feeling his stress melt away as he sank onto the well-worn barstool. The scent of aged wood and spilled drinks filled his senses, mixed with the lingering aroma of perfume and sweat. He set his glass down on the rough surface of the bar, admiring the way the light played off its imperfections.

"You ladies are like a breath of fresh air," Biscuit confessed, taking in the warm smiles and genuine gazes of the three women beside him. "I've met too many gals with nothin' but heartache to offer."

"Maybe you were just lookin' in the wrong places," Lisa suggested, her voice soft and soothing like a summer breeze. Her words felt like a balm to Biscuit's weary soul.

"Or maybe I was just waitin' for y'all to come along," Biscuit countered playfully, a glint of hope shining in his tired eyes.

As their conversation flowed and laughter filled the dimly lit bar, Biscuit felt a growing connection with these women who seemed so open-hearted compared to those he had encountered in the past. For once, he dared to imagine that maybe this time, he might find something worth holding onto.

Amidst the clinking glasses and boisterous conversations, Biscuit couldn't help but feel grateful for this unexpected encounter - a small but powerful beacon of light amidst the shadows of his past mistakes.

The women's laughter echoed through the night like church bells on a Sunday morning, their eyes twinkling with amusement. Biscuit felt a warmth spread through his chest like the sun rising after a long winter night. It had nothing to do with the whiskey and beer he'd been nursing throughout the evening but everything to do with the companionship of these kind and welcoming women. He smiled back at them, surprised by their genuine reception. "Y'all sure know how to make a man feel welcome," Biscuit said, his voice tinged with gratitude. The women scooted closer, eager to continue their conversation as the hours passed. Their voices melded together in a symphony of friendship and curiosity. "Tell me something, Biscuit," Lisa asked, her dark curls bouncing as she leaned in. "What made you become a city bus driver?" Biscuit rubbed his chin thoughtfully, considering her question. "I guess I just like helpin' people get where they need to go," he answered honestly. "I ain't no superhero or nothin', but it feels good to be doin' my part." "Sounds like you got a big heart," Denise remarked, her eyes filled with appreciation. "Not many men would admit to somethin' like that." "Maybe they should," Biscuit replied, feeling encouraged by her words. "Ain't no shame in carin' 'bout others." "Here, here!" Veronica chimed in, raising her glass in agreement. Biscuit followed suit, the clink of his tumbler against hers ringing out like a toast to newfound friends and camaraderie.

As the night wore on, their conversation shifted from lighthearted banter to deeper, more profound topics. Biscuit opened up about his friendship with Calvin and his guilt for not always being there when needed. The women listened intently, their compassion and understanding radiating from their every word. "Sounds like you're turnin' over a new leaf," Lisa observed, her hand resting gently on Biscuit's arm. "We all make mistakes, but what matters is learnin' from 'em and movin' forward." Biscuit felt a sense of catharsis over him as he absorbed her wise words. "Y'all are wise beyond your years," he said, his eyes misting with emotion. "I never thought I'd find such understandin' in a place like this." "Life's funny like that," Denise mused, her lips curving into a knowing smile. "Sometimes you find what you need when you least expect it - be it a good whiskey or good company."

As the last call echoed through the bar, Biscuit reluctantly pushed himself up, his heart heavy with the knowledge that the evening was ending. But as the women he had spent the night with exchanged phone numbers, promising to stay in touch, a spark of hope ignited. "Thank you for tonight," Biscuit said, his voice thick with sincerity. He couldn't deny the warmth and joy that had filled him during their time together. "Y'all have given me somethin' I didn't even know I was missin'." Lisa's eyes shone with genuine kindness as she replied, "Anytime, Biscuit. Don't be a stranger now, ya hear?" Biscuit nodded, feeling a weight lifted off his shoulders. For the first time in years, he felt pleased and grateful for the company of these incredible women.

Meanwhile, across the bustling city of Chicago, a modest brick house nestled in the quiet neighborhood of the west side. Calvin and Lena Steele sought refuge and solace after a long day. They were greeted by a warm and cozy atmosphere as they entered their bedroom. The walls were adorned with family photos, capturing moments of love and laughter frozen in time. A well-loved Bible rested on the nightstand, its worn spine a testament to years of use. After shedding his clothes, Calvin watched Lena move gracefully around the room, her pretty feet padding softly against the polished wooden floorboards. The soft glow of the bedside lamp cast warm, golden shadows on the walls, creating an intimate ambiance that enveloped them both. Lena slipped into a simple cotton nightgown, not as alluring as the silky one she had worn the night before but still breathtaking in Calvin's eyes. Her beauty transcended material possessions or fleeting moments; it was a timeless grace that radiated from within.

With a contented sigh, he leaned back against the plush headboard, his unwavering gaze fixed on her every movement. "Darlin', you always look beautiful," he murmured, reaching out to take her hand. His love for her shone through his eyes like a beacon of light amidst a sea of darkness. Lena felt her heart swell with warmth at his words, a simple yet powerful reminder of how much he cherished her. "Thank you, Calvin," she replied softly, savoring the feeling of his hand in hers. A blush rose to her cheeks, making her feel like a giddy teenager again. "It's been such a long day, but moments like this make it all worthwhile." "Moments like these..." Calvin mused, thinking of all the little instances throughout their day when they stole glances or shared knowing smiles. With their daily jobs as a city bus driver and a nurse, they were all too familiar with life's daily grind. But their love for each other and faith in God remained strong like an oak tree standing tall against the fiercest storms. "Jesus gives us strength," Lena added, her voice gentle yet full of conviction. "And when I look at you, our children, I know that everything we go through has a purpose."

Calvin's eyes welled up with tears as he thought of their son, Junior, and daughter, Ryder. These two young souls embodied the strength and compassion of their parents, a testament to their resilience and love. They were their pride and joy, the most significant achievement, and the legacy they would leave behind. "Every day, I thank God for you and the kids," Calvin confessed, his voice trembling with emotion. His arms tightened around Lena as he whispered, "You are my rock, Lena. Without you, I wouldn't have the strength or courage to face anything." In that moment, as they held each other close, their bodies fitting together like puzzle pieces, Calvin and Lena found comfort in their unbreakable bond and unwavering devotion – a love that transcended time, distance, and any challenges life could throw at them. As they stood embraced in the soft glow of lamplight, shadows danced on the walls around them, a reminder that their connection was sacred and destined to last a lifetime.

The gentle hum of cicadas filled the warm night air as Calvin and Lena Steele slipped between their bed's cool, crisp sheets. The moonlight filtered through the sheer curtains, casting a soft glow over Lena's face as she turned to face Calvin. His heart swelled with love at the sight of her, his fingers tracing the curve of her shoulder, feeling the warmth radiating from her skin. There was the beginning of a half-smile played at the corners of Lena's mouth, a mix of affection and teasing that made Calvin's heart skip a beat. In this intimate moment, their love for each other was palpable, filling the room with a sweet, romantic aura that enveloped them in a passionate embrace.

"Now, now," Lena scolded gently, her eyes twinkling with amusement. "Remember, the kids are in the house tonight."

"Shoot, how could I forget?" Calvin replied with a playful grumble. He sighed and leaned back against the pillows, gazing at the ceiling. But Lena couldn't resist teasing him a bit more. Their playful banter, filled with lighthearted energy and joy, was a testament to their enduring love and strong bond.

"You were quite noisy last night," she said playfully, her laughter like wind chimes on a summer breeze.

"Well, can you blame me?" Calvin shot back with a grin. "We were kid-free, and my wife was so beautiful, I couldn't help it." As he spoke, he reached for a small towel from the bedside table and folded it neatly before placing it between his teeth. His eyes met Lena's, a challenge flickering in their depths as if daring her to resist him.

"Better?" he mumbled through the fabric, eyebrows raised mischievously.

"Much," Lena responded with a contented sigh. She snuggled closer to him, resting her head on his chest and listening to the steady rhythm of his heartbeat. As they lay together in peaceful silence, Calvin's thoughts turned inward.

"Lord knows we need these moments," he thought, his chest tight with emotion. "This love, this family, it's worth fighting for."

Breaking the comfortable stillness between them, Calvin whispered, "Say, Lena?"

"Hmm?" she hummed, her voice muffled against his chest.

"Thank you for everything you do for us," he said sincerely. "You're my rock, darlin'."

"Always," Lena replied softly, her warm breath tickling his skin. "Together, we can face anything." And in that moment, as their hearts beat in perfect harmony, Calvin knew their love was a guiding light in the darkness.

"I promise to be quieter this time," Calvin murmured through the towel, his eyes twinkling with mischief and devotion. The soft scent of lavender from Lena's freshly laundered nightgown filled his senses, grounding him in the present moment.

Lena chuckled softly, her laughter like a soothing balm to his soul. Her eyes danced with love and understanding as she brushed a stray strand of hair behind her ear.

"You better be," she teased gently.

"Cross my heart," he vowed, his voice still slightly muffled but no less sincere. He reached out to caress Lena's cheek, marveling at the softness of her skin even after all these years together. The flickering streetlight outside cast shadows across the room, playing on worn wooden floorboards. But in that moment, all Calvin could see was the woman he loved more and more each day, lying next to him in bed.

He could feel her chest rising and falling against his own, their breaths mingling in a tender symphony. As they drifted off to sleep with their bodies entwined and their hearts aligned, Calvin knew that their love would guide them through any storm that came their way.

The bar's neon lights flickered, casting a hazy glow on the faces of Biscuit and the three women who sat with him. The dimly lit room was filled with the smell of stale beer, mingling with the faint scent of cigarettes and sweat. As they leaned closer, anticipation sparkled in their eyes, the excitement for what was to come palpable in the air. Biscuit's deep voice rumbled through the smoke-filled room as he began his joke. "Alright," he said, a mischievous grin across his face. "So, the horse walks into the bar. And the Bartender looks at him and says—" He paused for effect, drawing out the moment before delivering the punchline.

"Why the long face?" Their laughter burst like a melody, filling the room with warmth and joy.

Biscuit basked in their shared moment, feeling a sense of peace over him. It had been too long since he'd known such carefree moments, free from the weight of the city bus steering wheel and his past troubles. "Ready to head out?" asked Veronica, her eyes twinkling like stars in the night sky. Her curly hair framed her face, creating an almost ethereal glow around her. "Sure thing," Biscuit replied, his broad smile revealing his genuine happiness. The group moved toward the exit, their laughter still ringing in his ears. As they were about to step out into the cool evening air, Biscuit couldn't help but feel grateful for this perfect evening with friends who had lifted the heavy burden of his past from his shoulders.

With a gallant sweep of his arm, Biscuit held the heavy wooden door open for the trio of women. Each stepped outside, their eyes meeting his in appreciation for his chivalrous act. A warm rush of gratitude washed over him as he nodded, taking a moment to appreciate each woman. With her silky red lips curved into an infectious smile, Denise had been their group's quietest member. But her laughter was just as contagious and filled the air with joy. "Thanks, Biscuit," she said, her voice soft yet full of warmth. "Anytime, ladies," Biscuit replied, basking in the simple pleasures of friendship and shared laughter. The evening sun cast a golden glow on their surroundings, highlighting the vibrant colors of the nearby flowers and bringing a sense of peace and contentment to the moment.

CHAPTER 4

The crisp wind swept away the echoes of laughter as Biscuit gallantly held open the door for the last of the women. The neon lights from the bar cast a vibrant mix of blues and reds onto his face, highlighting his rugged features. A look of concern crept over one woman's face as she noticed the sudden change in Biscuit's demeanor. "Hey, what's wrong?" she asked with genuine care. Biscuit struggled to swallow, suddenly finding his throat dry. He muttered a name under his breath, barely audible. "Willow." The name left a bitter taste in his mouth, tarnishing the joyful atmosphere that had surrounded him moments ago. The woman followed Biscuit's gaze, her smile fading like sugar dissolving in the rain as she caught sight of the figure framed between two parked cars. The other women also turned, their expressions mirroring hers as they recognized the source of Biscuit's distress.

Their eyes briefly met before one of them spoke up. "We'll catch you later, Biscuit." Her tone was gentle yet firm, leaving no room for argument. With that, they left Biscuit alone to face his past. "Damn," he thought to himself, clenching his fists at his sides. "Why now? Why tonight?" "Get it together, Biscuit," he told himself sternly, taking a deep breath and squaring his shoulders. "You're not the same man you were. You can handle this." "Alright, Willow," he muttered, preparing himself for the confrontation. "Let's do this." Willow's stiletto heels clicked menacingly against the concrete streets, each step calculated and intimidating. Like a panther stalking its prey, she approached Biscuit with a daunting grace and poise. Her tight black dress hugged her curves, accentuating her alluring but dangerous beauty. The dim lighting caught the sparkle of her silver earrings, casting a devious glint in her eyes as she locked onto Biscuit with predatory intent.

"Long time no see, Biscuit," she purred as she drew closer, her voice dripping with venom. Her wicked smile revealed a perfect set of pearly white teeth, enhanced by her ruby-red lipstick and striking against her flawless complexion. She tilted her head to one side, her dark curls cascading over one shoulder while her icy gaze bore into his soul. "Did you miss me?" Willow taunted him with words like poison-tipped arrows aimed straight at his heart. Biscuit clenched his jaw, desperately trying to maintain his composure. He knew he couldn't show weakness now, not when so much was at stake. "Not particularly," he replied calmly, though fear gnawed at the edges of his mind. "Ah, but admit it, baby," Willow teased with a sly smirk, circling him slowly like a vulture above its prey. "There's still a part of you that can't resist me."

The sound of Biscuit's voice wavered as he spoke, his hands gripping the edge of the bar counter for support. Memories of a time when Willow's charms had entranced him flooded his mind, but he pushed them away. "Maybe once," he admitted, feeling the weight of their history between them. "But I've changed, Willow. I'm not the same man you used to manipulate." Her laugh was like a cold gust of wind cutting through the warmth of the bar. "Changed?" she scoffed. "How quaint. You're still just a lowly city bus driver. You could never be on my level." Biscuit maintained his composure, refusing to let her words chip away at him. "Maybe," he said calmly, meeting her icy stare head-on. "But at least I don't have to hurt others to feel powerful." A flicker of doubt crossed Willow's face before she regained her steely facade. "Is that so?" she challenged, her tone dripping with superiority. "Well then, there's nothing left for us to discuss."

The festive atmosphere that had filled the room only moments ago seemed to fade away, replaced by a heavy and suffocating presence in the form of Willow. Biscuit could feel her calculating gaze bearing down on him like a vice, squeezing tighter with every passing second. "Enough's enough, Willow. I want you out of my life for good. You've caused enough damage," Biscuit's voice rang out clear and unwavering, cutting through the low murmur of conversations and drawing the attention of everyone in the room. "Damage?" Willow scoffed, her heels clicking against the worn wooden floor as she advanced towards him. "Is that how you see it? I thought I made you better, Biscuit." "Better?"

Despite himself, Biscuit let out a bitter laugh, his anger simmering just beneath the surface. The tension between them was palpable, filling the air with an almost physical weight. "You nearly destroyed me. Manipulated, lied to, used me for your twisted games." "Life is just a game, darling," Willow sneered, unaffected by his accusations. She drummed her fingers against her arm as she leaned in closer. "And I know how to play it." "Maybe so," Biscuit conceded through gritted teeth, his fists clenched at his sides in frustration. He took a deep breath, attempting to push aside the memories of pain and betrayal that threatened to consume him.

The silence that engulfed the room seemed to stretch for an eternity. The tension was thick and suffocating, crackling with an intensity that anyone in every corner of the bar could feel. Willow's steely gaze bore into Biscuit, her eyes cold and unforgiving. But beneath the surface, a flicker of emotion danced in her irises - was it fear? Regret? Biscuit couldn't tell, but he saw it there nonetheless. "Fine," she spat, breaking eye contact as she turned away from him. "Have it your way, Biscuit." His jaw tightened as he locked eyes with her, each refusing to back down.

The air almost vibrated with their unspoken challenge, drowning out the faint sound of the jukebox playing in the corner and the low murmur of voices around them. "I'm not playing," Biscuit declared, his voice unwavering. "I've got people who care about me. Calvin, Lena, Junior, Ryder. They're my family." A cruel smile spread across Willow's lips at the mention of his loved ones, her eyes narrowing maliciously. "Ah, the Steeles," she taunted. "Such a picture-perfect family." The mention of his friends ignited a fire inside Biscuit, filling him with a fierce determination. He could almost see their faces - Calvin's reassuring grin, Lena's warm embrace, Junior's bright optimism, and Ryder's fiercely protective gaze.

They were more than just friends; they were his lifeline. "That's enough on my family, Willow," he warned through gritted teeth. "I mean it." She closed the distance between them until they were only inches apart, her perfume overwhelming but unable to deter Biscuit's unwavering stance. "Or what?" she challenged, her breath hot against his face. He could feel her trying to break him with her piercing stare, but he held on to the memory of the Steeles - their love and support giving him strength. "You don't scare me, Biscuit," she sneered. "Maybe not," he replied in a low voice, his grip tightening on his fists by his sides. Despite the weight of Willow's stare, he stood tall and defiant with the support of his chosen family firmly in his mind.

Biscuit's voice was firm and resolute, his words ringing like a challenge as he stood tall before Willow. "I've learned from my mistakes," he declared, drawing an invisible line in the sand between them. His jaw was with a lot of tension, and his eyes shone with determination. "I won't let you control me again." Willow laughed the sound cold and mocking, her eyes glittering in the dim light. "Control?" she scoffed, her lips twisting into a sly smile. "I never controlled you, Biscuit." But as she spoke, something else flickered through her gaze – a hint of vulnerability or rejection. In the blink of an eye, Willow turned on her heel and strode towards another seat, her posture defiant and her glare like ice. She threw herself down onto the worn leather booth, crossing one leg over the other in a show of nonchalance. Waving him off dismissively, she added, "Enjoy your newfound freedom."

Standing alone in the dimly lit bar, Biscuit couldn't help but feel the smoky haze wrap around him like a cloak of uncertainty. The shifting neon lights cast eerie shadows on the peeling wallpaper and the grimy linoleum floor beneath his feet. He could hear the faint hum of the jukebox, playing an old soul tune that somehow managed to pierce through the noise of patrons' laughter and clinking glasses. Despite the busy atmosphere, all Biscuit could focus on was Willow and the past that seemed determined to haunt him. "Get it together, man," he muttered, his nervous fingers drumming a frantic rhythm on the sticky countertop. Biscuit glanced towards the booth where Willow sat, her shadowy silhouette outlined against the dim light. Even from this distance, he could sense her presence – toxic, insidious, like a slow-acting poison coursing through his veins. "Hey, buddy," the bartender called out, jolting Biscuit from his reverie. "You need another drink?" Shaking his head, Biscuit swallowed hard as he tried to calm his racing heart. "Nah, just my tab," he replied hoarsely, his voice betraying his inner turmoil. As the bartender shuffled off to retrieve his bill, Biscuit's thoughts drifted back to the

Steeles – Calvin, Lena, Junior, and Ryder. They were his family, his rock, his anchor in the stormy seas of life. It was for them and himself that he'd finally found the courage to break free from Willow's grasp. "Your tab," the bartender said gruffly, thrusting a crumpled receipt into Biscuit's hand. "Take care." And with that final warning echoing in his mind, Biscuit left the bar behind and stepped into the cool night air, feeling a sense of relief and freedom.

Biscuit's fingers trembled as he fished through his pocket, searching for a few crumpled dollar bills. He slapped them on the counter with shaky hands, smoothing out their creases with great effort. Willow's laughter rang across the room, causing Biscuit to flinch involuntarily. He clenched his fists, gritting his teeth in frustration. "Enough," he whispered, trying to drown out her mocking voice. "You've made it this far. Don't look back." Despite his inner turmoil, Biscuit pushed away from the bar and strode towards the door.

With each determined step, he felt the weight of Willow's controlling presence begin to recede like a bad dream, slowly fading into the morning light. As he reached for the heavy wooden handle, he paused momentarily, steeling himself against the urge to glance over his shoulder. "Never again," he vowed silently, gripping the handle tightly. "I won't let Willow control me any longer. I owe it to my family – and myself." With a final surge of resolve, Biscuit swung open the door and stepped out into the night air, leaving behind Willow and his painful past.

The soft glow from the bedside lamp cast warm, flickering shadows on the bedroom walls, illuminating the family portrait hanging above their dresser. Lena slipped back into her simple cotton nightgown, the fabric whispering against her skin as she moved gracefully. Calvin lay on the bed, watching her with a tender smile, his dark curls still damp and sticking to his forehead from their recent lovemaking. He admired how the light danced off every curve of her body, accentuating her beauty in a way that took his breath away. "Even in that plain nightgown," he murmured, his voice filled with love and admiration, "you're stunning." "Calvin, you always know just what to say," Lena replied softly, a blush spreading across her cheeks. She moved to sit beside him, intertwining her fingers with his and squeezing them gently.

Before Lena could respond further, there was a soft knock at the bedroom door. Calvin's eyes widened slightly – he hadn't expected or wanted interruptions tonight. He whispered to Lena, "I was quieter this time, right?" She stifled a chuckle, realizing that the intrusion had broken the moment. "It's not your fault, Cal. The walls are thin, and our kids have ears like hawks." "Maybe we need to invest in some soundproofing," Calvin joked, although his thoughts were already straying to their tight budget and whether they could afford such an expense. As a hard-working city bus driver providing for his family, there were always more expenses than money could stretch. "Or maybe we could just move out to the countryside," Lena suggested playfully, knowing that neither of them would ever leave the west side of Chicago – their home, community, and roots. "Perhaps someday," Calvin agreed wistfully, envisioning a quiet and peaceful life away from the hustle and bustle of the city.

But for now, he knew their place was here, with their family, friends, and church. Lena's gentle laugh echoed in the quiet room, a soothing balm to Calvin's frayed nerves. "Who is it?" she asked in a barely audible whisper. "Junior," came the muffled response, followed by a brief pause. "Can I talk to you for a second?" Calvin looked at Lena, his eyes filled with surprise and curiosity. What could their son want at this hour? A smile tugged at the corners of Calvin's mouth. "Of course, son. What's on your mind?" Junior's voice trembled with excitement and a hint of nervousness as he responded from behind the door. "Y'all can sleep in a little longer tomorrow morning. I want to make breakfast – nothing fancy, just wanted to try my hand at it and see what happens."

The warm, tender gaze shared between Lena and Calvin spoke volumes without a single word between them. The exhaustion from their night's activities was etched in their eyes, a testament to their sacrifice for their son's joy. In these simple moments, amidst the chaos of everyday life, they found solace and tranquility. It was a silent reminder of how blessed they were to have each other – someone to share their joys and burdens with. "Alright, Junior. Just don't burn the house down, okay?" Lena replied, her voice playful yet filled with love for her son. "Promise, Ma. Goodnight!" Junior said before bouncing off towards the kitchen, his footsteps echoing down the hallway like a lively drumbeat.

As Calvin lay back on the bed, his mind drifted to to-morrow's breakfast. He could already imagine the enticing aroma of buttery toast and fluffy scrambled eggs wafting through the air, mingling with the rich scent of Lena's freshly brewed coffee. The mere thought brought a con-tented smile to his face.

"Who would've thought our boy would be so eager to cook?" Calvin mused, a proud glimmer in his eyes. "Rose must be rubbing off on him," Lena responded fondly, saying that Rose was their family matriarch who taught them about faith and the importance of nurturing loved ones. "Or maybe he just wants to give us a break,"

Calvin pondered aloud, overflowing with gratitude for their kind-hearted son who always seemed attuned to the needs of others.

"Either way, we are truly blessed," Lena murmured as she reached to rest her hand on Calvin's arm. It was a silent prayer of thanksgiving shared between them, a quiet acknowledgment of their love and commitment to each other. As sleep finally began to calm them, Calvin and Lena took comfort in their little family, an unbreakable unit amidst the world's chaos.

With a wide, beaming grin threatening to split his face, Junior pivoted on his heels and continued his mad dash down the dimly lit hallway. The animated wallpaper that lined the walls – covered in vibrant wildflowers and woodland creatures – blurred past as he skidded to a stop outside Ryder's bedroom door. His heart drummed at an exuberant pace, a heady mixture of excitement and nerves coursing through his veins like electricity. "Ryder, guess what?" he exclaimed, his voice trembling with anticipation, raising his knuckles against the worn wooden door. The suspense was palpable as he waited for her response.

"Whatcha got, little brother?" Ryder asked, her dark eyes sparkling with curiosity as she swung the door open wide. Strands of her messy hair framed her face, adding to her disheveled charm. "Mom and Dad said I could make breakfast tomorrow!" Junior practically shouted, unable to contain his joy any longer. His brown eyes practically glowed with pride and excitement. "I can't believe they agreed!" he added, his voice an octave higher than usual as he struggled to contain his enthusiasm. "Wow, Junior, that's something!" Ryder chuckled indulgently, folding her arms across her chest and raising an eyebrow in amusement. The silver moonlight streaming through her window cast a gentle glow on her features, making her look ethereal and wise beyond her years.

"So, what's on the menu?" she asked playfully, leaning against the door frame and inquisitively tilting her head. "Uh... I'm still working on it," Junior admitted sheepishly, rubbing the back of his neck and avoiding her gaze. He chewed on his lower lip nervously, already brainstorming ideas for his culinary debut. Images of fluffy pancakes and sizzling bacon danced through his mind, but Junior needed to find something simple yet satisfying – a meal that would bring a smile to the faces of his loved ones. "Rose taught me some basic stuff," he thought fondly, remembering how the family matriarch had taken him under her wing, sharing her love for Jesus and her passion for nurturing others through food. "I can pull off something she showed me."

His determination to make this meal special for his family was unwavering. "Alright, you better impress us all with your culinary skills," Ryder teased, her playful smirk contrasting against the fraying wallpaper that adorned her bedroom walls. "Whatever it is, I'm sure it'll be great," Ryder assured him, her voice softening as she caught a glimpse of the determination across her younger brother's features. Ryder knew all too well how much Junior cherished their family and how eagerly he sought to lighten their burdens in any way he could. She recognized that same fire in Junior's eyes that she often saw reflected in her own when she set her mind to something. "Thanks, Ryder," Junior murmured gratefully, his cheeks flushed with emotion. "I just want to do something nice for them." "Of course, little bro," Ryder replied affectionately, reaching out to ruffle his curly hair with an endearing smile. "Now get some sleep – you've got a big morning ahead of you."

"Goodnight, Ryder," Junior whispered as he left his sister's room and padded down the hall to his own. As he settled into the embrace of his threadbare sheets, he couldn't help but feel overwhelmed with gratitude for the simple blessing of family. The love they shared, the memories they cherished, and the comfort they found in each other's presence filled his heart. As he recalled Rose's teachings about how Jesus could show love in ordinary actions, he felt renewed purpose and determination. "Lord, help me make tomorrow special for them," he whispered into the darkness, his prayer blending with the distant sound of a passing train outside his window. It was a simple request, born from the boundless love he held for his family – and a humble testament to the strength that had carried them through every challenge life had thrown their way. As they drifted off to sleep, both siblings took solace in the weight of their love for family and an appreciation for life's simple joys. In their dreams, Junior and Ryder could see the immense power within each small, heartfelt gesture.

CHAPTER 5

The dim light in the corner booth of the bar cast a shadow over Willow's face, her once bright and lively eyes now listless as they stared into the empty glass she held between her slender fingers. The remnants of her drink, now just a few drops, clung to the sides of the crystal glass, much like the heartache that clung to her chest. She had been nursing it for what felt like an eternity, hoping it would somehow dull the sharp edges of pain left behind by Biscuit's departure. "Damn him," she muttered bitterly, her voice barely audible above the low hum of conversations filling the room. It was a slow Sunday night, with only a handful of patrons around the bar.

Their hushed whispers and soft laughter seemed to mock Willow's misery, yet their glances drifted back to her, drawn by some invisible force to witness her torment. "Gettin' another one?" asked the bartender, his towel slung over his shoulder as he leaned against the counter. Willow forced herself to look at the empty glass and shook her head in defeat, setting it down on the table with a thud. "No, I think I've had enough." Her thoughts drifted back to Biscuit, and she couldn't help but acknowledge the painful truth that gnawed at her insides: she hadn't been the kind of person she would have put up with for as long as he did. Her cunning ways and manipulative behavior had been too much, even for someone as loyal as Biscuit. Yet, being alone terrified her - a foreign concept she had never mastered. "Look at it this way, Willow," she mused to herself in a desperate attempt to find comfort in her own words. "You've managed to drive everyone away, so what's one more?"

She sighed heavily, her shoulders drooping with the weight of her loneliness. The emptiness inside her seemed to grow with each passing moment, and she longed for a chance to turn back time, make amends for her mistakes, and prove to Biscuit that she was worthy of forgiveness. But as the seconds ticked by, she could feel hope slipping away. "It's never too late," she whispered, her voice trembling with uncertainty. Then, like a flicker in the darkness, a surge of determination stirred within her. "Maybe I can still find someone who believes in me." And just as the thought crossed her mind, the door to the bar swung open with a sudden gust of wind, causing Willow to look up in surprise. Could this be a sign of fate? Her heart raced with anticipation as she waited to see what would unfold next.

Willow couldn't escape the weight of curious stares from the other bar patrons, their gazes flickering in her direction like moths drawn to a flame. Each glance felt like a physical touch, as if they could sense the turmoil within her, the storm of emotions threatening to overtake her completely. She shifted uncomfortably in her seat, trying to shake off the feeling of being watched by unseen eyes. "Alright, Willow," she muttered, steeling herself for an intense internal conversation. "You're a big girl now. It's time to take a good, hard look at yourself." She lifted her chin defiantly and stared straight ahead as though addressing her reflection in an invisible mirror. "Well," she began sarcastically, pointing an accusatory finger at herself, "sometimes you just have this effect on people." "Excuse me?" Willow's eyebrows shot up in surprise and anger.

The few remaining patrons in the bar glanced her way, but she didn't care. She needed to get to the root of her problems and understand why Biscuit had left her behind.

"You've got it all – a stunning figure, a gorgeous face – but that attitude?" Willow leaned back in the booth, the black cloud of defeat looming over her head. Sitting there contemplating her life choices, she noticed a couple of patrons slowly walking past her, their eyes wide with curiosity. They looked at Willow like an everyday car wreck, and Willow couldn't help but feel like they were right. Perhaps she was just too damaged for anyone to love genuinely. "Fine," she said stiffly through gritted teeth, barely audible above the low hum of the bar. With a dramatic flourish, Willow mimed, zipping her mouth shut. Then, she took her car keys from her purse and placed them on the table with a resounding clink. She vowed to remain silent and not hurt anyone, or herself, any further.

Her hands folded in her lap, and Willow took a slow breath to contain the hurt that threatened to burst forth. "Damn him," she muttered under her breath. "Damn Biscuit for making me feel this way, and damn me for letting him get under my skin." Tears welled up in her eyes, but she refused to let them fall – not here, not now. She was stronger than that; she had to believe she was. It was the only thing keeping her from completely falling apart. As Willow sat there alone and heartbroken, she vowed to find a way to change and become someone better and worth loving. She refused to let Biscuit's actions obliterate her.

And maybe, just maybe, she could salvage some small piece of happiness from the wreckage of her life.

The soft tinkling of glass against wood broke through the room's stillness, causing Willow to snap out of her thoughts. She looked up to find a sharply dressed man approaching her table, confident strides echoing across the polished wooden floor. His dark beard perfectly framed a set of pearly white teeth that shone beneath a charming smile, and her eyes couldn't help looking at the gleaming gold watch adorning his wrist. Despite never seeing this man before, something about him made Willow feel oddly at ease. "Hello there, beautiful," he said smoothly, his voice like liquid honey. "You seem too sad for a night as lively as this." Willow forced a small smile, trying to hide the ache Biscuit had left behind. "Well, you know what they say – there's always a party pooper." The man chuckled and slid into the seat opposite her, his presence exuding confidence and charm. "My job tonight is to make sure your pretty face stays smiling. Let the whole world see what I see right now." He winked at her, sending a rush of warmth to her cheeks.

Curiosity prickled at Willow's skin as she gazed across the table at the stranger before her. "Who are you?" she asked, unable to resist voicing her question. The man's lips curved into a warm smile as he answered, "Name's Lenny."

He extended his hand towards her, and she clasped it in her own after a moment of hesitation. She couldn't help but feel the connection from the warmth and strength radiating from his grip. Despite the sadness in her voice, Willow couldn't deny the tiny spark of excitement that flickered to life within her. "Nice to meet you, Lenny," she said politely. "Likewise. Let's put some life back into your eyes," Lenny replied with a mischievous glint.

With practiced ease, he popped the cork off a bottle of champagne, the sound echoing through the nearly empty bar as he poured each a glass. Bubbles fizzed and danced within the liquid, mesmerizing Willow as the light reflected off its amber hue. "Cheers," Lenny said, raising his glass in a toast. "Cheers," Willow echoed, clinking her glass against his before taking a delicate sip. The sweet tickle of champagne on her tongue caused a spontaneous giggle to escape her lips. "See? That's better already," Lenny remarked with an approving grin. Willow toyed with the stem of her glass, momentarily lost in thought. She had never been one to open up to strangers easily, but there was something about Lenny's presence that made her feel safe and at ease. Perhaps it was how he carried himself - confident and self-assured like he owned every room he walked into - or it was simply the sparkling champagne talking. Either way, she felt content and unburdened in his company for this moment.

Willow's voice was laced with intrigue as she asked, "Is that so?" She couldn't deny the subtle pull of Lenny's charm and the way he carried himself – like a king ruling over his kingdom. His confident demeanor drew her in, making her feel alive and free. "Cheers to turning frowns upside down," Lenny said, holding his glass for a toast. Willow's lips turned up at the corners as she clinked her glass against his, the sweet scent of champagne filling her nostrils. She took a tentative sip, the bubbles dancing on her tongue and sending a delightful tickle up her nose, causing her to giggle uncontrollably. Lenny grinned wide-ly, clearly pleased with himself. "See? Smiles already," he declared, raising his glass again for another toast. As they sat beneath the stars, Willow felt more at ease than she had in weeks. But when Lenny asked, "Now tell me, beautiful lady, what's got you so down?" she couldn't help but feel a twinge of sadness. "Let's just say I had to let go of som eone..." Her words trailed off as she thought of Biscuit's stern expression and the hurt in his eyes when he turned away. A pang of guilt tugged at her heart, but she pushed it aside, focusing on the warmth and understanding in Lenny's gaze instead. "Ah, I see," Lenny said softly, swirling the champagne in his glass as if lost in thought. The tiny bubbles caught the light like stars twinkling in the night sky. "Sometimes, letting go is the hardest thing to do."

Willow's lips curved into a wistful smile as she listened to the soft murmur of the conversation around her. She couldn't help but let her gaze drift to the empty stage in the corner of the bar, where a grand piano sat silent and abandoned, collecting dust like a forgotten treasure. At that moment, Willow was overwhelmed by the feeling that her life without Biscuit was like an unfinished song, the melody haunting her thoughts and leaving her with a profound and palpable sense of incompleteness.

Lenny reached across the table, his hand brushing against Willow's. The warmth of his touch sent a shiver down her spine, a comforting sensation that chased away the coldness that had settled in her bones. His voice was gentle yet firm as he spoke, his words like a soothing balm for her troubled mind. "Sometimes," he said, "a fresh start is what we need. A chance to rewrite our stories, to find new melodies." Willow looked up at him, tears glistening in her eyes, reassured by the truth in his words.

But even as she nodded in agreement, the thought of leaving Biscuit behind still weighed heavy on her heart. It felt like an anchor dragging her down, keeping her from moving forward towards a new beginning. Yet deep down, she knew that Lenny was right. Sometimes, starting anew was necessary for growth and healing. Perhaps it was time for Willow to embrace this fresh start and create a new melody for herself that didn't include Biscuit but held endless possibilities for happiness and fulfillment.

The dim bar lights flickered off Lenny's gold watch as he raised his hand consolingly. He nodded empathetically, a glint of understanding in his eyes. "I know how that goes," he said softly, his deep voice carrying a soothing tone. Willow appreciated his attempt to comfort her and shook her head, strands of her hair catching the light as she did so. "Enough about me," she insisted, trying to push away her troubles for the moment. "What brings a man like you to a place like this on a Sunday night?" Her curiosity was piqued, and she couldn't help but study Lenny's enigmatic smile. "Business, my dear," Lenny replied mysteriously, tapping his gold watch with a sly smirk. "All work and no play makes Lenny a dull boy." Despite his words, an unmistakable playful undertone made Willow wonder if there was more to him than met the eye. The low murmurs from the other patrons' conversations and clinking glasses around them were momentarily forgotten by Willow as she laughed at Lenny's charm. The sound echoed through the bar, adding to the lively atmosphere. At that moment, Willow fell for Lenny's charisma. "Well then, let's make sure you're anything but dull tonight," she said with a mischievous grin, raising her champagne glass again, the bubbles fizzing excitedly inside.

Lenny's glass clinked against Willow's with a gentle chime, their laughter mingling and creating a soothing melody that drowned out the whispers of their past. Chatter still filled the bar and the soft glow of neon signs, but for Willow, the only thing that mattered was the mysterious stranger sitting next to her. As they shared stories and sipped on glasses of champagne, Willow found herself drawn to Lenny's charismatic charm and piercing gaze that seemed to hold secrets. As she let herself forget about the ghost of Biscuit and embrace this moment, she couldn't help but feel a sense of freedom in Lenny's company. "I deserve this," she thought, trying to push away the guilt that gnawed at her – a night of laughter and forgetting, even for a little while.

As the night wore on, the vibrant hues from the neon bar sign cast a mesmerizing glow upon Willow's face, highlighting her features in shades of blue and green. The lively jazz band playing in the corner added to the atmosphere, their soulful music drowning out the chatter of other patrons. With each sip of champagne and every whispered secret shared between them, Willow felt a weight lifted off her shoulders. She couldn't deny the allure of this new man – the promise of new beginnings, the anticipation of fresh adventures. "Here's to new friends," she toasted, her eyes sparkling in the low light. "New friends," Lenny echoed with a grin. "And new adventures." As he winked at her playfully, Willow couldn't help but feel a familiar thrill coursing through her veins – something she hadn't felt in far too long.

As the smooth, mournful melody of the saxophone echoed through the dimly lit club, Willow's mind drifted away. The night he stretched before them was full of endless possibilities and shimmering hope. For the first time in a long while, she allowed herself to believe that something better awaited her on the horizon. She leaned close to Lenny and asked, "What do you think is the most important thing in life?" Lenny considered her question, his fingers gently swirling the bubbly champagne in his glass. "I'd say it's savoring every moment as if it were your last, cherishing the people and experiences that truly matter, and living with no regrets." Willow nodded, pondering his words as she took in the sultry atmosphere of the club. "No regrets, huh? That sounds like a daunting task." "Perhaps," Lenny conceded with a smile. "But I've found that life is too fleeting to waste on what-ifs and could-have-been." He reached across the table and tenderly brushed his fingers against hers. "What about you, Willow? What do you think is the most important thing?"

Willow's eyes shone with determination as she answered, 'Change.' The word seemed to carry a weight of power. 'The ability to evolve, grow, and learn from our mistakes. Without change, we'd be stuck in the past.' Lenny nodded, his expression serious. 'Words of wisdom,' he remarked, impressed by her insight. 'And a fitting sentiment for a night like this.' He raised his glass, and Willow followed suit. 'May we embrace change and all it brings,' she declared boldly, clinking her glass against his. 'Cheers to that,' Lenny agreed enthusiastically. They sipped their champagne, the bubbles tickling their noses, as they surrendered to the music and the enchanting possibilities ahead.

CHAPTER 6

The morning sun crept through the thin lace curtains, casting a warm, golden light over the bustling Steele family kitchen. The aroma of burnt coffee lingered in the air, mixing with the sharp sizzle of bacon as Calvin and Lena moved into the kitchen in perfect harmony. After years of marriage, they had mastered navigating the tight space together, anticipating each other's actions like a graceful dance.

"Something smells...unique," Calvin commented with a playful smirk, his eyes meeting Lena's as they both caught a whiff of smoke. "Alright now, Junior," Lena called out to her son, her fingers deftly started weaving braids into Ryder's hair at the kitchen table. "Remember, your dad likes his bacon a little less...well done." She sent an endearing smile towards her son, who intently focused on frying the bacon before him, trying to avoid getting more smoke in his eyes.

"Ma, you know I'm still refining my technique," Junior replied with pride, coughing slightly as he flipped the charred strips in the pan. It may not have been the perfect breakfast feast he had envisioned, but he hoped his efforts would still bring a smile to his father's face. Lena couldn't help but chuckle at her son's optimism, knowing he inherited it from her family. She admired Junior's strong bond with his loved ones and ability to see the bright side in even the most challenging situations.

Junior beamed as he presented his latest creation to Ryder with a mischievous glimmer in his eye. "Here's some extra crispy just for you," he declared, offering her a plate filled with blackened bacon strips. "Thanks, Junior," she replied sarcastically, raising an eyebrow in mock appreciation as she took one of the burnt offerings between her fingers. With a loud crunch, she bit into it and nodded with exaggerated satisfaction. "Mmm, simply divine. Truly gourmet stuff here." Junior playfully nudged her in response, the love and camaraderie between them evident in their lighthearted banter.

Calvin, who had just finished buttoning up his crisp white bus driver uniform behind the counter, stepped into the sibling squabble. His deep, warm voice cut through the tension like a soothing balm. "Now, let's be kind to one another," he chided gently, a hint of amusement dancing in his eyes. "Junior is doing his best, and that's all that matters."

Ryder's lips curved into a genuine smile as she bit her brother's charred bacon. She could see the gleam of pride in her father's eyes as he watched Junior's cooking experiment, and she couldn't help but feel a twinge of admiration for her younger brother – even if the breakfast wasn't perfect.

Meanwhile, Lena observed the growing tension between her children from the corner of her eye. As a mother, she knew it was her job to diffuse the situation before things got out of hand. With quick thinking, Lena changed tactics and clapped her hands together, gesturing towards the door. "Alright, everyone, it's time to get ready for our day," she announced cheerfully. We don't want to be late!"

As she led her children towards the door, Lena felt an overwhelming rush of love for her family. Despite their chaotic mornings and burnt bacon mishaps, they are bound together by unbreakable bonds of faith and resilience. Their shared faith was a strong foundation that connected them, and at the end of the day, that was all that truly mattered.

As they exited the house and into the bright morning sunlight, Lena paused for a moment to silently pray. "Lord," she began earnestly, "we ask for your guidance today as we embark on our daily journeys. Please help us to treat each other with patience, kindness, and support. And maybe—maybe—grant Junior some culinary improvement."

As the Steele family emerged from the warmth of their cozy home, they were met with a refreshing burst of crisp morning air. The sun's first rays were beginning to peek over the rooftops of the quiet neighborhood. Calvin held open the station wagon door for his wife and children, a proud smile gracing his lips as he watched them settle into their seats. "Everyone buckled up?" he asked, glancing back at Junior and Ryder in the rearview mirror. They gave him a thumbs-up, and with that, he pulled out onto the road, the smooth hum of the station wagon filling the air around them.

As they cruised along the tree-lined streets, Calvin reached down and turned the radio dial, filling the car with soulful R&B from the 1970s. The velvety voice of Al Green crooned through the speakers, and Calvin couldn't resist tapping his fingers on the steering wheel in time with the rhythm. The music seemed to transport them all to another time and place as they approached their destination.

Lena's eyes shone with a nostalgic glimmer as she leaned back against the car seat, her head tilted towards the soft melody of Al Green's voice. "Your father used to sing this song to me when we were dating," she reminisced, a wistful smile gracing her face as memories flooded. "He's always had a soft spot for Al Green."

"Can't help it," Calvin admitted, his lips curving into a fond smile at the mention of his favorite artist. "The man knows how to put your heart into words."

Lena squeezed his hand affectionately and gazed out the window at their two children in the backseat. "Isn't this just perfect?" she said, warmth spreading through her voice and radiating from her expression. "Our little family, all together."

"Nothing better," Calvin agreed, his gaze lingering on his wife before turning to look at their children. His heart swelled with love for them, and he was grateful for every moment they could spend together.

"Dad, can I ask you something?" Junior piped up suddenly, leaning forward between the front seats and interrupting the comfortable silence.

"Of course, son. What's on your mind?" Calvin asked, turning slightly to give Junior his full attention.

"Do you think I could be as strong as you one day?" Junior asked earnestly, his eyes wide with curiosity and admiration.

Calvin's heart swelled with pride and love for his son. "Son, you're already stronger than you know," he replied with a gentle smile, glancing at Junior through the rearview mirror. "You've got your mother's kind heart and my determination. You'll do great things, Junior." His unwavering belief in Junior's potential, a beacon of inspiration, instilled confidence in his son and inspired those around him.

Junior beamed at his father's words, feeling a sense of reassurance and confidence wash over him.

As they drove through the bustling streets of Chicago, Calvin couldn't help but silently pray for his children's future. He knew they would face their fair share of obstacles but also believed in their strength, resilience, and bright future. His hopeful prayer filled the car with optimism, inspiring those around him to look forward with hope.

"Lord, watch over my children," Calvin thought, his grip on the steering wheel tightening ever so slightly. "Guide them to becoming strong, loving individuals like their mama."

With Al Green's soulful voice echoing through the car and the warm sun rising higher into the sky, Calvin Steele knew there was no better blessing than the love of his family – and he wouldn't trade it for anything in the world.

"Alright now, y'all have a good day," Calvin said with a warm smile, turning to face his children. "And remember what your grandma Rose always says: 'Keep Jesus in your hearts.'" His voice was filled with an overwhelming sense of love and pride as he looked at his two children growing up so quickly before his eyes, a testament to the strong bond and affection in their family that warmed the hearts of those around them.

"Will do, Dad," Ryder replied with a playful eye-roll before grabbing her backpack and jumping out of the car. As she stepped onto the sidewalk, she took a moment to take in the bustling schoolyard and the excited chatter of her peers. She felt grateful for her loving family and knew she was lucky to have them, even if they sometimes smothered her with their well-intentioned advice.

"Love you guys," Junior added, following his sister onto the sidewalk. He breathed deeply, feeling his father's words settle on his chest. He hoped that he could carry the strength and wisdom of his family with him as he navigated the challenges of school. "Love you too," Calvin called out, watching their retreating figures until they disappeared into the crowd of students. A pang of nostalgia hit him as he recalled his school days when life seemed more straightforward and the future was full of endless possibilities.

As he shifted the car back into drive and pulled away from the school curb, Calvin's thoughts turned to the long day ahead. The countless passengers who would rely on him to get them safely to their destinations, the steady hum of the bus engine, and the familiar rhythm of the city streets. He closed his eyes for a moment and took a deep breath, feeling grateful for his job and the sense of purpose it gave him.

Calvin Steele entered the bustling bus station, the thick scent of diesel fuel and the inviting aroma of freshly brewed coffee filling his nostrils. As he weaved through the crowd, exchanging warm greetings with fellow drivers whose faces bore the marks of years spent navigating Chicago's busy streets, he couldn't help but feel a sense of camaraderie. Suddenly, a familiar voice called out from behind him. It was Biscuit – Calvin's friend since high school – signing in for the day at the main counter. Their long-lasting friendship was reflected in how their buses were always parked side by side in the lot. "Morning, Biscuit," Calvin greeted with a clap on the shoulder as they headed towards their respective vehicles. "You know, I was just thinking about how we need to remind ourselves not to get caught up with any pretty passengers we see daily." Biscuit chuckled, shaking his head. "Man, ain't that the truth. But sometimes it's easier said than done."

"Tell me about it," Calvin agreed with a pensive look. He knew too well about Biscuit's tendency to fall for the wrong women. Losing his heart and common sense seemed an ongoing theme in his friend's life. "Preach, brother," Biscuit replied with a raised hand for a high five, which Calvin eagerly returned. The sound echoed through the lot, drawing amused glances from nearby drivers. Climbing into their buses, they started their engines – their purpose clear and their mission set. As Calvin deftly maneuvered his bus out of the station and onto the city streets, his thoughts drifted to his dear mother, Rose – who had worked at the post office for thirty years before retiring – and her teachings of hard work and unwavering faith that kept him grounded through life's ups and downs. Each turn of the steering wheel felt like a heavy burden on his shoulders – not just for himself but also for Biscuit.

As Calvin's bus rumbled down the street, he could feel the vibrations humming beneath his fingertips as they gripped the steering wheel. The west side of Chicago sprawled before him, a maze of busy streets and worn buildings that held the hopes and dreams, as well as the joys and sorrows, of its residents. His mind returned to his conversation with Biscuit and their mutual understanding of staying true to their families. As he rounded a bend, Hodies – a familiar breakfast spot – came into view. The morning sun glinted off its windows like a beacon, momentarily blinding Calvin as he squinted to see inside. And then he saw her – Willow – sitting at a booth with a man whose features were obscured by the angle. Curiosity ignited, but he quickly reminded himself to focus on his responsibilities. "Lord, help me," he whispered before continuing his route.

CHAPTER 7

Lenny settled back in the booth at Hodies, the worn leather cushioning him as he leaned against it. His eyes followed the Waitress's every move as she swayed her hips while walking away, a pen tucked behind her ear. The curves of her body were like nothing he had ever seen before, and he couldn't help but let his gaze linger on them for a moment longer. He quickly tore his eyes away, reminding himself he didn't want to be caught admiring other women while out with Willow. "Can't let her see me checkin' out the talent," he thought, a subtle smirk crossing his face. "Not when I'm tryin' to keep up appearances." As Willow spoke about the fire on Madison last night, Lenny nodded along but was distracted by his thoughts.

He couldn't shake the feeling that Willow could see right through him, that she could sense his wandering attention earlier. "Uh, yeah, real tragedy," he replied, hoping his voice sounded more confident than he felt. "Whole family lost everything, didn't they?" "Yep," Willow sighed, her eyes narrowing as if she could sense something Lenny wasn't sharing. "Makes you think about what's important in life, doesn't it?" Lenny's stomach churned with guilt and unease, knowing that there were things he was hiding from Willow and everyone else around him. He couldn't help feeling like someone would eventually uncover his secrets and ruin everything he had worked so hard to maintain.

The traffic light outside Hodies flicked from red to green, its shiny surface reflecting the blue sky above. Calvin eased his foot onto the accelerator, the bus jolting forward as he tried to shake off the unsettling image of Willow dining with a mysterious man. His grip on the wheel tightened, the cool vinyl groaning beneath his tense fingers. "Damn," Calvin thought, stealing one final glance at the sunlit window of Hodies before it disappeared from view. "Who's that guy Willow's sitting with? What's going on there?" Inside the bustling diner, clinking silverware and lively chatter filled the air as patrons enjoyed their meals. Willow discreetly observed Lenny's wandering gaze, her heart pounding against her ribcage. She cleared her throat, maintaining a nonchalant demeanor as she shifted the conversation. "So, do you come here often?" Her voice carried a tinge of annoyance, but she attempted to mask it with a casual tone of interest.

Lenny's mischievous face was dappled with the morning sunlight streaming through the window, casting playful shadows across his chiseled features. "Well, if I'm on this side of town, perhaps I'll drop in from time to time," he said with a sly grin, raising his coffee cup to his lips and taking a slow, deliberate sip while never breaking eye contact with Willow. She couldn't help but think, "Can't trust a man who can't keep his eyes where they belong." Meanwhile, Calvin expertly navigated the bustling streets of Chicago, the rhythmic hum of the bus engine providing a steady backdrop to his deep thoughts. As he turned a corner, the sight of children laughing and playing in a nearby park tugged at his heartstrings, reminding him of his family waiting for him eagerly at home. The children's joyful sounds and carefree energy made him smile as he continued toward his destination.

Calvin's grip on the steering wheel tightened as he maneuvered through the bustling streets of Chicago. The cacophony of car horns and chatter from passersby filled his ears, but a storm of emotions consumed his mind. "It's not my business," he repeated to himself, determined to stay focused. The bus rumbled beneath him, providing a solid foundation for his inner turmoil. Suddenly, a familiar voice cut through the noise - "Hey, Mr. Steele!" Looking up in surprise, Calvin caught sight of Mabel, one of his regular passengers, waving her handkerchief at him from the back of the bus. A small smile tugged at his lips as he recognized her kind face. "How's your mama doin'?" she asked with genuine concern. His tense shoulders relaxed slightly as he responded, "Mom's doing well, thank you." Mabel nodded in relief and settled back into her seat. "Give her my best," she added kindly. "I will," Calvin promised with a grateful nod, returning his attention to the busy streets ahead. Despite the chaos around him, the warmth of Mabel's compassion had managed to soothe his troubled soul for just a moment.

The pleasant atmosphere at Hodies suddenly stopped as the Waitress returned to Lenny and Willow's table. Her smile faltered, sensing that something was amiss between the two. "You have a phone call," she said, her eyes darting between them before gesturing towards the restaurant's wall-mounted phone. Lenny raised an eyebrow, surprised by the interruption during their breakfast together. He gave Willow an apologetic smile before excusing himself from the table. Willow watched him go with a tense expression, her mind swirling with questions and doubts about what he could be hiding.

As Lenny crossed the room to answer his call, Willow returned to her steaming cup of coffee. She held it in her hands, feeling its warmth radiate through her fingers. Despite the uncertain situation with Lenny, she knew she had the strength and resilience to face whatever lay ahead.

"More coffee, hon?" The Waitress interrupted her thoughts, breaking through her reverie. Willow nodded absently, keeping her gaze fixed on Lenny as he talked on the phone with his back turned to her.

"Thank you," she murmured when the Waitress placed the fresh mug in front of her. She wrapped her hands around it, drawing comfort from its familiar warmth. As the sounds of clattering dishes and lively conversations filled the air around her, Willow took a deep breath and mentally prepared herself for the upcoming conversation with Lenny. She knew he would be back soon and was, and she'd be ready when he was.

Willow took the opportunity to study her surroundings as Lenny's back was turned. The diner was familiar with its grease-streaked windows, well-worn booths, and cracked vinyl upholstery. The comforting scent of bacon frying on the grill filled the air. She glanced at the chipped Formica tabletop and then down at her eggs, feeling oddly deflated. "Everything okay with your meal, dear?" The Waitress asked slyly as she refilled Willow's coffee cup for what seemed like the 100th time. Willow forced a tight-lipped smile and replied tersely, trying not to show irritation. As she poked at her eggs, little rivers of yolk ran across the plate like spilled secrets.

Her mind raced, searching for any clue about Lenny's true intentions. "Good," the Waitress said with a wink before sauntering away and leaving Willow alone with her thoughts. "Who even calls a restaurant these days?" Willow mused, her eyes fixed on Lenny's hunched figure by the phone. A pang of jealousy washed over her as she wondered who could be so important that he would interrupt their breakfast together. Was it someone from his past? A partner in crime?

"Damn it," she muttered under her breath, gripping the fork tightly. No matter how hard she tried to convince herself that she didn't care, something about Lenny intrigued her more than she wanted to admit. "Here's your toast," the Waitress announced triumphantly, setting down a plate in front of Willow. She tore her gaze away from Lenny and looked up, forcing another tight-lipped smile. "Thank you," Willow said through gritted teeth, trying to hide her frustration. Slowly and deliberately, she buttered a slice of toast, focusing on each swipe of the dull knife to keep her mind from wandering. "Anytime, sugar," the Waitress replied with a voice dripping in sarcasm as she walked away, leaving Willow to her thoughts.

As she nibbled on her toast, Willow's mind swirled like the steam rising from her coffee. If Lenny was hiding something, she was determined to find out – and, if necessary, use it to her advantage. But for now, all she could do was wait. "Sorry about that," Lenny apologized as he slid back into the booth across from Willow. "It was just an old friend calling to catch up."

"Really?" Willow raised an eyebrow skeptically. "At this hour?"

"It's strange, I know," Lenny admitted, nervously rubbing the back of his neck. But some people have no sense of timing, I guess."

"Indeed," Willow agreed coolly, sipping her coffee. Her eyes locked onto his, searching for any sign of deception. She knew she couldn't trust him yet but couldn't deny her strong pull towards him.

Within the sterile walls of the county hospital, the peaceful hum of life swirled in a symphony of activity. Like graceful performers on a stage, doctors and nurses navigated through the chaos with swift, purposeful movements. Lena Steele, clad in a crisp white nurse's uniform with matching stockings, stood at a counter with medical charts. The acrid scent of antiseptic lingered in the air as she leaned against the counter, her fingers tracing the lines of text on the pages.

"Hey, Lena!" Sheila's voice broke through the bustling corridors, interrupting Lena's thoughts. Her footsteps echoed on the polished floors as she approached from behind. "So, how was it? Your night away from the kids?" The clattering of metal instruments underscored her question.

Lena turned to face her coworker, a warm smile spreading across her face and brightening her pretty brown eyes. "Oh, Sheila," she replied, a hint of mischief in her tone as she recalled the evening. "You know I love my babies more than anything. But let me tell you – when Calvin finally got those kids out of the house –" She shook her head fondly, a soft chuckle escaping her lips as she reminisced. The lingering scent of Calvin's aftershave mixed with the faint aroma of antiseptic in her mind. "I thought the neighbors were going to call the police with all the noise we made!"

Sheila's laughter joined Lena's, filling the room with a deep, hearty sound that echoed off the walls. Her hand came down playfully on Lena's back, causing the charts in her grasp to rustle and dance. "Well, girl, you deserve some fun now and then!" Sheila exclaimed with a twinkle in her eye, her voice warm and affectionate. Memories of her early days of marriage bubbled to the surface, and she could almost hear the sound of her husband's laughter as they spun around their tiny living room, the record player crooning a romantic tune.

"Let's talk more about it during lunch break, alright?" Sheila suggested, leaning in conspiratorially. Lena nodded eagerly, still smiling at the simple joy she and Calvin had shared. Her heart felt full of gratitude for their love and companionship. "Sure thing," she replied gently to her stray curl.

Feeling energized by their conversation, Lena set off down the corridor, her white stockings swishing quietly against each other as she moved from room to room. As she checked vitals and adjusted IVs with expert precision, memories of Calvin flooded her mind – his strong hands tucking away loose strands of hair, his unwavering devotion to their family, and how he'd led them all in prayer each evening.

However, these thoughts only strengthened Lena's resolve as she looked into each patient's eyes. She knew there was more to do than administer medication or change bandages; she was a vessel for God's love, and her mission was to share that love with everyone who crossed her path. "Lord," she prayed silently, "give me the strength and wisdom to carry out Your work today." And as she continued her rounds, Lena felt a sense of divine purpose guiding her every step, filling her with peace and fulfillment.

Lenny's vintage Buick glided smoothly through the city streets, its engine purring like a contented feline among the chaotic chorus of car horns and distant chatter. Beside him, Willow sat in silence, her fingers nervously twisting the hem of her skirt as she mulled over the unanswered questions. The faint tobacco scent clung to Lenny's faded denim jacket, mingling with the delicate fragrance that lingered on Willow's skin from earlier. "Alright," Willow finally murmured, her lips pressed together as she fidgeted with the fabric between her fingers. She couldn't help but steal glances at Lenny, his strong jawline and piercing dark eyes holding an air of mystery. Unable to contain her curiosity any longer, she hesitantly spoke up. "Um, Lenny?" Her voice was barely a whisper. "Was everything okay with that phone call earlier?" Lenny's brow furrowed as he glanced at her, considering her question. He heaved a heavy sigh and drummed his fingers against the steering wheel, the rhythmic tapping filling the car's interior.

"Look, Willow," he began slowly, his voice rough like gravel scraping across the pavement. "That call... it was complicated." He exhaled heavily and kept his gaze fixed on the road ahead. "But you don't need to worry about it right now." Willow bit down on the inside of her cheek, weighing whether or not to pry further. She knew deep down that delving into Lenny's tumultuous world could spell danger, but her desire for power and control urged her onward.

Willow's cunning gaze bored into Lenny, her sharp eyes assessing him as she pressed for answers. She could feel the tension in his body as he gripped the steering wheel tightly, his jaw set and shoulders rigid. "Complicated how?" she persisted, determined to unravel the mystery behind his guarded demeanor. After a pause, Lenny's voice came out strained and low. "It's not important right now," he replied, evading her question. But Willow was not one to back down easily. "Just trust me on this one, alright?" he added, desperation creeping into his tone.

She relented, crossing her arms over her chest in frustration. She knew that gaining Lenny's trust would be the key to unlocking the power she craved. But she also couldn't shake off the feeling that there was more to his secrecy than he let on. "Fine," she gave in but made sure to add, "But so that you know, I'm not some naive little girl who needs protecting."

Lenny glanced her way, a faint trace of admiration flickering in his eyes before disappearing behind a mask of concern. As they continued driving through the bustling city streets, Willow couldn't help but feel the weight of their unspoken secrets between them like a heavy burden. But she was determined to uncover the truth, no matter what it took. "I understand," she whispered to herself, steeling her resolve.

As Lenny sat behind the wheel of his car, navigating the streets of Chicago, Willow couldn't help but feel overwhelmed by the cacophony of honking horns and flashing lights. She anxiously twirled a lock of hair around her finger, the coarse fabric of her skirt starkly contrasting her delicate touch. Her mind replayed the image of Lenny's face when he answered that phone call - a subtle tenseness, a fleeting look of fear that she couldn't shake. "Look, Willow," Lenny finally spoke up, his grip on the steering wheel tightening as he hesitated briefly. She knew there was something he was trying to tell her, something that made him uneasy. "I gotta be honest with you," he continued, his voice low and filled with an unexplainable sense of foreboding. "If we keep...seeing each other, you'll find out some things about me.

Things that might scare you." His unspoken secrets hung heavy in the air, causing Willow to struggle for breath. "But if you decide to walk away," he added, his eyes never leaving the road ahead, "I won't hold it against you." His words sent a chill down her spine as she contemplated the unknown depths of Lenny's past. Should she be cautious? Yes. But there was also an undeniable magnetic pull between them, like an invisible thread pulling them closer and closer together. It was as if their fates were intertwined and bound by an unseen force. "Walk away?" Willow echoed, her voice barely above a whisper. The idea felt impossible - separating herself from Lenny would be like ripping apart a part of herself. Despite her fears and uncertainties, she wanted to stay by his side. "Yeah," Lenny replied with forced nonchalance, though the shadows in his eyes betrayed his genuine emotions. "You know, if you think it's too much to handle."

"Is this too much for you?" Willow's words echoed through the car, her mind racing with the implications of what Lenny had just said. She couldn't deny the powerful allure of control and danger that he represented. His mysterious aura drew her in, offering a glimpse into a world she couldn't resist. "Is this about the phone call earlier?" Her voice remained steady, but her heart was pounding against her chest. "What kind of world am I getting myself into?" Lenny looked determined as he replied, "I don't want to drag you into something you're not ready for. But believe me, life with me is not easy." "Maybe I don't want easy," Willow retorted, meeting his intense gaze without hesitation. "Maybe I want something real. Someone who isn't afraid to show me their true self."

Lenny's murmur was thick with emotion as he spoke her name, his concern evident. "I don't want you to get hurt," he confessed. "Then don't let me," she whispered, touching his arm. The warmth of his skin sent a jolt of electricity through her body, cementing their connection in a way that both thrilled and terrified her. After a long moment of silence, Lenny finally relented. "Alright. But remember, you asked for this." As they continued driving through the city streets, Willow knew Lenny would forever change her life. She didn't know what lay ahead for them, but she was sure of one thing: she would never look back. Pulling over to the side of the road, Lenny turned towards Willow with a serious expression on his face. In the background, a street vendor called out prices for fresh fruit, and children played in the nearby park. All Willow could focus on was the sound of her heartbeat pounding in her ears.

His brow furrowed with concern and determination as he spoke, his eyes fixed on hers with intense focus. "Listen, Willow," he began, his voice low and serious. "As I said, if you stay with me, you'll discover some things about me. Things that might scare you." He paused, searching her face for any sign of doubt. "That's my world, and if you want to get out of this car right now, open the door and leave." She hesitated, shifting in her seat as she studied

Lenny's face for any hint of insincerity. But all she saw was genuine honesty and vulnerability in his dark irises. Instead of taking the easy way out, she focused on the tiny beads of sweat forming on his forehead and the nervous movement of his throat as he swallowed hard. Without hesitation, she made him her focus.

"Are you scared, too?" she asked softly, searching for understanding in his eyes. "Every damn day," he replied, a hint of vulnerability slipping into his tone. "But that's just how it is." "Can't we face it together?" she whispered, her voice trembling. "Willow, I don't want to drag you into my mess," he said, his voice heavy with a thousand unspoken burdens. "But if you think you can handle it..."

Instead of dwelling on the moment's intensity, Willow laughed softly, her eyes twinkling with mischief. "Last night was...incredible," she admitted as she remembered their spontaneous lovemaking under the pale moonlight, their passion echoing through the empty streets. "Your toes will eventually straighten out soon enough," she teased, referring to Lenny's impressive work. A smile tugged at the corners of his lips as he glanced down at his feet. His worn sandals and mismatched socks did little to hide the evidence of their late-night adventure. "That's why you got me out here wearing sandals and socks," he joked, a lighthearted chuckle escaping him. The somber atmosphere seemed to lift, replaced by the sweet memory of a shared joy. Willow giggled, pointing at his socks – one striped, the other dotted – the absurdity of it all only adds to their connection's beauty.

"There's a lot more where that came from if you have more socks," Willow playfully challenged. "But I'm not leaving today." She felt a surge of determination rooted in the knowledge that whatever lay ahead was worth facing together. Lenny's dark eyes met hers, their depths holding a warmth that set her heart ablaze. The cityscape of Chicago rolled past them, a living canvas of grit and vibrancy highlighting the lines and curves of the aging buildings and abandoned factories that lined their path. "Alright, then," Lenny said after a moment, his voice a mix of relief and resolve. As the car hummed beneath them, Willow felt a strange mix of exhilaration and fear. She knew Lenny's world was fraught with danger and uncertainty, but she couldn't help herself. In the back of her mind, she wondered if this was what it meant to live genuinely, to embrace the unknown and let it shape you.

"But you're going to see some things," Lenny warned, his voice gravelly but sincere. "And I expect you to live by the code." "Code?" Willow asked, her curiosity piqued. The corners of her mouth tugged into a slight frown as she tried to gauge his seriousness. Lenny glanced at her, his eyes serious once more. "I can't show you the street code, but you must respect it. I hope you understand what I'm saying to you." He drummed his fingers on the steering wheel, an anxious rhythm echoing his words. Willow didn't fully understand, but she knew that Lenny had helped her with the hurt she felt from Biscuit. Somehow, he had made her happy again. And for now, that was enough. She watched the lines in his face soften slightly, etched with concern and something else she couldn't quite place. "Okay," she agreed, taking a deep breath to steady herself. "I'll try my best." As they continued down the road, the sun casting dappled shadows through the trees overhead. "Look, Willow," Lenny said, breaking the silence. "I know this ain't easy for you, but trust me when I say I'd never let anything happen to you. "Thank you, Lenny," Willow murmured, her heart swelling with gratitude.

As they drove past a group of children playing stickball in the street, Willow couldn't help but feel a pang of nostalgia for her childhood. The simple days when life's biggest worry was a scraped knee or a lost toy. Now, it seemed like everything was teetering on a knife's edge, one wrong move away from disaster. They turned onto a quieter street, the shadows growing longer as evening approached. Willow let out a sigh, her thoughts swirling with anticipation and concern.

Amid the hustle and bustle of the county hospital cafeteria, two friends sat across from each other at a small, circular table. Lena Steele and Sheila each cradled a steaming cup of coffee in their hands, the rich aroma providing comfort amidst the chaos of their daily lives. The sharp tang of scrambled eggs and bacon mixed with the sweet scent of freshly baked muffins that wafted through the air. Around them, trays piled high with steaming hot dishes were carried to various tables, accompanied by the clinking of silverware and chatter of lively conversation. But for Lena and Sheila, the world seemed to fade away as they leaned in closer to each other, their voices hushed and conspiratorial.

The fluorescent lights above reflected in Sheila's bright eyes as she asked about Lena's upcoming vacation plans. "Will you be taking the kids with you?" Her curiosity was palpable, mirroring the excitement bubbling inside Lena. With a playful roll of her eyes and a light laugh, Lena replied sarcastically, "Oh yeah, we're just gonna leave them behind like luggage." They both erupted into laughter, the sound echoing off the walls of the bustling cafeteria. After a moment, Lena's expression turned more serious as she took a sip from her lukewarm coffee. The bitterness seemed to linger on her tongue, reminding her of the long nights spent soothing her children back to sleep in their home on Chicago's west side. Yet despite the challenges of raising a family in such an area, Lena couldn't help but feel grateful for the love that filled their home every day – a mother's love that made it all worthwhile.

"Can you imagine how quiet our house would be without those little ones running around?" she mused aloud, her gaze drifting aimlessly over the sea of faces in the cafeteria. "Sometimes, I swear, it feels like they're the only thing keeping me going." "Kids have a way of doing that," Sheila agreed, nodding as she took another swig of her coffee. Her children were older now, but she still remembered the feeling of their tiny hands clinging to her legs as she tried to cook dinner or do the laundry, their laughter echoing through the rooms of their modest home. "Anyway," Lena continued, her eyes brightening as she shared their new arrangement with Calvin's mother. "Rose will start keeping the kids once a week on Wednesday night while we attend our bible study class." She swirled the last coffee around her cup, the steam rising lazily. "Ooh, now that's a plan!" Sheila exclaimed, raising her eyebrows in approval.

She leaned back in her chair and crossed her arms, clearly impressed. The corners of her mouth lifted in a knowing smile as she remembered how helpful her family had been when her children were younger. Lena grinned, feeling a warm relief at the thought of having one less thing to worry about. "That's an essential thing for us, you know? To get Junior and Ryder taught the way we want them to be, and at the same time, Calvin and I get to bless each other with the fullness of God on Bible study night!" "Exactly," Sheila agreed, nodding enthusiastically. "Everybody gets to hear the name of Jesus with joy!" She clapped her hands together in delight as the two women burst into laughter, drawing the attention of a few nearby diners.

As they giggled, Lena couldn't help but think of the impact this change would have on her family. She imagined Junior and Ryder sitting attentively with Rose, their Bibles on their laps, absorbing every word of wisdom from the matriarch's lips. And she knew those teachings would shape her children into strong, compassionate individuals like their grandmother. "Alright," Lena said with a contented sigh, her laughter subsiding and her eyes meeting Sheila's once more. "I think we've solved all the world's problems for today." She smiled warmly at her friend, grateful for their shared laughter and support. "Sounds about right," Sheila agreed, chuckling softly. As they prepared to return to their duties, Lena felt a renewed sense of purpose and hope for the future. "Look at the time!" Sheila's voice snapped Lena back to reality.

She followed her friend's gaze to the large clock on the wall, its hands pointing ominously toward the end of their lunch break. "Alright, girl, we better get back to work," Sheila said with a sigh, standing up and grabbing her tray. "Yep, time flies when you're having fun," Lena replied, following suit. She glanced down at the remnants of her meal, now a collection of crumbs and half-empty coffee cups.

As she picked up her tray, she longed for more time to laugh, share stories, and be present with her dear friend. As the two women made their way to the dish return area, Lena couldn't help but feel a swell of gratitude for her relationship with Sheila. Their conversations always left her feeling uplifted, inspired, and ready to tackle life's challenges. Lena and Sheila parted ways with a shared smile, each heading back to their respective duties. As Lena walked down the brightly lit hospital corridor, she reflected on her conversation with Sheila. "Thank you, Lord," Lena whispered under her breath, her steps echoing through the empty hallway. "For my family and for your love that carries us all."

CHAPTER 8

Lenny carefully parked the sleek, black car outside the imposing warehouse. The building rose before them, its massive frame casting a shadow over the surrounding area. Weathered and worn red bricks bore the weight of time and neglect. "Look, Willow," Lenny spoke, his voice tinged with worry, his brow furrowed in concern. "I need you to stay here. I'll be right back." His eyes locked with hers, searching for understanding. Willow paused, her lips pursed as she contemplated his words. She studied the man before her - an unexpected presence in her life, bringing with him a rush of excitement she hadn't experienced in years. Her voice was tentative as she made her request. "Let me come with you, Lenny.

I want to learn the code and experience your world." Lenny hesitated, torn between shielding her from the darker elements of his life and allowing her to share in his reality. He ran a hand over his stubbled jaw, a sigh escaping him. "Whatever happens inside, you won't be able to unsee it. Once you step in, everything changes." His eyes bore into hers, silently pleading for her to reconsider. "I understand," Willow replied, determination etched on her face. She reached out to touch his arm, seeking reassurance in the warmth of his skin. "But this connection between us feels different, Lenny. I'm happy for the first time in a while." "All right," he conceded, his voice soft but resolute. "But you need to relax and chill while I do what I must do."

As they gracefully emerged from the car, Willow's heart was filled with excitement and apprehension. The unknown lay before them, and she couldn't help but wonder what challenges and adventures awaited. However, she was determined to do whatever it took to preserve the newfound happiness she had found with Lenny. She glanced at him, her eyes searching for any sign of doubt or hesitation. Yet all she saw was a committed determination. With a deep breath, they stepped forward into the unknown future, ready to face whatever obstacles may come their way.

The night air was crisp and biting, causing Willow to wrap her arms tightly around herself for warmth. She could feel the weight of the unknown looming behind the warehouse doors, but she steeled herself with determination for what she felt was a love she had found in Lenny. "Are you ready?" Lenny's voice was low and intense, sending shivers down Willow's spine. "Let's do this," she replied, her resolve solidifying in her chest. The warehouse door groaned open like a beast awakening from slumber, releasing an intense aroma of gasoline mixed with the faint scent of marijuana. Despite her churning stomach, Willow fought to keep her composure. She couldn't afford to falter now, not when she was on the verge of uncovering the secrets of Lenny's mysterious world.

"Stay close," Lenny whispered, words sending shivers rippling down Willow's spine as she followed him into the dimly lit warehouse. Her wide eyes took in the frantic scene before her, a chaotic dance of men moving about like shadows, carrying bags of money and loads of drugs with stern, unyielding expressions etched onto their faces. "Who are these people?" Willow thought, her mind reeling with questions that threatened to overwhelm her. She couldn't believe she was here, surrounded by dangerous strangers in this illicit world. But despite her fear, Willow clung tightly to Lenny's side, trusting him to guide her through the tumultuous chaos and keep her safe. Her emotions were a whirlwind inside her chest, threatening to burst forth at any moment, but she forced herself to stay calm and focused on following Lenny's lead.

"Is everything okay?" Lenny inquired softly, his gaze searching Willow's eyes for any hint of uncertainty. "I'm fine," Willow replied, swallowing hard. "I'm fine." "Good." Lenny gave her hand a reassuring squeeze and continued guiding her further into the warehouse. As they walked past the men, Willow felt their eyes assessing her, like wolves sizing up an unsuspecting lamb. She fought to remain unfazed by their scrutiny, but doubts raced through her mind. "Can I handle this?" she wondered, her heart rate accelerating. "And what will it mean for Lenny and me if I can?"

Despite the fear eating away, Willow knew one thing: she had willingly entered this world of shadows, and there was no turning back. For better or for worse, this was her reality now, and she would support Lenny through it all. "Remember," she reminded herself, taking a deep breath to steady her nerves. "You're doing this for us."

Lenny strode up to a group of men gathered under the harsh glare of fluorescent lights, their identities obscured by long shadows. They stood beside stacks of plastic-wrapped bricks - the merchandise. Confidence oozed from Lenny as he addressed the men in a firm, unshakable voice. "Do I need to inspect this?" he asked, eyeing the product. One of the men, towering and imposing, met his gaze with a stoic expression, arms crossed over his chest, straining against the fabric of his leather jacket. "Need us to count your money?" he retorted. Lenny's jaw clenched as he responded, standing tall with evident tension, a silent vow to protect the woman at his side from the ominous atmosphere. "You know me, man," he asserted. "Your call, boss," the man conceded with a shrug, never breaking eye contact. "You're the one taking the risks." Lenny glanced back at his loyal companions, nodding for them to proceed with the bags of money, sealing the deal. He turned to Willow, his hand resting gently on her shoulder. "Stay here," he murmured as she watched him depart, her admiration for his unwavering strength mingled with concern. "Is this what it means to stand by him?" she pondered, her heart heavy. "To witness his risks for our happiness?" The transaction was swift - money for drugs - and Lenny exchanged a lingering gaze with the other leader, a silent agreement passing between them. "Until next time," they murmured, parting ways.

"Let's go," Lenny said, mustering a forced smile as he returned to Willow's side. Lenny's hand, slick with sweat, intertwined with hers as he guided her back through the dimly lit warehouse. During the eerie silence, Willow wondered if her mind was a chaotic maze of fear and longing. "Is this my life now?" she pondered silently. "Will I ever truly find my place in this world?" As they emerged into the cool night air, the sound of the door slamming shut behind them resonated with finality. At that moment, Willow realized that regardless of the challenges ahead, she had decided. She was determined to stand by Lenny, unwavering, no matter the sacrifices that lay in store.

The soft hum of the car's engine filled the quiet, rhythmic pitter-patter of raindrops on the windshield as Lenny steered away from the dimly lit warehouse. Willow gazed out the window, her reflection distorted amidst the streaks of rain on the glass. The haunting images of the men and the tightly wrapped bricks lingered in her mind, replaying like a relentless movie reel she couldn't switch off. "Listen," Lenny began, his voice gentle but resolute, concern furrowing his brow as he glanced at Willow. "I don't want you involved in my business."

Willow drew in a deep breath, nodding in understanding. She turned to meet Lenny's gaze, seeking solace amid the whirlwind of emotions. "It's just... overwhelming. But I'll manage," she assured him. "Okay," Lenny replied, though not entirely convinced, opting to let the matter rest. The car coasted in silence, the rhythmic squeak of the wipers on the windshield providing a backdrop to the steady drumming of rain on the roof. Willow watched the streetlights cast a hazy glow over the slick pavement, feeling as though the outside world was slipping away with each passing moment.

In an unexpected moment, Lenny turned to her, his face breaking into a wide grin. "So, how about we go for a leisurely shopping trip?" His suggestion brought a smile to her face, the weight on her heart lifting ever so slightly. "I suppose you're still keen on the sandals-with-socks look?" she teased. "There's nothing quite like experiencing some good old toe-curling comfort," Lenny chuckled, his laughter filling the air with warmth. In that instant, Willow was overwhelmed with affection for the enigmatic man who had rekindled joy in her life.

As they whisked down the street, the passing scenery, with its rows of brick houses and the faint glow of store lights, seemed to reflect the shift that had taken place – both in herself and their relationship. The rawness of Lenny's reality began to color her once-innocent perceptions. Yet, regardless of what lay ahead, she was resolved to confront it all as long as they faced it together. In a silent gesture, Lenny reached out and clasped her hand, his touch conveying strength and reassurance.

Calvin maneuvered his bus through the bustling streets near the county hospital, leaning eagerly forward in his seat. The blaring cacophony of car horns filled the air as he squinted through the windshield, searching for a familiar figure among the crowd. His heart raced with anticipation, knowing that Lena's shift would soon end. He couldn't wait to see her face light up with joy when their eyes met.

"Come on, come on," he muttered, gripping the steering wheel tightly. As he approached the traffic light ahead, he knew it held the key to a brief moment of connection with his beloved wife amidst the chaos of the city. If it turned red, he would have to move on without her, but if it stayed green, they would share a few precious moments before their duties pulled them apart again.

"Lord, just a little longer," he silently prayed, his eyes flickering back and forth between the traffic light and the bustling sidewalk.

Standing at the bus stop, he saw Lena, adorned in her pristine white nurse's uniform, jogging gracefully toward the stop. Her complexion was slightly flushed from the exertion, and as she motioned for him to wait, her wedding band shimmered in the sunlight. Calvin's heart swelled with adoration and pride at the sight of her, recognizing her unwavering commitment to her profession, akin to his own. "Hey, Lena!" a passenger from the rear of the bus called out, acknowledging her presence. "I didn't realize you were married to the driver!" "Yes, that's my Cal," Lena responded with a smile, maintaining her pace. "Almost there, my love," Calvin whispered, extending the duration of the green traffic light. Every passing second felt like an eternity, yet he kept his gaze fixed on his beloved wife as she drew nearer.

Finally, Lena reached the bus stop, her chest heaving with effort. She placed one hand on her knee, trying to catch her breath before stepping onto the bus. As Lena straightened up, their eyes met, and Calvin felt a warmth spread through his chest, banishing the chill of Chicago's streets. "Made it," she gasped, smiling at him as she swiped her pass and sat nearby. "Sure did, sweetheart," he said softly, allowing himself to wink in her direction before pulling away from the curb. The traffic light had just turned red, but Calvin didn't care - his heart was whole, enough to carry him through the day.

"Hey, can we get going already?" a gruff voice barked from somewhere behind Calvin. "Got places to be!" another chimed in. But Calvin didn't care. He held the bus in place. His eyes fixed on Lena. "Patience, folks," he said with a smile, feeling the warmth of their connection banish the cold air seeping through the cracked windows. "Love is worth waiting for." "Damn right, it is," muttered an older woman seated near the front, her knitting needles clicking away as she worked on what looked like a vibrant afghan. She cast a glance at the younger passengers, daring them to argue. "Sorry, everyone!" Lena called out, panting as she climbed aboard the bus. A drop of sweat glistened on her forehead. "Take your time, Lena," Calvin told her gently, his eyes never leaving hers. "We've got all day."

The scent of lilacs filled the air around Calvin as Lena settled into her seat, a gentle fragrance that found harmony with the faint antiseptic smell lingering on her crisp white uniform. She leaned in towards him, her breath warm against his ear as she whispered, "Thank you, baby." Calvin felt the warmth of her words wrap around him, and he glanced at her, his eyes shining with love. "Any time, sweetheart." He turned back to face the road, his hands gripping the steering wheel with renewed vigor. It was just one small moment in the tapestry of their life together, but these moments made it all worthwhile. "Alright, people," he announced, pulling away from the curb, the chorus of complaints fading into the background. "Next stop, destiny." "Or downtown Chicago," Lena added with a chuckle, nudging him playfully. "Same difference." "Same difference," Calvin agreed, a smile playing on his lips as the bus continued navigating their beloved city's crowded streets.

For a moment, their hands met, fingers intertwining with a familiarity that spoke volumes of their love. The warmth of her touch seemed to seep into his very soul, and when she pulled away, he felt the ghost of her hand still resting upon his. "Lord, I'm grateful for this woman," he prayed silently, feeling a swell of gratitude pulse. Behind them, an old lady's voice pierced the murmurs of discontent still in the air. "That's love right there," she declared, loud enough for everyone to hear. "Instead of complaining, someone should say Amen." A few scattered 'Amens' echoed through the bus, and Calvin felt pride in his chest. The old lady's words were like a balm, soothing the sting of the passengers' impatience.

"God bless you, ma'am," he said, glancing in her direction through the rearview mirror. She nodded, her wrinkled face alight with approval. "God bless you both," she replied, her eyes twinkling as they met his. "And may He be with you always." Calvin knew life wasn't a smooth ride; it had bumps and twists along the way. But with Lena by his side and their love to guide them, he felt ready to face whatever challenges lay ahead. "Next stop, destiny," he thought, smiling as the bus rumbled on through the streets of west side Chicago.

Calvin maneuvered the behemoth through the dense Chicago traffic. The bus engine rumbled beneath his feet. His eyes darted between the rearview mirror and the crowded streets, a steady rhythm of focus. Lena sat beside him, her presence a quiet comfort, an anchor in the chaos. "Remember when the bus broke down on Lake

Street right before that bakery?" Lena mused, her voice soft against the backdrop of the city's noise. Calvin chuckled, recalling the memory. "How could I forget? We bought enough donuts to feed half the neighborhood." "Mrs. Thompson nearly cried when we brought them to her door," Lena added with a smile, her eyes crinkling at the corners. "Who knew sugar could bring such joy?" Calvin said, laughter warming his words. "Joy or diabetes?" Lena joked, her hand settling gently on his forearm.

"Maybe a bit of both." Calvin grinned, feeling the tender weight of her touch as he turned the wheel, navigating around a double-parked taxi. "Baby, you know how much I appreciate what you do for us, right?" Lena asked, her eyes searching his face. Her sincerity shone like a beacon amid the bus's din. "Of course, sweetheart," Calvin replied, his heart swelling with love for this woman who had stood by his side through thick and thin. "I'd do anything for you and the kids." "I know you would," Lena murmured, her fingers tracing a reassuring pattern on his arm. "Hey, Mr. Bus Driver!" shouted a young man toward the back of the bus. "When are we getting to Madison?" "Two more stops, son," Calvin called back, his eyes never leaving the road. He knew the route like the back of his hand – every pothole, every tight corner, every red light that took just a second too long.

"Can't wait to get home and see my babies," Lena sighed, her head resting on Calvin's shoulder briefly before straightening up. "I've missed their laughter." "Me too," Calvin agreed, his mind flickering to the image of their children – bright-eyed and full of life, ready to face the world with open hearts. He knew they would inherit the love and strength he and Lena shared. "Promise me something?" Lena asked, her voice barely audible above the chatter of passengers and the city's hum. "Anything," Calvin said, his hand squeezing hers briefly before returning to the wheel. "No matter what happens, we'll stay strong together, just like this," Lena said, her eyes shining with determination. "Forever, Lena," Calvin whispered, his soul echoing the truth of his words.

CHAPTER 9

Lenny guided Willow through the bustling department store, laughter and chatter filling the air as shoppers buzzed from one display to another. Her eyes, wide and sparkling like a curious child's, took in the vibrant displays of clothes with a mixture of delight and cunning calculation. Each outfit promised a new identity, another layer for her manipulative persona. "Look at this one!" Willow exclaimed, holding up a shimmering emerald blouse. "Isn't it just divine?"

He couldn't help but smile at her enthusiasm, feeling a sense of satisfaction in being able to provide for her.

Despite her calculating nature, something about seeing her genuinely excited tugged at his heartstrings.

"Go on, try whatever you want," Lenny encouraged, watching as Willow picked up a silky red dress and held it against her body, admiring herself in the mirror. The fabric seemed to catch the light, casting an alluring glow on her skin. "Are you sure?" Willow asked, a hint of disbelief in her voice. She glanced over her shoulder at him, searching his face for any sign of hesitation. It was a rare moment of vulnerability for the usually poised woman. "Absolutely," Lenny replied with a grin, his internal struggle momentarily forgotten. For now, he wanted to give her this small taste of happiness, even if it meant ignoring the darker aspects of their relationship. "You deserve it."

As Willow turned back to the mirror, a satisfied smile playing on her lips, Lenny couldn't help but feel the weight of his decisions bearing down on him. He had chosen to align himself with a woman whose motivations could be personal vendettas and a desire for power. Yet, he couldn't bring himself to regret it entirely. There was something undeniably magnetic about her, something that drew him in despite his better judgment.

As they continued to browse the store, Lenny felt a familiar knot of anxiety growing within him. The choices he had made and the secrets he had kept were like a noose around his neck. But for now, as he watched Willow twirl in front of the mirror, laughing with delight as she transformed into a dream vision, he allowed himself to forget the darkness that loomed. "Thank you," Willow whispered, her eyes shining with gratitude as she wrapped her arms around him tightly. And for a moment, standing there amidst the chaos of the department store, Lenny could almost believe everything would be alright. Almost.

Calvin gripped the wheel of the city bus tightly, the vinyl surface slightly sticky in his sweaty palms. The engine's hum vibrated through his body as he navigated the bustling streets of Chicago's west side. Calvin could hear the chatter of passengers mixed with the distant sounds of car horns and rumbling trains. The familiar scent of exhaust fumes wafted through the open windows, a reminder that he was nearing the end of his shift. He glanced over at his wife, Lena, who sat near the front of the bus.

The soft afternoon light filtered through the window, glowing her caramel skin warmly. Her white stockings clung to her shapely legs, drawing Calvin's gaze like a moth to a flame. His heart swelled with love and desire, the intense emotion that threatened to distract him from his duties as a bus driver. "Pay attention, baby," Lena whispered, a blush coloring her cheeks as she noticed his wandering eyes. She tucked a stray curl behind her ear, her fingers brushing against the delicate gold cross hanging around her neck. "We're almost home." "Can't help it," Calvin admitted with a sheepish grin, forcing himself to focus on the traffic ahead. "I'm just so glad this is my last trip today. I can't wait to get home and spend time with you." Lena's smile widened, her dimples deepening as she regarded him affectionately. As Calvin navigated the crowded streets, his thoughts wandered to their family waiting at home. Their children would be eager to share the day's adventures, and Rose, his mother, would undoubtedly have prepared a hearty meal for them all.

"Stay focused, Calvin," Lena admonished gently, her eyes twinkling with mischief. "You know how important your job is—not just to us, but to everyone who relies on you to get them home safely." Calvin nodded, his love for Lena and their family fueling his determination to be the best husband, father, and bus driver he could be. He knew that his work was more than just a way to provide for his loved ones; it was also a testament to his faith and resilience in adversity. With a renewed sense of purpose, Calvin pressed onward, eager for the day to end and the evening to begin. As the bus rounded the corner onto their street, he couldn't help but steal one last glance at Lena.

"Speaking of which," Calvin continued, his calloused hands gripping the steering wheel tighter, "when's our next

Bible study night with Mama and the kids?" Lena's lavender perfume mingled with the diesel fumes from the bus, creating an odd yet comforting aroma that filled the air around them. Lena smiled coyly, her dark eyes shimmering with amusement. She glanced away momentarily, watching the brick buildings and bustling storefronts of Chicago pass by before meeting his gaze again. "Whenever it is, it's not tonight," she teased, tucking a stray curl behind her ear. "Now watch the road, Mr. Steele."

Calvin chuckled, the sound rumbling deep in his chest. "Alright, alright," he conceded as they approached a red light. "I'll keep my eyes on the road—for now." He winked at her playfully before concentrating on the traffic ahead.

Moments like these—simple, unassuming exchanges steeped in familiarity and affection—have made it all worth it. "Almost there," Lena murmured, her hand resting on his shoulder, a gentle reminder of the love that anchored them both. He could feel the warmth of her touch even through the fabric of his uniform. Calvin nodded, his heart swelling with gratitude and anticipation. With a renewed sense of focus, he navigated the crowded streets of Chicago, eager for the day to end and the evening to begin. "Home sweet home," he whispered, already envisioning the laughter and love that awaited them behind their front door.

Lenny stood at the cash register, his arm draped over a mountain of Willow's new clothes. The scent of new fabric and the hum of fluorescent lights filled the small store. As Lenny leaned on the counter, he couldn't help but feel the weight of his actions tugging at his conscience. He glanced at Willow, whose eyes sparkled with disbelief and giddy excitement as if she were floating on cloud nine. "Your total is $247.65," Nicki announced from behind the register, her voice smooth as honey. She had the beauty that could stop traffic, but Lenny knew better than to get lost in it at the moment. He nodded and handed over the cash, ignoring how her fingers brushed against his own. But Willow, ever observant, caught the lingering eye contact between him and the cashier. Something unspoken passed between them as if they shared a personal connection.

"Here's your receipt," Nicki said, stretching her hand toward Lenny. She held onto it just a moment too long as he reached for it, forcing him to offer a subtle nod of acknowledgment before finally releasing her grip. "Thanks," Lenny muttered, his eyes flicking back to the woman behind the counter.

"Enjoy," Nicki said sweetly, her gaze shifting to Willow. For a moment, Willow remained frozen, caught in the web of Nicki's knowing stare. It was as if the cashier had somehow managed to look past Willow's casual demeanor and straight into the dark heart of her intentions. Then, without another word, Nicki turned her attention to the next customer, leaving Willow standing there, lost in thought. Willow clutched her bags tightly, trying to make sense of the interaction she'd just witnessed. Lenny could feel Willow's eyes boring into him, her calculating mind working to decode the interaction she'd just seen. He knew she was cunning and manipulative, but he also knew he had been mostly honest with her. "Is everything alright?" Lenny asked, his eyes searching her face for any sign of distress. "Yes, of course," Willow replied quickly, smiling as she fought to push her doubts and fears aside. "Did you know her?" Willow asked, her tone deceptively casual.

"Old acquaintance," Lenny replied, not wanting to reveal more than necessary. He could see the gears turning in Willow's head, her curiosity piqued, but he needed to steer her away from Nicki and back to the task. "I think we should focus on the next steps, don't you?" "Of course," Willow agreed, but Lenny knew she would file away the information for later, like a snake coiled and ready to strike. Willow replied quickly, "I'm overwhelmed by all these new clothes." "Ah, well, I figured you deserved a little something after everything we've been through," he said, brushing a strand of hair from her face. "Are you hungry? We could grab some lunch before heading home."

"Sure," Willow replied, her mind racing as they walked away from the register. She knew to tread carefully, always keeping in sight that Lenny lived in a world of secrets and hidden dangers. For now, though, she chose to revel in the thrill of the shopping spree and the happiness it had brought her, even if only for a moment.

As they strolled through the busy mall, laughter and conversation filled the air, along with the scent of buttery popcorn from a nearby stand. The world outside their little bubble felt distant, and Willow found herself almost able to forget the twisted path that had led them here. "Let's try that diner over there," Lenny suggested, pointing to a cozy-looking eatery tucked in the corner of the mall. "I've heard good things." "Alright," Willow agreed, her eyes flicking back to the store where Nicki continued to work as if she could somehow unravel the mysterious connection between them with just a glance. "Hey," Lenny said gently, his hand on her arm bringing her back to the present. "Let's focus on us for now, alright? We'll figure everything else out later." "Okay," Willow responded, nodding her head. But deep down, she knew that it wouldn't be long before the truth would come crashing down around them, as unstoppable as the setting sun that cast long shadows across the west side of Chicago.

The sun was now casting a warm golden light over the bus station as Calvin and Lena strolled hand in hand toward their car. A gentle breeze ruffled their clothes, carrying the irresistible scent of freshly baked bread from Mrs. Baker's bakery just around the corner. Calvin couldn't help but smile as he breathed in the familiar aroma, thinking back to countless dinners at home when Lena would bring in a loaf to share with the family.

He looked at his wife, her hair dancing like a dark waterfall in the wind. The way the sunlight accentuated the curve of her cheek made his heart swell with love for her. The corners of his eyes crinkled as he let out a contented sigh. Life wasn't always easy, but moments like these reminded him that it was worth it – for the love they shared and the family they'd built together.

"Hey, what's going on tonight?" a familiar voice called out, breaking the momentary spell. Biscuit jogged up to Calvin and Lena, wiping sweat from his brow after a long day driving the city bus. Calvin tore his gaze away from Lena, disappointment flickering across his face like a shadow. "Nothing much," he replied, trying to keep the annoyance out of his voice. "Just cooking dinner for the kids." "Sounds nice," Biscuit said, his voice tinged with melancholy. It was no secret that he didn't have much in the way of the family himself, which seemed to weigh on him more heavily some days than others.

Calvin glanced over at his wife, then back to Biscuit, a sigh escaping as he nodded in agreement. "Yeah, come on over if you want," he said, trying to sound more enthusiastic than he felt. He just hoped Biscuit's presence wouldn't take away from the precious family time they had together. "Thanks," Biscuit said, his eyes lighting up with gratitude. "I appreciate that." Biscuit's eyes darted back and forth between Calvin and Lena. "Nah, I'm not inviting myself over for dinner this time. Spending family time together sounds nice at the end of a hard day in these streets."

Lena playfully nudged Biscuit in the ribs, her grin making the laugh lines around her eyes crinkle. "It's not like you're not trying in these streets daily to make a family too."

Their laughter filled the air, the sound bouncing off the surrounding buildings like a sweet melody against the backdrop of the city's constant hum. Lena turned and headed towards their car, her heels clicking on the pavement with each step. Calvin watched her go, feeling that familiar warmth in his chest that always swelled when he looked at her. But as her footsteps faded into the distance, he couldn't help but feel a sense of urgency pressing down on him.

He leaned closer to Biscuit, his voice barely above a whisper as if sharing a secret that only the two were privy to. "Please, don't get back with Willow." The name hung heavy between them, a reminder of past mistakes and the turmoil they had caused. Biscuit sighed, his eyes clouding over with memories of her. The soft curve of her hips and her laughter seemed to dance along his skin – those moments were hard to forget, even when the darker side of her nature tainted them. "I won't, man. But damn, she had some traits that are hard to forget."

Calvin took a deep breath, grasping for the right words to offer his friend. He knew that Biscuit's heart was in the right place, even if it sometimes led him down the wrong path. "You deserve better, Biscuit. You're a good man; don't let her pull you back in." "Thanks, Calvin," Biscuit said, his voice hoarse with emotion. They shared a knowing look. Then both turned their gazes toward the car where Lena stood waiting, her silhouette outlined by the fading sunlight. As they walked towards her, Calvin prayed silently that his friend would find the strength to resist the siren call of his past and that their family could remain a beacon of hope and love amidst the chaos of life in these streets.

CHAPTER 10

The luxurious condo towered above Lake Michigan like a sentinel guarding the shoreline. The setting sun glowed on its new glass, reflecting the rippling waters below. Inside, the floor-to-ceiling windows offered a breathtaking panorama of the lake, stretching out infinitely. It would have been mesmerizing to anyone who took a moment to appreciate it. "Hey, Lenny," Willow called from the bedroom, her voice tinged with frustration and hope. "What about this one?" She emerged wearing a slinky red dress, its hemline daringly high. Her thick legs seemed endless as she sauntered toward him, hips swaying with every step.

But Lenny barely glanced her way, too engrossed in his phone call. His brow furrowed, eyes focused on some distant point beyond the glass. He muttered into the receiver, "Yeah, I got it. Don't worry." Willow's lips curled in irritation, her eyes flashing with impatience. She had always been able to command attention effortlessly, and Lenny's preoccupation tested the limits of her tolerance. She knew that if she could bend him to her will, there were a few obstacles she couldn't overcome. Lenny barely registered her presence, his attention consumed by the urgent conversation on the other end of the phone. He paced back and forth, the thick shag carpet beneath his feet muffling his steps.

Aware that she needed a new strategy, Willow took a deep breath before stepping out of the bedroom, wearing nothing but a towel wrapped around her body. Her heart raced as she stood there, challenging Lenny's attention with all the confidence she could muster. The towel slipped from her grasp and fell to the floor with a soft thump, leaving her vulnerable in the dim glow of the condo's golden lights. At last, Lenny hung up the phone and turned to look at her, his eyes widening in surprise. "Well, now," he drawled, taking in her appearance with an appreciative gaze. "You sure know how to make a brotha forget his troubles." "Is it working?" Willow asked coyly, arching an eyebrow as she struck a sultry pose.

"Can't say I've ever seen a better outfit on you," Lenny replied, smiling slowly. His voice was thick with desire, but a hint of vulnerability was underneath. It was as if he knew what game she was playing but couldn't help himself from being drawn in anyway. Willow's heart soared as Lenny's admiration washed over her, erasing the frustration she had felt earlier. She moved closer to him, her bare feet whispering against the plush carpet. "Does this mean I finally have your full attention?"

"It seems like it," Lenny admitted, his eyes never leaving hers. Lenny sighed, rubbing the back of his neck as he met her gaze. "Willow, we're playing a dangerous game, and I can't afford to make any mistakes."

"I know," she murmured, reaching out to trace a finger along the curve of his jaw, her touch feather-light. "But we could use a little break from all that stress, don't you think?" "Maybe," Lenny conceded, his expression softening. "But promise me one thing, okay?" "Anything," she replied, her voice laced with sincerity. "Promise me you won't let this change us," he said, his eyes searching hers for the truth. "We've gotta stay focused on what matters most."

Willow hesitated for a moment, considering his words. She had never been one to make promises she couldn't keep, but something about Lenny's vulnerability stirred a new, unfamiliar emotion within her. "I promise," she whispered, her eyes locked on his. "Good," he murmured, pulling her close and wrapping his arms around her naked form. As they stood there, wrapped up in each other, the tension between them seemed to dissipate like mist fading into the evening air. But even as Willow reveled in Lenny's embrace, a small part of her mind couldn't help but wonder if she could keep the promise she had just made.

The rich aroma of roast chicken and garlic mashed potatoes filled the cramped dining room, teasing the taste buds of everyone present. Calvin, Lena, Junior, and Ryder gathered around the worn wooden table, their eyes bright with anticipation as they took their seats. The flickering light from above cast warm shadows on their faces, making the humble room feel like a sanctuary. "Lord, thank you for this meal and the hands that prepared it," Calvin prayed, his deep voice reverberating. "Bless our family and help us continue growing in your love." "Amen," they chorused, their voices blending in perfect harmony.

Laughter and conversation bubbled up as they dug into the mouthwatering meal. The sound of cutlery scraping against plates mingled with the loving banter, creating a symphony of warmth that filled the air. Calvin felt a surge of pride for his family and gratitude for their unwavering support as they passed around dishes, sharing spoonfuls of food and cherished memories.

"Hey, Dad," Junior said between bites of creamy mashed potatoes, glancing towards the front door. His voice held an undercurrent of concern, reflecting the empathy he'd inherited from Calvin and Lena. "Is Biscuit coming tonight?"

Calvin's eyes met Lena's across the table, exchanging a glance heavy with meaning. He shook his head slowly as he reached for a piece of chicken. "No, son. Biscuit has other things on his table tonight." He felt a pang of worry for his long-time friend but hid it behind the calm mask he wore for his family.

"Maybe we should pray for him too," Ryder suggested, her strong-willed independence shining through as she looked out for those important to her family. "An excellent idea, sweetheart," Lena agreed, her compassionate nature evident in the warmth of her smile. She reached out to clasp Calvin's hand, gently squeezing it as they bowed their heads in silent prayer. Calvin's thoughts turned inward as the family settled back into the conversation. If Biscuit could only find his way back to the Lord, he might be able to break free from the cycle of falling for the wrong woman.

"Hey, Junior," Calvin said, snapping back to the present. "Why don't you tell us about your Sunday school lesson today? I heard you learned something interesting." Junior's face lit up at the opportunity to share his knowledge, his optimism shining bright. "Well, we talked about forgiveness and how Jesus wants us to forgive even those who've hurt us the most." "Sounds like a valuable lesson," Calvin said, approving. "Remembering that we're all human and make mistakes is important. Sometimes, it takes a little understanding and forgiveness to help someone get back on the right path." As the conversation continued around the table, Calvin felt grateful for the love and strength that tied them together. They were a family forged by blood and faith - a beacon of hope and inspiration for one another in an ever-changing world.

Across town, Biscuit found himself in a less-than-wholesome situation. Earlier that day, he had met a girl on his bus route – a young woman with wild, curly hair and eyes that sparkled like the city lights outside. She had been waiting at the stop near the factory where she worked, her hands stained with grease, but her smile bright and inviting. He knew he shouldn't have invited her over, but something about her made him throw caution to the wind.

They were at his house, laughing and rolling in passion like teenagers. In their carelessness, they stumbled and rolled off the edge of the kitchen table, crashing onto the worn linoleum floor with a resounding thud. The impact left them both flat on their naked backs, gasping for breath and wincing from the pain. "Ouch," Biscuit groaned, rubbing his sore back as he stared at the water-stained ceiling. "I think I might've hurt myself." "Sorry 'bout that," the girl replied, her voice breathless and tinged with laughter. "Didn't mean to get that carried away like that."

Biscuit couldn't help but chuckle softly despite the discomfort. But as Biscuit lay there, his laughter faded, replaced by a growing sense of unease. What was he doing here? This life wasn't for him – or it shouldn't have been. He'd always tried to do right by others, even when he struggled to do right by himself. For a brief moment, he thought about how this impulsive act could have jeopardized his back and everything. "Can we do this tomorrow?" Biscuit asked suddenly, still wincing as he rubbed his aching back. "I think I hurt myself." "Sure," the girl replied, her voice a bit more subdued now. "Right after I drop my son off at his father's house when I get off work. We can meet up then."

Biscuit stared at the ceiling, the cracked paint and water stains forming a map of his regrets. With each shallow breath, memories of women from his past flickered in his mind like snapshots – women who had come and gone, leaving him no wiser but undeniably older. "Man, what am I doin'?" he muttered, feeling the weight of each decision pressing down on him. But as the silence stretched out, he couldn't help but wonder if there was still time to change, to find something more meaningful than these fleeting encounters.

A smile tugged at the corners of his mouth as he turned to the girl beside him. She was pretty in a way that reminded him of the first girl he'd kissed behind the bleachers in high school. "Sounds like a plan," he said softly, surprising himself with the warmth in his voice. The girl propped herself up on one elbow, her brow furrowing in confusion as she glanced around the room. "Hey, have you seen my panties?" Her voice was vulnerable, and Biscuit felt a pang of guilt. "Uh, lemme check," he grumbled, gingerly lifting himself off the floor and scanning the cluttered room. His eyes finally landed on the discarded garment tangled in the legs of an overturned chair. He retrieved it and handed it to the girl with an awkward half-smile. "Here you go."

"Thanks," she said, rolling her eyes playfully as she pulled them on. "You know, Biscuit, you're unlike the other guys I've met. You seem different."

His heart clenched at her words, and for a moment, he found himself at a loss for what to say. Instead, he held her gaze, feeling an unspoken understanding pass between them. And as they lay there, side by side in the dimly lit room, Biscuit felt the first stirrings of hope – a fragile, flickering flame that whispered of redemption and the possibility of a better tomorrow. "Maybe we both need to make some changes," he mused, rubbing at the stubble on his chin. "Start choosin' better for ourselves." "Maybe so," she agreed, her eyes softening as she looked back at him.

The night he had fallen over Chicago's streets. Biscuit drove aimlessly through the gridlocked traffic, his old car humming softly beneath him. He let his mind wander as he maneuvered the car through the crowded lanes, eyes scanning the faces of passersby – women in their colorful dresses and men in their pressed suits. The warm breeze drifted through the open window. "Maybe tonight," Biscuit muttered, the words lost in the wind. He couldn't shake the feeling that somewhere out there was a woman who could be his wife material – someone who would give him stability and help him make sense of the randomness in his life. "Where you at?" he whispered, gripping the steering wheel tighter. Loneliness crept into his chest, settling heavily alongside memories of past loves gone wrong. Biscuit shook his head, trying to dislodge the feeling. "I ain't got time for all that."

As he approached an intersection, Biscuit noticed several police cars with flashing lights ahead. His heart skipped a beat, the familiar dread knotting in his stomach. The officers conducted a random checkpoint, stopping cars to check for DUIs and other violations. Biscuit knew he hadn't done anything wrong, but the sight of authority figures still made him uneasy. "Damn," he murmured, inching forward in the queue. "Just my luck." He glanced in the rearview mirror, straightening his collar and running a hand through his unruly hair. In his peripheral vision, he saw a young couple arguing on the sidewalk, their harsh words drowned out by the clamor of the city. Biscuit sighed; love could be as cruel as it was beautiful. He wondered if the right woman would ever enter his life.

"Alright, stay cool," he whispered as he approached the checkpoint. The officer waved him forward, his stern expression unchanging. Biscuit's heart pounded in his chest as he rolled down the window, the cool night air doing little to ease his nerves. While waiting in line, Biscuit couldn't help but notice the women walking by on the sidewalk. A woman with brown curls that bounced as she walked caught his eye. She wore a simple floral dress and a smile that hinted at a hidden secret.

He wondered if someone like her could be the one to bring him stability and happiness. He chewed on his lip, considering the possibility. "Could it be that easy?" he thought, the randomness of life weighing heavily on him. His heart yearned for something more, something meaningful. As Biscuit contemplated, a sudden knock on his driver's side window was jolting him back to reality. Startled, he turned to see a pretty Chicago policewoman standing beside his car, her expression unreadable. The streetlights cast a soft glow on her face, highlighting her sharp cheekbones and keen eyes.

"Good evening," Biscuit said, quickly rolling down his window. He attempted to mask his unease with a charming grin. "You're the perfect example of Chicago's finest." "License and registration, please," she said, her voice authoritative yet melodic. "Sure thing, officer," Biscuit replied, fumbling in the glove compartment for the documents. He handed them over with a shaky hand, hoping she wouldn't notice. As she examined his papers, Biscuit couldn't help but steal glances at her, admiring how her uniform hugged her curves. He tried to imagine what kind of life they could have together, but the vision seemed too good to be true. The policewoman narrowed her eyes, sizing him up. Biscuit's heart pounded, his palms growing clammy on the steering wheel. He knew he hadn't done anything wrong, but the uncertainty of the situation gnawed at him. "Stay cool, man. Just stay cool," Biscuit repeated to himself, trying to slow his racing thoughts. The officer's eyebrow arched upwards, and she gave him a once-over, taking in his worn denim jacket and the untamed beard that framed his face.

Her gaze swept through the interior of his car, lingering on the empty soda cans and fast-food wrappers scattered across the backseat. "Alright," she said, her tone neutral. "Now, if I see something going on, I will still ask you to step out of the vehicle." Biscuit's eyes crinkled at the corners as he grinned, trying to break the ice. "Hell, if that's what it takes, let me help you find something wrong." He reached for an empty bag of chips on the passenger seat, offering it to her with a flourish. The officer eyed him warily, but then her lips twitched into an almost imperceptible smile. It was the first sign of warmth Biscuit had seen from her since she approached his window, and he couldn't help but feel a sense of victory. "Have a lovely evening, sir," she said, handing his license and registration back to him.

"Thank you for making it beautiful," he replied with sincerity, feeling lighter than he had all night. She waved him through the checkpoint, and Biscuit eased his foot onto the accelerator, careful not to speed off too quickly. As he eased his car past the checkpoint, he watched the policewoman in his rearview mirror until she disappeared. He couldn't shake the feeling that their paths might cross again someday. Biscuit replayed the encounter in his mind, savoring the memory of the officer's hesitant smile. He thought about how hard it was to find someone who could understand his life, which seemed like a never-ending series of mistakes and fleeting relationships. His thoughts drifted to Calvin and his family, wondering if he would ever find that kind of stability and love.

"Maybe there's someone out there for me, too," he mused aloud, feeling a flicker of hope ignited within him. The streets of Chicago stretched before him, cloaked in darkness and dotted with the warm glow of streetlights. Biscuit drove on, his heart lighter than it had been in a long time, as he continued his search for meaning amid the chaos of life.

In Lenny's luxurious condo, the soft glow of the moonlight peeked through the curtains, casting shadows across the bedroom floor. Lenny lay sprawled out on his king-sized bed, his chest heaving with each heavy breath as he was in the tendrils of sleep. The room was silent but for the rhythmic sound of his breathing. Willow, however, was wide awake. The silky sheets clung to her like a second skin, and she could feel the tension running through her body – a living current of unease that pulsed in time with her racing heart. She couldn't help but think of all the people whose lives had been affected by her cunning manipulations. Was this what power felt like? It wasn't as satisfying as she had imagined. "Damn it," she muttered, fidgeting beneath the covers. Sleep wouldn't come, no matter how much she willed it to.

With a frustrated sigh, she slipped from the warmth of the bed, her bare feet touching the cool parquet floor. Padding silently over to the door, she cracked it open just enough to slip through, leaving Lenny undisturbed in his slumber.

As Willow entered the kitchen, she was in awe by the sleek modernity of the space. Stainless steel appliances gleamed beneath recessed lighting, and cherry wood cabinets lined the walls. It was a far cry from the cramped, dingy kitchens she'd grown accustomed to before Lenny. "Wow," she whispered, unable to contain her amazement. "Never thought I'd see a kitchen like this."

She never really saw herself as the domestic type, but she couldn't help feeling drawn to the shiny new gadgets and tools surrounding her. Willow wondered if this was the kind of life she could get used to after all – one of luxury and comfort. But at what cost? "Got to keep my eye on the prize," she reminded herself, her gaze hardening with determination.

Her stomach growled, demanding her attention. Willow decided to rummage through the pantry, hoping to find a late-night snack to quell her hunger and distract her from her scattered thoughts. The neatly organized food items greeted her as Willow opened the pantry door. She scanned the shelves for something that would satisfy her midnight craving, her fingers brushing over boxes of pasta, jars of peanut butter, and bags of chips. "Let's see what we've got here..." she mused, reaching for a can of fruit cocktail in the back of a shelf.

As her hand made contact with the aluminum container, she felt an unexpected shift beneath her fingertips. "W ha...?" she muttered, startled by the sudden movement. To her astonishment, a hidden compartment swung open like a secret door in a mystery novel, revealing even more stacks of tightly wrapped bricks that she instantly recognized — drugs. Her breath caught in her throat, her heart pounding wildly. "Of course," she whispered bitterly, trying to keep her voice steady. "It's never that simple, is it?" Willow stared at the concealed stash, her mind racing about what this discovery could mean for her future. She knew she had to tread carefully because Lenny was starting to look like a kingpin versus a corner boy.

"Stay calm, Willow. You're smarter than this," she reminded herself, taking a deep breath to steady her nerves. "Just find something to eat and act like nothing's wrong."

She closed the secret panel with trembling hands, ensuring it clicked back into place. She grabbed a bag of pretzels from the pantry and returned to the living room, hoping against hope that she could keep her newfound knowledge hidden away, just like the drugs behind the facade of everyday household items.

Sinking onto the plush couch, Willow hugged a cushion tightly against her chest as if it could shield her from the grim reality surrounding her. The soft fabric absorbed her tears as they began to flow, reflecting the flickering light from the streetlamps outside. "Look at what your greed has gotten you into," she chastised herself, choking back a sob. "Lenny's charm, his wealth, so blinded you.

The first morning light crept in through the gaps in the curtains, casting a warm glow onto the linoleum floor. The kitchen was alive with the sizzling of butter on the grill and the rhythmic tapping of Calvin's foot as he hummed an upbeat gospel tune. He stood at the stove, his bus driver uniform crisp and freshly ironed, flipping pancakes with one hand, his other engaged in keeping time with the music. Calvin's rich, baritone voice filled the room like a choir, and even without words, the Steele household knew that this man lived and breathed his faith.

"Morning, baby," Lena called out as she entered the kitchen, her white pantyhose hugging her legs as she adjusted the collar of her nurse's uniform. Calvin shook his head and looked at her, his eyes twinkling with admiration for the woman who had become his rock in life. "Look at you," he murmured, pausing to take in the sight of his wife as she prepared herself for another long day of caring for others. "Praise God from whom all blessings flow." Lena smiled and rolled her eyes playfully, knowing full well that Calvin was just as much a blessing to her as she was to him. "I can't do this with you right now," she said teasingly, giving him a quick peck before retreating to the other side of the house to gather her things.

Calvin sighed, feeling pride and concern as he thought about Lena's dedication to her work and their family. He knew she often carried the world's weight on her shoulders, but she never let it show. She was strong, just like his mother, Rose, and they had instilled that same strength in their children, Junior and Ryder. He flipped another pancake and glanced at the clock on the wall, noting the time with a furrowed brow. The kids would be up soon, and he needed to ensure they were ready for their day. With a silent prayer for strength and guidance, Calvin turned his attention back to the task at hand, knowing that if there was one thing his family could always count on, it was a hot breakfast and a warm embrace from their loving father.

CHAPTER 11

The sound of hurried footsteps reverberated through the hallway, signaling the imminent arrival of Calvin's lively children. In a perfectly timed entrance, Junior and Ryder burst into the room, their faces aflush with the infectious excitement of a new day. "Good morning, Dad!" Junior greeted, his voice betraying the transitional phase of adolescence. With swift movements, he settled into his seat at the table, eagerly helping himself to a plate piled high with delicious pancakes. Alongside him, Ryder mirrored his enthusiasm, her eyes sparkling with a blend of hunger and determination that Calvin knew all too well.

"Remember, today is Bible study night," Calvin reminded them, his tone severe but loving as he surveyed the scene before him. "Grandma Rose will be picking you up from school." The words had barely left his mouth before Junior nodded enthusiastically, sending syrup flying from his overstuffed mouth onto his shirt. Ryder, ever the cool and collected one, gave her father a thumbs-up, her eyes never leaving her breakfast. Calvin couldn't help but smile at the sight of his children, their youthful energy a constant reminder of the blessings God had bestowed upon him and Lena. Moments like these made the early mornings and long days worthwhile, and he was determined to cherish every second.

"Alright now, let's not forget anything today," he chided gently, knowing full well that Junior and Ryder were prone to leaving their belongings behind when caught up in the whirlwind of their daily lives. Just then, Lena reentered the kitchen, the crisp white of her nurse's cap starkly contrasting with the dark curls that framed her face. "And if you forget something," she added, her eyes dancing with amusement as she looked at her husband, "we'll be happy to bring it to Grandma's house, won't we, Calvin?"

Calvin fought to maintain his composure, the corners of his mouth twitching as he struggled to keep a straight face. "Absolutely," he agreed, forcing a smile onto his face, "but again, don't forget anything." As he watched his family sharing breakfast and laughter in the warm embrace of their kitchen, Calvin felt a surge of gratitude and love that threatened to overwhelm him.

The dim glow of a single table lamp cast shadows across Lenny's upscale living room, softening the harsh lines of the leather sofa and plush chairs. A haze of cigarette smoke hung in the air, giving the scene a gritty, film-noir atmosphere. The man at the center of it all, Lenny, sat with his crew in a circle, speaking in hushed tones. His eyes darted around the room, ensuring that none of their conversations would reach Willow, who was still asleep in the bedroom—or so he thought.

"Lower your voices," Lenny warned through gritted teeth, rubbing his temples as the stress weighed on him. He couldn't afford any mistakes now, not with everything on the line. "Hey, boss," Turk whispered, leaning closer to Lenny. He glanced over his shoulder, making sure no one was listening. "How are we gonna handle that situation with, you know, that guy?" "Sleepy time for whoever," Lenny replied cryptically, his gaze brutal and unflinching. Turk's eyes widened for a moment before he nodded, understanding the gravity of what his boss was implying. "Got it, boss. You can count on me," he said, determination etched in his features.

Lenny stared into the distance, his jaw clenched. He knew what had to happen, but that didn't make it any easier. This situation was the life Lenny had chosen and the path walked down willingly. And yet, as he looked around the room at the men he had come to consider family, sometimes Lenny couldn't help but wonder if he had made the right choices. "Damn it, Willow," he muttered, thinking about the woman sleeping just a few rooms away.

"Alright, boys," he said, trying to inject some authority into his voice. Lenny looked around the room, took a deep breath, and steeled himself for what would come.

As the men continued their tense conversation, Willow's heart pounded relentlessly. Sweat trickled down her temple as she pressed her back against the wall, just around the corner from the living room. Her ears strained to catch the hushed tones of Lenny and his crew, each word a dagger that twisted deeper into her soul. "Look, we just gotta be careful," one of the men muttered, his voice low and gravelly. "Stick to the plan, and everything will run smoothly." "Damn right," another chimed in, the clink of a whiskey glass punctuating his agreement. Willow closed her eyes, fighting to steady her breathing. She could feel the weight of her discovery bearing down on her – secrets that should have remained buried, now clawing at the surface like restless ghosts. She had always been to the darker side of life, but this time, this was beyond anything she could have imagined.

"Is there any other way?" Willow whispered to herself, the words barely audible even to her ears. The footsteps approaching sent a jolt of panic through her veins, and she held her breath, praying they wouldn't hear her ragged breathing. As the footsteps receded, Willow allowed herself a small sigh of relief. She knew she couldn't hide forever – sooner or later, they would discover her eavesdropping, and the consequences could be dire. "Damn you, Lenny," she thought bitterly, his brooding face flashing through her mind.

With her resolve strengthened, Willow pushed away from the wall and tiptoed back towards the bedroom, her heart pounding to the rhythm of newfound hope. As she swung the door open, her elbow knocked over a vase on the nightstand, and shattering glass cut through the silence. "Willow?" Lenny called out, concern lining his voice. Is everything alright in there?" "Y-yeah," she stammered, trying to force a casual tone. I just dropped something, is all."

"Alright then," he said, though she could hear the uncertainty in his voice. "Damn it, Willow," she whispered, the words barely audible. Her thoughts raced as the realization hit her like a cold slap – there was no turning back now.

The pit of Willow's stomach twisted into a tight knot as she recalled the excitement and allure that had once drawn her to Lenny's world. She took in a shallow breath, trying to calm herself.

Willow's hands trembled as she began to collect the broken shards of glass scattered across the floor. Each sharp fragment seemed to taunt her with its jagged edges, a reminder of the mess she had created—for herself. "Hey," Lenny called out softly from the doorway. Are you sure you're okay?" Willow looked up at him, her eyes shining with determination. "Yeah, Lenny. I'm alright." She nodded as the door closed behind him.

The low hum of conversation resumed, and she could feel her heartbeat syncopate with each measured word exchanged between Lenny and his crew.

The front door clicked shut, signaling the departure of Lenny's associates. The sudden silence was deafening, leaving Willow alone with her thoughts. She allowed herself to exhale then, her body trembling from the aftershocks of adrenaline that coursed through her veins. "Alright, Willow," she whispered, her fingers clutching the broom handle tightly. "You've dug yourself into this hole. As she swept the last broken vase, Willow glanced at the bedroom door, expecting Lenny to appear momentarily, but he didn't. "Time to put my thinking cap on," she mused, staring down at the pile of shattered glass.

With a sigh, Willow set the broom aside, her resolve hardening with each step she took toward the living room. The remnants of a now lifeless cigar lay smoldering in an ashtray beside the cracked window. The acrid smell filled the room, merging with the scent of stale whiskey that clung to the air like a suffocating fog. "Call me if you run into any issues," Lenny said, his voice firm and authoritative. "Will do, boss," came the muffled response before the door closed again. Willow knew her path had taken a dangerous turn. What once held the promise of excitement and adventure was now far from glamorous, and there was no escaping the darkness that enveloped her.

"Damn it all to hell," Willow muttered, her hands trembling as she fought back tears. She clenched her fists, nails digging into her palms, searching for something solid to hold onto. But all she found was the cold emptiness that had settled deep within her bones. It was true. Willow could almost taste the bitter tang of fear that coated her tongue. With determination, Willow strode across the room, the floorboards creaking beneath her feet. She hesitated as she reached the door, her hand hovering over the knob. If Willow opened it, there would be no turning back – no pretending that everything was fine, that her life hadn't spiraled out of control. "Here goes nothing," she thought, gripping the doorknob tightly. Willow turned it slowly, praying the hinges didn't betray her with a tell-tale squeak. As Willow sank into the worn-out couch, she knew she was treading dangerous ground.

The smell of diesel mixed with the aroma of fresh coffee as Calvin Steele leaned against the cool metal of the bench, his breath fogging up from the heat of his coffee. The warm liquid offered a slight reprieve from the chilly Chicago morning air as he took a sip, savoring the aroma wafting to his nostrils. "Damn, that's good," he mumbled, watching the bustling bus station come to life before him. Diesel engines roared and belched black smoke into the sky like angry dragons as they carried passengers through the city's veins.

The cacophony of drivers hollering to one another and passengers shuffling on and off buses created a symphony of controlled chaos—a melody Calvin had grown to love over the years. "Hey man," Biscuit said, sidling up next to Calvin, his cup of steaming coffee in hand. "How'd family night go?" He raised an eyebrow, his curiosity piqued by the possibility of some juicy gossip.

Calvin smiled at the memory of his children gathered around the television, their eyes wide with wonder as they watched the latest episode of their favorite show. His wife had prepared a delicious pot roast, and Rose, his mother, had regaled them with stories from her days at the post office. The warmth of the evening still clung to him like a comforting blanket, shielding him from the harsh realities of the world. "Family night was great, Biscuit," Calvin replied, the pride evident in his voice. "Mom even told the kids about how she used to take me to Sunday school and church when I was a boy." "Man, you're lucky to have a family like that," Biscuit said, taking a swig from his cup. "Wish I had someone looking out for me like that, too."

"Who says you don't?" Calvin clapped his friend on the back. "You're part of our family, too, you know. You need to find your path and learn from the past." He considered Biscuit's history with women and how it sometimes tested their friendship. But he knew his friend was seeking re-demption, and he would be there to support him every step of the way.

"Thanks, man," Biscuit replied, his smile returning as they sipped their coffee. They stood there in companion-able silence, basking in the familiar sounds of their work-place, ready to face whatever the day would throw their way.

Calvin's laughter filled the air, soft and warm like the steam from their coffee cups. "Kids were askin' about you, though. Told them you had other things on your plate."

"Aw, man," Biscuit said, rubbing his head sheepishly. His eyes sparkled with mischief as he added, "Yeah, well, I did have someone on my table last night. It hurt my back a little bit. You know how it is." Calvin shook his head, a small smile tugging at the corners of his mouth despite himself. He knew Biscuit's ways all too well, but he couldn't help worrying for his friend. He'd seen firsthand the damages a toxic relationship could cause; even now, the memories lingered in the recesses of his mind, painful reminders of another life.

"Please, not Willow," Calvin pleaded, concern etching lines on his face that weren't there before. He remembered the cunning and manipulative woman who'd brought chaos to their lives, her vendettas and power plays tearing at the fabric of everything they held dear. Years later, her name still sent shivers down his spine. "Man, no, not Willow," Biscuit assured him, holding his hands defensively. "Just some girl I met on my bus route the other day. I'm tryin' to avoid those toxic women, even if they have some secret sexy power." "Damn straight, it's powerful," Calvin agreed. "Promise me you'll be careful, Biscuit," Calvin said, his voice low and serious. "We've both been down that road before, and it ain't pretty." "Scout's honor," Biscuit replied with a grin, raising his hand in a mock salute. Calvin could see the sincerity behind his friend's playful words and knew Biscuit was trying to improve.

"But hey," Calvin said, his eyes twinkling with mischief, "I saw this gorgeous policewoman at a checkpoint last night. You didn't try anything with her, did you?" "Man, you know me better than that," Biscuit replied, feigning offense. He took a sip of his coffee before continuing. "I kept it movin' right along. Wouldn't wanna end up in jail by breakin' her heart or somethin'."

"Or maybe she told you to keep it moving?" Calvin teased, a knowing smile playing on his lips. He hoped that Biscuit's newfound resolve would keep him out of trouble for once. "Feels like you were there with me," Biscuit chuckled, playfully nudging Calvin. As they shared a laugh, Calvin couldn't help but feel grateful for this moment of camaraderie. Despite their contrasting lives, their friendship remained strong—a testament to their forged bond. Taking a final swig of their coffee, they tossed the empty cups in a nearby trash can and headed towards their buses. Calvin felt the comforting weight of his uniform as he walked, the familiar fabric a reminder of his cherished stability. This job was more than just a means to provide for his family; it symbolized the hard work and dedication that defined his life.

As Calvin settled behind the wheel of his bus, he glanced over at Biscuit. His friend was chatting animatedly with a group of passengers, his laughter echoing through the station. Calvin couldn't help but smile, knowing that beneath Biscuit's carefree demeanor was a man who truly cared for those around him.

"Lord, watch over us today," he whispered. He knew the west side of Chicago could be rough, but he also recognized the beauty in the people he served—their resilience, spirit, and determination to create a better life. With the push of a button, the engine roared to life, and Calvin steered his bus out onto the city streets. As he navigated the familiar route, he thought about his family waiting at home, their love sustaining him through every bump and turn.

Lena Steele sat at the nurse's station inside the county hospital, her pen moving across patient charts with practiced precision. The scent of antiseptic hung heavy in the air, mingling with the hushed murmurs of medical staff as they went about their duties, each focused on providing care and comfort to those in need. As Lena completed another chart and set it aside, she silently thanked Jesus for giving her the strength to balance her job while raising her family. Her love for Him and her family was her guiding force, her own North Star, leading her through life's challenges. "Hey, Lena," Sheila, a fellow nurse and friend, said as she sidled up to Lena's side, her chair squeaking in protest. A mischievous grin spread across her face like butter on warm cornbread. "My husband and I were wonderin'... how much would your mother-in-law charge to take our kids for Bible study on Wednesdays, too?"

Lena paused, her pen hovering above the paper. She shot Sheila a sidelong glance, taking note of her friend's eagerness. It was no secret that Sheila admired how Lena managed to hold everything together, even with all the demands of life pressing down upon her. Perhaps this request was less about Bible study and more about seeking guidance from someone. "Mother-in-law, don't charge nothin', you know that," Lena replied, her tone gentle but firm. "She believes in sharin' the Word of God with any child willin' to listen."

Sheila's eyes sparkled with gratitude, and Lena could tell her friend was holding back a sigh of relief. "Thank you, Lena. You're an angel, truly. Your mother-in-law must be proud to have you as a daughter." "More like blessed," Lena corrected with a soft chuckle. "But I'll pass on your kind words to her, Sheila." Lena's laughter filled the small space between them, echoing off the sterile walls as she clutched her side. "Oh, Sheila," she gasped, wiping a tear from her eye, "you always know how to crack me up." But when

Lena glanced back at her friend, she saw no amusement in Sheila's face—only sincerity. Confusion washed over Lena, and she raised an eyebrow, her laughter dying. "Oh, you're not playin', are you?"

"Girl, I'm as serious as a heart attack!" Sheila declared, her eyes pleading. "We just wanna hear each other be free and make all those loud love noises again without the kids around." "Child, he's done made enough noise since y'all got six little ones runnin' 'round!" Lena teased, shaking her head. She imagined the chaos of Sheila's home life, the cacophony of tiny voices clamoring for attention. "True," Sheila conceded with a sheepish grin. "But please, Lena. Ask your mother-in-law for us." Her eyes were wide and hopeful, like a child begging for a treat.

"Alright, alright," Lena sighed, biting back another chuckle. "I'll consider it." She paused, tapping her pen against the clipboard in thought. As much as she wanted to help her friend, Lena knew Rose already had her hands complete with their children. But then, an idea struck her. "But don't forget, vacation Bible school is comin' up soon! In the meantime, maybe drop them off at the library every weekend. They can always find a good book to read, which never hurts." Sheila's face brightened, and Lena could see the relief in her posture. "Thank you, Lena. You're a life-saver." "Anything for a friend," Lena replied, patting her shoulder before returning to her charts. The pen danced across the paper, filling the blanks with a practiced hand. "Lord," Lena murmured under her breath as she filled out another chart, "please guide us all in finding and keeping love in our hearts." With those whispered words, Lena Steele returned her focus to the task, her heart swelling with gratitude and purpose.

CHAPTER 12

Willow's forehead pressed against the cool glass of the window, her breath leaving ephemeral misty circles on the pane. She stared out at the street below, watching the sun dip lower in the sky, splashing hues of orange and pink across the horizon. The sinking sun mirrored her waning patience. "Uh-huh...Yeah, I'll talk to him about it," Lenny's voice droned on in the background, a continuous hum that filled the living room. His endless phone calls cast a heavy cloud over the room as if the walls were closing around them. The weight of the tension settled on Willow's shoulders, making her heart race with a mix of irritation and anxiety.

She couldn't take it anymore. Turning to face Lenny, she said wistfully, "I want to go for a walk." "Can you hold on a second?" Lenny asked into the phone, covering the receiver with his hand but not looking at her. "Are you serious? I need fresh air, Lenny. I can't breathe in here." Willow's voice trembled slightly, betraying her frustration. "Alright, alright," Lenny relented, a flicker of sympathy crossing his face. "Just give me five minutes." "Five minutes, Lenny. I'm holding you to that." Willow tried to sound stern, but the softening in her eyes betrayed her genuine desire: connection. "Promise," Lenny said, reassuring her before returning to his call. "Sorry about that. What were we saying?"

Lenny glanced at her, his eyes cold and distant, before waving her off dismissively and returning to his call again. The way he barely acknowledged her presence stung, but Willow masked her hurt behind a stoic facade. She was used to disappointment – it had been her constant companion. "Listen, I gotta go," Lenny said into the phone, his voice oozing with frustration. He slammed the receiver down, scowling at nothing in particular. "All these damn calls..."

Frustration bubbled within Willow, but she tried a different approach, her voice softening, calculatedly vulnerable. We could wear one of those new dresses you bought me and go to dinner tonight. She asked, desperate for a change of scenery and some real connection. The stale air of the condo seemed to close around her, the walls bearing witness to countless whispered secrets.

For a moment, Lenny stopped, considering her proposal. His brown eyes met hers, and she could see the internal struggle behind his gaze. Willow knew this was her chance to regain control and remind him of her body's power over his emotions. "Alright," he agreed, a defeated sigh escaping his lips. "One night out won't hurt." "Thank you," Willow breathed, her eyes shining with gratitude – or so she made it appear. As she walked out the door, anticipation lifted her spirits like a helium balloon tugging her toward the sky. She knew that getting Lenny out of their lair, away from the constant ringing of the phone, was a crucial step in reestablishing her dominance.

She felt renewed determination as they stepped out into the chilly Chicago evening, the wind tousling Willow's dark curls. Tonight would be a turning point for them. She was sure of it. "Let's make this a night to remember," she murmured.

Later that day, Lena stood at the bus stop, her eyes scanning the horizon for the familiar sight of Calvin's bus. As it rounded the corner, she felt a surge of pride in her chest, like the sun breaking through the clouds on a stormy day.

The cityscape of 1970s Chicago seemed to fade away as she focused on the man behind the wheel. "Number 47," she whispered, her love for Calvin eclipsing even the bustling world around them. She could see him now. His broad shoulders squared very confidently as he guided the bus towards her, his eyes bright and warm like the embers of a fire on a cold winter's night.

"Hey there, handsome!" Lena called out playfully as she stepped onto the bus, her heart swelling with pride as she saw the bright smile on her husband's face. He looked so alive in his driver's seat, his whole body radiating enthusiasm and warmth. It was as if she had been there when they first met; their love was new, and every shared moment felt like an adventure.

"Evening, Lena," Calvin said, chuckling as he welcomed his wife aboard. "Had a long day?" "Nothing I couldn't handle," she replied, her voice steady and robust. "Alright then," Calvin nodded, his gaze lingering on Lena for a moment longer before returning to the road ahead. "Find yourself a seat and enjoy the ride." As Lena made her way down the aisle, she played a flirtatious tease and a little game with him to make the ride home more enjoyable. She glanced over her shoulder and caught his eye in the rearview mirror. "Calvin," she asked innocently, raising her eyebrow and smirking, "do you think this run in my stockings looks terrible?"

Calvin's reflection in the mirror seemed to falter for a moment, his eyes darting between Lena and the road as he tried to process her unexpected question. Lena couldn't help but smile at his reaction, knowing she could still catch him off guard even after all these years. "Lord have mercy, woman!" Calvin exclaimed with a hearty laugh, shaking his head as he continued navigating Chicago's busy streets. "I don't think anyone on this bus could care about that little run when they've got a view like you."

Lena grinned, her heart full of warmth and love for the man who never failed to make her feel special, even in the smallest moments. As she settled into her seat, she knew that no matter what life had in store, they would face it together - hand in hand, side by side, and heart to heart. Calvin's eyes widened from being caught off guard, and he bit his bottom lip, blinking as he saw Lena in the rearview mirror. Her perfume drifted to him, bringing back memories of their wedding day - the sun shining down on them as they danced together beneath a canopy of flowers.

"It looks fine," he finally managed to say, his voice barely above a whisper. His grip tightened on the steering wheel, and the leather wore smoothly from years of use. "Fine?" Lena teased, her laughter tinkling like wind chimes as she pretended to be offended. A ripple of laughter spread through the bus, some passengers joining in the playful banter while others merely exchanged knowing smiles. It was impossible not to be touched by Calvin and Lena's love.

As the bus trundled on, the soulful melodies of a nearby radio muted the passengers' chatter. The music weaves itself into the fabric of their lives, filling the air with hope and promise. Marvin Gaye's voice crooned about finding joy through the struggles of life, and Calvin couldn't help but think of the incredible journey he and Lena had been on together. "Promise me something, Lena," he said quietly, catching her gaze in the mirror again. "Promise me that no matter how many runs your stockings get or how bumpy the road ahead might be, we'll always find our way back to each other." "Always, Calvin," Lena replied, her love for him shining in her eyes like the first light of dawn breaking over the horizon. "I wouldn't have it any other way." With a gentle nod, Calvin turned his attention back to the road, navigating the busy streets of Chicago with the same care and devotion he had always shown to his family.

Rose stood next to her aging car parked in front of the school, her hands on her hips as the sun cast a golden glow on her graying hair. A warm smile played on her lips as she watched Junior and Ryder emerge from the building, their laughter mingling with the chatter of other students. "Grandma!" Junior called out, his face lighting up at the sight of her. He raced towards the car, his backpack bouncing against his back, cheeks flushed from the sprint. Ryder wasn't far behind, her long brown hair streaming behind her like a flag.

"Hey there, my sweethearts," Rose replied as Junior clambered into the back seat. She ruffled his hair affectionately before turning to Ryder, who was already buckling her seatbelt. "How was school today?" "Same as always, Grandma," Ryder responded with a slight grin, her eyes sparkling. "But I got an A on my history test." "Aw, that's wonderful, honey!" Rose beamed, her pride evident. She knew how hard Ryder worked to get her grades.

Turning to Junior, she asked, "And how about you, young man?" "Everything's good, Grandma," he answered, his eyes shining sincerely. Despite any setbacks or challenges that came his way, Junior always sought to find the silver lining. It was one of the things Rose admired most about him. "Alright then," she said, sliding into the driver's seat and starting the engine. The car rumbled to life, a familiar sound that reminded her of all the memories they'd made together. "Now, let's get going. We've got bible study at my house tonight, so I need your help to prepare."

"Sure thing, Grandma," Junior agreed, his voice filled with enthusiasm. Rose could see the influence her teachings about Jesus had on him. His faith and kindness were a testament to the love he'd learned from her. "Of course, Grandma," Ryder chimed in, her strong-willed independence shining through even in moments of agreement. She was always willing to help out when it came to family, and her loyalty was unwavering.

As the car pulled away from the curb, Rose's heart swelled with gratitude for these two amazing young people she called her grandchildren. At that moment, she knew their bond was unbreakable. "Grandma, can we stop by our house quickly?" Junior's voice wavered with a hint of desperation, his eyes scanning the street as if searching for a solution to his predicament. "I forgot my pajamas." Rose glanced over at Ryder, who rolled her eyes and shook her head in a silent, sisterly reprimand. The swaying elm trees that lined the sidewalk cast dappled shadows on her face, highlighting her strong-willed determination.

"No, Junior," Rose said firmly, her hands gripping the wheel with authority. "If you have to sleep naked, then you'll sleep naked. We won't disturb your parents tonight." She knew her grandchildren's parents needed peace after long work days. "Got it, Grandma," Junior sighed, slumping in his seat as the car pulled away from the curb. The dull hum of the engine mixed with the distant sound of children playing in a nearby park, a soundtrack to their childhood memories. He knew better than to argue with his grandmother when she had that determined look in her eye, which reminded him of the time she'd singlehandedly fixed the leaky roof in their home.

"Good," Rose said, her tone lightening like the clouds parting after a rainstorm. "Now, I want both of you to be on your best behavior tonight, alright?" She glanced in the rearview mirror, catching the reflection of her two precious grandkids. "Yes, ma'am," Junior and Ryder chimed in unison, their voices filled with respect and love for their grandmother. They understood the importance of these gatherings, where they could learn about their faith and how to navigate life gracefully and courageously.

As they continued driving down the familiar streets of their blue-collar neighborhood, Junior couldn't help but feel disappointed at having to sleep without his favorite pajamas. But he quickly pushed the thought aside, focusing instead on the evening ahead – a chance to spend time with his beloved family and learn from his grandmother's wisdom. "Remember, Junior," Rose said gently, catching his eye in the mirror. "Sometimes, we must let go of our comforts to grow." He nodded solemnly, his heart swelling with gratitude for the life lessons she'd instilled in him. At that moment, he knew how lucky he was – to have a loving family, faith to guide him, and a grandmother who taught him how to find silver linings amidst life's challenges.

Lenny and Willow entered the swanky Gold Coast restaurant, momentarily blinded by the dazzling chandeliers. The air was heavy with the scent of expensive perfume and the low murmur of hushed conversations. As they strolled through the dining area, heads turned to follow their progress, whispers spreading like wildfire. Willow reveled in the attention. Her deep red dress strikingly contrasted with the black and white attire of the other patrons. Lenny shifted uncomfortably in his tailored suit, feeling the weight of the stares as if they could see straight through him.

"Table for two, please," Willow said sweetly to the maître d', her brilliant smile never faltering. "Of course, madam," he replied, leading them to a candlelit table near a large window overlooking the cityscape. The flickering light cast dancing shadows across Willow's face, accentuating her high cheekbones and full, crimson lips. The red dress clung to her curves like a second skin, making it difficult for even Lenny to tear his gaze away.

"Wow," Lenny murmured, his eyes lingering on Willow's face. "I never knew that dress would look like this when we were in the store." Willow felt her chest tighten at his words, and for a moment, anger threatened to bubble over. She remembered earlier in the day when she had tried to model the dress for him, but his attention had been elsewhere. She wanted to snap at him, to call out his hypocrisy, but something stopped her. His gaze was genuine, and as she looked into his eyes, she realized he was finally paying attention to her. It was a small victory, a fleeting moment of connection in their twisted, shared existence. Swallowing her pride, she managed a half-smile. "Thank you, Lenny." The air between them lightened, the tension dissipating like steam from the hot plates carried by the waiters nearby.

They shared a genuine smile, a rare instance of honesty. "Have you decided what you'd like to eat?" Lenny asked, turning his attention to the menu. Perhaps the filet mignon," Willow replied, scanning the list of options. Or maybe the lobster thermos... You know how I love a good shellfish dish." "You can't go wrong with either choice," Lenny agreed, his eyes darting between the two items on the menu.

"Whatever we end up choosing," Willow said, her voice lilting with a hint of mischief. "I have a feeling tonight will be one to remember."

"Indeed," Lenny agreed. For now, they were just two people sharing a meal in an expensive Gold Coast restaurant. As they placed their orders and shared bites of their decadent dishes, Lenny focused on the present moment, hoping that the night would bring them closer rather than push them further apart.

CHAPTER 13

Grandmother Rose's kitchen buzzed with life as the late afternoon sun painted the room in a warm, golden hue. Junior could feel the heat of the oven on his cheeks as he scrubbed at a stubborn stain in the living room, the smell of freshly baked chocolate chip cookies drifting through the air and mingling with the hum of the vacuum cleaner that his sister, Ryder, pushed back and forth with determination. "Grandma, is everything clean enough yet?" Junior asked, wiping the sweat from his brow with the back of his hand. He looked around to see if anything else also needed to be cleaned.

"Junior, I'll let you know when it's enough," Grandmother Rose replied, her tone gentle but firm. She stirred a pot on the stove, her eyes never leaving her work. "You don't need to ask me every five minutes." "Sorry, I just... you weren't looking this way." Junior mumbled, glancing over at his sister for support. "Child, I see everything," Grandmother Rose said with a knowing smile that crinkled the corners of her eyes. She leaned against the kitchen counter, arms crossed over her apron, as the smell of fresh cookies wafted through the air. "Now, your attitude isn't helping you get this place any cleaner. Get yourself together and finish up."

Ryder rolled her eyes and pointed at the vacuum cleaner, urging him to continue. He sighed and returned to his task, praying that Jesus would help them finish their chores soon. Junior hunched his shoulders in frustration, the muscles in his back tensing as he scrubbed at a stubborn stain on the living room floor. He couldn't help but wonder how his grandmother always seemed to know what he was thinking. Was it some sixth sense that came with age? Or it was a gift passed down from Jesus Himself. "Lord, help me understand," Junior whispered under his breath, wringing out the soapy rag and wiping his brow.

"Talking to yourself now?" Ryder teased, smirking as she unplugged the vacuum cleaner and began winding up the cord. The whirring noise died down, leaving behind only the sound of their breathing and the ticking of the wall clock. "Focus now," Grandmother Rose scolded, her voice soft but firm. "There's still work to be done." "Sorry, Grandma," Junior mumbled, his cheeks burning from embarrassment. "Is it strange that I talk to Jesus, Ryder?" Junior asked his sister as they worked side by side, cleaning their small home's last remnants of dust and grime. "Strange? No, not really," she replied, shrugging her shoulders nonchalantly. "I mean, I don't do it myself, but if it helps you, then who am I to judge?"

"Thanks," Junior said, appreciating her understanding. Before Junior could dwell on it further, Grandmother Rose walked past him and lovingly rubbed his head, ruffling his dark curls. "You're doing a great job, Junior. Keep it up."

"Thank you, Grandma," Junior replied, feeling the frustration drain from his body as her words washed over him like a balm. He returned to his task with renewed determination, motivated by his grandmother's praise. Junior couldn't help but admire his sister's tenacity as he worked. Despite the tediousness of their chores, Ryder remained focused, her movements precise and efficient. Her intuition always seemed to guide her effortlessly through whatever challenges came her way, and Junior knew that she'd do anything to protect their family. "Junior!" Grandmother Rose called out, snapping him out of his thoughts.

"I think we're just about done here. You've done a great job, both of you."

"Thanks, Grandma," Junior replied with a smile, feeling a sense of accomplishment as he surveyed the spotless living room. "Let's get washed up and enjoy some of these cookies before they get cold," she said, turning off the stove and setting the pot aside. "And remember my darlings, it's not just about having a clean house; it's about working together as a family and finding joy in even the smallest tasks." Junior nodded, understanding that his grandmother's wisdom went beyond the simple act of cleaning. As they gathered around the table, he knew that the real reward wasn't the warm cookies or the immaculate home – the love and unity bound their family together through thick and thin.

Calvin and Lena Steele sat side by side in their favorite Chinese restaurant deep in Chinatown's heart. The red paper lanterns above them swayed gently, casting a warm glow on their faces. Servers hustled past, the scent of soy sauce and garlic wafting through the air, mingling with the shared laughter that filled the cozy space around them. "Alright, let's get the usual, shall we?" Lena suggested, her eyes sparkling with anticipation. She glanced over at Calvin, who nodded in agreement. "Sounds perfect," he replied, signaling for the waitress. "We'll have two orders of shrimp fried rice and some shrimp egg foo young."

"Very good," the waitress said, scribbling down their order before turning to leave. Calvin, wanting to impress Lena, quickly grabbed his silverware and handed it to the waitress with a theatrical flourish. "Here you go, ma'am," he said, grinning broadly. "I won't be needing these tonight." His confident smile faltered slightly when the waitress looked confused, but he pressed on, determined to show off his newly acquired chopstick skills. "Thank you," the waitress replied, still perplexed as she reached for Lena's next silverware. Lena shook her head, her smile comforting Calvin's nerves. "Oh, that's quite alright," Lena said, her voice gentle yet steady. "I'll be using my silverware; eventually, he will too."

"Could you give me his, and I'll hold it for later?" Lena asked the confused waitress. Obliging, she handed the silverware to Lena, who tucked it under her napkin with a knowing smile. The words were teasing, but there was no malice behind them, only love and understanding.

Calvin felt warmth spread through him at her words, knowing that Lena had seen through his attempt to impress her but had opted to play along anyway. He loved her all the more for it, marveling at how she always knew what he needed even before he did. As they waited for their meal,

Calvin remembered the countless times they had sat in this very spot, sharing stories of their day and discussing their plans. "Ready for the chopstick challenge?" Lena asked, her voice pulling him from his reverie.

Calvin fumbled with the chopsticks, his thick fingers struggling to hold them properly. The scent of Chinese food filled the air around them, adding to Calvin's embarrassment at being unable to devour his food. "See, I knew you'd need this," Lena laughed, holding up the fork she had kept for him. Her eyes danced joyfully in the dimly lit restaurant, the red paper lanterns casting shadows on her lovely face. "Ha, you know me too well," Calvin chuckled, grateful for her understanding and teasing. He took the fork from her outstretched hand, briefly touching her fingers. "Alright, alright," he admitted, using the spoon to dig into his shrimp-fried rice. "You got me." Though he knew they were playing around, deep down, he could feel how much their love had grown.

As he savored the medley of flavors on his tongue, Calvin couldn't help but think back to when they first met. They had been so young, barely scraping by on their blue-collar jobs. But even in those tough times, they always found a way to laugh and make the most of the life they had. "Remember our first date here?" Lena asked as if reading his thoughts. "We tried so hard to use the chopsticks that we ended up sharing one plate because we kept knocking it over." "We sure did," Calvin smiled, reminiscing about the memory. "And look at us now, still trying to conquer these chopsticks." "Maybe one day, Mr. Steele," Lena teased, raising an eyebrow. "Maybe," he agreed, feeling a swell of happiness. "But even if we never master the art of chopsticks, at least I know we have each other."

Their eyes met, and at that moment, Calvin knew again just how precious their love was. They'd built a life together.

"Cheers to that," Lena said softly, raising her glass of water. Calvin clinked his glass against hers, knowing that no matter what challenges life threw at them, they would always face them side by side.

The aroma of soy sauce and sizzling shrimp filled the air, mingling with the soft murmurs of conversation from neighboring tables. The red paper lanterns cast a warm glow on their faces as Calvin watched Lena take another bite of her shrimp egg foo young, her eyes shining with contentment. "Calvin, remember the first time we brought Junior to this place?" Lena asked between mouthfuls, a playful glint in her eye. "He must have been only five or six years old." Calvin chuckled at the memory. "How could I forget? The boy was so excited about those fortune cookies that he opened every single one before we even finished our meal."

Lena giggled, wiping the corners of her mouth with a napkin. "And then he declared that he would grow up to be the best bus driver in all of Chicago, just like his daddy." "By God's grace, he might just do it," Calvin said, pride swelling in his chest. He took a bite of his shrimp fried rice, savoring the familiar flavors. At that moment, he was grateful for the simple pleasures in life – good food, family, and love. "Speaking of driving, how's Ryder doing with her lessons?" Lena asked, concern knitting her brow. "I know she's been having some trouble with parallel parking." "Ah, she's getting better," Calvin reassured her, recalling the countless hours spent coaching his daughter behind the wheel. "I told her to trust her instincts and follow the guidance her mother and I provide. She's a smart girl; she'll get the hang of it soon enough."

"Thank the Lord for that," Lena sighed with relief. "I just want our children to be safe on these streets." "Amen to that," Calvin agreed, sipping his water. Calvin prayed silently, his heart swelling with love. "May we continue to grow together, guided by Your grace and wisdom."

Elsewhere in the city, Lenny and Willow found themselves nestled in a quiet corner of a dimly lit restaurant. The draped white linen table contrasted against the dark wood paneling surrounding them. A magnificent chandelier hung above, casting flickers of light that danced across Willow's face. It was an air of elegance she had never experienced, and her eyes sparkled with wonder as she took it all in. "Nobody's ever taken me someplace this fancy, Lenny," she said softly, her fingers tracing the delicate embroidery on the crisp cloth. The clink of silverware against China punctuated her words, mingling with the low murmur of conversation from the other diners. "This is nice. Thank you."

Her voice wavered slightly, betraying her unease at feeling out of place among the well-dressed patrons and fine China. She glanced around nervously, taking note of the men in tailored suits and women in elegant dresses, their laughter filling the air like champagne bubbles.

Lenny's gaze drifted to Willow's hesitant fingers, the unease in her voice creating a ripple in his chest. He reached for her hand with a reassuring smile and gently squeezed it. A violinist strolled through the dimly lit restaurant, bow poised elegantly above the strings. "Excuse me," Lenny murmured, catching the musician's attention with a subtle wave. The violinist raised an eyebrow, intrigued by the request, as Lenny quietly asked for a song he knew would resonate with Willow. The first notes of the haunting melody floated through the air, settling around them like a warm embrace. A single tear escaped from Willow's lowered lashes, betraying her vulnerability. She hastily wiped it away, but not before Lenny saw it.

"Hey, don't worry about it," he whispered, leaning closer until their foreheads nearly touched. The soft glow of the candles flickered in his eyes, revealing the depth of his sincerity. "You deserve somethin' special, Willow." "Thank you, Lenny," she murmured, her voice barely audible over the poignant strains of the music. She stared into his eyes, searching for traces of the manipulative instincts that often drove her actions. But at this moment, they were both just two souls, vulnerable and open, teetering on the edge of something unknown.

"Tonight, it's just us, all right?" Lenny insisted on his words, a promise enveloped in the low hum of conversation and clinking glasses around them. "No hustle and bustles." "Promise," Willow replied, a mixture of relief and uncertainty seeping into her thoughts. Could she truly set aside the life she'd built for herself, even for one night?

"Good," Lenny grinned, his doubts temporarily vanishing in the face of Willow's tentative smile. "Let's enjoy tonight and remember it when we're back in the thick of things." "Deal," Willow agreed, her voice stronger now, brimming with newfound determination. "I'll never forget tonight." And as the violinist's melody wound down, their hands remained entwined on the crisp white linen, symbolizing the fragile connection they'd forged amidst the chaos of their lives.

Meanwhile, Biscuit found himself alone in his small apartment. The TV's flickering light illuminated the room, creating eerie shadows that danced on the peeling wallpaper. He glanced around at the familiar clutter: the stacks of newspapers and magazines he never read, the empty pizza boxes, and the ashtrays overflowing with cigarette butts. This little space was all he had to call home, but it felt more open than ever tonight. "Damn," he muttered under his breath, his voice barely audible above the hum of the television. He switched channels but couldn't find anything worth watching, just more reruns and commercials for products he didn't need or want.

Placing a can of beer on the coffee table, he sank into the worn sofa with a sigh, feeling the familiar sag where the springs had given up long ago. The upholstery scratched against his skin, but it was a sensation that had become oddly comforting over the years. He tore open a big bag of potato chips, the sound mingling with the chatter from the television. It reminded him of a simpler time when he'd sit with Calvin on a Friday night, laughing and joking as they devoured junk food together.

He took a swig of the cold beer, savoring the familiar bitterness as it washed away the loneliness that threatened to overwhelm him. It wasn't enough to numb the ache in his heart, but it was better than nothing. Biscuit leaned back against the cushions, his gaze drifting towards the framed photograph of him and Calvin in their bus driver uniforms, grinning like fools after passing their exams. "Calvin, my man," he whispered, raising his can in a silent toast. "I wish you were here right now." He could almost hear his friend's laughter and feel the warmth of his presence beside him. But Calvin wasn't here. And Biscuit was left to face his demons alone, one beer and one bag of potato chips at a time. "Damn," Biscuit muttered, his eyes blankly fixed on the TV screen as if in a trance. The neon glow of the game show host's suit reflected off his glassy eyes, but it was clear he wasn't seeing any of it. His mind had wandered far away from the flashing lights and canned applause that filled the small room.

With a grunt, he absentmindedly scooped up a handful of potato chips and crammed them into his mouth, the salty crunch echoing through the apartment. As he chewed, crumbs tumbled onto his chest, joining the graveyard of chip fragments and beer stains on his stained white undershirt.

"Would I ever find someone like Lena?" he wondered, thinking of Calvin's wife. She was a woman who seemed to love her husband unconditionally. Her faith and devotion to her family were a beacon of light in the tough neighborhood they found themselves living in. "Someone who would stick by me, through thick and thin..." "Maybe one day," he whispered to the empty room, wiping a greasy hand on his pants. It left a streak of oily residue on the faded denim, but he hardly noticed, lost in thought. Instead of this quiet, solitary existence, he pictured himself with a loving wife and a home filled with laughter and happiness. "Can't give up now," he mumbled, taking another swig of beer. "Just gotta keep lookin'." Biscuit tried to reassure himself, believing the woman he would marry was waiting for their paths to cross. And when that day finally came, he'd be ready to give her his heart and share life.

"Calvin found his wife," he said quietly, glancing at the photograph of him and his best friend and Lena, their arms slung around each other's shoulders. "And I'll find mine. Gotta have faith." With a renewed sense of determination, Biscuit took another gulp of his beer, the bitterness on his tongue a reminder that life was full of challenges, but hope and love were waiting around the corner if only he could keep searching.

The rhythmic knocking on the door reverberated through the small, cozy house, pulling Junior from his momentary exhaustion. He rubbed his eyes and straightened his shirt before striding to the door with a determined smile, fueled by the teachings of Jesus that Grandmother Rose had ingrained in him. The hardwood floor beneath his feet creaked as he welcomed the mothers from the church. "Welcome, everyone," Junior greeted the church mothers as they entered the living room.

He couldn't help but notice their subtle glances at the freshly vacuumed carpet and spotless countertops, their eyes taking in the clean space. A swell of pride surged, knowing that he and Ryder had worked tirelessly to make the house presentable for their distinguished guests. "Junior, honey, this place looks wonderful. You and Ryder did an amazing job," said Mrs. Johnson, her voice warm and genuine. "Thank you, Mrs. Johnson," Junior replied with a grin, feeling satisfied with a job well done. "Y'all must've been workin' like bees all mornin'," added Mrs. Washington, her eyes twinkling with amusement.

"Ryder and I wanted everything to be just right for y'all," Junior explained, his hands instinctively brushing invisible dust from his pants. From the corner of his eye, Junior caught sight of Grandmother Rose standing by the kitchen doorway. Her knowing gaze fell upon him as she pointed at her eyes, then back to him, silently reminding him that she saw everything. He felt relief and apprehension; she was watching, but her presence also meant she trusted him to handle the gathering. As he passed Grandmother Rose, he felt a gentle squeeze on his shoulder – a silent gesture of encouragement.

The warm scent of freshly brewed coffee wafted through the air, mingling with the soft melodies of a gospel record playing in the background. Junior's eyes took in the vibrant colors of the afghan draped over the back of the couch, a hand-crafted gift from one of the church mothers. The living room was alive with laughter and shared stories as the women relaxed into their seats. "Junior, honey," called out Mrs. Jackson, her silver bangles chiming as she gestured toward him. "Would you mind fetchin' me a cup of that delicious coffee your Gran'ma Rose made?" "Of course, Mrs. Jackson," he replied, his heart swelling with pride for the family home they had so lovingly prepared for this special gathering.

As Junior poured the hot coffee into an elegant China cup, he couldn't help but overhear snippets of conversation from the living room. They spoke of faith, love, and the challenges of raising a family in these trying times. He realized then that these gatherings were more than just social events; they were a lifeline for these women, offering support, understanding, and the wisdom that only years of experience could provide. "Thank you for having us, Rose," said Mrs. Thompson, her warm smile lighting up the room. She adjusted her thick glasses, magnifying her eyes even more. "Of course, dear. It's always a pleasure," Grandmother Rose replied, her voice filled with love and warmth.

Junior returned to the living room, carefully balancing the cup and saucer in his hands. As he handed it to Mrs. Jackson, he exchanged a knowing glance with Ryder, who was now conversing with the other guests. A silent signal passed between them, acknowledging the success of their efforts and the importance of this moment. "Thank you, Junior," Mrs. Jackson said, sipping the coffee. "You and your sister have done a wonderful job making this house feel like a home." "Thank you, Mrs. Jackson," Junior replied, his cheeks flushing with pride. "We learned from the best."

He glanced at Grandmother Rose, who listened intently to one of the ladies recounting a story from her youth. The church mothers have always been passing down the wisdom and strength he saw in Gran'ma Rose through generations of the church from mothers who came before her. As the gathering continued, Junior marveled at his sense of unity and purpose in that room. The shared laughter, tears, and prayers bound them together, forging a connection that could withstand the trials and tribulations of life.

Meanwhile, in the dimly lit Chinese restaurant in Chinatown, Calvin Steele fidgeted with his silverware, the clink of metal against porcelain echoing in the quiet space. The scent of soy and ginger hung heavy in the air, mingling with the faint hum of conversation from nearby tables. Sweat trickled down Calvin's temple. Calvin glanced around the small restaurant, taking in the worn red lanterns swaying gently overhead, the faded paintings of dragons and phoenixes adorning the walls, the clattering of dishes, and the hum of conversation. It was a sanctuary, an oasis in the harsh desert of life's challenges.

Even though he felt out of place in his worn-out denim jacket and faded jeans, he was determined to keep up the facade of sophistication for Lena. "Calvin," Lena said, her voice gently nudging back to reality. She looked radiant in the low light, her dark curls framing her face like a halo. Her eyes sparkled with warmth and amusement as she reached across the table, her fingers brushing away the stray napkin clinging to his hand. "Uh, sorry," Calvin stammered, dropping the fork with an embarrassed smile. "I just wanted tonight to be special, you know?" With a playful smile, she touched his hand, her skin soft and warm against his calloused fingers. "Calvin, you don't ever have to act fancy for me.

I love you for everything you do for our family and me," Lena said softly, her eyes shining. His heart swelled at her words, and he couldn't help but think about how blessed he was to have Lena in his life. "Thank you, Lena," he murmured, gently squeezing her hand. "I just want you to know that no matter what, I'll always do whatever it takes to make you happy."

He set down the chopsticks on the table and looked deeply into Lena's warm brown eyes. A smile spread across his face, genuine and unrestrained. "I just want you to know that Wednesday night isn't about just one blessed event," he replied, his grin widening. "It's about never forgetting us."

"Us" is a simple word, yet it carries the weight of shared dreams, tireless prayers, and countless moments of joy and sorrow. Like a sturdy oak tree, their bond weathers the storms of life, growing stronger with each shared experience. The shared experiences—the ups and downs, the joys and sorrows—strengthen their bond and make the audience feel connected and empathetic.

Lena nodded, her fingers tracing delicate circles on the back of his hand. She seemed to understand the unspoken language of his heart. "Raising those kids is a blessing too, but one day, if everything goes right, they'll be on their own, trying to discover this," she said, gesturing between them. Her voice was a gentle melody in the hushed murmur of the bustling restaurant. "Exactly," Calvin agreed, squeezing her hand gently. They were more than just husband and wife, mother and father. They were soulmates, bound together by love as fierce and tender as the calloused fingers now entwined with her soft touch. "That's what it's all about."

"And I look for it every day with you," Lena whispered, her voice filled with love and determination. It was as though she had plucked the words from his thoughts and breathed life into them—a testament to their shared connection. This connection transcended words and found its expression in their unwavering support for each other, a support that was as solid as the ground beneath their feet.

As they shared their meal, savoring each bite and every stolen glance, the trials of life seemed to fade into the background. "Here's to us," Calvin whispered, raising his glass of lukewarm tea in a toast. Lena echoed his gesture, her eyes shining like stars in the dim light. "Forever," she vowed, clasping his hand tighter still. Their love was a beacon in the darkness, guiding them home.

The scent of freshly brewed coffee wafted through the air, mingling with the aroma of homemade cookies as the women gathered in Grandmother Rose's cozy living room. Soft laughter and familiar voices filled the space, creating an atmosphere of warmth and camaraderie. The light from the antique street lamp cast a golden glow on the worn but comfortable furniture, making the room feel like a sanctuary from the bustling streets of 1970s Chicago just outside the window. Their love was a comforting blanket in this room, shielding them from the world's harsh realities.

Rose smiled as she surveyed the scene, her heart swelling with pride at the community she had helped to foster. The Bible study had become a regular event for many families in the community, and tonight was no exception. Each week, they gathered together to share stories, offer support, and find solace in the teachings of the Good Book. It was more than just a gathering; it was a lifeline for these hardworking women, a chance to recharge their spirits and remind themselves that they were not alone in their struggles. "Ruth," Rose said, turning to her friend beside her, "How's your daughter doing in the Big Apple?" She leaned back in her favorite armchair, clutching a warm mug of coffee between her hands.

As Ruth began to answer Rose's question, Rose's thoughts drifted to her family. She thought of Calvin, her dedicated and loving son, who took great pride in his work as a city bus driver. She was grateful for the man he had become and knew that his children, Junior and Ryder, would carry on their family's legacy. Junior, a kind-hearted and optimistic teenager, always sought to find the silver lining in every situation. Rose knew that his empathetic nature helped him understand the struggles of others around him, and she couldn't help but feel proud of the young man he was becoming. Ryder, a strong-willed and independent teenage daughter, had inherited her grandmother's keen sense of intuition. Fiercely protective of her family, Rose knew she would face the world head-on, using her intelligence and intuition to navigate whatever challenges life threw her way.

Ruth's eyes glowed with pride as she spoke, the golden lamplight casting a warm glow over her features. Every wrinkle and line on her face seemed to soften in this light, revealing a lifetime of love and devotion. She spoke of her daughter, who was now working at a prestigious law firm, making a name for herself and building a successful career. Rose couldn't help but feel admiration for Ruth and her daughter. As she took a slow sip of her coffee, the rich taste spread across her tongue and filled her senses. The aroma of freshly brewed beans, the comforting warmth of the mug in her hands, and moments like these reminded Rose of the importance of family and their unwavering support.

She thought of Lena, her daughter-in-law, who worked tirelessly to provide for her family while still finding time to enjoy these precious evenings together. In this moment, surrounded by love and gratitude, Rose felt truly blessed.

Rose leaned back in her chair, gazing at the steaming mug. The rich aroma of coffee filled her nostrils as she listened to Ruth's words. "You must be so proud of her," Rose said, setting her mug on the worn wooden table. Wisps of steam curled and danced away from its surface as their children's dreams rose. Ruth's laughter rang out through the cozy living room, filling it with a warm, pleasant atmosphere. "Of course I am!" Ruth exclaimed, giggling joyfully. "She didn't get her talent for law from me. That's between her and God. But she's damn good at it too." Her infectious laughter spread through the room like wildfire, bringing smiles to everyone's faces. Rose couldn't help but feel a twinge of worry for her children as the laughter subsided. Life in Chicago was a constant battle, and the challenges grew daily. She glanced down at the well-worn leather cover of the Bible resting on her lap, finding solace in its familiar presence amidst the chaos of their city lives.

Gently clasping her hands together, Rose closed her eyes and whispered a silent prayer. Her heart felt heavy with love and concern for her family, whom she held dear. She thought of Calvin, his steady hands gripping the wheel as he drove his bus through the bustling streets; Lena, juggling her demanding job while pouring every ounce of love into her family; Junior, navigating the tumultuous waters of adolescence with unwavering optimism; and Ryder, fiercely guarding her loved ones as she ventured bravely into the world.

As if sensing her thoughts, Ruth spoke up from across the room. "Your children are a true blessing, Rose," she said warmly. "They possess your strength and resilience."

Tears pricked at Rose's eyes as she replied, "Thank you, Ruth. They are my greatest treasure." And she meant every word. Her family was everything to her, and she would do anything to ensure their happiness and safety.

As the evening wore on and the women shared stories and laughter in Grandmother Rose's cozy living room, their bonds grew stronger. Each one found solace and support in the others' presence, fortified by their unwavering faith and unconditional love. Together, they were ready to face whatever challenges life may bring.

CHAPTER 14

Amidst the hustle and bustle of a chaotic New York courtroom, Pam stood like an immovable tower of strength. Her smooth, dark skin glowed under the harsh lights, a testament to her unwavering determination. Adjusting her glasses precisely, she projected an air of unyielding confidence, as if she were born to conquer any challenge. "Thank you so much, Pam," her client gushed, their grip on her hand tight enough to crush steel. Pam smiled warmly, her eyes crinkling at the corners as she gently pulled away. The rough callouses on her client's palm reminded her of the hard work and sacrifices they had both made to reach this moment. "You're welcome," she replied earnestly. "Now go out and live your life. Just try not to get in trouble again."

The client's pale cheeks were flushed with emotion, their forehead dotted with glistening beads of sweat as they nodded vigorously. Their promise hung in the air, a weighty testament to their commitment to change. With that, they turned and bolted towards their waiting family, their arms opening wide for an embrace that had been long overdue. Pam watched with misty eyes as her clients disappeared into the waiting arms of their loved ones. The transformation in the client was striking-from a person weighed down by legal troubles to a hopeful individual ready to embrace a new beginning. The tears and heartfelt hugs were tangible testimony to her work's profound, life-changing impact. As she clutched her briefcase, its weight seemed to have lifted, as if the victory had also lifted the heaviness of the legal texts within. She couldn't help but feel joy and fulfillment knowing she had made a profound difference in someone's life.

The weight of her briefcase tugged at her shoulder, a constant reminder of the challenging work she had chosen. But as she continued to adjust the strap, she couldn't help but feel a sense of fulfillment and purpose in what she did - helping others through her profession. As she made her way out of the courthouse, her eyes caught sight of a young couple walking hand in hand, their laughter carried on the gentle breeze and mingling with the rustle of fallen leaves outside. It reminded her of her family back home in Chicago, and with each step down the courthouse stairs, she felt a surge of determination to continue making a lasting, positive difference in the world. Her heart was full, her spirit lifted by the joy and fulfillment of her work.

The bustling streets of New York welcomed her back into its rhythm as she disappeared among the sea of faces. The warm orange glow from the worn brick buildings of Harlem provided a comforting backdrop as Pam stopped outside a small take-out joint, grateful for a short break from the fast-paced day. The irresistible smell of chicken and waffles filled the air, luring her inside like a moth to a flame. Her stomach growled in anticipation as she pushed open the door, the cheerful jingle of the bell signaling her arrival. "Good evening, Miss," greeted a young man behind the counter, his eyes crinkling with genuine kindness. "What can I get for you today?" The warmth and comfort of the meal were a welcome respite from the day's challenges, offering Pam a moment of relaxation and peace.

Pam's eyes lit up as she scanned the menu board above, her anticipation growing at the thought of crispy fried chicken paired with fluffy waffles. The young man behind the counter greeted her with a warm smile, his kindness and warmth bringing a spark of joy to Pam's eyes. "I'll have the chicken and waffles, please," She said, her voice filled with excitement. The clanging of the old-fashioned cash register added to the lively atmosphere, and Pam took a moment to soak in her surroundings. Laughter and conversation echoed off the walls, mingling with delicious smells of Southern comfort food. A mother sat at a nearby table, trying to juggle a squirming toddler while attempting to eat her collard greens. Two older men at the bar engaged in an animated discussion about the latest baseball game, their catfish plates untouched. Suddenly, the young man's voice brought her back to reality. "Here you go, Miss," he said, placing a steaming take-out bag on the counter before her. "Enjoy your meal!" Pam smiled in gratitude, her heart warmed by the young man's kindness, and headed out into the world, eager to savor every bite of her savory meal.

With her heart full of gratitude, Pam replied with a wide and genuine smile. She could feel the warmth of the take-out bag in her hands as she stepped out into the bustling streets of Harlem. The sounds of car horns blaring, street vendors shouting their sales pitches, and the cheerful laughter of children playing on the sidewalk filled the air, welcoming her like an old friend. "Watch it, lady!" A man pushing a cart filled with fresh fruits narrowly avoided colliding with her, shaking his head in disapproval. "Gotta keep your eyes open!" Pam apologized with a murmured sorry and stepped aside to let him pass, continuing her journey towards her apartment. Her thoughts drifted back to the family she had helped earlier that day. She could still hear the Father's voice, relieved and grateful when the judge announced the verdict—these moments made all her hard work and sacrifices worth it.

The city street was filled with energy and movement as a newspaper boy called out from the corner, his voice carrying above the honking cars and bustling pedestrians. "Extra! Extra!" he shouted, waving the Daily News above his head. Across the street, a neighbor called out to Pam, their arms flailing excitedly. "How was your day?" Pam grinned in response. "Same as always, Mrs. Thompson," she yelled back, her voice filled with energy. "Fighting the good fight!" Mrs. Thompson smiled and made the sign of the cross before disappearing into her building. The sun beat down on the pavement, casting long shadows as people rushed by, their faces determined and focused as they navigated through the chaotic city scene. Despite it all, there was a palpable sense of community and camaraderie amongst the chaos, and Pam felt grateful to be a part of it all. This sense of community connected her to the city and its people.

With that familiar warmth of pride and satisfaction bubbling in Pam's chest as she approached her apartment building. She gazed up at the familiar brick facade, grateful for the place that had become her home over the years. The savory scent of take-out food filled her nostrils as she clutched the bag closer to her body, a small smile tugging at the corners of her lips. "Lord," she whispered, offering a silent prayer of gratitude. "Thank you for allowing me to make a difference in this world." Her heart swelled with determination as she vowed to continue serving those in need, no matter what challenges lay ahead. The evening sunlight cast a golden glow on the streets, a reminder that the world still had hope and goodness amidst all the chaos. Pam's unwavering determination to make a difference was truly inspiring.

With each step, Pam felt the weight of her exhaustion lifting. She took a deep breath, taking in the comforting scent of her apartment building - an amalgamation of cooking spices, laundry detergent, and familiar scents from her neighbors' homes. As she reached the top of the steps, she paused to take in the view of the city skyline that stretched before her, its lights twinkling like stars in the night sky. Unlocking her tiny studio apartment door, she was greeted by a jumble of mismatched furniture and eclectic decor - a true reflection of her unique and busy life.

Pam set her bag down on the cluttered table and let out a content sigh. Her apartment may be small, but it was hers - a symbol of her hard work and determination. The familiar sound of her fridge humming and the gentle ticking of the old clock on the wall brought comfort and nostalgia. She smiled as she kicked off her heels, feeling the coolness of the linoleum floor against her feet. "Ah, home sweet home," she whispered with a smile. She pressed her hands to her temples, massaging away the tension from a long day at work. "What a day it's been," she mumbled to no one in particular, grateful for this little haven she could call her own.

She was drawn to the sleek phone on the kitchen counter as she lowered herself onto the plush cushioned chair. With a resigned sigh, she picked it up and dialed the familiar number, her fingers hovering over the buttons momentarily before pressing down. "Hey, Mama, it's me," she said, her voice softening as she heard the dial tone give way to her mother's sweet voice. "I just wanted to let you know I made it home safely." The line crackled with warmth and familiarity as her mother replied, "Good, baby girl. How was your day? Did you assist that family you were telling me about?" "Yes, Mama, I did," Pammy answered with a sense of fulfillment. "They were able to obtain what they needed and are truly grateful." "God is good," her mother's voice echoed through the receiver, filled with genuine pride and love. "He's working through you to help others, just like I always knew He would." The kitchen felt warm and cozy as Pammy smiled at her mother's faith in her and their devotion to helping those in need.

Pam's heart swelled with emotion at her mother's words, a lump forming in her throat as the weight of her mother's pride and support settled in. She had fought for justice and carried on a legacy of faith and service, and her mother's acknowledgment meant everything to her. "Thank you, Mama. Your words mean more than you know." Her mother smiled warmly, her eyes brimming with love and admiration. "Alright, my baby girl, now it's time to rest. You deserve it. And don't forget to say your prayers before bed," she reminded Pam gently. "I won't, Mama. Love you." "Love you too, Pammy," her mother replied, the affection in her voice shining through like a ray of sunlight on a cloudy day.

Pam ran across the room, causing the wooden floorboards to creak beneath her feet softly. The familiar sound brought a sense of comfort and nostalgia. The room was gently illuminated by the warm, orange glow of streetlights peeking through the thin curtains, casting long and graceful shadows on the walls. As she reached her bed, Pam smoothed her hands over the faded quilt that covered it, marveling at the intricate stitches her mother had lovingly sewn many years ago. A wave of gratitude washed over her for all the sacrifices her parents had made to help shape her into the resilient and strong woman she is today.

"Thank you, Mama," she whispered as she allowed herself to sink into the luxurious, plush mattress. The soft fabric seemed to envelop her and offer comfort and rest after a tiring day. With a contented sigh, she closed her eyes and listened to the gentle whirring of the ceiling fan above her head. Its cool breeze brought a sense of calm to her frazzled nerves after a hectic day searching for justice. "Lord knows I needed this moment," she thought, her body sinking deeper into the familiar embrace of her bed. But just as she began to drift off, the grumbling protest of her stomach reminded her that it was time to refuel after a long day. Pam let out another sigh and opened her eyes, taking in the sight of the take-out bag sitting on the small table near the door. Its tantalizing aroma filled the room, beckoning her to satisfy her hunger and recharge for tomorrow's battles.

With a grumble of hunger, she pushed herself up from the bed and made her way to the worn sofa that dominated the small living space of her cramped apartment. Settling onto the sagging cushions, she retrieved the styrofoam container filled with golden-brown chicken and waffles, the mouth-watering smells enveloping her senses. Taking a piece of crispy fried chicken in her hand, she brought it closer to her lips, feeling the satisfying crunch under her teeth before being greeted with a burst of savory flavors that danced on her taste buds.

As she dug into her plate of golden fried chicken and fluffy waffles, the warm light from the TV danced across Pam's face. The anchorman's monotonous voice drifted in the background, a constant hum that blended into the comforting ambiance of her small, cozy apartment. With each delicious bite, Pam felt herself slipping further into a contented state of relaxation, lulled by the flickering glow of the television. Despite its modest size, her home exuded an energy of success and accomplishment from a day well-lived, with the promise of even more triumphs to come. Slowly, her eyes grew heavy, and she surrendered to the sweet embrace of slumber, still basking in her surroundings' warm, soothing glow.

Beyond the panes of her window, the vibrant streets of Harlem buzzed with energy and vitality, a tribute to the indomitable spirit of the community she tirelessly served. And while Pam was lost in slumber, her soul remained vigilant, ever connected to the pulse and rhythm of her beloved neighborhood.

A warm, spiritual feeling filled Rose's cozy living room, emanating from the soft, golden glow that filtered through her lace curtains. The ladies of the Bible study group were gathered around her, their voices a gentle hum as they discussed and reflected on the scriptures in their worn Bibles. The faint scent of Rose's homemade peach cobbler lingered in the air, inviting and comforting. Rose opened the front door as the evening drew close and bade her friends farewell. She couldn't help but feel a sense of satisfaction in providing a welcoming space for them to gather and grow in their faith. "Rose, that was a lovely evening," Marjorie remarked warmly as she slipped into her jacket. "You always make us feel so at home."

"It's my pleasure, Marjorie," Rose replied with a smile, patting her friend on the shoulder. "I hope you take with you what we discussed tonight. Remember that the Lord is always there to guide us through life's challenges." As she spoke, the room seemed to fill with a stronger sense of peace and warmth.

As the women began to file out, Ruth approached Rose with a grateful sparkle in her eyes. With a gentle squeeze, she held Rose's hand tightly. "Thank you for hosting us tonight, Rose," she said sincerely, her voice resonating with warmth and tenderness. "It was my pleasure," Rose replied, her smile growing wider as she wrapped her arms around Ruth. They stood there momentarily, basking in the soft light, two pillars of strength leaning on one another. Ruth pulled away slightly and looked into Rose's eyes, her shimmering with emotion. "I needed this tonight more than you can imagine. My heart has been heavy lately, but being here with you and the other ladies and discussing God's word has lifted me." The peaceful ambiance of their embrace seemed to echo the peace that filled Ruth's heart at that moment.

The warmth of Rose's words enveloped Ruth like a comforting hug. She nodded in agreement, her heart overflowing with gratitude for the love and support of her fellow believers. "His love is powerful," Rose said solemnly, affirming their shared faith. "It's what keeps us going, day after day." Ruth couldn't help but smile at the sense of community and connection she felt at that moment. They were a family in Christ, united by their faith and devotion. The familiar scent of their home filled her senses as she took a deep breath, feeling a sense of peace wash over her. Rose's fingers traced the worn cover of her Bible, a symbol of their shared beliefs. "Thank you, Rose," Ruth said softly, tears glistening. "I'll keep that in mind."

At that moment, she could feel the presence of God surrounding them all. Memories flooded Ruth's mind as Rose opened up the scripture and read about the Lord's

Supper. She remembered how Jesus had gone before them to prepare a place in his Father's house. A wave of comfort washed over her as she thought about the promise of eternal life with him. "I'm so glad he did that," Rose spoke softly, echoing Ruth's thoughts. A slow nod from Ruth accompanied her agreement. "Yes, it's comforting to know we have a place waiting for us when our time comes."

As the women's conversation hummed and swirled around them, Junior lay on the sofa, his body sinking into the plush cushions. A gentle creaking of floorboards caught their attention, drawing their eyes to him. His head rested on an embroidered pillow, one arm draped lazily over his closed eyes. The soft light from the lamps cast a warm glow over his features, the lines of worry and exhaustion smoothed away in this moment of peace. "Grandma," Junior called out, his voice quiet but full of warmth and love. Slowly, he opened his eyes and turned to look at her. The corners of his mouth lifted in a soft smile that reached his eyes. "I'm glad you and your friends discussed the Lord's Supper tonight," he continued, his gaze drifting to include all the women in the room. "It made me think of how important that moment is for all of us." Rose felt tears prick at the corners of her eyes at his words. Her grandson's faith and hope never ceased to amaze her, even in the darkest moments. She moved closer to him, her heart overflowing with love for this young man who clung to hope with every word and gesture.

Junior closed his eyes, drawing in a slow breath as he silently prayed. He thanked Jesus for the Lord's Supper, savoring the warmth and nourishment it provided him. The familiar scents of freshly baked bread and sweet grape juice wafted through the air, bringing comfort and tradition to his heart. At this moment, he felt deeply connected to his faith and community, grateful for the continued guidance and strength offered to him on his journey. Lessons from his grandmother flooded his mind, her voice echoing with words of love and support. "Every time I face something difficult or scary, I think about the love and encouragement I receive from you all," Junior admitted, his voice tinged with vulnerability. "My family and community are my rock, my foundation... it keeps me going, Grandma."

Rose's eyes shone with pride and love as she gazed at her grandson, noticing how the light caught in his hair and illuminated his features. She gently squeezed his hand, her weathered fingers a testament to a life filled with love and faith. At that moment, she couldn't help but feel overwhelmed with emotion, proud of the young man he was becoming. "Junior," she whispered, her voice thick with emotion, "you carry the love of Jesus and our family within you. It's a bright light that will guide you through life's darkest moments. You are destined for great things."

Junior's heart swelled with gratitude, and he felt the warm embrace of his family's love surrounding him. Junior knew he was where he belonged - supported, loved, and cherished by those who mattered most. And it all began with something simple yet powerful - breaking bread together, just like Jesus had done so long ago.

CHAPTER 15

The city lights flickered and danced on the windshield as Lenny's car glided through the dark streets of Chicago. Willow's perfume filled the air, wrapping them in a warm embrace. She sat beside him, lost in thought, gazing out the window at the city below. Her fiery red dress stood out against the muted colors of the night, a sharp contrast that only added to her beauty. Lenny couldn't help but gaze at her with genuine admiration, his voice soft and sincere as he spoke. "You look amazing tonight, especially in that red dress and that sweet perfume." Willow blushed, a hint of shyness creeping into her voice as she replied, "Thank you for such a wonderful evening." Lenny grinned, his eyes twinkling with amusement. "Just wait until tomorrow when I make you wear socks and sandals." They both laughed, enjoying each other's company. But then Lenny's expression turned serious as he said, "But first, I have to make a drop tonight." Willow felt a pang of unease at the mention of Lenny's dangerous job, but she pushed it away, choosing to trust him. "Okay," she said calmly, trying not to let her fear show. Despite everything, she still loved this man and believed in him.

Meanwhile, back at the Steele household, the soulful melody of a classic love song wafted through the air as the moonlight gently kissed every surface in the cozy living room. The worn yet comfortable furniture, faded floral patterns, and familiar dents witnessed countless family gatherings, laughter, and heartfelt conversations. "Come on, baby," Calvin called out, his voice full of love and excitement as he expertly placed the needle on a particular record. He knew each groove by heart, having played it hundreds of times since they first danced to it at their wedding reception. As the music filled the room, it seemed to transport them back to that magical evening when they fell in love again. The faint scent of jasmine lingered in the air, a reminder of their wedding venue. "You know this is our song," Calvin whispered, pulling his wife close in a tender embrace. At that moment, nothing else existed except for the two and the timeless love that bound them together.

As the sweet, nostalgic melody floated gracefully from the speakers, Calvin couldn't help but be overcome with a flood of memories - the highs and lows, the laughter and tears, the milestones and challenges they had faced together. He smiled fondly at their two children, Junior and Ryder, who were sleeping soundly upstairs in their rooms. And then there was his mother, Rose, whose unwavering support and love had been a constant throughout their journey as a family. "Calvin," Lena's voice chimed in from the doorway, pulling him out of his reverie. "I'll be right there; just let me finish putting on my shoes," she said with a slight hint of something special. Calvin nodded understandingly, knowing how demanding her job could be. As he waited for her, he swayed gently to the music that had brought back many cherished memories. He remembered their first dance under the twinkling stars, their hands intertwined and their hearts beating in perfect sync.

His eyes traced the lovingly displayed photographs adorning the walls, each a cherished memory of their journey together. The vibrant images captured every precious moment - from Junior's first wobbly steps to Ryder's beaming smile and the joy-filled family vacations they had shared. Each snapshot was a testament to their unbreakable bond and unwavering faith in each other.

At that moment, as he stood lost in thought, the bedroom door creaked open, and Lena emerged, her nurse's uniform crisp and clean against her glowing skin. Her smile was like a beacon, radiating warmth and love that lit up the room. Calvin could feel his heart swelling with pride and passion for this incredible woman.

Her beauty took his breath away as she approached him with soft steps. Her long hair cascaded down her back like a river of black silk, framing her face like a halo. The gentle curve of her lips and the sparkle in her eyes made him feel like he was seeing her for the first time again.

"Daaamn," he whispered under his breath, entirely captivated by her presence. His heart pounded in his chest, matching the rhythm of the music playing in the background. This was his amazing, beautiful wife, and he couldn't believe how lucky he was to have her by his side.

Lena's playful, twinkling eyes met Calvin's as she asked teasingly, "Did I keep you waiting long?" He couldn't help but let out a soft chuckle, the sound thick with love and adoration for the woman standing before him. His heart swelled with pride as he took in her uniform, each thread symbolizing her passion and dedication. It reminded them of all they had overcome together, the obstacles that had only strengthened their love. As the music swelled around them, Calvin reached for Lena's hand, their fingers intertwining like two puzzle pieces coming together perfectly.

With syncopated steps, they glided across the well-worn wooden floor, their hearts beating in perfect harmony. The familiar melody transported them back to when their love was young and untested. "Remember our first dance, Calvin?" Lena's voice was barely audible over the music, but her words carried a weight of nostalgia and longing. "Of course, baby," Calvin responded, his mind flooding with memories of that starlit night so many years ago. "We danced like there was no tomorrow." A small smile formed on Lena's lips as she leaned closer to her husband, her gaze locked on his as if seeking solace and strength in his unwavering presence. "Sometimes it feels like we've been dancing ever since," she mused softly, the love in her voice evident to anyone listening. "Maybe we have," Calvin thought.

Amidst the ups and downs, the struggles and triumphs that had marked their lives, Calvin and Lena never stopped dancing. Their bodies swayed in perfect harmony, each movement reflecting the love and understanding that bound their souls together. As he pulled her closer, Calvin felt as if every cell in his body resonated with hers, creating a symphony of love and belonging. "Life hasn't always been easy," Lena whispered, tears glistening, "but I wouldn't change a thing as long as I have you, Calvin." The warmth in his heart spread to his voice as he vowed, "Baby, I'll always be here for you." In that moment, their connection felt stronger than ever, strengthened by the trials they had conquered hand in hand. And so they danced on, lost in the music and each other's arms, celebrating the enduring love that had carried them through every challenge life had thrown their way.

Biscuit paced his cramped living room's worn and splintered floorboards, one hand buried deep in his pocket while the other clutched a tattered little black book. The faint scent of dust and old wood wafted through the air, mingling with the sharp odor of industrial cleaner. The distant train rattling past echoed through the thin walls of his apartment, reverberating off every surface as if trying to escape. The low hum of the television set provided a steady background noise, only occasionally interrupted by a loud commercial or gripping moment in the show. Biscuit's boots creaked with each step as he moved back and forth, creating a rhythm that matched the beating of his heart. A restless energy coursed through him, causing him to fidget and fiddle with objects around the room. It was as if he couldn't contain his thoughts within his own body and needed to expend them through physical movement.

Biscuit paced back and forth in his room, the desperation in his voice growing with each passing moment. He held a small black book in his hand, its pages filled with scribbles of countless girls, each name representing a fleeting encounter that left him unsatisfied. His eyes scanned the names, memories stirring within him - "Angie? No, she never understood me," he muttered, flipping to the next page. "Cynthia? She was too wild for my taste." But then, one name caught his attention, causing his heart to skip a beat. "Melanie," he whispered, recalling her soft brown eyes and the warmth of her laughter. For a brief moment, he allowed himself to bask in the memory before their last bitter argument overshadowed it. He sighed, running his fingers through his thick hair, searching for anyone to fill his void.

"Damn it," Biscuit heaved, feeling the weight of his loneliness settle upon his shoulders like a weighted blanket. The little black book lay open before him, its pages yellowed and dog-eared from years of use. He ran his fingers over the faded names, each holding a fleeting memory of passion and hollow connection. The peeling wallpaper came alive with eerie shadows in the dim lamplight of his cramped living room, mocking his desperate search for meaning beyond the mundane routine of driving the city bus. Biscuit's hand trembled as he closed the book, its finality echoing through the empty room. He could almost hear the distant echoes of laughter and whispered promises that had faded away. His heart raced, yearning for something real to fill his void.

With a frustrated grunt, Biscuit slammed his hand onto the coffee table, the book hitting the wood and echoing through the small space. The empty pages mocked him, taunting him with their lack of answers. He ran his fingers through his messy hair, the strands sticking up in all directions. Grabbing another beer from the six-pack beside him, he cracked open the cold can and took a long swig, feeling the familiar burn of cheap alcohol as it warmed his insides. Thoughts swirled around in his mind, and he couldn't help but mumble, "Maybe I should just give up on love and stick to my old ways of chasing women." But deep down, he knew that wasn't an option. There was a persistent itch in his mind, a thought that wouldn't go away no matter how much he tried to ignore it.

Biscuit thought about his friend Calvin and his unwavering devotion to his family. The sacrifices he made for them, both seen and unseen, were always at the forefront of his mind. Biscuit glanced around the small, cluttered space he called home, feeling the weight of loneliness settling on his shoulders. "I can't keep living like this," he mused, his gaze shifting to the room's dark corners as if searching for an answer. "I'm not getting any younger... I can't keep running in circles forever." His voice trailed off as he pondered the uncertainty of his future, unsure if there was a way out of this endless cycle.

As he stood in the kitchen, Biscuit's mind was consumed with thoughts of love and its elusive nature. The soft hum of the refrigerator provided a steady soundtrack to his musings. He couldn't help but wonder how he would ever find it or if it even truly existed. Like a wave crashing onto the shore, memories flooded back - Calvin's words from years ago, spoken during a game of cards and shared a bottle of whiskey. "You'll know it when you find it, Biscuit," he had said with conviction. "It's like a fire that burns within and never dies down, no matter what obstacles life throws your way." Biscuit couldn't shake those words, but the image of Calvin's face as he uttered them was still vivid in his mind. He longed for that kind of love that burned bright, fierce, unstoppable, and eternal. But how would he know when he found it? That question lingered as he gazed out the window at the starry night sky, searching for answers in the vast expanse above.

"Maybe you're right, Calvin," Biscuit's voice echoed through the empty room as he leaned over the little black book, his eyes fixed on its worn cover as if willing to reveal its secrets. The faint smell of whisky and smoke lingered in the air, a reminder of the many nights Biscuit had spent pouring over the pages searching for something real. He sighed regretfully and missed opportunities weighing heavy on his shoulders. But he wouldn't give up. Not after all this time. "I owe it to you, Calvin," he whispered, his voice barely audible in the stillness. "And I owe it to myself to find something real." With newfound determination, Biscuit took one last swig of beer before setting the can down next to the little black book. Love had eluded him for so long, but he wouldn't stop chasing it now. No, he would pursue it with the same enthusiasm that had once driven him to pursue the women whose names filled those tattered pages. And with that thought, a glimmer of hope sparked inside him as he closed the book and headed out into the night, ready to continue his search for true love.

A sense of peace drifted like a gentle mist, spreading through every nook and cranny of Grandmother Rose's home. She moved from task to task with fluid grace, her hands flitting about like a seasoned conductor leading her orchestra in perfect harmony. Junior sat slumped on the sofa, his youthful face marked with fatigue after a long day spent cleaning, cooking, and preparing for the upcoming Bible study. "Junior, honey, you've done so much today," Grandmother Rose said, her voice soft yet carrying an air of authority. She gently draped a warm blanket over his weary legs and kissed his forehead tenderly. "Rest now, child." The scent of lavender and fresh-baked bread wafted through the room, creating a cozy atmosphere that enveloped them in comfort and love.

"Thanks, Grandma," Junior's gratitude was sincerely whispered as his eyes lingered on his grandmother's retreating figure. Rose went down the narrow, dimly lit hallway, stopping outside Ryder's door. She gently pushed it open, revealing her granddaughter curled up on the bed like a delicate flower in bloom. The soft light of a bedside lamp cast a warm glow on her face, illuminating the determination and curiosity that burned within her. "Ryder, my dear," Rose murmured, not wanting to startle the girl from her peaceful escape into the pages of a book.

Ryder looked up, surprise flickering across her features before smiling radiantly. "Hey, Grandma," she greeted warmly, marking her place in the book and setting it aside. Rose leaned down and tenderly kissed her granddaughter's forehead, feeling an overwhelming surge of love for this young woman she had helped raise and guide through life. "You've been working hard today, too, child. Rest now," she spoke softly but with conviction. "Alright, Grandma," Ryder agreed with sincere respect and love for the woman who had shaped so much of who she was. As Rose left the room, she couldn't help but feel a swell of pride for the firm, loving family she had helped build and a renewed determination to protect them at any cost.

The store's neon lights flickered, casting an eerie glow on the damp pavement as Lenny pulled up to the curb. The low rumble of his engine filled the air, adding to the ominous atmosphere. Willow's chest tightened with unease, her fingers gripping the edge of her seat as she took in the scene before her. "Wait here," Lenny said, his voice betraying a hint of nerves as he glanced at her. "I'll be right back." "Right here?" Willow asked, her eyes narrowed in suspicion. "What for?" "Trust me," Lenny murmured, avoiding her gaze as he climbed out of the car and strode toward the entrance. As he disappeared into the shadows of the store, Willow couldn't shake off the feeling that something was amiss. The store held too many secrets, too many memories of Nicki and the unsettling way they had seemed...close. Too close. She shifted in her seat, fingers drumming impatiently against the door as she anxiously watched Lenny's every move. "Come on, Lenny," she muttered under her breath, the words barely more than a whisper as her heart hammered in her chest. "What are you up to?" Her question was answered too soon as Lenny reappeared, accompanied by Nicki. Willow's blood ran cold, her hands clenching into tight fists at the sight of them together. "What in the world is going on?" she whispered, her voice trembling with anger and confusion as she tried to make sense of the situation.

Willow could feel the tension radiating from Lenny as they approached the car. His eyes flickered back and forth between her and Nicki, who stood just outside the passenger door. Willow's anger simmered beneath the surface, threatening to boil over at any moment. "Nicki," Lenny started, his voice wavering slightly. "Why don't you get in?" "Excuse me?" Willow snapped, her fury pulsing through her body. "So, I'm supposed to sit in the backseat?" "Willow, would you please? "Lenny pleaded, his eyes seeking understanding. But Willow was past reason, her emotions clouding her judgment. "Her car's been out of commission," Lenny continued. "She needs a ride home." "A ride home?" Willow scoffed, the words tasting bitter on her tongue. "And I'm supposed to be okay with that, too?" "Willow—" Lenny began again, but she cut him off. Without another word, she swung open the door and climbed into the backseat. The two women locked gazes, a silent battle raging between them as Nicki's lips curled into a triumphant smirk. "Enjoy your ride," Willow snarled while sitting behind Nicki. As the car pulled away from the curb, Willow stared blankly into the night, her mind consumed by betrayal and hurt. She couldn't believe Lenny would choose Nicki over her after everything they had been through together.

The car purred softly as Lenny's eyes flicked back and forth between the road ahead and the rearview mirror. He stole a glance at Willow, and her face twisted with a storm of emotions that she refused to reveal to him—instead choosing to focus on the passing lights outside. Her mind churned with anger, betrayal, and confusion, leaving her feeling raw and exposed. "How did I end up here again?" she muttered, fiddling with her sleek hair and tugging at her dress. She felt like a fool in the backseat, dressed to the nines for a night that had gone wrong. Sensing Willow's distress, Nicki turned in her seat and winked in her direction. But Lenny remained oblivious, his attention still divided between the mirror and the windshield, tiny beads of sweat forming on his brow. "Hey, why don't I turn on the radio or somethin'?" he suggested, trying to break through the oppressive silence with some noise. "That's cool," Nicki replied as Lenny clicked the knob and filled the car with the smooth melodies of jazz music. However, even the sultry tunes couldn't dispel the tension that hung thickly in the air as Lenny's thoughts were consumed by what lay ahead: a random police checkpoint looming in their path.

"Look alive, ladies," Lenny's voice rang out, high-pitched and frantic, shattering the tense silence in the car. "We got ourselves a checkpoint comin' up." Willow's gut clenched as she saw the flashing lights up ahead, her heart sinking like a stone in her chest. Her eyes flicked to the bag beside her, filled with the product Lenny had eagerly agreed to transport. Panic flooded her veins, making her palms slick with sweat, and her thoughts raced at lightning speed. What do I do now? She begged for a way out of this nightmare but knew deep down that there was no escape. As they crept closer to the checkpoint, Willow's mind spun into overdrive. She couldn't afford to make a single mistake - one wrong move could spell disaster for all of them. The bitter taste of betrayal burned in her mouth, and thoughts of Lenny's betrayal threatened to consume her completely. And yet, as they rolled forward, she realized that her fate was inextricably linked with Lenny's - for better or worse.

Lenny's hands shook on the steering wheel as he gripped it tightly. The car weaved through the busy street, Lenny's eyes darting between the oncoming traffic and the open space to his left, where he intended to make a dangerous U-turn. The headlights of the cars in front of him glared in his eyes, but it was nothing compared to the fiery glare he received from Nicki in the passenger seat. "Where do you think you're going, Lenny?" she demanded, her voice sharp like a blade. Her long, perfectly manicured finger pointed aggressively beyond the checkpoint, like a queen commanding her subjects.

Willow felt her heart skip a beat at the sudden outburst, and there was even more fear coursing through her veins. She tried to swallow the lump in her throat, but it remained lodged there. "I just don't feel like dealing with police tonight," Lenny mumbled, refusing to meet Nicki's gaze as he checked the rearview mirror. In its reflection, he saw Willow's wide eyes filled with disbelief. "Dealing?" Nicki scoffed, rolling her eyes dramatically. "I've been on my feet all day working, Lenny. I deserve to kick back and relax when I get home. So, no U-turns tonight. Keep going straight." Her dismissive wave of the hand left no room for argument. Sweat beaded on Lenny's forehead as he reluctantly followed Nicki's orders, feeling defeated and trapped in this tense situation.

The ominous bag in the backseat seemed to pulsate with danger, its contents a mystery that Lenny dared not reveal to Nicki. It was like a ticking time bomb waiting to explode, its presence a constant reminder of the risk they faced. Lenny's pulse raced even faster as he eyed it nervously in the rearview mirror. He eased off the gas pedal, joining the snaking line of cars approaching the checkpoint. Willow's thoughts raced around her head like a trapped bird desperately seeking an escape. She couldn't believe she had gotten involved with Lenny and his shady business. The weight of guilt and fear pressed down on her chest, making it hard to breathe. She bit her lip, tasting the metallic tang of blood as she tried to calm herself down. "Y'all need to act normal," Lenny whispered urgently, his voice strained with tension as they inched closer to the checkpoint. "Normal?" Willow snapped, anger bubbling up from deep within her. "We are anything but normal right now." She glared at Lenny, her eyes blazing with frustration and fear. In the front seat, Lenny's knuckles started hurting from his tight grip on the steering wheel as he tried to keep his cool under pressure.

Lenny's eyes darted between the rearview mirror and the road ahead as their car inched closer to the checkpoint. Willow could feel her heart racing in her chest, her breath coming in short, shallow gasps. She tried to keep her hands from shaking, gripping the door handle tightly to anchor herself. Lenny kept stealing glances at her, worry etched into his features. "Willow," he said, his voice low and urgent. "I know this ain't how you thought tonight would go." "Damn straight," Nicki interjected from the front seat, a bitter laugh escaping her lips.

Her fists were clenched tightly in her lap, her knuckles filled with tension. "If you had just fixed my car as you promised, none of us would be in this mess." Willow's head snapped around, her eyes wide with shock. She hadn't known about that detail – another of Lenny's secrets. But there was no time for anger now; they drew closer to the checkpoint every second. The headlights of a nearby patrol car illuminated the road ahead, casting an eerie glow over their faces. Willow could see the sweat glistening on Lenny's forehead as he gripped the steering wheel tighter. She closed her eyes and took a deep breath, trying to steady herself before they reached their fate at the checkpoint.

The tension was palpable in the car as Lenny hissed at Nicki, his eyes darting back and forth between her and the rearview mirror. "Not now, Nicki," he growled, his voice low and urgent. "We need to focus on what's happening right now." Turning to Willow, he spoke with an air of desperation. "Listen, I need you to grab that bag and get out of the car. Meet me later after I drop off Nicki." Willow's eyes narrowed as she glared at him, her frustration evident in the tilt of her chin. "Are you kidding me?" she spat, her hands clenching into fists. "Bag, Willow," Lenny repeated, his voice rising urgently as he gestured towards the object. "I need you to take the bag." The car slowed to a crawl as traffic thickened, providing a brief moment of reprieve from the chaos inside. Seizing the opportunity, Nicki flung open the door and leaned out eagerly. "Come on, Willow," she urged, beckoning with one hand while gripping the door handle with the other. "It's now or never."

Willow drew a deep, shaky breath and reached for the bag with trembling fingers. The worn leather strap creaked under her grip as she slid out of the car, her high heels clicking against the cold pavement. She could feel Lenny's intense gaze burning into her back as she stood up straight, her eyes following the taillights of his car as it merged into the slow-moving line of traffic. "See you on the other side," Lenny murmured, his voice thick with emotion. A fleeting glance passed between them before he turned away, disappearing into the hazy unknown. A sense of unease settled in Willow's chest, the weight of uncertainty heavy on her shoulders as she took a hesitant step forward.

Willow stood frozen, her fingers tightly gripping the worn bag as Lenny's car inched closer to the checkpoint. Each second felt like an eternity as she waited for him to return. His strained voice echoed through the air, filled with worry and tension. "Give me about 15 minutes," he called out, his words laced with desperation. Willow's anger boiled just beneath the surface, threatening to erupt at any moment. She turned sharply on her heel, the click of her high heels echoing through the lonely street. Her red dress shone under the dim streetlights, a lone beacon of color amidst the dreary urban surroundings. Hot tears streamed down her cheeks, leaving trails in her carefully applied makeup. But then, she didn't care about appearances or social expectations. All she could think about was how she had ended up in this mess, a pawn in someone else's dangerous game. "Damn you, Lenny," she muttered under her breath, wiping away her tears with the back of her hand. "And damn me for falling into this trap."

CHAPTER 16

The bus stop stood out in the darkness, a lone beacon of hope surrounded by the quiet stillness of the night. Sporadically, the light flickered as if taunting her with the uncertainty of her current situation. She sat on the cold metal bench, shivering despite her thick coat, and glanced at her watch anxiously. Each passing second felt like an eternity, and she couldn't help but whisper, "Where are you, Lenny?" The longer she waited, the more anxious she became. One hour passed, and then another; each bus that rumbled past only seemed to mock her with its empty seats.

As she sat there alone, memories flooded back to her - memories of Biscuit. She thought about all the times they shared, simple moments that meant so much more than any extravagant outing with Lenny ever could. She remembered Biscuit's infectious laughter and unwavering kindness. He always knew how to make her feel special, even when they spent a lazy evening watching TV on the couch. "Maybe I should've been content with what I had," she mused, her heart heavy with regret. "I didn't need fancy dinners or expensive gifts. All I wanted was someone who truly cared about me." With a heavy sigh, she realized too late that she had let go of something special for something superficial. And now she was left waiting alone at a bus stop, hoping for a ride back to where her heart truly belonged.

"Hey, lady," a deep, gruff voice cut through Willow's thoughts like a knife. "You, ok?" She looked up to see a burly bus driver peering down at her through the open door of his vehicle. His eyes were weathered and kind but also a little curious. Willow mustered a weak smile and shook her head, trying to convey that she was okay. "Thanks, but I'm just waiting for someone," she replied, her voice barely audible above the loud rumbling of the bus's engine. The driver nodded in understanding and pulled away, leaving Willow sitting alone once more on the empty bench. With a heavy heart, she whispered into the night, "Come on, Lenny. Please don't make me regret this even more than I already do." Her words echoed into the darkness, accompanied by the gentle rustle of leaves and the distant traffic sounds. Tears pricked at her eyes, threatening to spill over as she waited silently for Lenny to arrive.

Willow's eyes darted across the deserted street, her gaze zeroing in on a pay phone illuminated by a flickering streetlight. Every muscle in her body seemed to be fueled with determination as she marched forward, the sharp click of her designer heels resonating in the stillness of the night. She barely registered the searing pain as one heel snapped beneath her weight, sending her stumbling along like a wounded animal. "Damn it," she muttered through gritted teeth, quickly yanking off both shoes and hurling them into the shadows. Now barefoot, she continued toward the pay phone, her mind racing about Biscuit and the life she wished she had chosen.

Meanwhile, at that exact moment, Biscuit lay sprawled on his sofa, crumbs from dinner still clinging to his disheveled shirt. A soft snore escaped him; his face slacks with exhaustion after a long day's work. The shrill ring of the telephone jolted him awake, leaving him momentarily disoriented as he fumbled for the receiver. "Hello?" Biscuit grumbled groggily, rubbing sleep from his weary eyes.

The faint sound of Willow's voice trembled over the line, a delicate and uncertain whisper. Biscuit's heart clenched at the sound, memories of their last argument flooding back to him. "Willow? What do you want?" he asked, his tone guarded and defensive. He was tempted to hang up, but something in her voice made him pause. "Can we talk?" Her words were fragile, like a glass house on the verge of shattering. Biscuit sighed, rubbing his temples in frustration. "What's on your mind?" Willow's fingers hovered over the cold metal of the pay phone as she struggled to find the right words. "I... I messed up, Biscuit," she finally admitted, her voice breaking with emotion. Tears glistened in her eyes as she continued, "I should've stayed with you." Biscuit felt guilt and anger rise within him, but it quickly dissipated as he heard the raw emotion in her plea. "Willow, I -" he started but cut himself off. He knew how manipulative she could be, but he couldn't ignore the hurt and vulnerability in her voice. "Please," she whispered, her voice thick with emotion. "I just need someone to talk to right now." Biscuit softened at her words and relented, "Okay... let's talk."

"Look, Willow," he said, his voice low and uncertain. He shifted his weight on the couch, his eyes darting around the room before settling back on her. "I can come to pick you up if you want. But I ain't promisin' anything more than that." Willow's heart skipped a beat at his offer, relief flooding through her. "Thank you," she breathed, her voice trembling with emotion. "That means more to me than you'll ever know." Biscuit nodded, a small smile tugging at the corners of his mouth. He pushed himself off the couch with a heavy sigh. "Alright," he said, running a hand through his hair. "Where are you?" Willow gave him the cross streets by the bus stop on 20th Street and waited anxiously for his response. "And... Biscuit?" she added softly before he could hang up. He paused, sensing the hesitation in her voice. "Yeah?" "Thank you," she whispered, her voice cracking with gratitude. Biscuit felt a pang in his chest at her words, knowing all too well the struggles she had faced. "See you soon," he murmured, ending the call. As he grabbed his keys and headed for the door, Biscuit couldn't help but wonder if this was just another mistake in a long line of regrets.

As the minutes ticked by, Biscuit's car pulled into the desolate parking lot adjacent to the 20th Street bus stop. The flickering streetlights were barely enough to illuminate the figure standing there - it was Willow, her bare feet and tear-streaked face telling a story of desperation. She hurried to his car, her steps quick and frantic, and opened the door before sliding into the passenger seat. "Thanks for comin', Biscuit," she murmured, her eyes downcast as she fiddled with her broken heels. His heart clenched at her vulnerability, but he tried to keep his walls up even as he felt them crumbling in her presence. He could see her breathing heavily, her trembling hands gripping the edges of her dress. Their tense silence spoke volumes, each trying to hide their pain behind a facade of strength. But in this moment, they were two broken souls seeking comfort in each other's company.

Their conversation was minimal as they sat in the empty parking lot, the only sound coming from the gentle hum of passing cars and the occasional chirp of a nearby bird. The car, parked at a reasonable distance, appeared to be gently now rocking back and forth with passion and determination with each shift of its weight. The aftermath of silence between them was palpable, thick with unspoken words and shared memories that hung heavy in the air. Biscuit knew he should be angry, yet all he felt was an overwhelming sadness for the woman beside him. "Willow," he finally said, breaking the silence.

His voice was low and laced with concern. "I don't know what's going on with you." She looked at him, her tear-filled eyes searching his face for answers. "I... I know," she whispered, her voice barely audible amidst the stillness. "Trust me," Biscuit insisted, his unwavering gaze locked with hers. "You can do so much better." As Willow stared into Biscuit's eyes, searching for truth and hope, she couldn't deny the reality of his words. But could she find the strength to change? It seemed like an impossible feat at that moment, but deep down, she knew it was possible if she just believed in herself.

The glowing orange streetlights cast a hazy glow onto the cracked pavement as Biscuit's car glided through the city's deserted streets. The faint hum of the engine and the occasional beep of a traffic light were the only sounds breaking through the heavy silence inside the vehicle. Willow sat in the passenger seat, her fingers tracing patterns on the cold glass window as her mind raced with regret and unanswered questions. How had she ended up in this familiar yet toxic cycle once again? The city lights blurred outside, reflections dancing across her face like ghosts. "Where do you want to be dropped off?" Biscuit's deep voice finally broke through the quiet. Willow hesitated before answering, her voice small and subdued. "I'll let you know soon. I can walk from there." Biscuit nodded, trying to hide the disappointment that threatened to seep into his tone. As they continued driving, Willow couldn't help but feel lost in this maze of city lights and emotions, unsure of where she truly wanted to be dropped off at this point in her life.

The car hummed steadily as they journeyed, the familiar landscape passing in a blur. Biscuit couldn't help but think about how he always seemed to fall for women like Willow - beautiful, manipulative, and utterly destructive. He knew he should have turned her away at the pay phone, but something deep within him couldn't bear to leave her stranded and alone. "Thanks for picking me up," Willow said suddenly, turning to face Biscuit. Her eyes were red-rimmed from tears, and her once flawless makeup was smeared across her cheeks like war paint. Her voice was shaky with emotion, yet there was a hint of defiance. "I appreciate it." "Sure thing," Biscuit replied gruffly, avoiding her gaze.

They rode silently for the rest of the journey, their tension palpable. Each lost in their thoughts and regrets. As they neared Willow's desired location, Biscuit pulled over to let Willow out, the sound of gravel crunching under the tires breaking the moment's stillness. The silence between them lingered for a few more moments before Willow finally broke it with a whispered "thank you," her voice filled with regret and longing as she hesitated before stepping out. Biscuit watched her, his heart heavy with conflicting emotions as he was ready to drive off without looking back.

"Take care of yourself, alright?" he gently reminded her, his hand lingering on her shoulder as she reluctantly opened the door to leave. The streetlights cast a dim glow over her features, illuminating the slight downturn of her lips and the shadows under her eyes. "Thanks, Biscuit," she whispered, her voice barely audible before she stepped out into the night and disappeared down the sidewalk.

As Biscuit drove home, his disappointment in himself grew heavier with each passing mile. He knew that his pattern of falling for toxic women like Willow only perpetuated a cycle of hurt and heartbreak. And yet, as he replayed the events of the evening in his mind, he couldn't shake the nagging feeling that perhaps there was still a glimmer of hope for Willow and himself - a chance to break free from their self-destructive tendencies and find true happiness together.

Willow's bare feet slapped against the pavement, echoing through the empty streets as she approached Lenny's condo. The chill of the night air seeped into her skin, sending shivers down her spine. She pulled her coat tighter, trying to ward off the cold. Willow couldn't help but replay Biscuit's words in her mind, each piercing her heart with regret for not being stronger when she had the chance. "Damn it," she muttered under her breath, anger and frustration bubbling inside her. Willow cursed herself for allowing Lenny into her life. She felt like a prisoner again, caught in his entangling web with every step closer to his door. Willow glanced down at her now-empty hands, grateful that the bag was no longer weighing her down. But the weight of her past mistakes still hung heavy on her shoulders.

As she neared the entrance to Lenny's building, Willow couldn't help but feel a sense of dread creeping over her. She took a deep breath and steeled herself for the upcoming confrontation, knowing Lenny wouldn't be happy about losing the bag. But she was tired of avoiding conflict and decided to stand up for herself this time.

Lenny lay in bed inside the dimly lit condo, his body tense with anticipation as he strained his ears for any sign of Willow's arrival. When he finally heard the click of the front door opening and closing, he fought the urge to jump out of bed and confront her immediately. Instead, he lay still and listened as her footsteps approached the bedroom before stopping abruptly.

"Did you think I wouldn't notice you weren't coming to get me?" Willow's voice was sharp like a knife, filled with anger and hurt. Lenny remained silent, keeping up his facade of sleep. He knew he had messed up, and there was no excuse.

"Fine," she huffed, storming into the bathroom and slamming the door behind her. The sound echoed through the room, symbolizing the rift between them. The shower turned on, its steady stream of water drowning out any further attempts at conversation. Lenny closed his eyes and sighed, feeling guilty for causing tension between himself and Willow.

The steamy water poured over Willow's trembling body, causing her to shiver and sigh. She closed her eyes, allowing herself a moment of vulnerability in the privacy of her shower. Tears mingled with the water streaming down her face, and she bit her lip to stifle a sob. At this moment alone, she couldn't escape the memories of Biscuit - his kind touch, unwavering loyalty, and how undeserving Willow felt of someone like him. But she refused to let herself drown in self-pity any longer. "Get it together, Willow," she whispered through gritted teeth, determination flaring in her chest.

It was time to make things right and escape Lenny's toxic life. And if there were even a sliver of hope for redemption with Biscuit, she would do whatever it took to prove herself worthy of his love and trust. Meanwhile, on the other side of the bathroom door, Lenny's heart raced at the sound of the shower. He knew he had been treading dangerous waters, mixing Willow with his business dealings, but it was too late, and he couldn't help himself. The thought of losing anything made his palms sweat and his pulse quicken.

The first rays of sunlight filtered through the cracked blinds, casting slivers of golden light onto Willow's closed eyelids. She resisted the urge to open them, wanting to savor a few more moments of peaceful bliss before facing the inevitable. Her body felt heavy and achy from tossing and turning all night, her thoughts consumed by the turmoil between her and Lenny. The silence in the room was deafening, broken only by the soft sound of her breathing. With a deep sigh, she finally willed herself to sit up and swing her legs over the edge of the bed. Despite her exhaustion, she couldn't stay in bed any longer. The sheets were tangled and messy, reflecting the state of their relationship. As she stood up and stretched, her night-gown slipped off one shoulder, revealing the lace trim of her bra. Willow's mind was racing as she reached for her discarded robe, thoughts of last night's events swirling like a chaotic storm. Anger and frustration simmered beneath the surface, threatening to bubble over at any moment. She loosely draped the robe over her body, leaving it untied as she made her way out of the bedroom with hesitant steps.

The moment Willow entered the kitchen, her throat constricted at the sight of Lenny, Turk, and the rest of his crew scattered around the room. Their eyes were like lasers, boring into her fragile form as she stood frozen in the doorway. Her heart skipped a beat, and she quickly pulled her silk robe tightly around her body, self-consciously covering herself up. The air was thick with tension, and Willow could practically taste it on her tongue. Something was amiss. "Good morning," she mutters, sounding casual as she approaches the refrigerator. She could feel their eyes following her every move, like predators sizing up their prey. "Oh look, it's the little princess," Lenny sneered, his voice dripping with sarcasm. "Why don't you pour yourself some juice? You must be thirsty after all that beauty sleep." With shaking hands, Willow reached for a pitcher of orange juice, barely able to keep her grip on the cool glass. As she poured, she couldn't help but wonder what had caused such an unusual silence among this rowdy group.

"Where's the bag, Willow?" Lenny's voice, calm but deliberate, pierced through the silence in the room and sent shivers down Willow's spine. Caught off guard, her hand trembled, and she over-poured her glass, spilling juice over the counter and creating a sticky mess. Her heart raced as she flinched, expecting someone to say something, but the room remained eerily silent, their gazes fixed on her with an unrelenting intensity. "Um...the bag?" Willow stammered, feeling a bead of sweat roll down her temple as she desperately searched for an explanation. But the faces of Lenny's crew offered no solace – only cold, judgmental stares that made her want to shrink away. "Clock's ticking, Willow," Lenny's voice took on a dangerous edge. "Tell me what happened to the bag." Panic tightened its grip around Willow's chest, making it hard to breathe as she felt the weight of their scrutiny bearing down on her. She frantically tried to think of a way out of this nightmare – just wanting to escape and forget everything that had led her to this moment. But deep down, she knew there was no escaping until she found a way to fix the mess she had created. "I... I don't know," she finally stuttered, trembling with fear.

Willow's eyes darted around the kitchen, her heart pounding like a drum as she desperately searched for a way to buy some time. The sound of their heavy breathing filled the otherwise quiet room, creating an oppressive atmosphere that threatened to suffocate her. Her gaze landed on the mop resting inside the pantry, and she approached it, grasping for anything to break the tension. But before she could reach it, Turk stepped forward and snatched it up, his movements smooth yet somehow menacing. "Allow me," he said in a calm, deliberate voice as he leaned closer to Willow. "Don't you worry about mopping that up, Willow? That's what I love to do: clean up messes." Lenny's voice cut through the air like a sharp knife. "Where is my bag, Willow?"

He paced back and forth across the kitchen, his face a mask of confusion but with an underlying current of anger that made the hairs on the back of her neck stand on end. The tension in the room was palpable, filling the air with an almost tangible weight that made it difficult for Willow to think straight. She began pacing as well, her mind racing as she frantically tried to come up with an explanation for the missing bag. But Lenny's angry voice echoed in her head every time she opened her mouth to speak, making it nearly impossible for her to form coherent thoughts. Sensing her hesitation, Lenny slammed his fist on the counter with a loud thud, causing Willow to jump in fear and make her heart race even faster.

"His words dripped with venom as he spoke, 'Last night didn't go as planned, I get it. But that's another issue for another day. Right now, I want to know where my bag is.' Willow felt like a bird trapped in a cage with hungry lions, their intense gaze fixated on her, waiting for her to make a mistake. Beneath the surface, fear was boiling, leaving her breathless and overwhelmed. 'Please, Lenny, I...' she stammered, but her voice cracked, unable to hold its ground. In the pit of her stomach, she knew there would be consequences if she couldn't find a way to appease him. How could she possibly explain the unexplainable? 'Tick tock, Willow,' Lenny growled, his impatience growing by the second. 'You'd better have a good answer for me.'"

As Willow paced back and forth, her mind spun with a whirlwind of potential explanations and scenarios, each more improbable than the last. She understood the importance of choosing her words with extreme care, fully aware that a single misstep could spell her undoing. The weight of fear bore heavily upon her shoulders, making each breath a struggle, yet Willow knew that now was not the time to display vulnerability. With a tremor running through her, Willow could only offer a silent nod, desperately hoping to discover an escape from this harrowing ordeal before it completely consumed her.

Willow's voice trembled as she looked into Lenny's cold, unyielding eyes. They were like ice, reflecting no emotion or warmth towards her. She took a deep breath, trying to steady herself as she spoke. "Lenny, you never showed up last night," she said, shaky and almost unrecognizable. "I just kept walking." Her throat tightened as she struggled to continue. "During my walk, one of my ex-boyfriends saw me and offered to give me a ride somewhere. I asked him to bring me here to you." The room felt tense, like a thick fog pressing in on all sides. Willow could feel her heart racing as she tried to navigate the delicate situation. She moved towards the couch, sinking into its cushions as if they were a lifeline. "My bag..." Lenny's voice was slow and deliberate, his gaze piercing into her. Panic rose in Willow's chest as she realized the gravity of the situation. "With everything that happened last night," she stammered, her voice cracking, "I must have left it in his car. He probably doesn't even know it's there." Her mind raced with possibilities, trying to devise a solution before Lenny's anger consumed them both.

Lenny lowered himself onto the seat beside her, his tall frame casting a shadow over Willow. Despite his calm demeanor, his eyes burned with an unwavering intensity. "So, let me get this straight," he said, his voice like a steady current despite the undercurrent of anger. "Another man now has the bag I entrusted to you?" Willow's heart raced as she felt herself being backed into a corner. "But he probably doesn't even know it's in the car!" she blurted out, desperation creeping into her voice. Lenny leaned in closer, his gaze piercing and unforgiving. "I didn't hear you mention the details of how my bag ended up out of your hands in the first place," he said, his words dripping with venom.

Willow's brown eyes darted frantically around the room, her mind racing with possible solutions to this dire predicament. She felt utterly trapped, like a cornered animal, by the imposing figures of Lenny and his crew. Her chest tightened as she fought to keep her fear from consuming her, her heart pounding loudly in her ears. "Alright, Lenny. I'll get your bag back, I swear," she promised, her voice barely a whisper against the hush of their menacing presence. "Just give me some time." A cold chill ran down her spine as Lenny's steely gaze bore into hers, his features set in a dangerous snarl. "Time is running out, Willow," he warned, each syllable sharp and cutting like ice in her veins. "And you don't want to know what happens if you can't deliver." As the heavy threat hung in the air like a dark cloud, Willow knew with a sinking feeling that she had no choice but to find a way to retrieve that precious bag quickly before it was too late.

Willow's heart pounded against her chest, a fierce rhythm that drowned out all other sounds. Determined, she sprang to her feet, her body ready to take action and make things right. But as she moved towards the door, Lenny's voice stopped her. His tone was cold and commanding as he asked, "Where do you think you're going?" Willow paused, her mind racing for an answer that would appease him. "Getting your bag, Lenny," she answered quickly, hoping it would satisfy his demands. Lenny stood tall and still, like a predator ready to pounce on his prey.

He slowly clapped his hands together, the sound echoing sinisterly in the silent room. His steely gaze swept over Turk and his other men, who all seemed to tremble under his authority.

With a chilling smile, Lenny spoke again. "Seems no clean-up needed on aisle seven today, boys." Turk shifted uncomfortably and finally spoke up. "Guess I was wrong," he admitted, his eyes never leaving Willow's face. "I apologize, Willow." Despite their apology, Willow could feel their eyes lingering on her every move with suspicion and judgment. She forced a confident tone as she replied, "No problem. I need to get dressed to retrieve Lenny's bag." Hurrying into the bedroom, she closed the door behind her and leaned against it, trying to steady her trembling body. Fear coursed through her veins as she realized the danger she had narrowly escaped yet again.

CHAPTER 17

B iscuit stood in his cramped living room, his eyes fixed on the mysterious bag on his cluttered coffee table. His fingers fidgeted nervously as he buttoned up his bus uniform, unable to shake the curiosity about its contents. Willow had always been a bit of a wild card, but drugs? It seemed improbable, yet people were full of surprises. A knock on the door snapped him out of his thoughts, and he hurried to answer it. He found Roland, one of his closest friends, standing on the other side. Without a word, they both made a beeline for the bag, their excitement palpable. "I can't believe this," Biscuit murmured as Roland carefully examined the contents. "I mean, I just stumbled upon it..." "Man, I have no idea where you got your hands on this stuff," Roland interrupted, looking up at Biscuit in awe. "But it's the real deal."

A dryness settled in Biscuit's mouth as shock coursed through him, compounded by the fact that it came from Willow. He wanted nothing to do with drugs, but a thought crossed his mind – could there be a way to profit from this? "Hey, Roland," Biscuit began tentatively. "Do you happen to know anyone who would be interested in buying these drugs?" "Are you kidding me?" Roland exclaimed eagerly, his eyes gleaming with anticipation. "This is worth a fortune on the streets." The possibilities raced through Biscuit's mind as he considered this newfound opportunity before them.

Biscuit's voice trembled with nerves as he spoke. "Alright," he said, trying to sound confident. "I don't care about the cost. They can have it for half the price, whatever that may be." Roland considered his offer silently for a moment before Biscuit added, desperation seeping into his tone, "I'll even give you a cut of the profits." Roland's expression remained stoic as he finally agreed, "Let me make some calls. I'll get back to you." Biscuit attempted to hand him the merchandise, but Roland shook his head. "No way, man. I'm not walking down the street with all that stuff." He glanced around nervously before continuing, "You keep it. I'll let you know once I find a willing buyer." The tension in the air was palpable as they parted ways, each hoping for a successful outcome.

The morning was cool and crisp, the sun shining bright in a cloudless sky. As Calvin pulled up to Junior's school, his warm hand rested on Lena's thigh, providing a comforting pressure. Children's laughter filled the air, mingling with the distant hum of traffic. Junior turned to his parents, his eyes alight with anticipation and excitement. "I can't wait till we go to the Wisconsin Dells this weekend!" he exclaimed, bouncing in his seat. "It's gonna be so fun!" Calvin smiled at his son's enthusiasm and ruffled his hair affectionately. "It's time we take a family trip out of the city for a change," he agreed, glancing over at Lena with a grin. "We all deserve a little break." Lena nodded in agreement, her gaze taking in the bustling schoolyard and the smiling faces of the other children and parents.

She knew they needed this escape from city life's constant noise and stress. "Alright, you two," she said, urging Junior and Ryder out of the car as they arrived at their destination. "Have a great day at school. We'll see you later." "Bye, Mom! Bye, Dad!" the kids chorused happily, slamming the car doors shut behind them as they bounded off towards their friends. As Calvin and Lena watched their children disappear into the crowd of students, Lena felt a surge of gratitude for the man beside her. Calvin kept their family anchored in love and faith, always supporting them through thick and thin. "Thank you," she whispered, leaning over to rest her head on his shoulder as they drove towards the hospital where Lena worked as a nurse. "For everything." Calvin glanced at her with a warm smile, his hand reaching over to entwine their fingers together on the gear shift. "For what?" he asked gently. "For being such an incredible husband and father," Lena replied, looking up at him with love. "For never giving up on us."

Calvin reached for her hand, entwining their fingers as they drove through the familiar streets of West Side Chicago. The sun started peering through the buildings, casting a golden glow over everything in its path. Lena couldn't help but smile at the warmth and comfort radiating from her husband's touch. "I couldn't do it without you, Lena," Calvin said softly, his voice filled with gratitude and love. They continued to drive in companionable silence, taking in the sights and sounds of their neighborhood.

As they neared the hospital where Lena worked, Calvin turned to her with a mischievous twinkle in his eye. "Hey, don't forget to pack those stockings for our trip," he teased, wiggling his eyebrows suggestively. Lena rolled her eyes playfully but couldn't hide her fondness for her husband's sense of humor. "Oh, you!" she laughed, swatting his arm playfully. "Get out of here!"

"Okay, okay," Calvin chuckled, pulling up to the hospital entrance. He leaned in to give Lena a lingering kiss, their love for each other evident in every touch and gesture. "Have a great day at work, baby."

"Thank you, Cal," Lena smiled, stepping out of the car and waving goodbye as he drove off. She took a moment to soak in the beauty of the morning before heading into the bustling hospital. Thoughts of their upcoming family trip filled her with excitement and happiness, and she was grateful for all that she had in life—especially her loving husband by her side.

The locker room at the bus station was a chaotic symphony of metallic clangs and the pungent smell of sweat mingling with thick diesel fumes. Biscuit stood before the rusted, dented locker, its once bright blue paint now chipped and faded. Fingers trembling, Biscuit clutched the mysterious bag tightly in both hands, unsure of what it contained but feeling a sense of urgency to hide it. After a moment's hesitation, Biscuit shoved the bag deep into the bowels of the locker and slammed it shut. The sound echoed through the space, mixing with Calvin's voice as he approached from behind. "Those kids are buzzing with excitement for their trip to the Dells this weekend," Calvin said, slapping Biscuit heartily on the back with a wide grin.

Biscuit managed to force a smirk, though his thoughts were anything but focused on the upcoming family trip. Calvin's sharp eyes narrowed slightly, sensing that something was off with his friend. "Hey, you driving Cicero today, too?" Biscuit asked, attempting to push aside the unease that weighed heavily on him. "Yep, just like every other day," Calvin replied, studying Biscuit intently. "You seem a bit off, man." "Listen, I need to talk to you later, alright?" Biscuit said, avoiding Calvin's gaze. "At the end of the line." Calvin furrowed his brow in concern before nodding in agreement. As Biscuit walked away, his mind raced with the potential consequences of his recent actions. He couldn't shake the feeling of guilt and anxiety that had settled in his gut like a rock.

The sound of soulful music seeped out from the speakers of Biscuit's bus as it weaved through the busy streets of Chicago. The beat was steady and soothing, contrasting the turmoil in Biscuit's mind as he gripped the steering wheel. His thoughts were clouded by the heavy weight of the bag now locked away in his locker, a constant reminder of his mistake. The familiar hum of the engine provided some relief, drowning out the relentless melody of worry that played in his head. As his regular riders filed onto the bus, their faces blurred by his distracted state, Mrs. Jenkins stood out with her warm smile and cheerful greeting of

"Good morning, Biscuit." It barely registered as he muttered a distracted response, his fingers tapping an anxious rhythm on the steering wheel.

The secret locked away in his locker gnawed at him like a persistent itch he couldn't scratch. As they trundled down Cicero Avenue, Biscuit's mind fixated on the daunting conversation he needed to have with Calvin. How could he possibly explain what had happened? Would Calvin understand, or would their friendship be irreparably damaged by Biscuit's mistake? He heaved a sigh, feeling the weight of his predicament settle like a stone in his chest. The soulful music continued to play in the background, but Biscuit had no solace in its familiar melodies anymore.

Willow's heart pounded like a wild animal in its cage as she strode through the parking lot, her eyes darting from car to car until they finally landed on Biscuit's beat-up Chevy. Her steps slowed, attempting to mask the desperation in her stomach. She approached the driver's side window, peering in with bated breath, hoping to see the bag sitting on the seat. Her heart sank as she saw it was empty, her fists clenching in frustration. She forced herself to keep her breathing steady, trying not to let the panic show on her face as she circled the car. Each successive window revealed nothing, only increasing her dread and hopelessness.

The final blow came when she attempted to check the trunk to no avail. Defeated, Willow leaned against the car momentarily, feeling defeated and exposed. "Damn it," she whispered under her breath, trembling with fear. Visions of Lenny and his ruthless crew flashed through her mind, each scenario more brutal than the last. She had always been a survivor, but this time, it felt like a noose tightening around her neck. With a deep breath, she squared her shoulders and marched away from the car, determination replacing the overwhelming helplessness inside her. As she disappeared into the shadows of the parking lot, she couldn't help but wonder if this was the end of the road for her.

Biscuit leaned heavily against the side of his bus, and the metal panels felt cool and rough against his skin. His heart raced as he tried to rehearse what he would say to Calvin, his best friend and confidant. The terminal buzzed with activity, but he could only focus on his ragged breathing. He looked up anxiously as Calvin's bus turned into the terminal, relief washing over him like a wave crashing onto the shore. Biscuit pushed off the bus. Biscuit's feet moved automatically towards his friend, but his mind churned with anxiety and doubt. "Calvin," he called out when his friend stepped off the bus.

"I need to talk to you about something." Calvin glanced at Biscuit, concern flickering across his face as he registered the gravity of the situation. "What's going on?" he asked, his voice steady and reassuring despite the worry gnawing at him. Biscuit took a deep breath before launching into his tale, recounting the events that had led to him bumping into Willow and her leaving something in his car. His voice was low and filled with regret as he explained everything to Calvin, who listened intently with a mix of shock and concern in his eyes. Together, they stood side by side, lost in their thoughts and emotions as they processed what had happened.

Calvin's gaze drifted beyond Biscuit, settling on a figure in the distance as they shared a moment of camaraderie. Willow, Biscuit's ex-girlfriend, stood with her arms crossed and her posture rigid, her eyes locked on them with an intense glare that sent a shiver down Calvin's spine. She raised her hand, beckoning Biscuit to approach her, and he reluctantly hesitated before considering whether to comply. "Uh, Biscuit...you see who's here?" Calvin asked, nodding towards Willow. Biscuit turned away, his face paling at the sight of her. "Yeah, I see her," he muttered, rubbing the back of his neck nervously. "What do you think she wants, man? We all know it's over between us." "Only one way to find out," Calvin said cautiously, watching Biscuit hesitate. Finally, Biscuit turned to Calvin with a pleading look in his eyes. "Man, I... I don't know what she wants. Let me go see." before finally taking a deep breath and walking towards his former love. "Be careful, brother," Calvin advised, watching Biscuit amble over to Willow, his shoulders hunched in unease.

The air crackled with tension as they began to speak, their voices too low for Calvin to hear from where he stood. Alone with his thoughts, Calvin couldn't help but worry for his friend. Biscuit tended to fall for the wrong type of woman, and Willow was no exception. As he watched them converse from afar, he prayed that Biscuit would be able to resist whatever manipulative tactics she might employ. "Stay strong, my brother," Calvin whispered under his breath, his eyes never leaving the scene before him. "You deserve so much better." Beads of sweat appeared on Biscuit's brow as he listened to Willow's words, his expression tense and uncertain. The palpable tension between them only seemed to grow as they continued talking, and Calvin could sense the unease radiating off them both, thick and suffocating.

Calvin could feel his protective instincts kicking in as he observed the interaction between the two. He couldn't shake the nagging feeling that something was not quite right, and he was determined not to let his friend get entangled in whatever scheme Willow might be weaving. "Hey, Biscuit! We should probably head back on our route soon!" Calvin called out, masking his concern as best as he could. He raised his hand to greet Willow, forcing a smile. "Hello, Willow." Willow barely acknowledged Calvin with a dismissive nod before leaning close to Biscuit, and her voice hushed as she whispered something meant for his ears only. Biscuit visibly flinched at her words but reluctantly nodded, his face reflecting a mix of fear and resolve.

"Remember, Biscuit," Willow's voice hissed through the air, sharp and commanding like a whip cracking against skin. Calvin caught the tail end of her message but couldn't make out the words - just the intensity in her tone. As she turned on her heel and stalked away, leaving behind a trail of tension and unease, Biscuit's gaze met Calvin's. His eyes pleaded for understanding and support, the weight of Willow's demands weighing heavily on his shoulders. Calvin knew better than to push his friend for answers; whatever Willow had demanded must have been significant, maybe even dangerous. "Stay strong, Biscuit," Calvin thought, placing a reassuring hand on his shoulder as he returned to his side. "We'll get through this together." Biscuit's grateful expression spoke volumes, their unspoken bond giving them strength in the face of whatever was to come. The two friends shared a solemn moment before returning to their duties, each carrying the weight of the encounter on their hearts as they faced the rest of the day with determination and resilience, the burden of the encounter heavy on them.

CHAPTER 18

A golden orb sank into the horizon as the sun descended, and long shadows stretched across the bustling bus terminal. The air was thick with rumbling engines and hissing brakes as buses lined up, their doors opening to disgorge streams of exhausted bus drivers. Across the street, Willow's eyes were fixed on the scene, her gaze darting from one vehicle to another in anxious anticipation of Biscuit's arrival. Her fingers tapped impatiently against her thigh, a subtle sign of the eager energy coursing through her. "Where are you, Biscuit?" she murmured under her breath, her eyes scanning the parking lot for any glimpse of his familiar figure among the sea of strangers.

Unbeknownst to her, Biscuit was hiding behind a tall, weathered pillar at the edge of the lot. His back was pressed tightly against the cold steel and concrete, his fingers gripping the rough surface for support. He peered out from behind the pillar, eyes scanning the area intensely. In the distance, he spotted Willow, and his blood boiled with anger and unease. She couldn't see him enter his car if he wanted to keep his plan intact. If she caught wind of the product she had left there last night, all of Biscuit's careful scheming would be ruined. "Damn," he muttered under his breath, his brows furrowing in frustration.

Despite knowing why Willow was so desperate to find him today - she likely thought he knew about the drugs she'd stashed away. Biscuit shook his head vehemently. She wasn't getting it back after everything she had done to him. He remembered all too well how she had wrecked his house during one of their tumultuous breakups, causing him to lose all the money he could barely afford. The drugs were payback, a way to make things right in Biscuit's mind. "Once Roland finds a buyer," he reassured himself in a low voice, "I'll just tell her someone stole the bag." But deep down, he didn't believe his own words; it was just a flimsy excuse to justify his actions.

The thought of dealing with Willow's wrath once the truth came out made his stomach churn, but Biscuit pushed it aside. He just needed to focus on staying away from his car for now. The air was tense as Biscuit watched Willow from a safe distance, her eyes scanning the area like a predator searching for prey. His heart raced as he remembered all the times she had manipulated and used him; now, it was his turn to take control. "Time to face the music," he whispered, trying to steady his nerves. Every fiber of his being wanted to put everything between them behind him, but a small part of him couldn't help but feel a malicious satisfaction at the thought of getting back at her. But he knew that, sooner or later, Willow would find out the truth – and there would be hell to pay when she did. For now, he clung to the hope that he could outsmart her – even if only for a little while.

Biscuit's heart raced as he paced the cramped locker room. The pungent smell of sweat and diesel fuel lingered in the air, making it difficult to catch a full breath. The worn lockers, coated with peeling paint, seemed to loom closer and closer, closing in on him like a trap. He clenched his fists, trying to push away the anxiety that threatened to consume him. But the weight of the drugs hidden in his locker hung heavy on his conscience, suffocating him like a thick blanket. Every tick of the clock sounded louder and more ominous, counting down the seconds until he would have to face the consequences of his actions.

Biscuit's hair was in disarray as he ran a trembling hand through it. "Damn," he muttered to himself, the weight of his predicament heavy on his mind. How had he managed to get himself into this mess? The sound of other drivers entering the locker room jolted Biscuit from his thoughts. He stopped pacing and stared at his locker, disbelief across his face. As if seeing it for the first time, the ugly metal suddenly felt like a prison cell, trapping not only the drugs but also his future – a future that was beginning to look darker and more uncertain by the minute. "Hey, man," Calvin's deep voice pulled Biscuit from his reverie. He hadn't even noticed his friend enter the room. Calvin's brow creased with concern as he took in Biscuit's haggard appearance. "You, okay?" "Uh, yeah," Biscuit replied, attempting to force a smile that didn't quite reach his tired eyes. "Just tired, I guess." Calvin sat beside him on the worn wooden bench, his dark eyes searching Biscuit's face. They had an unspoken understanding, a bond forged by years of friendship and shared hardships.

Calvin knew something was eating away at Biscuit, but he also knew better than to push too hard. Instead, he chose to wait, giving his friend space to come to him when he was ready. "Willow is meeting you on your route today," Calvin said quietly, never breaking eye contact with Biscuit. "I don't like how she's been hanging around lately –

like a snake in the grass, just waiting for the right moment to strike." Biscuit swallowed hard, feeling the knot in his stomach tighten even further. He knew he couldn't keep the truth from Calvin much longer, but the thought of revealing his secret filled him with dread and anxiety. His actions were becoming too heavy to bear, threatening to crush him at any moment.

Calvin stood up from the hard bench, his long, lean frame casting a looming shadow on the lockers behind him. The once lively and bustling locker room now felt heavy and sad as Calvin began to pack away his things. "Hey," he called out to Biscuit, his voice trembling slightly as if trying to pierce through a thick fog. "I know it's our family trip to the Dells this weekend, but you're welcome to come along if you want." He turned towards Biscuit, hoping for a smile or a laugh to break through the tension that hung like a dense cloud. But instead, all he received was an unreadable expression from his friend. Determined to reach out, Calvin pressed on. "You could even hang with the kids while I try to spend more time with my wife," he said with a nudge, attempting to lighten the mood. But Biscuit remained silent, and silence hung between them like an invisible barrier. "Something isn't right," Calvin thought to himself, worry etched across his face as he searched for any sign of connection from his friend.

Biscuit, lost in thought, barely registered Calvin's words. The images of Willow lurking outside consumed his mind, looming like a dark storm cloud above him. He could practically feel her presence suffocating him, causing his heart to race and his palms to sweat. He knew he had to figure out his next move and fast. The weight of the situation threatened to crush him, and he could feel desperation clawing at his chest, begging for release. "Calvin ...," Biscuit started, hesitating for a moment before finally finding his voice. His eyes darted around the room nervously as he spoke. "Can I get a ride home with you? My car was acting up earlier, and Roland said he'll come by later to check it out." Calvin studied his friend carefully, noticing the telltale signs of anxiety etched on Biscuit's face. He saw how his hands fidgeted with the hem of his shirt, a nervous tic that gave away his inner turmoil. Something was off, but Calvin didn't press for more information. Instead, he nodded in understanding. "Sure thing, man. I'll give you a ride."

"Thank you," Biscuit muttered, a flicker of relief passing across his face like a fleeting shadow. "I'll be right there in a few minutes. You parked on the usual side of the building, right?" "Yep, same spot," Calvin confirmed, grabbing his jacket from the locker and draping it over his shoulder. He left the room, giving Biscuit some much-needed space to collect himself. Left alone with his thoughts, Biscuit hesitated momentarily before opening his locker. The metal door creaked as it swung open, revealing the bag that contained his deepest, darkest secret. He stared at it, feeling bile rise in his throat and his heart pound against his ribcage like a relentless jackhammer. He slowly retrieved the bag with trembling hands as if lifting the world's weight onto his shoulders.

Willow anxiously tapped her fingers against her thigh as she sat on a worn bench across the street. Her eyes darted back and forth, taking in every movement around the busy bus terminal. The tension was evident in how she chewed on her bottom lip and worry etched into her features. Suddenly, a voice whispered behind her, causing Willow to jump with surprise. She turned to face Lenny, her heart pounding against her chest at his unexpected appearance. His piercing gaze bore into hers, unyielding. "Have you been watching me?" she stammered, feeling a rush of nerves course through her body. Lenny responded with a cold smirk and moved to sit beside her on the bench, his shoulder lightly brushing against hers. "Watching you ain't what you should be worried about right now, darlin'," he replied cryptically. "But I'll be here with you until this guy brings me my bag." A palpable tension settled between them, thickening the air as they fell into a heavy silence.

Meanwhile, Calvin sat in his car outside the terminal, his hands gripped tightly on the steering wheel as he prayed for strength. "Give me strength," he murmured under his breath before Biscuit's voice broke through the quiet. "Ready?" Biscuit asked as he opened the passenger door and climbed into Calvin's car. His usually bright eyes were now hollow and drained, causing Calvin to worry about his friend's sudden change in demeanor. With a forced smile, Calvin shifted the car into gear and pulled away from the terminal. Biscuit stared out the window, lost in thought, his mind racing as he contemplated the consequences of his actions. "Man, I wish I could just erase today," he muttered, clenching his hands tightly to keep them from shaking.

The words hung heavy between Calvin and Biscuit. "Sometimes, life gives us tough breaks," Calvin said, his eyes reflecting the streetlamp's light. He glanced over at Biscuit, who sat slumped in the driver's seat next to him. Biscuit looked back at him, grateful for his unwavering support but tormented by the secret he was keeping. If Calvin ever discovered the truth about that bag, their friendship would be shattered, perhaps beyond repair.

Biscuit swallowed hard and tried to find the right words. "Calvin...," he started, his voice cracking with emotion. "I, uh... I appreciate you, man. You've always been there for me." A small smile tugged at Calvin's lips as he reached over and clapped Biscuit on the shoulder. "Hey, that's what friends are for," he replied. "We stick together through thick and thin."

As they drove from the terminal, Biscuit didn't notice Willow and Lenny watching them from a nearby bench. The distant sound of cars honking and people talking filled the air as they entered the bustling city. The neon lights of signs and storefronts illuminated their path, creating a surreal scene.

But despite all this, Biscuit couldn't shake the weight of his secret or the fear of losing his best friend if it were ever to come out. He turned up the music on the radio, hoping to drown out his thoughts as they drove into the night.

The car cut through the silence as Calvin and Biscuit drove down the empty road. Tension hung heavy in the air, like a thick fog that refused to dissipate. Calvin, unable to bear the weight of it any longer, spoke up. "Whatever's going on with Willow, you know you can talk to me about it, right?" His voice was soft and understanding, his eyes never leaving the road ahead. Biscuit swallowed hard, his grip tightening on the gym bag in his lap. "I know, Calvin. Thanks. I need some time to figure things out, you know?" He couldn't meet Calvin's gaze, afraid of what he might see there. But he knew his friend would be there for him no matter what. Calvin nodded in understanding, knowing that sometimes people needed time and space to solve their problems. He glanced at Biscuit and saw the world's weight resting on his friend's shoulders. But they had faced challenges together before and would do it again.

"Take all the time you need," Calvin reassured him, reaching over to squeeze Biscuit's arm. "But remember, you're not alone in this." As they cruised down the boulevard, Biscuit's eyes caught sight of a glowing neon sign in the distance. The colorful lights danced across his face as excitement tinged his voice. "Hey Calvin, pull over at that fast-food spot up ahead, will ya?" he asked eagerly. It was a small moment of joy in an otherwise heavy day, and Calvin couldn't help but smile at his friend's enthusiasm.

Calvin's gaze lingered on Biscuit; his friend's eager eyes filled with an unexpected spark. "Sure thing," he said, begrudgingly pulling himself into Biscuit's excitement. "But remember, I have much on my plate with the family. We're planning that trip for this weekend." The engine rumbles softly in the background. Biscuit nodded, his expressive face lighting up at the mention of the upcoming family adventure. "I know, man. And hey, if things work out with Roland and my car, maybe I could tag along? If you don't mind, of course." Calvin shook his head, amused by Biscuit's sudden burst of energy. "Just focus on getting your car fixed first," he replied with a chuckle, not wanting to encourage premature plans.

The two friends began their walk down the familiar street on the west side of Chicago, their feet crunching on fallen leaves as they made their way toward the fast-food joint they frequented after long days of driving the city bus route. As they walked, Calvin couldn't help but notice that Biscuit seemed distracted, his eyes darting nervously like a cat watching a particularly elusive mouse. He couldn't blame him - there was always something on Calvin's mind these days. Responsibilities as a husband to Lena and a father to Junior and Ryder weighed heavily on him, along with the stress of planning their upcoming trip. But for now, Calvin pushed those thoughts aside and focused on enjoying this brief moment with his best friend.

Concern etched Calvin's voice as he asked, "Everything alright, Biscuit?" Biscuit's gaze remained fixed on their surroundings as he replied, "Uh, yeah, yeah. Just thinking about the car and everything, you know?" Calvin decided to drop it, his attention turning towards the lively neighborhood they always called home. Vibrant colors and diverse scents filled the air, reflecting the close-knit community they belonged to. They were just a stone's throw away from the fast-food joint, its iconic aroma wafting through the air like a homing beacon. The familiar smell evoked memories of countless meals shared with Biscuit, a comforting reminder of their unbreakable bond. "Let's grab some food and head back," Calvin suggested, his thoughts drifting to his family waiting for him at home.

He hoped Junior hadn't attempted to make bacon without supervision again, still haunted by the memory of burnt pork filling their house with smoke. And then there was Ryder's unfinished math homework, looming over him like an ominous cloud, begging for completion. "Sounds good," Biscuit replied nervously, his eyes darting around. Despite his friend's odd behavior, Calvin knew he could always count on Biscuit when it mattered most. They had been through thick and thin together, weathering life's ups and downs with unwavering loyalty. As they approached the fast-food place hand in hand, each carrying their own stories and struggles, both knew that no matter what challenges lay ahead, they had each other's backs.

Calvin's gaze followed Biscuit as he expertly weaved through the crowded fast-food joint, his sharp eyes scanning the room for their next target. Suddenly, they locked onto something across the room that seemed to mesmerize him. It took Calvin a moment to realize what had caught his friend's attention: a gorgeous woman standing in line just a few feet away from them. The warm lighting of the restaurant highlighted her features, making her appear almost ethereal. "Man, can you smell that?" Biscuit asked, his voice thick with appreciation. "Smell what?" Calvin inquired, briefly distracted by his mental checklist of family responsibilities. "Perfume, man. Perfume." Biscuit breathed deeply, seemingly unaffected by the heavy scent of grilled onions lingering in the air.

Calvin shook his head, knowing all too well where this situation was heading. "Biscuit, remember what I said. We're just here to grab some food and go. My family's waiting, and we have much to do before our trip," he reminded himself sternly. "Relax, man, I got this," Biscuit assured him, his voice oozing confidence. "I'll be quick, promise." "Look, if you aren't ready when I am, I'm leaving you behind. You hear me?" Calvin emphasized, worry etched on his face as he knew how easily Biscuit could get distracted by a pretty face.

'Trust me, Cal. It'll be fine,' Biscuit replied with a confident grin, striding towards the woman with a purpose that was hard to ignore. Calvin let out a resigned sigh, already bracing himself for the fallout of yet another one of Biscuit's attempts at romance. For now, though, he would have to trust that his friend would focus on their mission of getting food. 'Excuse me,' Biscuit said smoothly as he approached the woman, who introduced herself as Angela.

Her dark eyes sparkled under the harsh glare of the fluorescent lights. 'I think someone needs to worry.' 'And who should worry?' Angela asked playfully. 'Whoever thought it was okay for you to come here all by yourself,' Biscuit responded with a sophisticated tone. A smile tugged at the corners of Angela's lips. 'How do you know I'm not a black belt in karate? Maybe I don't need anyone's permission to be here alone.' 'Ah,' Biscuit said, momentarily forgetting about the looming confrontation with Willow, 'I just saw a stunning flower amidst all these weeds and couldn't resist saying hello.' His charm and confidence caught Angela off guard, and she couldn't help but laugh at his cheesy line.

As Biscuit continued to charm and flirt with Angela, Calvin stood in line behind him, his patience a testament to his unwavering trust in his friend. It wasn't that he didn't have faith in Biscuit's abilities; he couldn't help but worry about what might happen if Biscuit got too caught up in this woman and forgot about everything else. 'Come on, Biscuit,' Calvin muttered, his fingers drumming nervously against the wall beside him. He glanced at his friend, who seemed wholly captivated by Angela's every word and gesture. 'Remember what's truly important.' Despite his frustration, Calvin knew that deep down, Biscuit would always have his back. They had been through so much together - from childhood adventures to high school shenanigans - and their unbreakable bond had withstood countless trials and tribulations. But at this moment, as he stood at the cusp of a well-deserved family vacation, Calvin couldn't help but wish that his friend would remember that point and focus on that instead of getting lost in the allure of a beautiful stranger.

"Must be nice to have all the time in the world," Angela playfully teased Biscuit, her eyes sparkling like shards of sunlight dancing on the surface of a lake as she sipped her soda. Biscuit's laugh was like music to her ears, and he couldn't help but grin as he shrugged his shoulders nonchalantly, his gaze never leaving hers. He leaned confidently against the counter, his body language exuding ease and charm. Meanwhile, Calvin had managed to navigate his way to a faster line, his eyes darting between the cashier and his oblivious friend, who was lost in conversation with Angela.

The stark contrast between Biscuit's charm and Calvin's frustration adds to the tension. After what felt like an eternity, the cashier handed over the bags of food to Calvin, and he sighed in relief. Finally, they could get going. "Thanks," he muttered to the cashier, struggling to balance the bags in one hand as he reached for his wallet. With a quick nod of gratitude, he adjusted his grip on the bags and returned to Biscuit and Angela, who were still engrossed in their conversation. Calvin nudged Biscuit's shoulder with the bags, breaking them out of their bubble.

The faint rustling of paper accompanied the mouth-watering aroma of hot, greasy food that filled the air. Impatiently waving the bags, he barked, "Time to go." Biscuit glanced at Calvin before turning back to Angela, a knowing look passing between them. A surge of hope shot through him, wondering if this woman would be different from all the others Biscuit had fallen for. Calvin couldn't help but wonder if his friend would ever truly change. Biscuit had always been a dreamer, chasing after love and adventure, while Calvin focused on providing for his family. Deep down, Calvin knew that Biscuit envied the stable life he had built, even if he didn't always show it. "Hey," Biscuit said suddenly, breaking Calvin's thought. "Thanks for waiting, man. I know you've got a lot on your plate." The words hung in the air, with a hint of longing and admiration for the life his friend had created.

Calvin leaned against the doorframe, arms crossed and bags of food resting by his side. The savory scent of grilled onions and frying grease wafted through the air, making his mouth water, but he forced himself to focus on the task. His gaze was fixed on Biscuit, who seemed to have forgotten their need to hurry as he laughed and flirted with Angela. Calvin couldn't help but feel a twinge of frustration - they were on a time crunch, and Biscuit was more interested in impressing this woman than Calvin returning home to his family. His frustration was palpable, making the audience feel his sense of urgency. "Come on, man," Calvin muttered under his breath, watching Biscuit's hand gesture animatedly while he regaled Angela with a story.

He resented how easily Biscuit could charm others, even when there were more important matters. "Hey, Biscuit!" Calvin finally called out, trying to get his friend's attention. "We gotta go, man." Biscuit glanced over, his eyes apologetic momentarily before returning to Angela. "Just a sec, Cal. I'll be right there." Calvin sighed exasperatedly, shifting his weight from one foot to the other. He could feel the minutes ticking, each weighing heavier on him than the last. His thoughts turned to Lena at home, waiting for them to bring dinner. "Calvin, my man, can't you see I'm busy?" Biscuit said with a hint of annoyance in his voice. "Relax. We'll be out of here in no time." But Calvin couldn't relax - family came first, and he couldn't shake off the responsibility he felt towards them. "Sometimes I wonder about you, Biscuit," Calvin said with a shake of his head as he retreated to their car.

"Unbelievable," Calvin muttered, his knuckles tense as he gripped the steering wheel tightly. The hot sun beat down on the pavement, causing shimmering heat waves to rise. Calvin exited the car and slammed the door shut, his frustration boiling. He had been patient with Biscuit, but now he needed to confront him. "Hey, Biscuit. We need to get going," Calvin said, trying to keep his voice level despite the anger bubbling inside him. He looked over at Biscuit, who was still captivated by Angela's beauty.

Her long hair cascaded down her back in perfect waves, and her eyes sparkled in the sunlight. Biscuit seemed utterly lost in her gaze and barely registered Calvin's words. "Yeah, yeah, sure thing, man," he replied absentmindedly, his eyes never leaving hers. As if seeking her approval, he added, "You wouldn't mind giving me a ride, would you?" Calvin let out a frustrated sigh and glanced at his watch. His family was waiting for him at home, and he couldn't afford any more delays. He just hoped that Biscuit could find his way home without getting distracted again by Angela's enchanting presence.

Angela hesitated momentarily, her eyes flickering with uncertainty before nodding in agreement. "Sure, why not?" she responded with a casual shrug, but Calvin could see the hesitation in her body language. Frustrated but resolute, he made the difficult decision to leave Biscuit behind. He had always been fiercely loyal to his friend, but there came a point when it was necessary to prioritize his values and family above all else.

With a curt nod and a heavy heart, Calvin turned on his heel and strode back to his car. As he drove away from the fast-food joint, the familiar sights and sounds of the city surrounded him – honking horns, bustling sidewalks, and the faint smell of exhaust fumes. But his mind was elsewhere, consumed by the nagging feeling that something wasn't right.

Calvin glanced back at the restaurant one last time, catching a glimpse of Biscuit and Angela laughing together as they climbed into her car. He couldn't help but ache at the thought of leaving his friend behind, but he knew deep down that it was the right decision.

CHAPTER 19

Navigating through the city's west side, Calvin tapped his fingers rhythmically on the steering wheel, trying to ease his restless thoughts. The soulful melodies on the radio during his drive home echoed in his head, providing some comfort amidst the turmoil.

But even as he let himself get lost in the music and the familiar hum of the engine, there was no escaping the unease that had taken root in his chest since leaving Biscuit behind. As he approached an intersection, he saw a police officer holding a hand to slow traffic at a random checkpoint ahead. Vehicles were being stopped and inspected individually, and Calvin felt a surge of anxiety wash over him.

His grip on the steering wheel tightened involuntarily as he neared the checkpoint, but he reminded himself to stay calm – he had nothing to hide. Still, the sight of flashing lights and police officers looming in his path made him break out into a cold sweat. All he could do now was hope to pass through the checkpoint without any issues and make it home safely to his family.

The line of cars stretched for miles, red and blue lights flashing. Police officers swarmed between them like bees around a hive, their radios crackling with activity. Calvin couldn't help but notice the varying expressions on the faces of drivers pulled over; some showed defiance, others resigned, but most sat glazed over in fear and confusion. "Lord, keep us safe," he murmured under his breath, thinking of his wife and children waiting for him at home. As one of the officers made his way towards Calvin's car, shining a bright flashlight into the driver's seat, Calvin met his gaze with determination. "Evening, sir," the officer greeted him professionally. "We're conducting a sobriety checkpoint.

Mind if I ask where you're heading tonight?" "Home to my family, Officer," Calvin replied calmly, trying not to show his nerves. "Just got off work." Before continuing, the officer scanned Calvin's identification badge clipped to his shirt pocket. "City bus driver, huh? Long day?"

"Something like that," Calvin admitted with a half-smile. "But it's worth it, knowing I'm helping folks get where they need to be." The officer nodded understandingly, shining his flashlight around the interior of Calvin's car. "You haven't had anything to drink tonight, have you?" "Nothing stronger than coffee, sir," Calvin assured him truthfully.

As he neared the next part of the line, Calvin's heart began to race as he noticed a pair of German Shepherds sniffing their way through the maze of vehicles. Their black and tan fur glinted from the police lights as they diligently searched for signs of illegal substances. Calvin couldn't help but feel a sense of admiration for these police dogs, trained to detect even the slightest traces of wrongdoing. Their handlers, dressed in crisp uniforms, led them from car to car with confident strides. The dogs' noses twitched with excitement as they picked up on various scents, their tails wagging eagerly.

Calvin recalled stories he had heard about K-9 units and their impressive abilities. He remembered a time when his father had been pulled over and questioned by police and how afraid he had been as a young boy. His mother, Rose, had always tried to protect him from the harsh realities of life, but as he grew older, Calvin became all too aware of the challenges faced by those who looked like him in this city.

Offering a silent prayer to God for safety, Calvin returned to the road ahead. As he approached the K-9 unit checkpoint, something felt different. The air seemed charged with tension, and even the officers appeared uneasy. Calvin couldn't pinpoint what it was but knew whatever lay ahead would test his faith and determination.

"Stay strong," he whispered, trying to calm his nerves. "You've got your family depending on you." With a deep breath, he rolled down his window and prepared for whatever may come next.

The piercing sobs of children echoed through the tense air, wrenching at Calvin's heart as he bore witness to families being ripped apart. A distraught mother, her face stained with tears, frantically tried to comfort her wailing child as police officers handcuffed the father nearby. An older woman clung desperately to a young man's arm, begging for mercy from the cold, stone-faced officer. "Please," she pleaded, her voice quivering with despair. "He's all I have left." Calvin swallowed hard, feeling the weight of his family's love and dependence on him.

The countless nights spent working tirelessly to put food on the table and the peaceful Sunday mornings in church with Lena and their children he had flashed through his mind. He could only imagine the devastation and anguish those families were going through, and it shook him to his core. "Lord, protect us," he murmured, gripping the steering wheel tighter. "Alright, sir, pull up to the checkpoint," a sharp command from an officer brought him back to reality, motioning for him to pull up to the checkpoint ahead.

As Calvin's car crept closer to the checkpoint, an overpowering sense of unease washed over him, causing his hands to tremble on the steering wheel. The atmosphere here was different, more foreboding than any other checkpoints he had encountered. The officers stood at attention, their eyes sharp and alert, hands hovering near their holstered weapons. Calvin took a deep breath and reminded himself to stay calm and focused. "You've done nothing wrong," he repeated as he stared straight ahead. A stern-looking officer approached his window, demanding to see his license and registration with a curt tone. Calvin's heart raced as he handed over the documents, his mind racing about his family and their future.

"Calvin Steele... city bus driver, huh?" the officer noted skeptically, eyeing the identification closely. "What brings you out here tonight?" "Just heading home after a long day at work, sir," Calvin answered honestly, trying to maintain eye contact with the intimidating figure. "Wait right here," the officer instructed before returning to confer with his colleagues. As Calvin waited for an eternity, he silently pleaded for strength from above. He thought about his wife Lena and their children, the love and laughter that filled their modest home, and the unwavering guidance of his mother. No matter what happened at this checkpoint, Calvin knew there was no choice but to fight for them with every ounce. "Please help me make it through this," he prayed fervently, steeling himself for whatever lay.

The K9 officer led his furry companion around the car, its snout twitching feverishly as it scoured every nook and cranny for suspicious scents. When they reached the backseat, the dog's demeanor shifted, its ears perking up and tail wagging with excitement. It pawed at a bulky gym bag next to the back door, causing the officer's eyebrows to shoot up in surprise. "Sir, could you please step out of the vehicle?" the officer requested, his tone taking on a sterner edge. A perplexed Calvin complied, his heart racing as he tried to remain composed. This can't be happening, he thought anxiously. Nothing is incriminating in that bag, just Biscuit's workout gear. "Would you mind if we took a look inside this bag, sir?" the officer inquired cautiously, gesturing towards the gym bag. Calvin gulped before responding, "Go ahead." He tried to keep his voice steady despite his growing unease. "There's nothing in there but some clothes and sneakers."

Calvin's mind raced as the officer unzipped the bag, trying to piece together how those gym clothes could have triggered the dog's violent reaction. But a wave of dread washed over him when he saw the bricks of powdery substance nestled among the belongings. "Sir, can you explain what this is?" the officer's voice cut through the tense air. He held up one of the packages, studying it with a furrowed brow. "I... I don't know," Calvin stammered, his voice barely audible. "I've never seen that before. I swear." The officer's stern gaze bore into him, searching for any sign of guilt or deception. Calvin met his stare, desperately trying to convey the truth through his eyes alone.

He couldn't let this derail his life – not when his family depended on him. As the officer carefully pulled out the bricks of white powder from the gym bag, Calvin's heart pounded in his chest. Everything seemed to slow down around him, each second stretching into eternity while memories of his wife and children danced at the edge of his vision. "Sir, you're going to have to come with us," the officer's tone turned cold and stubborn, emphasizing the severity of the situation. "Wait, please," Calvin pleaded, his hands trembling uncontrollably. "There's been a mistake. I don't know anything about those drugs. They're not mine." But his words fell on deaf ears as the handcuffs clicked around his wrists, sealing his fate. As he was led away, Calvin caught glimpses of Lena laughing in their cozy kitchen, her contagious joy lighting up her face.

Calvin felt like he had stepped into an alternate reality where every sound and sight was amplified. The sharp snap of the handcuffs reverberated in his ears, their cold metal biting into his wrists. The flashing lights from the police cars bounced off the surrounding buildings, casting eerie shadows on the cold pavement below, creating a surreal atmosphere. He could feel the officer's firm grip on his arm, guiding him harshly towards the curb. "Have a seat here, Mr. Steele," the officer's voice was detached and hollow, lacking any hint of empathy, adding to the surreal atmosphere.

Calvin sank onto the unforgiving concrete, taking in his surroundings with shock and disbelief. As he waited for what seemed like an eternity, he couldn't help but think of his mother, Rose, and the values she had instilled in him since childhood - faith, resilience, and the importance of family. These were the pillars of his life as a dedicated bus driver and loving father. But now, sitting on this curb surrounded by chaos and uncertainty, he couldn't help but feel as if those very foundations were crumbling beneath him.

"Hey man, what'd they get you for?" A low, gravelly voice cut through the hazy air, drawing Calvin's attention to the man beside him. The question hung in the stillness, barely registering in Calvin's mind as he tried to shake off the shock that had left him numb. He blinked, his vision blurred, and he struggled to focus on the man's face before him. It seemed to swim before him like a mirage, a distorted image of reality. "Can you believe this?" A woman's voice called out from his other side, her tone thick with anger and disbelief. She shook her head, her hands gripping the metal of her handcuffs tightly. "I was just trying to get home to my kids."

Calvin felt a surge of empathy for the woman and all those surrounding him, each bound by their circumstance and the unforgiving hands of fate. As he looked around at the sea of faces, he saw a reflection of his struggles and disillusionment on the west side of Chicago. But even as their voices rose in protest and frustration, Calvin remained silent, lost in his thoughts and memories. "Rose," he whispered under his breath, the name a constant source of strength and comfort. His mother had always been the rock of their family, unwavering in her faith and determination to provide for her children. In this moment of uncertainty and fear, he could almost hear her voice, assuring him that everything would be alright and that God was watching.

"Hey, you, okay?" The woman's voice, soft and compassionate, broke through the cacophony of flashing lights and blaring sirens. She reached out a hand, her concern evident as she tried to catch Calvin's eye. But he couldn't respond; his words were trapped in his throat, suffocated by the heavy weight of injustice that crushed his spirit. As the chaotic symphony continued to play around him, Calvin Steele clung to the teachings of Rose - the matriarch who had held their family together through every hardship. He drew strength from her unwavering resilience and unshakable faith, knowing that he would need both to endure this trial and return to his family, who needed him now more than ever. The scene swirled with a frenzy of red and blue lights, like vultures circling overhead, waiting for their prey.

Calvin's eyes followed the sleek, powerful K-9 unit as it paced around his car, sniffing and scratching at every crevice. The German Shepherd was relentless in its pursuit, nose to the ground and tail wagging excitedly. Calvin knew there was nothing else to find, but he couldn't help feeling anxious as the dog circled his vehicle. He had always taken great pride in his work as a city bus driver, ensuring his vehicle was spotless and well-maintained. His car was no different - clean and polished, with no speck of dust. "Easy now, boy," an officer calmly commanded the dog, his keen gaze locked on its every move. Fingers hovered over the radio clipped to his shoulder, ready to call for backup at any sign of trouble. Beside him, another officer diligently took notes on a clipboard, eyes darting between the detainees and the canine's progress with focused intensity. "Anything yet?" a man seated next to Calvin asked anxiously, his voice barely audible among the chaotic symphony of sirens and shouts. Calvin could only shake his head in response, the knot in his chest tightening with each passing second as he waited for this tense situation to be resolved.

The K-9 handler, a burly man with a stern expression, finally reported to his partner that nothing else had been found. He nodded towards the group of officers, signaling that they could move on. "Alright, everyone, on your feet!" one officer barked, his deep voice commanding attention as he gestured for the handcuffed men and women to rise. "You're all going to county jail!" The words hung heavily, causing fear and confusion among the suspects. "Wait, what? For what? We didn't do nothin'!" cried out a young woman, her voice trembling with panic as she shuffled nervously in her restraints. Calvin felt a sudden surge of protectiveness towards her; she couldn't have been over twenty years old, and her wide-eyed innocence was painfully evident. "Lord, please watch over us," he thought.

"Save it for the judge," the officer's stern reply cut through the air like a sharp blade, pushing her forward with unrelenting force. Calvin clenched his jaw, struggling to contain the anger inside him. This entire situation was unjust, and he knew it - but he was powerless to fight back. In this moment of despair, he reached out for the comforting words of his mother, Rose, in his mind. "Give me strength," he thought, grasping her memory as solace. Suddenly, the roar of a powerful engine echoed through the street, drawing Calvin's attention to a large police patty wagon pulling up nearby. The back doors creaked open, revealing a cramped and dimly lit interior that resembled more of a cage than a vehicle meant for transporting humans. "Move!" the officer barked again, forcefully nudging them toward the intimidating van. As they stumbled forward, Calvin braced himself against the overwhelming sense of injustice that threatened to consume him. "God is with us," he whispered, holding onto his faith like a lifeline in adversity.

Calvin Steele sat hunched in the back of the patty wagon, a cold metal seat pressing into his spine. His hands were tightly cuffed behind his back, the sharp edges digging painfully into his wrists. The vehicle lurched and swayed as it bumped along the potholed streets of Chicago's west side, jostling the passengers like rag dolls. The loud engine rumble and the harsh squeak of wipers against the windshield filled the cramped space. All around him, the motley crew of inmates muttered and shifted, their breaths heavy with the stench of sweat and fear. "Man, this is a rough ride," grumbled one young man sporting a black eye and split lip.

Calvin could feel a twinge of sympathy for the injured inmate, knowing all too well the pain that came with being taken into custody. But he pushed it aside, focusing instead on his thoughts and regrets. "Shut up and sit down!" snapped a burly officer from the front of the wagon, breaking through Calvin's thoughts. As the patty wagon continued its journey, it made several stops to pick up more disgruntled passengers. Each new arrival brought with them a fresh wave of desperation and despair that seemed to cling to the cramped space like a thick fog. Calvin couldn't help but feel sorrow for these men, even as he struggled with guilt and shame for ending up in this situation himself.

At one particular stop, the wagon lurched as an older man named Clyde stumbled through the doors. He tripped over his feet, barely able to steady himself before collapsing onto the narrow bench next to Calvin. His face was flushed and mottled, a stark contrast to the bloodshot whites of his eyes. His clothes were rumpled and wrinkled, reeking of alcohol and sweat. These were all unmistakable signs of a long night spent inebriated. With a resigned sigh, Clyde tried to straighten himself up, failing miserably as he slumped against the wooden bench. "Name's Clyde," he slurred with a shaky grin, offering his hand to shake.

Calvin hesitated before reluctantly taking it, feeling out of place among these hardened criminals. In truth, he couldn't quite believe how he had ended up here – sitting in the back of a patty wagon with a group of strangers who seemed to have accepted their fate with resigned in-difference. He thought of his wife and children at home, his mother, Rose, waiting for him after work, and the city bus he used to drive with pride. The weight of his mistakes bore down on him like a heavy boulder, making it difficult even to take a deep breath. "Ah, Brother," Clyde drawled, leaning in too close for comfort. "You seem like a good man caught up in bad business." Calvin grimaced but remained silent, the knot in his stomach tightening with each passing moment.

The wagon's wheels clattered and jolted over the rough pavement, creating a cacophony that echoed through Calvin's mind. He desperately tried to focus on the rhythm, hoping it would drown out the mounting dread that threatened to consume him. But no matter how hard he tried, he couldn't escape the reality of his situation or the memories of his family that haunted him with every bump and jostle of the patty wagon. The heavy scent of sweat and despair hung in the air, only adding to his suffering. "Hey, don't worry, kid," Clyde said, his voice surprisingly gentle as he placed a hand on Calvin's shoulder. "We've all been there. Gotta keep your head up and trust in something bigger than yourself." Though grateful for the older man's encouragement, they did little to quell the storm within him. As the patty wagon continued its relentless journey through the dark streets of Chicago, Calvin closed his eyes and sent up a silent prayer, clinging to hope that this was just a temporary detour on the long road home.

The overwhelming stench of body odor and stale sweat permeated the air like a thick fog, assaulting Calvin's senses with each labored breath. But it was the pungent odor of liquor emanating from Clyde's breath that made him gag and his eyes water. He desperately tried to breathe through his mouth, but it only intensified the taste of the various disgusting scents mixing in the cramped space. "Ya know, I can always spot a newbie," Clyde slurred, leaning closer to Calvin as if he were sharing a deep secret. The smell of alcohol on his breath was suffocating, filling every corner of Calvin's being. "You don't belong here." Calvin wrinkled his nose and fought off the nausea creeping up his throat.

He swallowed hard before responding. "Can you please not talk right now?" Clyde let out a small chuckle, blowing another gust of foul breath directly into Calvin's face. "Yeah, I suppose it's a bit unbearable now, huh?" He leaned back against the cold metal wall of the police wagon, giving Calvin some much-needed breathing room. "Thanks," Calvin muttered, rubbing his head against the wall to block out the overpowering smells and sounds around him. He longed to tune it all out – the putrid odors, the constant noise, the crushing weight of knowing he wasn't where he was supposed to be. But no matter how hard Calvin tried to escape into himself, reality refused to release its grip on him. He clenched his jaw and focused on the vibrations of the wagon beneath him, searching for any semblance of solace amidst the chaos.

He replayed the events that led to this moment, each scene playing out in vivid detail behind his closed eyelids like a film reel: the sudden arrest by rough-handed officers, the confusion in his mind as he tried to make sense of it all, the sharp pang of fear that gripped him tightly. And now, trapped in this suffocating metal box, he couldn't help but wonder how things might have turned out differently. His heart beat frantically against his ribs, and sweat coated his palms as he imagined the worst possible outcomes. But then, unexpectedly, a voice broke through his thoughts. "Hey, man, don't beat yourself up too much," Clyde said, his voice surprisingly clear and steady above the chaos. "Every storm runs out of rain eventually." Calvin's eyes snapped open, and he turned to look at Clyde, who sat beside him with a calm expression on his weathered face. Was that supposed to make him feel better? To give him hope in this dire situation? "Is that supposed to make me feel better?" Calvin asked, unable to hide the bitterness in his tone.

Clyde shrugged nonchalantly. "Maybe," he replied. "Or maybe just knowing you ain't the only one who's been through some rough times will help you keep your chin up." For a moment, Calvin studied Clyde's face, searching for any sign of deception or mockery. But all he saw was raw empathy and understanding. Could it be possible that Clyde was right? That this terrible moment would eventually pass and become nothing more than a distant memory? With a heavy sigh, Calvin leaned against the wagon's wall again and closed his eyes. For now, there was nothing he could do but wait – and hope that, in time, things would get better.

Calvin shifted his gaze away from Clyde and peered out the small, barred window of the patty wagon. The vibrant sounds of the bustling city streets outside seemed to swirl around him, a symphony of honking horns and distant laughter that comforted and disheartened him. He closed his eyes and inhaled deeply, trying to find solace amidst the overpowering stench of liquor and body odor that filled the cramped space. "Please guide me through this," he whispered silently, seeking strength in adversity. And as if in answer to his prayer, memories of his family bloomed behind his closed eyelids like a series of vivid photographs.

He saw his beloved wife, Lena, with her infectious smile, standing at the kitchen stove as she stirred a pot of her famous beef stew. Calvin's heart swelled with pride as he remembered teaching their son Junior how to cook – the satisfying sizzle of extra crispy bacon on the stove – and how they had shared it with Ryder, who had reluctantly taken a bite to prove just how tough he was. "Please," Calvin choked out, his voice barely above a whisper. "I have a family. I can't let them down." But the officer remained unmoved by his plea, repeating the same dismissive response he had heard countless times before.

The silence in the back of the patty wagon was suffocating, darkness pressing against Calvin's eyes as he struggled to find peace. "Y'know," Clyde said suddenly as his voice cut through the stillness like a knife, snapping Calvin back to reality. The older man's words echoed in his mind, reminding him of the family he left behind - a wife and two kids worried sick about him. Calvin opened his eyes and studied Clyde momentarily, taking in the lines etched into his weathered face and the sadness lurking in the depths of his bloodshot eyes.

Without thinking, he leaned over and placed a comforting hand on Clyde's shoulder. "Then let's make a promise to each other," he said quietly, his voice firm with resolve. "Let's promise we'll keep fighting for our families, no matter how hard things get. We'll do whatever it takes to make it back to them." Clyde hesitated momentarily before nodding, a ghost of a smile playing at the corners of his mouth. "You got yourself a deal, Calvin," he said. "Deal," Calvin agreed firmly. As the patty wagon continued its bumpy journey through the streets of Chicago, Calvin clung to the image of his family in his mind's eye, their love and warmth giving him strength in the darkness. Finally, they arrived at their destination –the county jail's parking lot–the sound of gravel crunching under the wagon's tires. Calvin closed his eyes momentarily, steeling himself for what was to come.

CHAPTER 20

T he heavy metal doors of the patty wagon swung open with a loud, grating creak, releasing a noxious odor of stale alcohol and sweat into the night air. The inmates stumbled out, their eyes burning from the harsh glare of the jail's fluorescent lights as they struggled to regain their balance on solid ground. One particularly drunken man failed miserably, his feet tangling together as he fell face-first onto the unforgiving asphalt. A collective wince rippled through the group as blood immediately pooled beneath his dazed face.

"Get him outta the way!" barked one officer, his voice thick with impatience. He grabbed the inebriated man under his arms and dragged him to the side. "Medics will be here soon enough." Turning back to the rest of the disoriented group, he barked out orders. "Keep it moving, people! Single file now. Let's go!" Still reeling from the whirlwind of events that led him here, Calvin stood in stunned silence, his eyes fixed on the chaotic line of inmates before him. This was nothing like what he had seen on TV. Despite his fear and confusion, he couldn't help but remember his mother Rose's words about staying on the right path. Her unwavering faith in him had been etched into his mind since childhood, and now more than ever, he wished he had listened to her advice.

"Hey, hey, you!" A gruff voice snapped Calvin out of his daze. He looked up to see a burly officer gesturing impatiently at the line of prisoners ahead of him. Calvin quickly joined the ragtag group, his steps feeling mechanical as they shuffled toward the looming building ahead. The walls rose high around them, casting a foreboding shadow over the scene below.

"Man, this ain't how I pictured spendin' my day," muttered Clyde, a familiar figure a few spots ahead of Calvin in line. His words slurred slightly, a testament to his earlier drunken revelries. Calvin couldn't help but silently agree, his heart heavy with shame and fear. How had he ended up on the wrong side of the law? He could still remember the comfort and stability of his old life, now so far removed from his reality.

"Race, fellas!" another officer barked as they neared the entrance. The sound cut through the air like a sharp whip, signaling their arrival to the officers inside. Calvin could feel a cold sweat forming at the base of his neck as they crossed the threshold into the unknown.

The cacophony hit Calvin like a physical blow as they entered the county jail's intake unit. The air was thick with tension and desperation, a palpable energy that seemed to cling to every surface. The smell of sweat and fear hung heavy in the air, mingling with the strong scent of disinfectant. Disarray ruled here, with inmates shouting at one another or crying out in frustration while officers barked orders over the unit. It was chaotic and overwhelming.

"Move! Get in line!" an officer yelled, pushing and prodding them forward like cattle. Calvin's heart raced as he tried to process the chaos surrounding him. Being incarcerated was nothing like the life he knew outside these walls; it was terrifying and dehumanizing.

"Alright, everybody in!" the officer commanded, shoving Calvin, Clyde, and the others into a cramped holding cell. The metal door slamming shut echoed through the room, sending a chill down Calvin's spine. "Someone will come to get you for processing. Hold tight." His words were cold and uncaring, a stark reminder of the harsh realities of life inside the jail. Calvin could only hope that his time here would be short-lived.

The wiry man with sunken eyes snapped at the officer, desperation and anger evident in his strained voice. "Whatcha mean 'hold tight'? Like we have no choice but to cling on for dear life up in this hellhole!" Another inmate's urgent cry rang out, tinged with fear and a sense of urgency. "When can I make a call? I gotta let my family know where I'm at!" But their pleas fell on deaf ears as the officer barked at them to quiet down before slamming the heavy metal door shut behind them. The cell was cramped and dimly lit, the air thick with the scent of sweat and despair.

Calvin could feel the weight of so many bodies pressing in on him, suffocating him. He took slow, measured breaths, struggling to keep his panic at bay. "Man, you look like you ain't never been in a place like this," Clyde slurred, his words slurring together as he leaned against the cold concrete wall. "Keep your head up, Calvin. You'll make it through this. Remember who you are, and don't let this place change you." But Calvin couldn't help feeling overwhelmed by the chaos and uncertainty around him. The thought of his mother, Rose, her face a beacon of hope even in the darkest times, gave him some solace. "Lord, give me strength," he whispered, trying to find peace amidst the turmoil. "Help me endure this ordeal and protect my family while I'm gone."

"Step up, next in line!" An officer's harsh, commanding voice boomed down the narrow corridor, sending a shiver down Calvin's spine. He stood among a line of other inmates, shuffling forward in unison as they were herded toward their destination. The dim lighting cast shadows on the grimy walls, amplifying the musty smell of sweat and despair that hung like a thick fog. Calvin tried to block out the lewd comments and wild laughter from his fellow prisoners with the rhythmic clicking of a camera in the distance. "Name?" barked the photographer as Calvin approached the height chart, his eyes avoiding the gaze of those around him. "Calvin Steele," he muttered under his breath, already feeling a sense of shame wash over him when the flash went off, capturing his image for eternity in this hellish place. "Right hand first," another officer commanded as they fingerprinted each inmate.

Calvin hesitated momentarily before pressing his ink-stained fingers onto the paper, leaving behind a dark, indelible mark as a reminder of his downfall. Looking at the black streaks on his fingertips, he couldn't help but feel like he was staining more than just the paper. He was tarnishing his life, his family's name, and everything he had worked hard to build and protect. "Here's your new uniform," a third officer said gruffly, thrusting an orange jumpsuit into Calvin's hands. "Strip down and put it on."

Calvin forced himself to swallow the lump in his throat as he entered the small, windowless room designated for changing. The stark white walls seemed to close in on him as he reluctantly undressed, one piece of clothing at a time. With each discarded garment, he felt a part of his dignity slip away until he stood vulnerable and exposed before the prying eyes of authority. "Place your clothes in the bag," the officer instructed, watching with a sense of satisfaction as Calvin obeyed, knowing he had complete control over this broken man.

"Alright, bend over and cough," the officer's voice echoed through the stark, concrete room, devoid of warmth or compassion. "Alright, bend over and cough," he ordered again, his tone flat and still emotionless. Calvin's heart raced as he gritted his teeth, fighting back tears as he complied—the cold floor bit into his bare feet as he stood, feeling utterly exposed and vulnerable. The humiliation was almost unbearable.

"Spread your fingers and toes," the officer barked, his words cutting through Calvin's shame like a knife. Calvin did as he was told, trying to block out the reality of what was happening to him. Each command felt like a violation, stripping away his dignity and humanity.

"Open your mouth for inspection," the officer ordered, and Calvin reluctantly obeyed. The sound of latex gloves snapping on and off filled the silence, making Calvin shudder with disgust. He closed his eyes tightly, wishing he could escape this nightmare.

"Alright, you're done. Get dressed and head back out." As the officer's footsteps faded, Calvin released a shaky breath and slowly opened his eyes. The jumpsuit in front of him seemed to mock him, its bright orange color a stark contrast to the bleakness of his surroundings.

As Calvin pulled on the scratchy fabric, it felt like he was slipping into a new identity that threatened to consume who he had once been. His hands trembled as he fumbled with the zipper, struggling to accept this harsh new reality. "Lord, please let this be a mistake," he prayed silently, his heart heavy with remorse. "Let my time here be short, and help me find a way to make things right."

Calvin's shoulders drooped with defeat as he clutched the tattered mattress and other jailhouse necessities. The once proud and dignified man now looked broken, stripped of all sense of self-worth. Beside him, Clyde tried to offer comfort as they stood in the noisy hallway, shouting and slamming doors echoing off the walls. "Welcome to my world, just for today," Clyde said, his voice barely audible above the chaos. "Please let this be your last time here." Calvin wanted to respond, but the words stuck in his throat like a lump of cold porridge. Instead, he raised his eyes heavenward, silently pleading for divine intervention to end this nightmare.

But there was no mercy to be found as an officer barked at them to move forward, shoving them with a force that sent Calvin stumbling over his own feet. The noise level only intensified as they entered the general population area, filled with hooting and hollering from existing inmates who sized up the newcomers like fresh meat at a butcher's counter. Calvin could feel their hostile gazes bearing down on him, their lewd remarks and taunts making him shrink into himself. "Stay close to me," Clyde muttered, expertly navigating through the chaos. He had been through this before, and Calvin was grateful for his guidance, even though it did little to ease his fear.

But then a burly inmate shouted out from behind his cell bars, fixating on Calvin with predatory eyes. "What're you in for?" he demanded, his tone laced with aggression. Panic surged through Calvin as he hesitated, unsure of how to answer. Should he tell the truth? Would it make him seem weak? He struggled with these thoughts and felt the man's stare drilling into him like a physical force. But before he could respond, Clyde stepped protectively in front of him. "Leave him alone," he snapped at the inmate. "He's had enough for one day." The man snorted dismissively and turned away, but Calvin could still feel his menacing gaze on his back.

"Thanks," Calvin whispered to Clyde, his voice barely audible. He clung to every word of his mother's prayers and teachings, seeking strength and protection in this unforgiving world. As they walked toward their assigned cells, Calvin couldn't help but feel like he was drowning in a sea of hostility and violence. But he held onto Clyde's words, determined to endure this ordeal with their support. And as he lay down in his cramped cell that night, he prayed for forgiveness, redemption, and a chance to make things right again.

CHAPTER 21

Calvin's heart raced like a runaway train as he cautiously stepped into the cell. The heavy iron door creaked behind him, its rusted hinges groaning in protest. A chill ran through his body, causing goosebumps on his skin. The air was thick with a musty scent, and the faint sound of dripping water echoed off the walls.

He never could have imagined that he would end up in such a place, a world away from the warm embrace of his loving family and the familiar routine of his job as a city bus driver. "Lucy, I'm home," Clyde slurred from behind him, his voice laced with intoxication. Calvin turned to see Clyde grinning weakly, his bloodshot eyes betraying the long night of excessive drinking. "Man, am I glad to see you," Calvin admitted, his voice trembling with fear.

A familiar face by his side in this unknown and hostile environment comforted Calvin. "Hey, we're in this together, right?" Clyde clapped him on the back, causing him to stumble forward slightly. "One night in hell won't kill us." Calvin forced himself to nod, though his stomach churned with anxiety and dread. He looked around the cramped cell, taking in the stained concrete walls and cold metal bunk beds. A solitary toilet stood in one corner, offering no privacy or dignity for whoever used it. As he thought of his family anxiously awaiting his return home, praying for his safety, it felt like a sharp blow to the gut.

"Look, just try to get some sleep," Clyde suggested, his voice low and soothing as he flopped onto the lower bunk and closed his eyes. All the cells around them were small and cramped, with gray, cold concrete walls. Distant shouts and metal clanging echoed through the halls, a constant reminder of their confinement. "Tomorrow morning, you'll be back with your family where you belong." Calvin couldn't help but scoff at the idea; it felt like an impossible dream.

"Sleep? In here?" he whispered incredulously, his gaze darting nervously around the cell. The only light came from a small window high up on one wall, casting long shadows across the room. But as much as he wanted to resist the idea, he knew Clyde was right; he needed to conserve his energy and focus on getting through the night.

"Lord, give me strength," Calvin murmured, sinking onto the top bunk's thin, lumpy mattress. It offered little comfort for his weary body.

"Hey, Calvin," Clyde called up from below, his voice calm and steady. "Remember that time you fixed up your mom's old Chevy? Even if you never did, pretend you did, and you stayed up all night working on it, laughing and talking until the sun appeared." A small smile tugged at Calvin's lips at the thought, a brief moment of light amidst the darkness of their current situation. "Yeah, now I remember. That was a good night."

"Just pretend you're back there, alright?" Clyde suggested. "You'll get through this and come out stronger on the other side." Calvin nodded in agreement and closed his eyes, trying to picture that night. He held onto the image like a lifeline, praying for the strength to endure and the chance to return to the life he knew before this nightmare began.

The incessant tick-tock of the jailhouse clock reverberated through Calvin's mind, a constant reminder of his captivity. In his fitful sleep, he was plagued by nightmares of cold iron bars and unfeeling concrete walls. His restless body jolted awake, drenched in sweat and consumed by anger. How had Biscuit's foolish actions brought him to this desolate place? It made no sense; Calvin had always been cautious, keeping his head down and staying out of trouble. Yet here he was, confined and cut off from his loved ones because of someone else's recklessness. "Damn you, Biscuit," Calvin muttered into the darkness, his voice heavy with resentment.

The morning sun rose too soon, illuminating the cruel reality of life behind bars. The jarring clanging of cell doors opening sent shivers down Calvin's spine as he reluctantly joined the other inmates assembling in the narrow hallway. Led by stern-faced guards, they trudged towards the mess hall, their footsteps weighed down by despair. "Line up! Get your food!" barked the guard at the entrance. Calvin hesitated, taking in the dismal scene before him - the greasy trays, the slop-like gruel that passed for breakfast, and the hostile glares on the faces of the serving inmates. A wave of nausea washed over him as the putrid smell of overcooked oatmeal assaulted his senses.

The guard's harsh voice echoed through the jail, cutting through the tense silence. "Move it, Steele!" he barked, shoving Calvin forward with a rough hand. Calvin reluctantly grabbed a tray and held it out, trying not to grimace as the slimy substance plopped onto the cheap plastic.

"Think you're too good for this grub, huh?" sneered one of the servers, his lip curled in disgust as he eyed Calvin up and down. "Didn't say that," Calvin mumbled, keeping his expression neutral. "Just ain't used to it, is all." The server's eyes narrowed further at Calvin's response. "Better get used to it quick," he spat, turning his attention to the next inmate in line.

Calvin moved away from the counter, momentarily relieved to escape the hostile atmosphere. But as he walked, a massive figure suddenly appeared beside him, muscles bulging beneath a tight-fitting jail-issued shirt. The man's voice was a low rumble as he leaned in close, making Calvin flinch instinctively. "Hey, new guy," he drawled, his tone almost friendly. "I got some snack cakes back in my cell. It's top-notch stuff. Do you want some? You just gotta come get them." Calvin couldn't help but stare at the man warily, unsure of his intentions. Was this a genuine offer of kindness or something more sinister? He quickly scanned the room for any sign of safety or support in this cold and daunting environment. "Thanks, but I think I'll pass," Calvin replied cautiously, though his hungry stomach grumbled in protest. He turned away and hurried off, hoping to end the conversation before anything else could happen. But his mind raced with questions about what might happen next in this unpredictable place filled with hardened criminals and tense power dynamics.

Calvin cautiously sat at one of the long metal tables, his fingers tracing the cold surface as he surveyed the crowded mess hall. The clattering of trays and loud, gruff voices filled the air, making it difficult for him to focus on anything else. His stomach churned as he looked down at the unappetizing food before him, trying to will away the nausea that threatened to rise. Suddenly, a voice jolted him out of his thoughts. "New guy, huh?" Calvin turned to find Clyde, his cellmate, giving him a knowing nod. "I saw that big guy talking to you. Don't go for those snack cakes." "What do you mean?" Calvin asked, his brow furrowed in confusion. "Let's just say there's more than sugar in 'em," Clyde said with a heavy sigh, scanning the room before leaning in closer. "You don't want any part in his... business."

The implications of Clyde's words hit Calvin like a ton of bricks, causing his heart to race and his throat to tighten. "Is he... serious?" he whispered, unable to hide the fear in his voice. "Dead serious," Clyde confirmed before eating his meal. "You're lucky it was your first night here, and besides, the nightmares were enough. You didn't have to hear what goes on after lights out. It ain't pretty." Calvin swallowed hard, feeling his already nonexistent appetite disappear entirely. Biscuit's face flashed through his mind, and anger boiled within him. That old friend of his had played a significant role in landing him in this hellish place, all because of his weakness for women. With clenched fists under the table, Calvin struggled to control his emotions.

"Hey, man, don't let it get to you," Clyde advised, noticing Calvin's tense posture. His broad shoulders were hunched up, and his jaw clenched tightly as he stared at the unappetizing meal before him. "Keep your head down, eat what they give you, and avoid trouble. That's what I'm going to do." Calvin nodded, attempting to heed Clyde's advice. He picked up his fork and hesitantly stabbed it into the gray mush that was supposed to be breakfast, forcing himself to take a small bite.

The texture was slimy and unappealing, and the taste was even worse. But he knew he needed the energy to survive in this place. "Thanks, Clyde," Calvin managed to say after swallowing with difficulty. "I appreciate the help." "Anytime," replied his cellmate with a reassuring pat on the back. "We gotta look out for each other in here. That's the only way we'll make it." Through the barred windows, Calvin could hear the distant sounds of shouting and clanging metal - reminders of the harsh reality of jail life. But he couldn't afford to let anger consume him inside these walls. He needed to survive this ordeal - and do whatever it took to clear his name.

Calvin's heart pounded against his ribs, threatening to burst through his chest as the hulking inmate sauntered towards him with a sly smirk. The man's well-oiled muscles bulged against his skin, making him seem more intimidating. "Hey there, pretty boy," he growled, getting uncomfortably close to Calvin's face. The stench of sweat and aggression emanating from the man was suffocating. Calvin's fear was palpable, his voice shaking as he replied, "Absolutely nothing's going on." His eyes darted around the crowded mess hall, desperately searching for an escape route. But all he saw were hardened criminals and guards watching intently. "Aw, come on, don't be like that," the inmate cooed, placing one massive hand on Calvin's shoulder. The weight felt like a boulder crushing down on him. Just when Calvin thought he couldn't take it anymore, a guard's voice boomed over the noise of the mess hall. "Steele!" they called out from the entrance. "You got a visitor." Relief flooded through Calvin at the sound of those words, a wave of comfort and hope amid his fear.

He shrugged off the inmate's grip and practically ran towards the guard, eager to leave this frightening encounter behind him. He could feel the inmate's gaze burning into his back as he walked away.

The guard led Calvin down a sterile hallway, their footsteps echoing loudly in the silence. Every step brought him closer to the visitation area, where families gathered to see their loved ones behind bars. A symphony of hushed voices and muffled sobs filled the air, a constant reminder of the pain and loss that permeated this place. Calvin scanned the room, taking in the weary faces of parents, siblings, and partners visiting their incarcerated loved ones. His heart sank when he spotted children clinging to their mother's hands, their wide eyes filled with confusion and sadness. He silently prayed that Lena had spared their children from this grim reality, unable to bear the thought of Junior and Ryder seeing him in chains like this.

As he shuffled forward, his gaze finally fell upon Lena, her face a mixture of determination and anguish as Calvin was released from his handcuffs. He could see her holding back the tears, forcing a smile for his sake. She was always the heartbeat of their family, even more so now when he was at his weakest. Her dark hair cascaded over her shoulders, framing her features contorted with emotion. Yet, despite the turmoil in her eyes, she remained strong for him.

"Calvin," she whispered, her voice trembling with emotion as they locked eyes through the thick glass partition. His heart ached at the sight of her, knowing that he couldn't reach out and hold her close. "I'm here, baby."

"Thank you for coming, Lena," Calvin replied, his voice wavering with emotion. He admired her for being strong enough to visit him in this place. She was his rock, his anchor in this stormy sea they were navigating together. "I don't know what I would do without you."

Lena's hand reached up to press against the cold glass panel that separated them. She wanted nothing more than to feel his touch, to comfort him in any way she could. "I'll always be here for you, Calvin."

Their gazes never wavered as they held on tightly to the phones on either side of the partition. They knew their words would be monitored and recorded, but they didn't care. All that mattered was being able to communicate with each other.

"Hey," Calvin said softly into the receiver, fighting back tears that threatened to spill over.

"Hi," Lena replied, her voice breaking with emotion as she took in his weary appearance. The once-confident man she knew was now worn down by his time behind bars.

But even in this bleak setting, their love remained unbreakable. It was a source of strength for both of them, a glimmer of hope in the darkness surrounding them.

"I'll always be here for you." Lena's voice cracked, betraying the storm of emotions surrounding her composed exterior. The weight of their situation bore down on her like a heavy cloak, but she refused to let it crush her.

Calvin took a deep breath, trying to remain strong for both of them. He longed to reach out and comfort Lena, but he spoke softly, "I'll always be here for you, no matter where I am." His words were a promise, a lifeline that connected them even when they were miles apart.

At that moment, Calvin realized how much Lena had sacrificed for him. She was his rock; now, with him gone, she was shouldering an even heavier burden. But despite the pain and uncertainty, Lena found strength in her faith. "God will see us through this," she whispered, drawing comfort from the thought.

"He won't let us down," Calvin agreed firmly. They had come so far together through countless trials and tribulations, and he believed they would make it, too.

But Lena couldn't help but feel overwhelmed by its unfairness. "This isn't fair, Calvin," she said, her voice trembling with emotion. And in that moment, Calvin's heart broke for her.

"I know," he replied quietly. "But don't worry. I'll be home soon, and we'll get this all sorted out." He hoped his words would comfort Lena, who was looking at him with tears.

"How did this even happen?" she asked, her mind swirling with unanswered questions and fears for their future.

Calvin met her gaze, and they both spoke in unison, their voices heavy with irony, "Biscuit." The mention of Calvin's longtime friend brought a brief moment of unity between them. Biscuit had always been one to make mistakes, and now his past had caught up with him – dragging Calvin down with it.

As they sat in the cramped visitation room, they both could hear the distant sounds of other conversations, and stifled sobs filled their ears on the sides of the glass. The weight of the world outside pressed in on them, but they focused on one another, seeking solace in their persistent connection. Each word spoken between Lena and Calvin was a testament to their unbreakable love and resilience. "Remember our promise, Lena," Calvin said, his voice filled with unwavering conviction. "No matter what, we'll face everything together." "Always," she whispered back, determination shining in her eyes. "We'll get through this." And so their conversation continued, hushed tones carrying a sense of comfort and strength amidst the pain and uncertainty surrounding them.

Bound by their faith and unwavering love for each other, they drew courage from one another, knowing that together, they could overcome any obstacle. "Keep praying, baby," Lena urged gently. God is watching over us, even in here." Calvin nodded, his heart swelling with gratitude for the woman sitting before him. "I will, Lena. I know He's with us now." Their faith is a beacon of hope in the darkness of their situation.

Calvin's lips curved into a small smile as he shared his disoriented thoughts with Lena. "I was supposed to be heading to the Wisconsin Dells with you and the kids this weekend," he said, shaking his head in disbelief. "Instead, I'm sitting here in Cook County Jail." "Life sure has a way of twisting our plans," Lena replied wistfully, her mouth turning up slightly despite the tears threatening to spill over again. "Twisting them into an ironic rhyme," Calvin agreed with a weary chuckle. Though it may only bring temporary relief, their shared sense of humor felt like a soothing balm on their heavy hearts.

"Have you thought about your job, Calvin?" Lena's brow furrowed with worry as she voiced her concern. "Do you think they know about what happened?" Calvin let out a sigh as he ran a hand through his hair. "I don't know, baby. But at least this mess happened during my vacation time." "True, but I worry about what they'll say when they find out," Lena confessed, her fingers tracing invisible patterns on the cold countertop. Her practical concern for their future was evident in her every word.

Despite the weight of their circumstances, Calvin's voice remained steady and robust as he assured Lena, "Whether they know or not, we'll handle it." She could see the determination shining in his eyes, which only strengthened her resolve. Tears streaked down her face, but she refused to let them break her composure. "Right now, getting you back home matters most," she declared, her unwavering love for him evident in every word.

Calvin's heart swelled with love for this incredible woman who had captured his heart. He whispered his gratitude to her, blinking back tears that threatened to fall. "I don't know what I'd do without you."

"Lean on me, Calvin," Lena urged him, her voice dripping warmly and strongly. "Together, we'll fight through this and come out stronger for it."

As they continued to talk, Calvin felt the weight of their situation pressing down on him. But in that moment, with Lena by his side and their love surrounding them, he knew they could overcome anything life threw at them.

"Pray," Lena reminded him gently. Her words were like a soothing balm to his soul. "God is watching over you, even in here." She leaned closer to the glass separating them, her breath fogging up the surface momentarily before disappearing. "I need you home soon." She stood up from their chairs with a playful wink and a glimpse of her white stockings.

A mischievous smile played on Calvin's lips as he watched her discretely model her white stockings for him. He couldn't help but think how lucky he was to have someone like her. He couldn't resist teasing her as soon as she picked up the phone again. "You alone could get me to break this glass right now." They laughed at his joke, their shared humor momentarily easing the heaviness in the air. Together, they would face whatever challenges came their way, and their love would only grow stronger with each passing day.

Lena's face turned grave as she spoke about breaking free. Her voice was serious, and her eyes were intense. "Your mother is working to get you out today, Calvin," she said. "Rose went to the bail bonds place with the kids." At the mention of Junior and Ryder, Calvin's heart constricted, a pang of sorrow sweeping through him. He ran a hand through his hair, the weight of their young faces heavy on his mind.

"How are they doing?" he asked, his voice betraying his worry. Lena's expression softened as she reached out to touch the glass between them, offering comfort. "Don't worry about them," she reassured him. "They are stronger than you think. They have been our pillars of strength throughout all of this. They have unwavering faith that everything will work out."

Calvin blinked back tears, pride swelling in his chest for his family. Despite all they had been through, their resilience and determination never ceased to amaze him. In moments like these, he was reminded just how much he needed them – and how much they needed him to keep fighting.

"I'll pray and trust in God's plan for us," he stated firmly. "And I promise, Lena, I'll be home soon." Her response was soft but filled with emotion. She replied, "Good, because we need you, Calvin. All of us." In that moment, their connection transcended the cold barrier that separated them. Together, they would face whatever challenges lay ahead with love and faith guiding their way.

Rose sat across from the bail bond agent, a stocky man with a thick, bushy mustache that seemed to twitch with every nervous movement. The cramped and cluttered office was packed with anxious souls, each pleading for their loved one's release from jail. Papers were stacked high on every surface, teetering precariously like the uncertain fate of those they represented. The air was thick with the scent of stale cigarette smoke, a constant reminder of the countless tense conversations that had taken place within these walls. Rose could feel her heart racing as she waited for the agent to address her case.

"Ma'am, I understand your situation," the agent said, his voice strained as he attempted to focus on Rose amidst the chaos around him. "But I need you to understand. We have procedures to follow."

"Procedures?" Rose muttered under her breath, her eyes narrowing at the agent as she assessed the situation. She knew everything about procedures from working at the post office, but this was different – family. "Sir," Rose began, her voice stern but with a tinge of motherly concern, "I know you have a lot on your plate, but my son needs me. And I won't leave here until you help me get him out." The agent looked into her eyes and seemed to see something that made him pause. It was as if he suddenly understood the strength of a mother's love. He glanced around the room, then back to Rose, finally giving her full attention.

"Alright, ma'am," he sighed, reaching for a stack of papers. "Let's go over the terms of Calvin's release." As the agent explained the conditions and fees involved, Rose nodded, her expression remaining stubborn and determined. She was used to navigating complex situations, having raised Calvin as a single parent after her husband passed away. Her unwavering faith had always been her guide, and it did not falter now. As the negotiation continued, Rose couldn't help but quietly pray for a favorable outcome.

"Alright then," she declared with a steely determination, her voice carrying the weight of her unwavering resolve. As the discussion concluded, she swiftly signed the necessary papers, her actions a testament to her unyielding commitment. The agent, momentarily forgetting his weariness, acknowledged her resoluteness as he rose to attend to the next desperate family. Rose, her heart filled with gratitude, knew it was not just this man she was thanking but also the unshakeable strength of her faith that had brought her this far. With Calvin's release now set in motion, she turned her thoughts towards the grandchildren eagerly waiting outside, their anticipation and hope palpable. They needed their father just as much as she needed her son. Her heart swelled with hope and expectation for their reunion and the joy that would again fill the house, a testament to the power of a mother's love and determination.

The frigid wind relentlessly nipped at Rose's cheeks, sending shivers down her spine as she stepped out of the dim bail bond office and into the crisp Chicago air. She pulled her woolen shawl tighter around her shoulders, determined to shield herself from the biting cold as she approached her trusty Buick. The worn leather of her purse dug into her frozen fingers, a small reminder of her sacrifices to get here. Determinedly, she whispered, "Let's bring my son home," her breath visible in the icy air. Junior sat in the car's backseat. His face was pressed against the chilled window pane, and his breath created little puffs of condensation with each exhale. Beside him sat Ryder, her gaze fixed on the world outside, the lines of worry etched onto her young features. They were on a mission to bring the one they loved back home, a mission that began with enduring the physical discomfort of the cold, a testament to their determination and resilience.

Their eyes, bright with anticipation and tinged with a hint of anxiety, flicked to the door as it creaked open. "Grandma?" Junior asked hesitantly, his voice cracking with the last remnants of adolescence. His gaze shifted nervously between Rose's face and the doorway, unsure of what news awaited him. But his ever-present optimism remained, clinging onto hope even in uncertainty. "Let's get your father and bring him home," Rose announced confidently as she gracefully slid behind the wheel. Her words brought on an explosion of relief from the two teens. Junior let out a whoop of joy while Ryder's eyes glistened with unshed tears, her emotions too overwhelming for words. A small, weary smile tugged at Rose's lips as she looked at these two young souls who had been through so much together. Her heart swelled with love and pride for them, a love and pride that she ensured were felt in every word she spoke.

"Thank you, Jesus," Rose whispered reverently as she turned the key in the ignition, the engine roaring to life with a practiced turn. A sense of gratefulness washed over her as she thought of all the moments God had carried her family through. She glanced at Ryder, who wiped her tears away with her faded, well-worn sweater sleeve. "Let's go get Dad," Ryder said, determination shining through her watery eyes. Rose nodded, gripping the steering wheel tightly as they started their journey. The road stretched before them, lined with tall trees and endless possibilities. But they were not alone - their love for one another and the strong faith instilled in them by their mother would see them through. "Home," Rose whispered, her eyes fixed on the winding road ahead as they returned to their family. "We're bringing you home, Calvin." Junior reached for Ryder's hand in the backseat, their fingers entwining like a symbol of their unbreakable bond. They leaned their heads against the frosted windows, their breaths fogging the glass again. But this time, it was not from sadness or fear - it was filled with hope and determination as they embarked on their journey together.

Junior's eyes widened with hope while Ryder clenched her jaw to hide her worry, the tension palpable between them. They both knew the gravity of the situation and how it could tear apart their family. The drive to the jail was filled with anticipation and silent prayers, each family member clinging to their faith and holding onto any hope. As they pulled up to the brick building, Rose parked the car and turned off the ignition, the engine's hum fading into the background. The three of them piled out, huddling together against the biting wind, their breaths visible in the frigid air. Their hearts pounded as they waited anxiously near the entrance, their minds racing with thoughts of Calvin walking out those doors and returning home to where he belonged. Finally, after what felt like an eternity, Calvin emerged from the jail, his face drawn from his harrowing experience. But as soon as he saw his family waiting for him, a spark of life returned to his tired eyes, filling them with renewed strength and determination.

Rose's heart skipped a beat when she caught sight of her son, Calvin, walking towards her. She couldn't contain her joy and rushed forward to embrace him. Their hug was full of love and relief, each holding onto the other as if they had been separated for years. Calvin buried his face in his mother's shoulder, momentarily allowing himself to be vulnerable. He whispered a heartfelt apology, his voice cracking with emotion. Rose shushed him gently, stroking his back in a comforting manner. "You're home now," she said softly, the weight of worry finally lifting off her shoulders. "That's what matters." Next, Ryder stepped forward, her eyes glistening with unshed tears. She hugged her father fiercely, her strong-willed nature shining through even in this tender moment as she held onto him like a lifeline in the stormy sea of emotions that had engulfed them all.

Tears welled up in her eyes as she pressed her cheek to her father's chest. "Welcome home, Daddy," she murmured, her voice muffled by his embrace. Calvin's heart swelled with love for his daughter, grateful to be back in her arms after so long. Finally, it was Junior's turn. He wrapped his arms around his father, his small frame disappearing in Calvin's strong embrace. "I prayed for you, Dad," he whispered earnestly. "I knew God would bring you back to us." Calvin couldn't hold back his tears any longer as he squeezed his son tight. "Your prayers worked, son," he said, his voice choked with emotion. "Thank you." As Calvin stood there, surrounded by the love and warmth of his family, he couldn't help but think of Biscuit - his loyal friend. A shadow of doubt still lingered in his mind - thoughts of the consequences of his actions and their impact on his family. However, he pushed those concerns aside and basked in the moment with his loved ones.

CHAPTER 22

Calvin's home's living room was illuminated by the warm glow of countless candles, filling the space with a serene aura. The air was alive with the sound of prayer and heartfelt conversation, mingling with the savory scents of homemade fried chicken, collard greens, and cornbread. As the church members raised their hands in praise or clasped them together in supplication, Calvin felt surrounded by love and support from his tight-knit community.

"Thank you, Lord, for bringing our brother back to us," Pastor Reynolds' voice echoed through the room, gravelly and tender. "Guide him through this difficult time and let him find solace in Your embrace." Standing at the center of the circle, Calvin closed his eyes and let the prayers wash over him like a soothing balm. He felt Lena's hand squeeze his own, a silent show of solidarity that filled him with gratitude. "Remember, Jesus is always with you," she whispered into his ear.

As the prayer ended, everyone moved to the dining room, where a potluck dinner was to be served. The atmosphere was filled with joy and jubilation as plates were piled high with delicious food, and laughter reverberated in the air. "You have to try some of Miss Betty's pecan pie, Calvin," someone exclaimed enthusiastically. "It's simply divine!"

Amidst the boisterous gathering, Junior was the only one who heard a faint knock at the door. Curiosity flickering across his features, he excused himself from the table and went to answer it. When he opened the door, Biscuit stood there, his eyes downcast and hesitant. "Hey, Junior, do you think I could speak to your father?" he asked quietly.

At that moment, Calvin appeared behind his son with a furrowed brow filled with tension. "I can handle it, Junior. Go on back inside," he said, his voice firm yet gentle. "Remember Jesus," Junior said softly before retreating to the dining room. Calvin and Biscuit were alone on the doorstep with a palpable tension in the air, the laughter and chatter from inside only accentuating it.

Marks of resentment etched Calvin's face, a man who refused to forgive, blaming Biscuit for his current predicament. As Biscuit appeared, Calvin's bitterness erupted in harsh words. "Typical of you to show up only when there's food to be had," he sneered. The air between the two old friends thickened with unspoken grievances, a tense pause stretching until Lena approached, her arms wrapping around Calvin's waist. Her touch softened his features, and her voice carried the weight of love. "I'm just grateful to have you back home," she whispered. Turning to Biscuit, she pleaded, "Calvin, we must let go of our anger and forgive. Our faith teaches us the importance of forgiveness and releasing negative emotions."

Calvin met his wife's gaze, struggling against the tight hold of resentment within him. He knew she was right and that forgiveness was necessary, but letting go of the hurt that consumed him felt impossible. With a deep breath, he tried to release some of the tension in his shoulders. "Come inside, Biscuit," Calvin relented, gesturing towards their warm, welcoming home. "We'll talk later." As they stepped back into the warmth and love of their gathering, Calvin held onto a glimmer of hope that forgiveness and reconciliation were attainable, not just for himself and Biscuit but for their entire community.

The voices of their fellow church members rose together in prayer, filling the room with hope and love. Calvin closed his eyes, letting the words wash over him like a soothing balm, chipping away at the hardened shell of anger that had encased his heart for so long.

Lena's gentle touch on his arm in that moment of vulnerability was like a soothing balm to Calvin's raging emotions. She whispered, conveying wisdom and understanding, "Please, Calvin, see the bigger picture. We need Biscuit's help to clear your name. Don't let anger consume you." Her words struck a deep chord within him, and he could feel the bitterness slowly dissolving, replaced by an understanding of what truly mattered.

With a heavy sigh, Calvin turned to face Biscuit, who watched the scene unfold with guilt and trepidation. The tension between them lingered momentarily before Calvin spoke, his voice low and controlled, "Alright, man. Let's put this behind us." A look of profound relief washed over Biscuit's face as they embraced, the warmth of their friendship starting to rekindle. "Thank you, Calvin," Biscuit murmured, his voice thick with emotion. "I'm so sorry for everything." As they pulled apart, Calvin looked into his friend's eyes, searching for answers. His curiosity and concern now overshadowed the remnants of his anger.

"Tell me, Biscuit," Calvin began, his voice firm but compassionate. "How did all this happen? And more importantly, what will we do to fix it?" Biscuit hesitated for a moment before gathering the courage to confess his mistakes. His gaze shifted to the floor as he spoke, the weight of his actions bearing down on him. "I... I got mixed up with something stupid, Calvin," he admitted with a heavy heart. "I didn't know how to stop it. But I promise I'll do everything possible to help you clear your name."

Calvin nodded firmly, his jaw set in determination. "We'll figure this out together, Biscuit. But we must be honest with each other from now on, you hear me?" Biscuit met his gaze with a renewed sense of purpose and gratitude. "Yes, Calvin," he agreed, his eyes shining with determination. As the two friends stood side by side, surrounded by their family and community's unwavering love and support, Calvin knew that no matter what challenges lay ahead, they would face them together. With that knowledge, he felt a sense of peace settle within him, a calm assurance that they would find a way to right the wrongs and heal the wounds of the past.

"Alright then," Calvin said with a determined nod, clapping Biscuit on the shoulder. "Let's get to work." The two friends turned towards their future, ready to tackle whatever obstacles came their way.

"Let's not worry about this tonight, Calvin," Biscuit said, looking around at the gathered family and friends. We'll talk in the morning, alright? Just enjoy being back home with your family." Calvin sighed, feeling a sense of peace at his friend's words. He knew Biscuit was correct—there would be time for answers and explanations later. But for now, he just wanted to soak up every moment with his loved ones.

"Alright, Biscuit," he agreed, smiling at his wife and children beside him. "Tonight, we celebrate and give thanks for my return." "Sounds like a plan, brother." Biscuit grinned, clapping him on the back before joining the gathering.

As they walked towards the buffet table, Biscuit's eyes were drawn to a beautiful church member standing nearby. Her long golden hair cascaded down her shoulders in loose waves, and her bright smile was as radiant as the sun. He felt a familiar stirring inside - an old habit he knew he should break.

But just as quickly as the desire had sparked, it was extinguished when he caught sight of Rose's disapproving gaze from across the yard. She'd seen him looking, and there was no hiding from the matriarch's watchful eye.

"God is so good," Biscuit murmured under his breath as he tore his eyes away from the woman and nodded in Rose's direction. He didn't need any more trouble in his life, especially not now when he had a chance to make amends with Calvin and set things right. "Sure is," Calvin replied with a hint of amusement. Let's get some food before Mama walks over here and scolds us both."

Calvin and Biscuit joined the bustling crowd of well-wishers, filling their plates with the bounty of home-cooked dishes spread out before them. A chorus of laughter and chatter filled the air as friends and family caught up with each other over plates piled high with food. As Calvin filled his plate, he couldn't help but feel a sense of warmth and belonging that he hadn't experienced in a long time. The love and support of his family and community enveloped him like a comforting embrace, and he knew they would always be there for him no matter what challenges lay ahead.

"Hey," Biscuit said softly, nudging Calvin's arm as they settled at the table. "You know I'm sorry. About everything?" Calvin met his friend's gaze, searching for any signs of insincerity or deceit. But all he saw was genuine remorse and the promise of redemption in Biscuit's eyes. "I know, Biscuit," Calvin replied quietly, offering a small smile. "We'll get through this together. We can overcome anything as long as we've got each other and our unbreakable bond." "Damn straight," Biscuit agreed, raising his fork in a toast. "To friendship and forgiveness." "To friendship and forgiveness," Calvin echoed, clinking his utensil against Biscuits before digging into his food with renewed vigor, feeling grateful for the warm meal and even warmer company around him.

The Steele family home felt alive again with the sounds and scents of a long, blessed day. The laughter of children playing in the yard mingled with the hum of conversation from the adults on the porch. The tantalizing aroma of fried chicken and collard greens wafted through the air, tempting everyone to return for seconds. "Calvin," Rose called out, her voice gentle but firm, "Come on now, honey. It's time." The lively chatter quieted at her words, and all eyes turned to Calvin. He glanced around at the faces of his family and friends - faces that showed concern, love, and unwavering support. At that moment, he felt a surge of gratitude, bolstering his resolve to face whatever challenges lay ahead. "Alright, Mama," he said, nodding as he stood up from his seat at the table.

As if guided by a shared understanding, the group formed a circle around Calvin. They placed their hands on his shoulders, arms, and back, creating a living tapestry of love and faith. Their touch was comforting and grounding, reminding him he was not alone in his struggle. "Lord, we come to you today," Pastor Williams began, his voice strong and clear, "to ask for your guidance and protection for our brother Calvin. He is facing trials and tribulations, but we know that with your help, he can overcome them." "Please, Father," Lena added, her hand gripping Calvin's tightly, "give my husband the strength to persevere and the wisdom to make the right choices. We trust your plan for our family and know you will see us through this difficult time." "Show him the way, Lord," Biscuit said solemnly, his usually cheerful demeanor replaced with deep sincerity. "Help him navigate these troubled waters and keep him safely back with us."

As the prayers continued, Calvin felt a warmth spreading through him, emanating from the hands of those who loved him most. Each word and plea for divine intervention seemed to wrap around him like a protective shield, fortifying his spirit against the darkness that threatened to engulf him. "Thank you," he whispered, tears welling as the last prayers' last echoes faded. "Remember," Rose said softly, her hand lingering on Calvin's arm, "you are never alone. The Lord is with you always, and so are we." Calvin nodded, swallowing past the lump in his throat. Though his future remained uncertain, the love and support of his family and friends had given him newfound strength. He knew he could face whatever lay ahead with their help and God by his side, despite the overwhelming anxiety about the unknown that still gnawed at his heart.

CHAPTER 23

Calvin's heart pounded against his chest, a thunderous rhythm echoing through the underground tunnels of the Chicago subway. The fluorescent lights flickered above him, casting eerie shadows on his face and reflecting the storm brewing inside him. His fingers clenched and unclenched in frustration as he gritted his teeth against the anger and uncertainty that threatened to consume him. The cityscape blurred past as Calvin emerged from the station and made his way through the bustling streets of Chicago, each step heavy with the weight of his thoughts.

His mind raced with worries about his family, their future, and the looming sense of unrest that seemed to permeate every corner of the city. He longed for an escape, a moment of peace amidst the chaos. Calvin climbed onto rocks overlooking Lake Michigan, seeking solace in a familiar spot. The vast water expanse stretched before him, seemingly endless and ever-changing. Closing his eyes, he listened to the gentle lapping of waves against the shore, trying to find calm within himself.

"Yo, Cal!" a voice called behind him, shattering the stillness. The unmistakable scent of Italian beef sandwiches filled the air, bringing a small smile to Calvin's face even before he turned around to see his friend Biscuit approaching. "Better be dipped," he muttered playfully, finally facing his long-time friend. "Is there any other way to experience one of Chicago's finest things?" Biscuit grinned mischievously, holding out a paper-wrapped sandwich for Calvin. They dug into their sandwiches, savoring the familiar taste of home with each bite. Their silence was comfortable and easy, built upon years of shared history and camaraderie, a bond that made Calvin feel deeply connected and a part of something greater.

But then Biscuit cleared his throat, his expression turning serious. "I'm sorry for what I did, and I can't say it enough," he said, his eyes filled with genuine remorse. "All I want is for this storm to end," Calvin sighed, setting aside his sandwich and looking at Biscuit expectantly. "Tell me the real story, Biscuit. How did this happen?" Biscuit hesitated momentarily, his gaze drifting to the lake as he collected his thoughts. "You know I stopped messing with Willow a while back," he began, his voice quiet and strained. "But one day, she called me, asking what I was doing. I told her the truth – nothing. She asked if I wanted to do something, and I said yeah." Calvin shook his head, disappointment etched on his face. "You've gotta stop being so weak, man. Especially for that girl, after what happened last time."

Biscuit's voice trembled as he spoke, his gaze fixed on his fidgeting hands. "I know, Cal," he admitted. "And I never meant for any of this to hurt you or your family. I just... I wasn't thinking clearly at the time." Calvin's anger dissipated, replaced by a deep sorrow that weighed down his entire being. "None of us were," he murmured, his eyes glistening with unshed tears. "But now we're all paying the price, Biscuit. We have to find a way to make things right." A fierce determination ignited in Biscuit's eyes as he turned to face Calvin. "Whatever it takes, Cal," he vowed. "We'll fix this mess together." They sat side by side, their backs against a weathered tree trunk, gazing out over the calm lake waters. Despite the weight of this mistake and all the regrets, Calvin couldn't help but feel a glimmer of hope amidst the darkness. With Biscuit by his side, they usually could weather any storm and emerge stronger on the other side.

They stayed there until the moon rose, casting a cool glow on the rippling water. Calvin and Biscuit walked along the lakeshore, their footsteps crunching against the soft sand and creating a steady rhythm to their conversation. The gentle lapping of waves against the shore provided a soothing backdrop to their words as they navigated the complexities of life. Biscuit's smirk seemed out of place, given the gravity of the situation. "I did stop messin' with Willow a while ago," he said, shoving his hands into his pockets. "But man, it was a slow week with the ladies, and when she called, I just... fell for it." Calvin's eyes scanned the water as if searching for answers in its depths, and his brow furrowed in concern. "Man, you need to get some control," he retorted. "Especially with her. You remember what happened last time, right?" Biscuit's shoulders slumped as he let out a heavy sigh. "Of course I do. She tore up my place before she stormed out. That's why I didn't invite her over this time. We just met and talked in the car, and that was it."

The realization hit Calvin like a lightning bolt, illuminating the situation in a new light. "Is that how the bag ended up in your car?" he asked, his eyebrows raising in surprise. Biscuit's guilty expression and sheepish rubbing of the back of his neck confirmed Calvin's suspicions. "But I wasn't thinkin' straight at the time, man," Biscuit admitted with remorse. "I just wanted to have some fun, you know?" A mixture of disappointment and frustration swirled in Calvin's mind as he processed Biscuit's words. "You had to see that Willow was playing you, Biscuit. And now it might cost me everything." The weight of the conversation hung heavily between them, the silence broken only by their heavy breaths. Biscuit's earlier smirk was nowhere to be seen, replaced by a solemn expression. "Listen," Calvin began, his voice betraying his frustration, "why didn't you just call her and tell her to come get her bag? You could've avoided all of this." "Cal, believe me, that was my first thought," Biscuit pleaded, desperation evident in his eyes. "But when I saw what was inside that bag, I freaked out, man. She was using me for something dirty. I just wanted to get rid of it and be done with it. You know I don't mess with drugs."

Calvin's footsteps were heavy and angry as he kicked a small rock, sending it flying across the beach. He stopped walking and turned to face his friend Biscuit, his eyes dark with frustration. "Everything ain't always a hustle, Biscuit," he snapped. "Sometimes, you gotta think about the consequences. For me, for my family." Biscuit nodded solemnly, his gaze filled with regret and understanding. "I get it, Cal. And I will do whatever it takes to make this right." As they stood on the shore, their silhouettes etched against the night moonlight, the two men knew their bond was being tested like never before. The crashing waves at their feet seemed to echo their inner turmoil but also held the promise of redemption – if only they could find the strength to weather the storm together.

Calvin's eyes traced the pattern of the waves crashing against the jagged rocks, their relentless force mirroring the turmoil in his mind. The knot in his stomach tightened, a physical manifestation of his anger and betrayal. Despite the chill from the wind whipping off Lake Michigan, Calvin's emotions were still boiling. "I knew Willow could be into almost anything but the lowlife drug game," Biscuit admitted, his voice wavering with guilt. "But that didn't stop you from getting involved with her again," Calvin shot back, his disappointment and hurt evident in his dripping tone. "It was a slow week," Biscuit attempted to defend himself, running a shaky hand through his hair. "But I see now that it was a mistake. Maybe Roland has information on where Willow got the drugs without me telling her about it. They can help us fix this mess." The words tasted bitter in Calvin's mouth as he realized how deeply he had been dragged into this dangerous world by someone he thought was his friend.

"Great plan," Calvin responded sarcastically, his eyes narrowing. "We're gonna contact a drug dealer and ask him to find us another drug dealer to tell the police that I mistakenly got his drugs so they can let me go free?" The two men locked eyes, fully aware of their plan's absurdity and futility. A heavy silence settled between them, the weight of their dire situation hanging in the air like a dark cloud. Calvin sighed, defeated, and turned towards the dark water, feeling the weight of impending doom. "Damn," he muttered under his breath, his shoulders slumping in resignation. "I'm goin' to jail." Without another word, he turned and began walking down the lakeshore, leaving Biscuit alone to watch his friend's retreating figure disappear into the night. The only sound was the gentle lapping of the lake against the shore, starkly contrasting the chaos and danger surrounding them.

The following day at the bus station was tranquil as Biscuit pulled in, his eyes darting left and right in search of Willow. He knew she had a knack for appearing when least expected, and he couldn't afford any more trouble. His hands tightened around the wheel as he steered his car through the lot, scanning the sea of tired faces for that familiar sinister smile. The air smelled of gasoline and exhaust, hinting of late summer heat. "Coast looks clear," he muttered, a sigh of relief escaping him. He decided to park in Calvin's usual spot, the emptiness of which was a stark reminder of the mess they were in. As the engine shuddered to a stop, Biscuit stared at the faded yellow lines beneath the tires, guilt weighing heavy on his chest. "Damn it, Cal. I'm sorry." "Hey, Biscuit!" one of the other drivers called out from across the lot, giving him a friendly wave.

Biscuit forced a smile and waved back, trying to suppress the unease gnawing at the edge of his mind. He took a deep breath and drove onto his regular route through the west side of Chicago. The streets were bustling with life, children playing on the sidewalks while their parents chatted idly on porch steps. It was a scene Biscuit knew well, but today, it felt different. The once vibrant colors seemed muted and dull under the weight of recent events. Dark clouds loomed in the distance, threatening to burst open and wash away any sense of normalcy in this neighborhood.

"Next stop, Jackson and Pulaski," he announced over the speaker, his voice feeling hollow and distant even to himself. As passengers filed on and off the bus, Biscuit couldn't help but let his thoughts drift back to Calvin. "Man, what did I get you into?" Biscuit whispered to himself, his knuckles turning white as he gripped the wheel. Images of Calvin's face, filled with confusion and betrayal, played on a loop in his head. He thought about Rose, Calvin's mother, and how she had always been his second mother.

Her fierce love for her family was legendary, and Biscuit couldn't bear disappointing her. "Snap out of it," he told himself, shaking his head to clear the fog of guilt. "Gotta focus on the road." Biscuit tried to lose himself in the city's rhythm as the bus hummed. He knew he couldn't turn back time or erase his mistakes, but maybe there was still a chance to set things right for Calvin, Lena, and himself. "End of the line," he called out as they reached the final stop, his voice filled with renewed determination. Passengers filed out onto the sidewalk, leaving Biscuit alone in the driver's seat, his eyes fixed on the horizon. "Whatever it takes," he whispered, gripping the wheel tightly. "I'm going to fix this, Cal. I promise."

The bus's windows had a golden hue over the worn seats with the sun dipping low in the sky. Biscuit caught sight of his reflection and was struck by how much older he looked than he felt. He sighed, absently running a hand over the stubble on his chin. "Come on now, Biscuit. You've got a job to do," he told himself, taking a deep breath and exhaling slowly. The weight of guilt still clung to him like a heavy coat, but he knew he couldn't afford to let it consume him. Not now, when there was still so much work ahead of them. "West Side!" Biscuit called out at the next stop, his voice carrying its usual warmth despite the turmoil. A group of girls, all laughter and light, climbed aboard. They giggled as they dropped their change into the fare box, casting flirtatious glances on Biscuit's way. "Hey there, Mr. Bus Driver," one of them said with a sassy wink, her bright red lipstick matching the curve of her smile. "Mind if we sit up front with you?" "Be my guest," Biscuit replied, smiling back despite himself. It was impossible not to be charmed by their youthful exuberance, and for a moment, he allowed himself to forget about Calvin and the mess he'd made.

"Thank you kindly," another girl chimed in, her long eyelashes fluttering as she settled into the seat next to Biscuit. The other girls followed suit; their excitement was palpable as they chattered and giggled. "Y'all sure know how to brighten a man's day," Biscuit said, his spirits lifting as they traded playful banter back and forth. He felt a weight lifted from his shoulders, at least for the moment. "Next stop, folks!" he called out, pulling up to the curb. As the passengers filed on, Biscuit caught sight of a man in a worn leather jacket slipping aboard at the tail end of the line. Willow's complex accomplice, Lenny, moved through the crowded bus with a graceful ease that belied his size. Unaware of the newcomer's identity, Biscuit continued flirting with the girls. He didn't notice Lenny sitting at the back, his dark eyes locked on the driver and his antics. "Mr. Bus Driver," one of the girls purred, her voice dripping with flirtation, "you sure know how to make a girl feel special."

"Aw, now, it ain't nothin'," Biscuit replied, his laughter ringing out genuine. For a brief moment, he could almost forget about Calvin and the guilt that threatened to consume him. But then he felt it again - that nagging sensation of being watched - and unease crept over him like a shadow. He tried to pass it off as paranoia from his earlier encounter with Willow, but he couldn't shake it off. "Next stop!" Biscuit called out again, trying to sound confident despite the tightness in his chest. He glanced at the rearview mirror but saw nothing except rows of anonymous faces staring back at him. "Everything all right, Mr. Bus Driver?" one of the girls asked, her concern evident in her furrowed brow. "Y-yeah, I'm fine," Biscuit stammered, forcing a smile. "Just got a lot on my mind, is all." "Maybe we can help take your mind off things," another girl cooed, leaning closer to Biscuit with a seductive grin. But even as they continued to flirt and tease, the nagging feeling persisted, tightening its grip on Biscuit's heart.

With a jolt and a hiss, the bus stopped at the end of its route. Its brakes released with relief as if they had been holding their breath for too long. Biscuit stood up, feeling every muscle in his body protest against another day of driving. He stretched with a weary smile, trying to shake off the weight of the day's events that had settled on his shoulders like an unwelcome passenger. The girls he had picked up earlier had long since disembarked, leaving echoes of their laughter and flirtatious comments that now reverberated through Biscuit's mind.

"End of the line, folks!" he called out into the semi-empty vehicle, his voice echoing against the walls. The remaining passengers shuffled past him towards the doors, offering mumbled thanks as they stepped out into the early evening light. Biscuit began walking down the aisle, his eyes sweeping each empty seat as if searching for something lost. It was a ritual he had been performing for years—part of the job but also a way to find closure at the end of each shift. Today, however, it held new meaning: a chance to let go of the gnawing guilt that clung to him like a second skin from an earlier incident.

Biscuit cautiously approached the last occupied row, his heart pounding with fear. The man sitting there had a menacing glare that seemed to pierce right through him. As Biscuit spoke, he could feel the weight of the man's intense gaze bearing down on him like a heavy iron press. "Excuse me, sir," he stammered, trying to avoid eye contact and failing miserably. But Lenny wasn't easily ignored. He rose slowly to his full height, towering over Biscuit like a dark cloud ready to burst. "This is the end of the line for you," he growled, his voice gravelly and dangerous. "You'll have to get off the bus until I leave again." Biscuit's palms began to sweat as he nervously turned to look out the window, hoping for any sign of rescue. The skies were clear, the sun casting long shadows from the nearby buildings, mocking him with its brightness. "Wouldn't be an issue if it were rainin'," he muttered, but Lenny was not amused. With deliberate slowness, he moved closer until their reflections were side by side in the glass.

The heat radiating off him was suffocating, making Biscuit want to disappear into nothingness. "So," Lenny said casually but with a veiled threat. "What are you lookin' for out there?" Biscuit could feel himself shrinking under Lenny's intense gaze, unable to speak or move. "Uh, nothin' in particular right now," he managed to squeak out eventually, unable to tear his eyes away from the unrelenting stare of Lenny's dark eyes. But Lenny had other plans; he always did. "I have an idea," he continued, his voice still light but with a palpable menace lurking underneath. "You see, a specific bag belongs to me." Biscuit's heart began to race even faster as he realized what was coming next. He knew he couldn't deny Lenny—or the consequences that might follow. "Do you want to help me find it?" Lenny asked, his voice low and dangerous like a coiled snake ready to strike. Biscuit gulped, his throat suddenly dry as a desert. He knew he had no choice but to agree, feeling the weight of all his past mistakes settling heavily on his shoulders. Despairingly, he thought this would be another one to add to the list.

Biscuit's heart pounded furiously in his chest, the fear and guilt swirling inside him like a storm. His fingers involuntarily tightened around the steering wheel, the worn leather grooves familiar and comforting beneath his touch. Beside him, Lenny's intense dark eyes seemed to bore into his very soul. Biscuit bit his lip, torn between confessing everything and keeping silent.

He could sense Lenny's anger and disappointment and knew he deserved it. After all, he had been foolish enough to mess around with Willow again, but he never knew she was with someone like Lenny and that he would be confronted by him about it now.

Sitting across from now Biscuit, Lenny leaned forward and rested his elbows on his knees, his expression unreadable. "Y'know," he said calmly, "I know you used to mess with my girl." Biscuit's eyes widened in shock and horror. His throat felt dry as he struggled to form a response. "What girl?" he stammered, his voice cracking with nerves.

Lenny's cold and emotionless tone sent shivers down Biscuit's spine. "Willow," he said flatly as if stating a simple fact. "Mr. Funny Man." Biscuit gulped as a bead of sweat trickled down his temple. He couldn't believe this was happening.

Trying to lighten the mood, Biscuit forced a weak chuckle. "Ah, yeah, that was long ago," he mumbled nervously.

But any attempt at humor fell flat as the tension in the air thickened, suffocating him. Lenny wasn't amused or fooled by Biscuit's feeble laughter.

"Regardless of when it happened," Lenny continued sternly, "Willow told me you have my bag." Biscuit's pulse raced even faster, his mind racing as he tried to respond. He knew he was caught, and there was no way out.

Lenny leaned in so close to Biscuit that he could smell the faint scent of fear on his breath. "You'll return my bag to me soon," he said in a low, menacing voice. "Without anything missing. Do you understand me?"

Biscuit could only nod, feeling like a trapped animal unable to escape. He whispered, "Y-yes," unable to meet Lenny's intense gaze. Instead, he stared at his trembling hands, feeling small and helpless under Lenny's powerful presence.

Lenny's abrupt rise from his seat was like a tiger uncoiling, every movement deliberate and precise. "Good," he said with a finality that sent shivers down Biscuit's spine. As Lenny stepped off the bus, the weight of his words lingered in the air like a dark cloud. Biscuit watched through the window as Lenny strode across the pavement, his steps confident and purposeful. He climbed into a waiting car, its glossy black exterior reflecting the city, and it quickly sped off, leaving Biscuit more alone than ever.

The quiet hum of the idling bus seemed to amplify Biscuit's thoughts, which raced in a whirlwind of fear and regret. He couldn't shake the image of Calvin, his loyal friend, locked away for a night because of their actions. How had he let things get so out of control? Biscuit wiped the sweat from his brow, trying to calm himself as he took in the city around him. His past mistakes felt like an unshakable burden, pressing down on his chest like a leaden anchor. What was he going to do now? How could he ever find redemption for all the lives he'd ruined—including his own? The answer seemed to elude him, disappearing into the dusky Chicago sky like a wisp of smoke.

As the bus pulled from the stop, another passenger climbed aboard, ignorant of the turmoil brewing in Biscuit's mind. With trembling hands, Biscuit gripped the steering wheel and tried to focus on driving as the weight of his actions loomed over him like a dark storm cloud. The streets of Chicago were now bathed in darkness, the only light from sporadic streetlights casting an eerie glow on the cracked pavement. Biscuit drove cautiously, his eyes darting around for any potential danger. But his thoughts were elsewhere, consumed by regret and guilt. "Damn," he muttered under his breath, the word dripping with self-condemnation.

Memories of Willow's face plagued him – her crooked smile, her dark hair falling in waves around her face. He squeezed the steering wheel tighter, recalling how her eyes had glinted with both playfulness and something more profound, a warning that he had foolishly ignored in his state of lust. Biscuit could feel the weight of his actions crushing him like a heavy burden on his chest. He knew now that his danger was facing the consequences of the law like Calvin's and entering the unforgiving world of the streets where survival is a constant battle. Every car horn or noise outside made Biscuit jump, his nerves on edge and beads of sweat forming on his forehead as he navigated the chaotic city streets.

Biscuit's heart raced. "Keep it together, man," he whispered as he took a deep breath, his hands trembling slightly. He could still hear Calvin's voice echoing, urging him to do the right thing and be strong for his family's sake.

Biscuit had always admired Calvin - his unwavering loyalty and dedication to his loved ones was something he aspired to. But now, it seemed like an impossible task. Pushing away the memories, he focused on the road ahead, determined to make things right and prove that he could be a man worthy of Calvin's friendship and trust. The weight of his mistakes pressed heavily on Biscuit's shoulders as he prayed silently, seeking guidance from above. He knew he had to confront his wrongdoings, seek redemption, and somehow extricate himself from Willow's dangerous grasp. "God help me," Biscuit whispered, feeling the weight of his past actions bearing down on him. "I've got to fix this mess I made."

A thin, wispy mist hung low to the ground like a ghostly shroud, obscuring the sounds of distant sirens and laughter. Biscuit's hands gripped the wheel tightly, his knuckles filling with tension. "Somethin' botherin' you, driver?" The lone passenger's sharp and intrusive voice pierced through the heavy silence. She was an older woman, her face etched with lines of hardship and perseverance. "Nothin'," Biscuit replied hastily, avoiding her intense gaze in the rearview mirror. He focused on the road ahead, trying to push away memories of that fateful night with Willow. If only he'd had the strength to resist her alluring but dangerous pull. "Seems like somethin' on your mind," the woman persisted, shifting in her seat to better view him. "You've been drivin' like you got a devil on your tail." Biscuit clenched his jaw, his heart racing as he remembered Willow's seductive smile that concealed her true wickedness. "Just tired, ma'am," he lied, his voice tense with effort. "Uh-huh," she murmured skeptically, her sharp eyes seeming to see right through him. "Well, just remember, young man, we all have our demons to face one day."

"Best to do it head-on before they drag us down with them." The weight of her words settled over him like a thick shroud, suffocating and inescapable. He swallowed hard, feeling the anxiety and fear rise inside him. As much as he wanted to brush off her concerns, he knew she was right. He couldn't keep evading the truth and running from his problems; it was time to face them head-on. "Thank you, ma'am," he said quietly, his voice barely audible over the low hum of the bus's engine. He caught a glimpse of her tired eyes in the rearview mirror, seeing a glint of understanding and empathy that gave him some solace. "I'll... I'll keep that in mind." She nodded in response, sinking back into her seat with a heavy sigh. "You've got a good heart, driver. Don't let it go to waste." With each passing moment, Biscuit drew in a shaky breath, determination building within him. As the bus rumbled through Chicago's dark and lonely streets, he knew he was barreling towards his fate – and there was no turning back now. "God help me," he whispered again, steeling himself for what lay ahead on this fateful journey through the night.

In their bedroom on the other side of town, Calvin's broad shoulders were hunched over as he sat on the edge of their creaky bed. His large hands were clasped together tightly, like a vice grip, as if he was trying to hold on to something slipping away. The soft glow of the bedside lamp cast warm light across Lena's concerned face, her eyes searching for answers in the deep furrows of her husband's forehead. Calvin took a deep breath, the air thick with responsibility and unspoken emotions, and began to speak, his voice resonating with his unwavering sense of duty, a duty that the audience could feel weighing heavily on his shoulders.

"Baby," he said, his voice cracking with frustration. "It's all because of Biscuit messin' around with Willow." He couldn't bear to look at Lena as he spoke, instead focusing on the worn-out floral bedspread beneath him. "I never thought I'd see the day when Biscuit let a woman get the better of him like this." His voice carried the weight of disappointment and disbelief, drawing the audience into the emotional turmoil of the situation.

Lena bit her lip, disappointment clouding her usually bright eyes. She had always admired Biscuit's loyalty to Calvin and their family, but now she was forced to face the reality that even good men could fall victim to temptation. She knew they couldn't dictate who Biscuit loved, but the situation had spiraled out of control, casting a heavy shadow over their lives.

"What has she done this time?" Lena asked, her voice barely audible in the tense silence between them.

"Willow put that bag in Biscuit's car on purpose," Calvin replied, his voice laced with anger and betrayal. "She knew exactly what she was doin', knowin' full well eventually it would cause problems for all of us." He clenched his jaw tightly, trying to contain his rising temper. "We have no idea where she got those drugs from or who she's workin' with. This situation ain't just about their relationship anymore – it's puttin' our whole family in danger."

Lena's heart ached at the sight of her husband's anguish. Calvin had always been a rock for their family, guiding them through life with an unwavering faith in God and a steadfast commitment to his work as a city bus driver. But now, as the weight of Biscuit's mistakes threatened to drag them all under, she could see the cracks beginning to form in his stoic facade.

"Calvin, my love," she said softly, moving closer and resting a comforting hand on his arm. "We can't control what other people do, but we can control how we respond. And we've always been fighters – we'll get through this together."

Calvin's gaze lifted to meet Lena's, unable to hide the exhaustion and worry etched into his features. But as she spoke, her words wrapped around him like a warm blanket on a cold night, soothing his frayed nerves. He knew she was right – their family had faced hardships before and had always emerged stronger. Whether it was when Lena had to work two part-time jobs for years to make ends meet, or Rose's unyielding dedication to their spiritual well-being, this family's history of resilience was a beacon of hope. "Thank you, baby," Calvin whispered, his voice strained with emotion as he looked at his wife with gratitude and love. "I don't know what I'd do without you." A small smile tugged at the corners of Lena's lips as she gently squeezed his arm, her touch offering reassurance and strength. "Lean on God, and lean on me," she replied softly. "Together, we'll find a way through this storm and emerge even stronger."

Lena's eyebrows furrowed like dark storm clouds, showing worry and determination on her face. Her heart squeezed with pain for Calvin as she processed the gravity of the situation before her. She closed her eyes and silently prayed for strength to help her husband through this trial. "Calvin," she said softly, reaching out to cup his face with her warm, steady hands. The love in her eyes shone brighter than the dim glow of the bedside lamp, radiating warmth and reassurance. Her voice was unwavering, like a beacon of hope amidst their stormy emotions. "Baby, I know it's hard," Calvin admitted, his gaze locked with hers. "But it's overwhelming." Lena leaned in closer, her thumb gently stroking his cheek soothingly. "Listen to me," she whispered, her voice laced with conviction. "God didn't bring us this far just to leave us stranded. We'll get through this together like we always do. He's the same God." She paused momentarily, allowing her words to take root in their hearts.

She leaned closer to Calvin with deliberate slowness, her breath warm against his skin. He caught a flickering glimpse of something beyond comfort in her eyes - an invitation, a promise of solace for his soul and weary body. "Tonight," Lena murmured, her lips barely brushing against his, "let Him handle everything else. Let me take care of you." A gentle kiss enveloped them in a sanctuary from the chaos outside, where only their two bodies existed. As she pulled away, her fingers found the switch on the lamp, plunging the room into encompassing darkness.

Outside the four walls of their bedroom, the world faded away, leaving only the shared warmth of their bodies and the steady thrum of their beating hearts. Hushed prayers escaped Calvin's lips into the stillness of the night as Lena's arms tightened around him, seeking comfort and strength in each other's embrace. And in that moment, their unwavering faith shone like a guiding star amidst the shadows, leading them towards the hope that dawn would bring.

CHAPTER 24

Biscuit's tired eyes roamed wearily over the bustling bus terminal, the flickering streetlights casting eerie shadows across the pavement. The pungent smell of exhaust filled his nostrils, the distant sound of a street musician's saxophone drifting through the night air. Biscuit felt the weight of the day bearing down on him. His shoulders slumped with exhaustion from the constant hustle and bustle of the city. He carefully approached his car, each step echoing loudly against the surrounding buildings. "Man, what a life," he muttered to himself, his voice barely audible above the chaotic noise of the city. As he neared his car, he caught sight of Willow leaning casually against a lamppost, her silhouette illuminated by the dim lights.

A wave of unease washed over Biscuit as he reflexively tightened his grip on the keys in his pocket. "Have you broken any hearts today?" she called out nonchalantly as she strolled past him. Her voice was like dark honey, dripping sweetness but tinged with danger. Biscuit hesitated for a moment before mustering up the courage to respond. "Can't say that I have, Willow," he replied, trying to keep his voice steady despite the nerves coiling in his stomach. "What about you?" Willow smirked, her eyes sparkling mischievously in the dim light. "Oh, just another day in paradise," she said with a hint of sarcasm. Biscuit clenched his jaw, thoughts of Calvin and his family flooding his mind and anger bubbling within him at how their lives had been affected by this woman before him. It was all because of her.

Biscuit's heart thundered in his chest, beating against his ribs like a jackhammer tearing through the pavement. He couldn't let Willow walk away without confronting her about what she had done to him. His footsteps quickened as he closed the distance between them, determination fueling his every move. "Hey!" he called out to her, his voice strained with emotion. Willow turned to face him, a mischievous glint in her eyes. A sly smile crept across her face as she leaned in, pressing a quick kiss against his lips before pulling back with a cruel laugh that echoed through the empty street. Her perfume lingered in the air, taunting him even as she spoke. "You thought you were special, didn't you?" she taunted, her words laced with malice. Biscuit's fists clenched at his sides, struggling to control his anger. "I never said I was special," he replied through gritted teeth, forcing himself to swallow the lump in his throat. "But Calvin and his family are special to me, and because of what you did to me, Calvin got caught up in this mess."

For a brief moment, Willow's confident facade cracked, revealing a flicker of shock that darted across her face. But just as quickly, it vanished, replaced by her usual air of arrogance. Biscuit moved closer to her until they were inches apart, their faces almost touching. He could see the uncertainty in her eyes, but it was clear she wasn't willing to give in just yet. "Drop the act, Willow," he challenged, staring into her eyes with unwavering determination. He sensed the unease beneath her mask of defiance and knew there was more to her than this cold-hearted witch she was pretending to be. "I know there's more to you than this. You don't have to hurt people like this." "Is that so?" Willow replied, her voice dripping with sarcasm and defiance. But Biscuit could sense the flicker of doubt in her eyes, knowing he had struck a nerve. "And what makes you think you know me better than anyone else?"

Biscuit's voice softened as he held Willow's gaze, his eyes pleading with her to listen. "I've seen it," he said, his voice laced with conviction and understanding. "I've seen the jealousy in your eyes when you look at Calvin and his family. But you don't have to keep pushing people away, Willow. You could be a part of something real, too." Willow's breath caught in her throat as Biscuit's words hit her like a punch to the gut. Anger surged through her, and she pushed him away with a force that surprised even herself. "Shut up!" she snapped, her eyes blazing with fury. But deep down, she knew that he was right. She couldn't deny her longing for the close-knit relationships around her.

Her chest heaved as she tried to regain control of her emotions. "You don't know anything about me," she spat, trying to hide the vulnerability that threatened to escape. But Biscuit could see through her facade and knew he had struck a nerve. He saw how she avoided his gaze, and her shoulders slumped slightly beneath her leather jacket. "Maybe I don't know everything," Biscuit admitted, his voice filled with sadness and determination. "But I know enough to see that this isn't who you must be, Willow. You have a choice." As his words lingered between them, Biscuit hoped they would somehow break through the walls she had built around herself and give her the courage to choose a different path.

With a final, fiery glare that seared the air and left a lingering bitterness, Willow spun on her heel and began to walk away. The streetlights cast an eerie glow on the cracked pavement as she moved further into the night, her boots clicking lightly against the concrete with each determined step. "Willow..." Biscuit called out after her in a voice filled with desperation and anguish, but the din of the city swallowed his words. He clenched his fists, frustration boiling inside him like a kettle about to whistle, each moment bringing another surge of regret. "Damn it," he muttered through gritted teeth, watching her retreating figure grow smaller and smaller in the distance.

What was it going to take to get through to her? To make her see reason and understand there was another way? As if in answer to his silent pleas, a young boy with dirty clothes and tangled hair approached him from behind, holding a newspaper with trembling hands. "Latest edition! Only ten cents!" he called out with a hoarse voice. Despite his inner turmoil, Biscuit smiled and reached into his pocket for change. As he handed over the coin, he couldn't help but feel betrayed and used, anger burning within him like wildfire. He clenched his fists tighter, fighting the urge to chase after Willow and demand answers. But deep down, he knew it was futile. He had fallen for her trap, and there was no changing the past now.

His heavy footsteps echoed through the deserted streets as he went to a local bar, seeking solace in a cold beer. The dimly lit establishment was alive with the bustle of patrons, their laughter and chatter bouncing off the dark wood-paneled walls. A jukebox blared soulful tunes in the corner, filling the room with nostalgia. The bartender, a grizzled man with calloused hands, wiped down glasses with practiced precision.

Biscuit settled onto a worn barstool, ordering a single beer from the no-nonsense bartender. He took small sips of the chilled drink, hardly noticing the pretty woman who tried to flirt with him. Her playful smiles and coquettish giggles held no appeal; all he could think about was the mess he had gotten himself and Calvin into. "Damn you, Willow," he muttered under his breath, his gaze fixated on the amber liquid swirling in his glass. His mind raced with thoughts of how to make things right, but every possible solution seemed to lead to even more trouble. He knew he couldn't outrun the consequences of his actions forever, but facing them head-on felt like walking into a lion's den.

As the first rays of sunlight filtered through the kitchen window, they cast a warm, golden glow over the small table where Junior and Ryder sat patiently waiting for breakfast. Their father, Calvin, stood at the stove, his tall frame hunched over as he flipped pancakes with an unsteady hand. The sweet scent of maple syrup filled the room, mingling with the faint aroma of coffee brewing on the counter. Calvin's mind seemed to drift further away with each attempt, and his movements were slow and deliberate as if he were carrying the weight of the world on his shoulders. "Almost ready, kids," he said quietly, sounding more upbeat than he felt. Junior and Ryder exchanged a sympathetic glance, understanding the heavy burden on their father's shoulders.

"Take your time, Dad," Junior replied in a soft voice beyond his years. He leaned back in his chair, trying to find a silver lining. "We're not in a rush." "Speak for yourself," Ryder chimed in playfully, a faint smile appearing as she tried to lighten the mood. "I'm starving." Despite being grateful for his children's unwavering support, Calvin managed a weak chuckle despite himself. As he attempted to flip another pancake, his hand trembled uncontrollably, and it slipped from the spatula, falling onto the floor with a soft splat. A trail of batter followed in its wake, leaving a messy pattern on the linoleum like a Jackson Pollock painting come to life.

"Shoot," Calvin muttered, his frustration threatening to boil over like a pot of hot syrup. He bent down, his stiff back protesting, to pick up the fallen pancake from the kitchen floor. His eyes were red-rimmed from lack of sleep, deep bags weighing heavily underneath them. The weight of his troubles carved deep lines into his face, etched with worry and exhaustion. Junior and Ryder, their hearts heavy with empathy for their father, exchanged worried glances.

Their love for their father, a powerful force, was evident in their eyes, a testament to the depth of their bond. It was a love that transcended words, a care that knew no bounds. They knew their father was feeling the brunt of these grueling days. They wished there was something more they could do to help, some way to ease his burdens. "Hey, Dad," Junior said hesitantly, trying to offer assistance. "Do you want me to take over for a bit? You know, give you a break?" He knew his father took great pride in providing for their family, but he also knew that even the strongest people sometimes needed a little help.

"Thanks, son," Calvin replied with a grateful smile, his voice catching with emotion. "But I've got this." He appreciated Junior's offer more than words could express, but he also knew it was up to him to find a way to keep going – for himself and his family. With a renewed determination that was palpable in the air, Calvin turned back to the stove, flipping another pancake with a steadier hand. As the warm morning sun streamed through the window and filled the small kitchen with golden light, Calvin's unwavering determination shone brightly, a beacon of hope in the face of adversity. His determination, a testament to his resilience, was a source of inspiration for his children and the audience. It might not be much, but it was enough to keep going – one day, one pancake, one moment at a time.

Lena's gentle tone and warm hand on Calvin's arm brought comfort and relief. Her dark curls cascaded around her face as she glided past him to take over at the stove, her eyes filled with understanding. "Thanks, baby," Calvin murmured gratefully, his voice barely audible over the sizzle of batter in the pan. He stepped back, mesmerized by Lena effortlessly flipping a pancake high into the air, its golden edges glistening in the light from the nearby window. As Lena expertly took charge of breakfast, Calvin sank into a seat at the small kitchen table between Junior and Ryder. The sun's rays danced across the surface, illuminating every tiny imperfection in the worn wood and reminding him of all the meals shared here over the years. With a deep sigh, he felt the weight of his troubles pressing down upon him.

"Hey, Dad." Junior's voice broke through Calvin's thoughts as he scooted closer, his warm brown eyes brimming with compassion. "It'll work out, you know. We got your back, no matter what." "My brother's right," Ryder said, her tone fierce and protective. She leaned in to join the embrace, wrapping her arms around her father's shoulders. "We're family, Dad. We stick together." "Thank you, both," Calvin whispered, feeling their love enveloping him warmly. At that moment, he knew he needed their support to make it through the day ahead. With a shaky breath, he began to pray silently, seeking guidance from the Lord in these trying times. "Father," Calvin thought earnestly, his heart heavy with worry. "Grant me your strength today so I may carry this burden and be the man my family needs me to be."

Lena's cheerful voice sliced through the tension in the room as she announced, "Breakfast is ready, everyone." She set down a plate piled high with golden pancakes in front of Calvin, each fluffy stack adorned with melting pats of butter. The aroma of warm syrup and fresh batter filled the air, mingling with the gentle rays of sunlight streaming through the window. "Thank you, Lena," Calvin said with a grateful smile, his voice strong and determined as he reached for her hand. "You're my rock, and I don't know what I'd do without you." Lena squeezed his hand reassuringly, her warm touch sending a wave of comfort through him. "God brought us together for a reason, Calvin," she replied softly. "We'll face this challenge like we've faced everything else – together, as a family." As they sat at the table, surrounded by their home's familiar warmth and love, Calvin felt a spark of hope ignite within him. Though the road ahead was uncertain and daunting, he knew they would find the strength to face whatever life had in store – as long as they were together.

The doorbell's shrill ring sliced through the warm, cozy atmosphere of the kitchen, shattering the fragile peace that had settled over Calvin and Lena. The couple shared a brief, silent glance, their eyes reflecting worry and curiosity, before Lena gracefully rose from her seat and approached the door. Calvin's heart began to race with anticipation, his grip on his fork tightening as he braced himself for whatever challenge was about to present itself. "Rose!" Lena exclaimed with palpable relief as she swung open the door, revealing Calvin's mother standing on the doorstep.

Rose's face was a beacon of joy and determination, her bright smile lighting up the dark morning. "What a pleasant surprise!" "Good morning, everyone!" Rose declared with her trademark enthusiasm, stepping inside and clapping her hands for emphasis. "Come on; this is when we start counting our blessings!" Calvin couldn't help but feel gratitude for his mother's unwavering faith and optimism. With her infectious energy filling the kitchen, Rose crossed the room and took in the half-prepared breakfast spread with an expert eye. "Darling," she turned to Lena with a smile, "would you mind if I take over here?" Lena readily agreed, grateful for the extra support. "Please, go right ahead," she replied gratefully. "Thank you."

As Rose resumed cooking even more breakfast, Calvin couldn't help but feel a sense of comfort wash over him. He watched as his mother expertly flipped another pancake onto a plate, her movements graceful and precise. "Calvin, Lena, do you remember Ruth from the church? And her daughter Pam?" Rose asked, breaking through his thoughts. "Yeah, we remember," Lena answered with a nod, her eyes shining with intrigue. "Isn't she living in Harlem or something like that?" Calvin chimed in, suddenly curious about their old acquaintance. "Ah, yes, she was," Rose confirmed with a smile, her eyes twinkling with excitement. "But she recently moved back to Chicago and called me this morning. She asked if she could help with your case." Calvin and Lena exchanged stunned looks, their hearts racing at the unexpected news.

They had been struggling to find a way to navigate their current situation, and now it seemed that divine intervention had arrived in the form of an old friend. "Really?" Lena gasped in disbelief, her voice barely audible as emotions threatened to overwhelm her. "Really," Rose confirmed with a gentle nod, her smile growing wider as she served more breakfast to Junior and Ryder. "Now, let's eat up and start this day on the right foot!" As they gathered around the table again, Calvin couldn't help but marvel at the power of family and faith. His heart swelled with gratitude for the strong, resilient women beside him who always knew how to lift his spirits.

Calvin's gaze fixated on his half-eaten pancake, its golden edges glistening in the morning light. The sweet, sticky syrup oozed from the sides, creating a moat around it that beckoned to be devoured. His fingers tapped anxiously on the edge of his plate, mimicking the racing thoughts in his mind. "We'd love her help, but we can't afford that New York lawyer rate," he said softly, his voice laced with worry and uncertainty. Rose stood with her hands firmly planted on her hips, radiating strength and determination as she surveyed her son and daughter-in-law. "Money is not the issue we need to worry about right now," she declared. "Pam expects to see you both this morning."

Lena's hand trembled as she clutched onto Calvin's under the table, her eyes wide with fear. "Where?" she asked in a barely audible whisper. "At the courthouse," Rose answered, her tone urgent and determined. "I told her you would meet her before your arraignment today." Calvin exchanged a glance with Lena, their hearts beating in unison as they faced the unknown together. Questions and concerns swirled in his mind like a chaotic vortex, threatening to consume him. But amidst all the uncertainty and fear, one thing remained steadfast: their unity as a family, rooted deep within their faith and love. "Alright," he finally agreed, releasing a shaky breath as Lena squeezed his hand reassuringly. "We'll go."

Rose's warm, amber eyes softened with affection as she looked at the couple. "Good," she nodded, her voice gentle and reassuring, a source of comfort and security in the storm. "Don't worry about these kids; I will get them to school." With that, she moved towards Calvin and Lena, enveloping them in a comforting embrace. Her favorite perfume, a delicate blend of roses and vanilla, filled the air around them, bringing back memories of childhood moments in her arms. Calvin closed his eyes, savoring the familiar smell and drawing strength from his mother's embrace. "Get out of here," Rose whispered, gently nudging her son and daughter-in-law towards the hallway. "Go get dressed. You don't have much time."

As they left the kitchen, Calvin's thoughts turned inward, his heart swelling with gratitude for his mother's unwavering support. "Thank you, Mama," he murmured, his voice trembling with emotion as Lena squeezed his hand tightly. "For everything." "Of course, baby," Rose replied tenderly, her eyes shining with love and pride, a beacon of hope in the darkness. "Now go on. We have a big day ahead of us."

Rose's old station wagon rumbled and gasped as it approached the imposing brick building of the school. Junior and Ryder sat in the backseat, their backpacks between them, filled with worn textbooks and dog-eared notebooks. "Junior, Ryder," Rose began, her voice gentle yet firm as she navigated the car toward the drop-off area. "I want you to know how grateful I am for you being part of this family. You do not know how important it is — how you carry yourselves and the love you show others. It can make all the difference, especially our family." Junior glanced over at his sister, noticing the faint smile that graced her lips. He knew she was taking their grandmother's words to heart, just as he was. The silver lining was there if they chose to see it, which Rose, with her profound wisdom and guidance, had taught him from a young age. "We love you too, Grandma," he said quietly, meeting her gaze in the rearview mirror. His eyes shone bright with emotion, reflecting the depth of his connection to her and the rest of their family.

The car pulled up to the curb before the school, and Rose looked determinedly at her grandchildren. "Remember," she said, her voice firm but kind, "everything will be fine. Just keep your heads held high and never forget who you are." Her hand gently touched their shoulders as she spoke, reassuring them they were not alone in this journey.

Her eyes held a wisdom gained from years of experience and struggle, a strength that seemed almost tangible in the air around them. Then, her tone shifted to caution as she added, "And please, focus on being good in school. We don't need more issues adding to what we're already going through."

Ryder's intuition kicked in, honed by years of observing and learning from the world around her. She knew the importance of their roles as students and family members, and her voice rang out firmly and determinedly. She replied, "Right, Grandma. We'll make you proud, we promise." Junior nodded in agreement, his heart swelling with love and pride for his sister and grandmother. They had been through so much together, but he knew they could face whatever challenges life threw at them with their support and guidance. The sun shone on them, casting golden light over the three generations gathered outside the school, symbolizing their unbreakable bond and determination to persevere through anything.

Rose's voice was soft, barely above a whisper, as she spoke. Her eyes glittered with unshed tears, reflecting the fading sunlight filtering through the car window. "Alright then," she said, her words heavy with emotion. "Off you go." Junior and Ryder leaned forward one by one to press their lips against their grandmother's cheek, their affectionate gestures speaking volumes. As they exited the car, the crisp autumn air enveloped them, carrying the familiar scent of fallen leaves and woodsmoke. The sidewalk was littered with a carpet of reds and oranges, each leaf crunching satisfyingly underfoot. They shared a look, a silent understanding passing between them, before heading towards the looming school building – each taking their path, yet forever connected by the unbreakable bonds of family and love.

CHAPTER 25

The imposing gray stone structure loomed ahead, casting a shadow over them as they parked. Calvin killed the engine, and for a moment, the only sound was the ticking of the cooling car. He looked into Lena's warm brown eyes, searching for reassurance amidst his wife's weary expression. The weight of their situation settled heavily on their shoulders, making each step they would take towards the courthouse feel like trudging through quicksand. The air was tense and heavy with anticipation. "How did we get here, Lena?" Calvin asked, his voice barely above a whisper. "Calvin," Lena said softly, gripping his hand, "as long as we have love, we can get through any-thing." She squeezed his hand reassuringly, her wedding ring glinting in the sunlight. Calvin took a deep breath, steeling himself for what lay ahead. He knew he needed to be strong for Lena, their family, and his mother, Rose, who had always taught him the importance of resilience and unwavering faith.

"Alright, let's do this," he said with determination now etched in his features. Hand-in-hand, they stepped away from the car and approached the grand entrance of the courthouse. The marble columns stretched high into the sky, giving the building an air of authority and gravity. The doors opening and closing echoed throughout the lobby as people entered. As they made their way towards the entrance, Calvin couldn't help but feel a sense of purpose and strength from Lena's presence by his side. Together, they would face whatever challenges lay ahead.

The heavy wooden doors creaked as they pushed them open, and the sounds of the bustling courthouse washed over Calvin and Lena like a tidal wave. The steady hum of chatter and the shuffling of feet on the marble floors filled their ears, along with the occasional clang of metal from law enforcement officers' equipment. Lawyers in sharp suits and determined expressions rushed past them, their briefcases swinging at their sides. As they made their way through the chaotic maze of people, Calvin's heart raced in his chest, his grip on Lena's hand tightening with each step. He couldn't help but think about their children waiting and hoping for the best possible outcome. His mind drifted back to their humble beginnings on the west side of Chicago, where they had worked tirelessly to build a life together. But now, as they stood on the brink of uncertainty, he drew strength from Lena's unwavering support. "Whatever happens," Calvin whispered into her ear as they approached the courtroom, "we'll face it together." "Always," Lena replied with a firm nod, her voice a pillar of determination. And with that reassurance, they walked through the doors and into their unknown future, ready to confront whatever lay ahead with courage and unity.

The familiar scent of old leather and waxed wood wafted through the air, enveloping Calvin as he scanned the bustling crowd. Amidst the chaos, his eyes settled on a figure that stood out like a beacon – Pam. Her poised and polished appearance starkly contrasted with the frantic energy around her. Her heels clicked against the marble floor with confidence and purpose with each step. Calvin couldn't help but feel a sense of nostalgia wash over him as he remembered their high school days together. Back then, Pam had been a gangly teenager with wild curls and an infectious laugh. Now, she exuded an aura of calm and control, perfectly tailored in a sleek suit and styled hair. "Calvin, look," Lena whispered excitedly, her grip tightening on his arm. He smiled, admiring how Pam had blossomed into a stunning and sophisticated woman. Her genuine smile and warm greeting filled their hearts with joy as she approached them. "It's so good to see you both," she said sincerely.

Calvin's voice was full of admiration as he gazed at Pam, "Wow, look at you. You've come so far since we were just kids running around the streets of Chicago together." Her eyes twinkled with shared memories as she replied, "Back then, we didn't have a care in the world, did we?" Lena chimed in, her gratitude evident in her tone, "We're so grateful to have you on our side, Pam. Thank you for taking on Calvin's case." With a resolute expression, Pam assured them both, "Of course. I will do everything in my power to help you both." As they talked, Calvin couldn't help but reminisce about the simpler times they had shared growing up on the west side of Chicago. The three of them had been inseparable, navigating the trials of adolescence together. He felt a surge of gratitude for the unwavering friendship that had carried them through life's storms. Bringing himself back to the present, Pam wanted to roll up her sleeves and declare, "Alright, let's get to work." Amidst the chaos of the courthouse, Calvin knew they were lucky to have Pam by their side. And now more than ever, those words rang true.

Pam's voice was filled with genuine gratitude as she replied, her eyes shimmering with emotion as they landed on Calvin and Lena. "Thank you both," she said, touched by their words. "But I should be the one thanking you. You two have always been an example of real love, and that's something I will never forget." At that moment, Calvin felt a surge of pride wash over him, but he couldn't help thinking about all the struggles he and Lena had faced together. The long hours they had both worked to support their family, the countless sacrifices they had made; it hadn't been easy, but their love for each other had remained unshakeable.

Pam's question brought them back to reality. "Can you believe it's been over twenty years since we first met?" she asked, her voice tinged with nostalgia. She reached up to tuck a loose strand of hair behind her ear, revealing a pair of sparkling gold hoop earrings that caught the fluorescent lights in the courthouse. "It feels like just yesterday," Calvin admitted, gently squeezing Lena's hand. As they stood there, the frantic noise of the courthouse faded into the background, and all that mattered was their deep connection. Bringing everyone back to focus, Pam cleared her throat and looked around the bustling room. "Alright," she said determinedly. "Let's find a conference room and get to work. We don't have much time left."

Calvin's jaw was set with determination, his eyes glinting with unwavering resolve. He knew that no matter the rocky road ahead, he could count on his family and friends' unshakeable strength and support to guide him. They walked through bustling corridors, chatter and footsteps reverberating off the walls like a symphony. Amid it all, Calvin couldn't shake the memory of his mother, Rose, and her wise words from years ago: "Life will test you, my son, but always remember that love and faith are your greatest allies." The thought brought comfort and reassurance amidst the world's chaos around him.

Calvin's voice wavered slightly as he addressed Pam, his childhood friend and now his ally in this difficult time. "Hey, Pam," he said, trying to project confidence and strength despite his turmoil. Memories flooded back of happier times, like when they all went to the park together with Junior, who was just a baby then but so full of pure joy, laughing and clapping his hands. Pam's smile widened as she, too, recalled that day. "Of course, I remember," she replied fondly. "Back then, we never could have imagined where life would take us. But one thing remains unchanged – the love between you and Lena. It's something extraordinary."

Her words touched Calvin's heart, and he felt emotion build up. "Junior and Ryder are lucky to have parents like you," Pam added earnestly. Lena's eyes glistened with unshed tears as she nodded in agreement. "Thank you, Pam," she whispered, her voice filled with gratitude. As the three of them entered the conference room and closed the door behind them, shutting out the chaos of the courthouse, Calvin couldn't help but feel a renewed sense of hope. With Lena by his side, Pam fighting for him, and the unwavering love of his family in his heart, he knew there was nothing they couldn't face together. The air in the room seemed to shift as their bond strengthened, shielding them against whatever challenges lay ahead.

The bright sunlight filtered through the classroom windows, casting a warm, golden glow on the tiled floor. Junior couldn't help but feel a sense of contentment wash over him, the kind that came from making a difference in someone else's life. His gaze drifted to Carmen; her brow furrowed in concentration as she struggled with schoolwork. A familiar pang of empathy tugged at his heart, and he couldn't help but think of all the late nights spent with Ryder, hunched over books and laughing until their sides hurt. With a soft sigh, he made his way over to her desk, the sound of his sneakers squeaking against the linoleum tiles. "Hey, Carmen," he said gently, a flicker of concern crossing his features. "There's no need to look so sad when there's so much to be happy about. We haven't even seen a roach in school today." He couldn't help but grin, the memories of their shared laughter echoing in his mind. Carmen looked up at him, a small smile pulling at the corners of her mouth. She laughed softly, her pencil rolling across the desk as she shook her head. "You're right," she said. "Being cockroach-free is something to be happy about."

Junior's heart swelled with relief as he caught sight of her bright smile. He knew all too well the weight of sadness and how easily it could consume a person, and he was determined to be the kind of friend who could keep it at bay for Carmen. After all, Grandmother Rose had always taught them that Jesus watched over those in need, and Junior made it his mission to ensure Carmen never felt alone in her struggles. "See? Even in challenges, there's always something to be grateful for," he exclaimed, his warm brown eyes twinkling with determination. "Now, let's tackle this lesson together, alright?" The joy of overcoming challenges and finding reasons to be grateful filled the room, inspiring them both with a sense of triumph.

Carmen's voice overflowed with gratitude as she thanked Junior, her dear friend. Like a comforting blanket, the warmth of their bond radiated between them as they tackled the task at hand. Sunlight poured through the windows, casting a glowing beam over their work area. Laughter and chatter echoed in the room, creating an uplifting atmosphere of joy and camaraderie. As Junior helped Carmen, he couldn't help but feel he was fulfilling a higher purpose, doing what Jesus wanted him to do in that moment.

Carmen sighed deeply, her fingers twisting at the frayed edges of her math book. She gazed back at the pages filled with numbers and equations, feeling overwhelmed and alone. "Sometimes it gets tough," she confessed, "and I wish I had someone to help me more often." Her dark eyes shimmered with unshed tears as she looked up at Junior, who could see the weight of her struggles reflected in her gaze. "It's just me, my mom, and sometimes my dad when he's around," she explained, "and neither one likes helping me with homework."

Junior's heart ached as he remembered his nights spent huddled around the kitchen table with his family, trying to make sense of their lessons amidst the chaos of life on the west side of Chicago. He knew the frustration of feeling lost and alone in the struggle to understand schoolwork. But he also learned firsthand the power of friendship and support. And he was determined to offer that same support to Carmen, no matter what it took.

Gently, he reached out and placed a comforting hand on her shoulder. His warm and steady touch offered a sense of security amidst the chaos. His smile was genuine, the corners of his eyes crinkling as he spoke. "Hey," he said softly, "you don't have to go through this alone." Carmen's eyes scanned his face, searching for any hint of insincerity before finally settling on a small but grateful smile. "Thank you, Junior," she whispered, her voice catching with emotion. "That... that means more than you know." "I've got your back," he reassured her, gently squeezing her shoulder before returning to the task. Together, they would figure this out and face whatever challenges lay ahead.

Junior's heart ached as he listened to Carmen's words, her troubles settling heavily upon him like a thick fog. He could feel the weight of her worries and struggles, knowing all too well how easy it was to be consumed by them. As he gazed at the cracked linoleum floor, illuminated in golden hues by the afternoon sunlight, an idea sparked in his mind. His thoughts churned like gears, each clicking into place until he had a plan. Swallowing back any hesitation, Junior's voice rang out with newfound confidence. "Hey," he said, "What if you come to our house and study? I know we have a lot going on, but we can all learn together - me, you, and my sister Ryder. Would that be okay with you and your family?" The warmth of inspiration flooded him, and he couldn't help but feel hopeful for their shared future.

Carmen's eyes were hopeful, like the first twinkling stars appearing in the deepening twilight sky. Her dimples deepened, and her smile widened, revealing perfect teeth that glinted in the fading light. She nodded eagerly, her long dark hair cascading over her shoulders like a silk waterfall. "If it saves Dad from trying to help, I'm sure it'll be fine," she said, determination shining in her eyes. "But I'll ask him first since he was going to pick me up today." Junior's heart swelled with pride at her responsible attitude. "Great!" he exclaimed, his excitement bubbling like a freshly opened soda pop bottle.

He could already picture them all gathered around the kitchen table - Carmen, her father, and Ryder. Textbooks spread before them, pencils scratching against the paper as they worked through the problems together. It would be hectic, maybe even chaotic, but it would also be filled with warmth, love, laughter, and camaraderie. And let's not forget that Carmen was beautiful, too, making the scene all the more perfect in Junior's mind. "I can't wait to meet Ryder," Carmen said, her worries momentarily forgotten as she leaned back in her chair, the beginnings of a genuine smile playing at the edges of her lips. "Trust me, this will be fun," Junior replied, chuckling softly. He knew that Ryder would most likely be skeptical initially, but he also knew that deep down, she'd appreciate the opportunity to use her talents for a good cause.

"Thanks, Junior," Carmen's voice was soft and full of emotion, her eyes sparkling with gratitude. In moments like these, when kindness and compassion flourished, Junior saw life's beauty in its purest form. The sunbeams filtered through the windows, casting a warm, golden glow over the room and the other classmates. As Junior basked in the comforting embrace of their newfound friendship, he felt a sense of hope and determination for the future - one filled with understanding, support, and the unbreakable bonds of friendship.

As Calvin, Lena, and Pam peered into the courthouse's small, dimly lit conference room, a thick tension hung like a heavy fog. The musty scent of old books and stale coffee mixed with the sharp tang of fear made Calvin's skin prickle with unease. He caught Lena's wide-eyed gaze and gave her a reassuring smile before following Pam inside. The click of her heels on the dingy linoleum floor echoed through the room, adding to the sense of foreboding. She exuded an aura of authority and determination that demanded attention with every step. "Listen closely, Calvin and Lena," Pam began as she slammed her briefcase onto the table with a resounding thud. She pinned them both with an intense stare, her tone grave and unwavering. "I need you to understand that our most challenging charge is for distribution – due to the large amount they found in the bag."

Calvin's stomach was knotted with the thought of being torn from his family, their shared home, and the life they had painstakingly built. Lena's hand found his, firm grip anchoring him in the present. They exchanged a glance brimming with unspoken understanding: they would confront whatever came their way with the same resilience and faith that had seen them through past trials. Pam, their lawyer, regarded them with compassion, aware of the gravity of her words but also acknowledging the value of honesty. She paused, allowing the seriousness of the situation to sink in before continuing. 'I won't sugarcoat it - this is a serious charge. But I want you to know your bail will hold. We will fight this to the end, no matter what happens in that courtroom.' Calvin felt a warmth spread through his chest at Pam's words. It wasn't a promise of a trouble-free future but a pledge to stand by them through the storm that brought some solace. He looked at Lena, her grip on his hand unwavering, and saw the same determination in her eyes that Pam exuded. 'Thank you, Pam,' Lena whispered, her voice thick with emotion. 'We appreciate everything you're doing for us.' Pam nodded, a hint of a smile playing at the corners of her mouth. She knew they had an arduous journey ahead but also saw the strength and love that bound Calvin and Lena together. It was that very love, she believed, that would be their most potent weapon in the fight to come.

The courtroom buzzed with an undercurrent of hushed whispers, its heavy air pressing on Calvin like a leaden blanket. He stood alone, hands clammy and heart pounding in his chest, as the judge's gavel fell with a resounding crack. "Order in the court," the judge commanded, his voice like gravel on a dirt road. The room quieted to a suffocating silence. Calvin felt like drowning in a sea of legal jargon and stern faces. The judge's words washed over him, indistinct waves silenced by the weight of it all. His mind raced, thoughts splintered between images of imprisonment and loss – Rose, his mother, weeping alone in her kitchen, the kids growing up without their father's steady guidance.

The judge cleared his throat, his gaze fixed on Calvin, a bead of sweat rolling down the defendant's face. 'Mr. Steele,' he said sternly, tapping his gavel on the desk for emphasis. 'Do you understand the gravity of the accusations against you?' Calvin's hands trembled as he nodded, barely managing to respond. 'Yes, Your Honor.' The judge leaned forward, his eyes piercing. 'I advise you to take this matter very seriously. Please, take a seat.'

As they sat in the car after their long day in court, Calvin's heart raced, and his mind felt like a jumbled mess. The leather seats beneath him were worn from years of use, mirroring his fraying emotions. Lena reached out and took his trembling hand in hers, her touch warm and comforting. Her eyes bore into his, filled with worry. 'Calvin, are you okay?' she asked softly, concern etched into every line of her face. He could barely meet her gaze as he struggled to hold back tears. 'I don't know,' he finally admitted in a shaky voice. 'It was just so overwhelming in there.'

The dust motes danced in the sunlight that streamed through the windshield, starkly contrasting the heavy atmosphere inside the courtroom. Like a fish caught in a net, Calvin couldn't shake off the trapped feeling. But then he looked at Lena; her unwavering support gave him strength. She was always his rock, even when he felt he was falling apart. 'I felt so... lifeless,' he continued, his voice barely above a whisper. 'Like everything was out of my control.' Lena's hand tightened around his, radiating love and reassurance. 'You're not alone in this, Calvin,' she said firmly. 'I'll stand by you no matter what happens. God has a plan for us, even if we can't see it yet.' For a brief moment, he believed her words and let himself find solace in her unwavering faith in him—their shared faith in a higher power brought hope amid their turmoil.

Calvin's hands gripped the steering wheel tightly as he sat in the car with his wife, Lena. His forehead was creased with worry lines, and his jaw was clenched. He shook his head, hoping to dispel the dark cloud that seemed to have settled over him. "I'm glad the kids didn't see me like that today," he finally spoke up, his voice trembling slightly. Lena reached over and placed her hand on his, offering a comforting touch. "Me too, but you're only human, Calvin," she reminded him gently. "You're allowed to be scared. We all are. But we'll get through this together, trusting God's grace and guidance." The sound of passing cars and chattering pedestrians filled the air as they sat in the parking lot, providing a sense of normalcy amidst their current struggles. Calvin couldn't help but watch enviously as people strolled by, seemingly unburdened by the weight that pressed down on his chest.

Calvin's fingers tightened on the steering wheel as he pulled out of the courthouse parking lot. The weight of the day's events pressed down on him, but Lena's hand on his gave him a sense of strength and comfort. "Let's go get our kids," he said, determined to keep moving forward. "Together," she replied softly with a reassuring smile. As they drove home, the sky turned orange and pink, a reminder that there was still beauty amid their struggles. Calvin felt a glimmer of hope ignite, knowing that they could overcome anything with Lena by his side and their faith in God.

CHAPTER 26

T he sun set behind the school, casting a warm orange and pink glow over the busy schoolyard. The old brick building basked in the beauty of the vibrant sky. Excited shouts and laughter filled the air as students of all ages streamed out of the wide double doors, their backpacks bouncing on their shoulders. Calvin Steele navigated his car through the chaos, his grip tightening on the steering wheel as he searched for his children among the sea of faces. Beside him, his wife Lena leaned forward, her soft eyes scanning just as intently. "There they are," she said with a smile, pointing towards two familiar figures standing near the playground. Junior and Ryder, their son and daughter, stood next to their new friend - a cute little black girl with colorful braids tied neatly with ribbons. As soon as Junior spotted them, he dashed towards the car, his grin stretching from ear to ear as he bounded with youthful energy.

Junior's sneakers pounded against the pavement as he raced toward the car, his backpack bouncing against his back. He leaned down to catch his breath and peer into the open window, excitement and eagerness written all over his face. "Mom, Dad!" he exclaimed. "Is it okay if we bring Carmen home to study with us tonight? She called her father, who said it was fine with him as long as it's fine with you." Calvin's fingers drummed against the steering wheel as he exchanged a knowing look with Lena, his wife. Her lips quirked up in a smile as she nodded, and he turned back to Junior. "Yeah, as long as it's okay with her family," he said, feeling a swell of warmth in his chest growing at the thought of helping a young girl who seemed to be struggling just like his children once were. Calvin motioned towards Carmen and Ryder, who stood patiently by her side. "Let's meet your classmate."

Junior's grin stretched from ear to ear as he turned to his dad, giving him a tight hug. "Thanks, Dad," he exclaimed, relieved to see his parents' faces after a long day at school. He patted the car's top in gratitude before returning to join Ryder and Carmen. Calvin watched with pride as his son walked away, amazed at the kind-hearted young man he had raised. Junior always found the silver lining despite their family's challenges in every situation. Lena leaned closer to Calvin, her floral perfume blending with the warm scent of freshly baked cookies wafting from the bakery down the street. "Remember when we used to work on homework together? Those were simpler times," she said softly, a wistful gleam in her hazel eyes.

A fond smile played across Calvin's lips, and his mind flooded with memories of studying under the old oak tree in Lena's backyard. He watched as the three children, Junior, Ryder, and Carmen, ran towards the car, their laughter echoing through the colorful autumn leaves. "Looks like he found a cute one, just like his old man," Calvin chuckled, glancing at his wife beside him. She smiled back, her eyes filled with love and pride for their kids. The sound of backpacks bumping against each other filled the air as the trio climbed into the car, each vying for the best seat. Calvin basked in the warmth of the late afternoon sun as he started the engine, grateful for moments like these that reminded him of the power of love and faith. "Everyone buckled up?" he called out, receiving enthusiastic responses from the backseat. With a contented sigh, Calvin pulled away from the curb, knowing that no matter the challenges ahead for his family, they would face them with unwavering love and support. He stole one last glance at Lena before focusing on the road ahead, feeling blessed to have her by his side as they navigated life's journey together.

The children's laughter filled the air as they piled into the car. Calvin couldn't help but smile; it was a sight that would never grow old for him. He watched as Junior held the door open for Ryder and Carmen, a genuine act of chivalry that warmed his heart. "You should have seen Mr. Thompson's face when he tried to explain algebra?" Junior asked, grinning at his sister and Carmen. "He looked like he was trying to solve the world's hardest riddle." "I bet!" Ryder chimed in, her eyes sparkling with mischief. "Y'all should've seen Carmen," Junior added, nudging her playfully. "She was the only one who could figure it out. She saved the whole class!" "Aw, stop it," Carmen said, blushing and ducking her head, though she couldn't hide the proud smile across her face.

Calvin started the engine, the steady hum of the car bringing him back to reality. The courthouse had been weighing heavy on his mind all day, but seeing his children happy and carefree was enough to lift some of that burden. He glanced at Lena and noticed the same relief reflected in her eyes. As the car pulled away from the school, the sun dipped lower in the sky, casting long shadows across the streets of Chicago. Calvin's thoughts turned inward, reflecting on their challenges and the strength they drew from each other. He knew that, as long as they stood together, there was nothing they couldn't overcome. "Hey, Dad," Ryder piped up, breaking his reverie. "Can we stop for ice cream on the way home? So, once we finish all our homework, we can have it!" Calvin shared a glance with Lena, her smile warm and encouraging. "Alright, just this once," he agreed, the weight of the courthouse momentarily forgotten in the light of his family's love and laughter.

Later that evening, Biscuit stood at the door of his supervisor's office at the bus station, feeling like a deflated balloon. His face was sad and drawn, making him almost unrecognizable from the spirited man who had once charmed everyone in the bus station with his infectious laughter. "I'm not feeling well, Bill," he said softly, leaning against the doorframe as if it were the only thing holding him up. "Could I take some sick time? Maybe a week until I feel better, if that's okay?"

Bill, his supervisor, looked up from the papers on his desk and eyed Biscuit with concern. He noticed how Biscuit's hands trembled and the dark circles under his eyes that made him seem ten years older. "Of course," he said, rising from his chair and giving Biscuit a sympathetic pat on the shoulder. The gesture felt too light, like a father comforting a wounded child. "Take the time you need, and I hope you get better soon." "Thanks, Bill," Biscuit muttered before leaving the office, each step heavier than the last.

The engine of Biscuit's car hummed to life as he climbed into the driver's seat. He was consumed with finding Willow, a persistent itch he couldn't scratch, a nagging thought that wouldn't let him rest. He drove aimlessly through the streets of Chicago, his eyes scanning every street corner and alleyway for any sign of her familiar figure.

He walked through the neighborhoods, asking anyone who might have seen her, but to no avail. Each shrug of the shoulders and shake of the head only fueled his desperation further. The weight of his mistakes bore down on him like a lead blanket, dragging him deeper into despair. The realization that time was running out weighed heavily on his mind.

He gripped the steering wheel tightly and thought about Calvin and how much he had already lost due to his poor judgment. "Damn it, Willow," he whispered, frustration evident in his voice. "Where are you?" A sense of helplessness washed over him as he continued his search for the woman who held his heart in her hands.

The streets of Chicago seemed to mock him, offering no solace or answers to his racing mind. Willow's disappearance weighed heavily on him, her absence a constant reminder of his failures and the mounting danger she faced. As he drove through another unfamiliar neighborhood, Biscuit muttered under his breath, urging himself to find Willow before it was too late. But with each passing hour turning into days and days blending into an endless haze of worry and exhaustion, Biscuit couldn't shake the sinking feeling that perhaps he was already too late to fix the damage he had caused.

The bright neon lights of Biscuit's go-to cheeseburger joint flickered in the darkness, beckoning him forward with promises of comfort food and temporary escape from his troubles. The scent of sizzling beef and onions filled the air, mingling with the distant rumble of the elevated train tracks overhead. Leaning against his car for support, Biscuit could feel the weight of exhaustion pulling at every muscle in his lean frame, but he knew he couldn't rest until he found Willow and made things right.

The words escaped his lips in a mumble as he unwrapped the greasy burger with trembling hands. Each bite was a rush of flavor, the first authentic meal he'd had in days. His thoughts were a whirlwind, but he allowed himself to bask in the simple comfort of the food for a fleeting moment. Yet even as he chewed and savored each mouthful, the hairs on the back of his neck stood on end, an unexplainable sense of unease washing over him. A sudden chill ran down his spine, and he knew without looking that he wasn't alone. Slowly, hesitantly, he turned and saw her – Willow, standing just a few feet away with her smug smile, almost predatory. Her presence sent shivers down his spine and left an uneasy feeling settling in the pit of his stomach.

"So, I hear you've been trying to find me today," she said as she stood before him, her stance confident and unyielding. Her voice dripped with disdain, like poison from a serpent's fangs. Her eyes gleamed like a cat toying with its prey, and Biscuit felt caught in her web. His stomach tightened with anger as he clenched his teeth, trying to hold back his emotions. "Willow," he muttered through gritted teeth.

In one swift motion, he crumpled up the remains of his burger and tossed it onto the hood of his car. The wrapper hitting the metal echoed through the empty parking lot, adding to their tension. "First, I don't know why you did this to me or sent your new man Lenny looking for me either." Disgust and frustration swirled inside him like a tornado, threatening to tear him apart. He could feel his heart racing and his hands shaking as he tried to keep his composure before her.

But despite his anger, he couldn't help but notice how beautiful she looked in the dim light of the streetlamp above them. Her long hair cascaded down her back in waves, and her piercing eyes seemed to glow in the darkness. She was still the same woman he thought he had fallen in love with all those years ago, but now she had a hardness he didn't recognize.

Biscuit's thoughts were interrupted by Willow's cold laugh. "You think you can just walk away from me like that? After everything we've been through?" she taunted him.

He shook his head, trying to push down the memories that threatened to overwhelm him. "I had no choice," he said firmly.

Willow's expression softened slightly, but her eyes remained hard. "Well, I guess we'll just have to agree to disagree on that," she said with a haunting laugh before turning and slowly walking away, wanting to leave Biscuit alone with his thoughts and regrets.

Willow's laughter was like ice, cutting through the air between them. "Did you return the bag to Lenny?" she asked as she spun around to gaze again at Biscuit's face. Biscuit's mind raced, images of Calvin's family flashing before his eyes. He knew what was at stake, and he also knew that Willow held all the cards. He clenched his fists, his nails digging into his palms, trying to hold onto some semblance of control.

"Look," he said, his voice barely above a whisper. "I don't know what kind of game you're playing or what you want from me, but I ain't gonna let you hurt Calvin or his family any more than you already have." A flicker of something – was it surprise? – passed over Willow's face before her mask of indifference returned. Biscuit saw that moment of vulnerability, and for the first time since this nightmare began, he felt a glimmer of hope. Maybe, just maybe, he could find a way out of this tangled mess he'd gotten himself into.

Biscuit's throat tightened, and the words he wanted to say were trapped like a caged animal. His silence spoke volumes, and Willow seized the opportunity to twist the knife further. "Wow, so your guy Calvin got pinched for the product, and you still need to get Lenny back his stuff soon." Her hands clapped together sarcastically, echoing off the surrounding buildings' brick walls. "You know how I felt when you broke my heart."

She stepped closer, her breath warm against his face, her voice seductive and dangerous. "How does it feel now?" The scent of her perfume, once comforting, now felt like poison. Biscuit stepped back, grounding himself in the memory of Calvin's smile and his family's laughter. Those things mattered not this twisted game Willow was playing. "Doesn't matter how it feels," he said, his voice low and steady. "You won't break me."

A satisfied grin played at the corners of her lips as she turned to walk away, her heels clicking on the pavement like a ticking clock. "When faced with this dilemma and heartbreak, you must figure out your next move while life still moves around you," she called over her shoulder. "The good thing about you in the past is that you always seem to bounce back regardless. Now we're playing a chess game, and it's your move, baby."

Biscuit watched her walk away, her cruel laughter still ringing in his ears. He leaned against his car, the cold metal seeping through his clothes, grounding him in the present moment. Chess game, huh? Biscuit thought. The problem was that he only knew how to play checkers. The train rumbled overhead, drowning out the city's noise and shaking him from his thoughts. Biscuit's jaw clenched with determination as he got into his car and started the engine. It was time to make a move.

There's a warmth coming through the thin curtains in the Steele family's cozy kitchen as Calvin and Lena busied themselves with their morning routine. Calvin and Lena moved about in perfect synchronization, like a well-oiled machine. One would butter bread while the other filled lunch bags with fruits and snacks, their movements slow and deliberate. Yet, despite their practiced routine, an unspoken tension hung heavily in the air. Calvin's gaze drifted to the calendar hanging on the wall, its pages marked with important dates and reminders. His eyes lingered on the circled date in red – the upcoming court hearing that weighed heavily on his mind. Letting out a weary sigh, he ran a hand through his hair while Lena watched him with concern etched on her face.

"Calvin, we just have to have faith that everything will work out," she reassured him, her eyes steady and full of love. She set down the peanut butter knife and reached out to squeeze his hand, grounding him for a moment. Calvin nodded, knowing she was right. But despite his wife's comforting words, the weight on his chest still lingered. He thought about the tests of his faith throughout this ordeal but knew he couldn't let his family see his doubt. They needed him to be strong. The power of faith, a guiding light in their darkest hours, inspired him to keep going.

"Alright, kids! Time for school!" Calvin called out, and his voice filled with determination as it echoed through the tiny house. The children, Junior and Ryder, responded with a sense of readiness, their bags slung over their shoulders and a spark of anticipation in their eyes. "Morning, Dad!" Junior greeted them with a bright smile, his resilience shining through even in these challenging times. Always the silent strength, Ryder hugged her father tightly, her unspoken support a testament to her resilience in the face of their shared worries.

"Ready to go?" Calvin asked, grabbing the car keys and gesturing towards the door. The children nodded, and together, they piled into the family car. As Calvin pulled out of the driveway, he took a deep breath, steadying himself for the day ahead. He knew he had to be vital for his family, and he prayed that God would give him the strength to navigate the challenges that lay before them. For now, he focused on the simple joys of life – like driving his children to school and listening to their laughter as they joked in the backseat. In these moments, the Steele family's unity was palpable and a powerful source of connection and support for each member.

"Remember what Grandma Rose always says," Junior piped up from behind, sensing his father's internal struggle. "When life gets tough, we only need a little faith and love." The Steele family's shared faith, a legacy passed down through generations, was a beacon of hope and a steadfast anchor in their challenging times, filling them with hope and reassurance.

Calvin smiled, glancing at his son through the rearview mirror. "You're right, Junior. We'll get through this together." And with that, he tightened his grip on the steering wheel and drove on, his family's love and faith guiding them every step of the way. Over the next few days, the rhythm of life continued in the Steele household as Lena flipped pancakes on the stove, their sweet aroma filling the room. Calvin sat at the table, his fingers stained with newsprint as he absorbed the day's headlines.

"Hey, Carmen, do you need help with that math problem?" Ryder offered one afternoon, peering over her shoulder at the textbook. Her dark curls bounced with enthusiasm, and her eyes sparkled with intelligence.

Carmen glanced up, a mixture of relief and gratitude shining in her eyes. "Thanks, Ryder. You're good at this stuff." "Ryder's our math whiz," Calvin chimed in from the living room, where he sat reading the newspaper. A proud smile spread across his face as he looked up and met Lena's gaze. "She got that from her mama." "Sure did," Lena agreed, beaming with pride from the kitchen as she stirred a pot of savory stew. She wiped her hands on her apron, symbolizing her dedication to nurturing her family.

As Carmen observed the interactions between the Stee-les, she couldn't help but feel a warmth that enveloped her like a soft blanket, a sensation foreign yet comforting. The love and unity that pulsated within these walls were something she had never experienced before, and she cher-ished it, even if she knew it couldn't last forever. Each day, when her father pulled up outside the house to pick her up, he honed the horn impatiently. Carmen would sigh, reluctance in her every step as she gathered her things and said her goodbyes. "Thank you so much for letting me come over, Mr. and Mrs. Steele," she'd say with genuine gratitude, hugging them tightly.

"Anytime, sweetheart," Lena would reply, her eyes soft and understanding. She brushed a stray hair from Car-men's face, her touch gentle and motherly. As Carmen stepped out into the cool Chicago air and made her way to her father's car, she couldn't help but glance back at the warmth of the Steele home. The laughter and love that emanated from within starkly contrasted with the silent car rides with her father. She hesitated momentarily, feel-ing the wind's chill on her cheeks and the weight of her father's impatience in the air.

"See you tomorrow, Carmen!" Junior called out from the front porch, his voice full of optimism. He leaned against the railing, his eyes bright with the promise of another day filled with friendship and support. "See you tomorrow," Carmen whispered to herself, a small smile playing on her lips as she looked forward to another day surrounded by the love and support of the Steele family. The warmth from their home seemed to follow her even as she climbed into the cold car, and she knew that no matter what happened, the Steeles had left an indelible mark on her heart.

Carmen and her father drove away from Calvin's house, their car disappearing around the corner just as Biscuit pulled up in his vehicle. He parked discreetly a few places down, wanting to avoid drawing attention. The old Chevy he drove had seen better days, but it was reliable, much like Biscuit. "Calvin..." he whispered, gripping the steering wheel tightly as regret began to gnaw at him. He watched through half-closed eyes as Calvin's family gathered on the porch, their laughter carrying through the evening air. They were enjoying each other's company, seemingly oblivious to the storm brewing on the horizon, which Biscuit knew he was responsible for bringing.

Seeing them so happy and carefree only intensified the pain in Biscuit's heart. His guilt weighed heavily on him, leaving a lump in his throat that refused to budge. A thought crossed his mind - maybe it would be better if he disappeared from their lives for good. He glanced at the rearview mirror, considering the possibility of driving away and never looking back. But deep down, he knew he couldn't abandon them. His loyalty to Calvin and his family ran too deep despite his mistakes. This unwavering devotion had kept him by Calvin's side all these years, even as he stumbled and fell into one dire situation after another.

"Damn it," Biscuit muttered, wiping a hand across his face. "Forgive me, Calvin," Biscuit whispered, his voice barely audible as he gripped the steering wheel tighter. "I'll find a way to make this right."

With a heavy sigh, Biscuit turned the key in the ignition, reviving the engine with a grumble, and guided his car through the streets of Chicago, each twist and turn reflecting the turmoil in his heart.

CHAPTER 27

The city lights blurred together, a kaleidoscope of color that did little to ease his mind. Lost in thought, Biscuit found himself in the little village, parking outside a cozy Mexican restaurant, El Sol Naciente. The warm glow of its windows promised refuge from the chill of the night. He needed to clear his head, and the spicy scent of grilled meats and fresh tortillas wafting through the air was just the distraction he needed.

"Evening, sir," greeted the waiter as Biscuit entered, the small bell above the door tinkling with the announcement. "Table for one?" "Uh, yeah. Thanks," Biscuit replied, his eyes scanning the room for an empty seat. The waiter led him to a small table near the back, handing over a menu before disappearing into the kitchen. As Biscuit perused the menu, his gaze fell upon a familiar face across the room. Could it be? He blinked, trying to dispel the illusion, but the woman remained, her features unmistakable. He rose from his seat, feeling excitement and nervousness intertwine like ivy around his chest, and approached her table.

Biscuit's voice was barely above a whisper as he spoke, his tone filled with disbelief and wonder. "Pam, is that you?" he asked, eyes wide and searching. "I can't believe it's you." Pam looked up from her meal, and her brow furrowed in confusion until recognition dawned in her eyes. "Oh! Biscuit, hi!" she exclaimed, a genuine smile spreading across her face. "It's been ages since we've seen each other. What brings you here?" Biscuit took a deep breath, trying to calm the fluttering of his heart that had suddenly taken over. "Needed some fresh air," he replied, his words tumbling like marbles on a hardwood floor. "Just needed to clear my head."

He couldn't help but notice the weight in her expression and wondered what could be troubling her. Was their chance encounter more than just a coincidence? "Late dinner before heading home," Pam explained with a small smile that didn't quite reach her eyes. Biscuit knew that look all too well - something was weighing on her mind. "Mind if I join you?" he asked, his voice almost hesitant as he gestured towards the empty chair at her table. "We can catch up a little." Pam nodded, giving him a warm welcome as he took a seat. The restaurant buzzed with soft chatter and tinkling glasses, but for them, it felt like they were the only two people in the room. As they talked and laughed, Biscuit couldn't shake the feeling that this was precisely where he was meant to be at that moment.

As Biscuit settled into the worn seat, his mind raced with memories of their shared past. He couldn't help but admire Pam's strength and intelligence, which always made her stand out in their rough-and-tumble world. She was a bright light in a sea of darkness. And now, she could be the key to making things suitable for Calvin and his family—a chance at redemption for himself. "Listen, Pam," Biscuit began, his voice low and serious, like a low rumble of thunder in the distance. "There's something I gotta tell you about Calvin, about what's been going on lately."

"Go on," she urged, her eyes narrowing in concern as she leaned closer. The tension was thick between them, the weight of their shared history hanging in the air like a heavy cloud. "The whole situation with him and his family... It's my fault," Biscuit confessed, the words tasting bitter on his tongue like a mouthful of bile. "I messed up, Pam. And I need your help to fix it." His shoulders slumped as he admitted his mistake, feeling the weight of guilt pressing down on him like a physical force.

With a sense of finality, she swiftly tucked her papers into a worn leather briefcase, the familiar sound of the latch clicking shut. "Man, you haven't changed at all," Biscuit remarked, trying to lighten the mood. He rubbed his nose and feigned a sniffle, pretending to have caught a cold. "Luckily, I just got some sick time off from work," Pam replied with a hint of amusement as she raised an eyebrow. "Oh really? Well, I hope you feel better soon, Biscuit. Because my profession is in law." Biscuit hesitated for a moment, taken aback by this revelation. "Wait, you're a lawyer?" Pam nodded, her eyes narrowing slightly. "Yes, I am. And now I'm representing our friend Calvin for the mess you got him into." Her disappointment was palpable, heavy like the lingering smoke from the flickering candles on the table.

Biscuit felt his chest tighten, the all-too-familiar weight of guilt settling on him again. He could see the hurt in Pam's eyes, which only fueled his desire to set things right. The edges of her pretty irises shimmered with unshed tears, and her jaw was clenched tight. But first, he needed to know how much she knew about the situation. "So, what exactly do you know about what happened?" His voice trembled slightly as he spoke, betraying the turmoil.

"Enough to know that you played a part in it," she replied curtly, her gaze unwavering. Her words struck him like a slap in the face, revealing just how deep her pain and anger ran. "Listen, Pam. I never meant for any of this to happen." Biscuit's voice cracked with emotion as he pleaded for understanding. But Pam remained stoic, her icy tone cutting through the air like a sharp blade. "Your words mean very little right now," she said, her eyes narrowing into thin slits of disappointment and betrayal.

Biscuit's voice trembled with desperation as he pleaded, "But actions speak louder than words. Just allow me to prove myself and help fix the situation." The silence between them stretched like a taut rope, each second feeling more prolonged than the last. Pam took a deep breath, her gaze fixed on Biscuit, before finally speaking in a barely audible whisper. "Let's hope you're as dedicated to helping Calvin as you say you are because if you're not, you'll have more than guilt weighing on your conscience."

The dimly lit Mexican restaurant provided little comfort for Biscuit as he awaited Pam's response. The flickering candlelight cast shadows across the cracked and stained walls, adding to the moment's tension. In contrast, a single flame danced in Biscuit's eyes, reflecting his fear and determination.

Feeling speechless and vulnerable, Biscuit struggled to find the right words. His heart hammered against his chest, threatening to burst through his ribcage at any moment. Fighting against his dry throat, he stammered, "You were always brilliant." His gaze shifted away from her momentarily, taking in their surroundings—worn red vinyl seats and a chipped Formica table.

Pam's sharp sarcasm cut through the air as she scoffed at his mention of prayers. She leaned back in her chair, crossing her arms over her chest in a defensive gesture. A slight smirk played on her lips as she asked with raised eyebrows, "When was the last time you prayed, Biscuit?"

With a determined look, he met her gaze head-on. The sincerity in his expression was unmistakable as he spoke softly, "When I saw you across the room." His hand reached out for hers to no avail, a silent plea for forgiveness. "And I pray that you believe me when I apologize for everything." Biscuit hesitated, his fingers gripping tightly onto the edge of the wooden table. A weight seemed to settle on his shoulders as he prepared to share his story. Pam studied him momentarily, her dark eyes searching his face for any signs of deceit or manipulation. The faint sounds of laughter and clinking glasses from other tables faded into the background as they engaged in this silent battle of wills. Finally, she said, uncrossing her arms and sitting up straighter. Her voice held a hint of sternness but also a touch of understanding. "You know how much of a mess this is." Her words hung in the air, heavy with the weight of their complicated history.

The weight of responsibility bore down on Biscuit's shoulders, threatening to crush him. But he knew that with Pam by his side, they might have a chance at fixing the mess he had made. "Alright," Pam said, leaning in close and lowering her voice to a conspiratorial tone. "Tell me everything, and don't leave out a single detail." As Biscuit began to recount the events of that fateful day, the memories played out in his mind like a vivid movie reel. Each frame was etched with guilt and regret as he realized how much damage his recklessness had caused. He had been so caught up in his desires and needs that he had failed to consider the consequences of his actions. Now, it was up to him to make things right.

Biscuit felt a heavy weight lifted off his chest with each word he spoke. It was cathartic to confess his mistakes to someone he knew finally would listen without judgment. And as he looked into Pam's eyes, he saw a glimmer of hope – not just for Calvin and his family, but for himself. For the first time in a long while, Biscuit felt like there was a faint light at the end of the dark tunnel he had been stuck in. He knew the road to redemption would be tough and filled with challenges, but he also knew he couldn't turn back now. This was his chance to make things right and create a better future for himself and those around him.

CHAPTER 28

Biscuit's heart pounded against his chest like a relentless drum as he parked the car a few houses down from Calvin's place. His weary eyes took in the familiar sight of the home of his friends, the place where they had shared countless memories and inside jokes. He could almost hear the joyful laughter and easy camaraderie that used to fill their gatherings back when life was simpler, and responsibilities seemed far away. Guilt gnawed at him like a hungry dog, reminding him of all the missed opportunities and broken promises. But he needed to see them – to remind himself of what mattered. "Get it together, man," he muttered under his breath, trying to shake off the heavy weight on his shoulders. With a deep, steadying breath, he exited the car and approached the familiar front door, steeling himself for whatever awaited him. The windows glowed with warm light, beckoning him closer with each step.

The cozy living room was the epitome of studiousness. Junior, Ryder, and Carmen sat around the dining table, surrounded by textbooks and notebooks scattered haphazardly like fallen leaves after a storm. The room was filled with a soft hum of concentration and the occasional rustle of paper or scratch of a pen against a page. Despite the quiet ambiance, each student was deeply immersed in their work. With his father's kind eyes and easy smile, Junior chewed on the end of his pencil while pondering an algebra problem. Ryder, her dark hair tied back in a tight ponytail, scribbled furiously in her notebook, her brow furrowed in determination. Carmen bit her lip as she traced the lines of a sketch in her art book, her whole being consumed by the creation before her. "Jesus, give me strength," Biscuit whispered as he hesitated momentarily before raising his hand to knock on the door.

Calvin stood tall by the window, his eyes tracing the familiar streets of his neighborhood with the bustling sounds of children playing and birds chirping filled the air, mixing with the occasional car passing by. His gaze drifted over to his children and Carmen, their young minds working on a project at the kitchen table. A surge of pride swelled within him, warming his chest like a cup of hot cocoa on a cold winter's day. The sunlight streaming through the window illuminated their faces, adding an extra glow to their bright expressions.

The sudden knock at the door broke through Calvin's reverie, causing him to startle slightly. Curious, he glanced at his family before going to the door. With a turn of the key, he swung it open to reveal Biscuit standing there, looking like a wilted flower under the weight of his frown. The once vibrant colors in Biscuit's hair had faded, and his usual smile was replaced with a somber expression.

Calvin couldn't help but feel sympathy for his friend as he invited him into their home. Biscuit's presence added a layer of tension to the cozy atmosphere, like a dark cloud looming over their usually cheerful space. But even now, Calvin couldn't deny his warmth towards his family and their simple yet fulfilling life together.

Calvin's eyes met Biscuit's with a firmness that brooked no argument. "Lord have mercy," he said, his voice low and commanding. He lifted one eyebrow in a silent challenge. "If you want to come into this house, leave that frown outside where it belongs. We don't do that here." Biscuit hesitated as he took in the warm, inviting interior of the Steele home. It starkly contrasted the dark cloud that seemed to follow him everywhere since his mistakes had been brought to light. But despite his reservations, he stepped forward, willing himself to leave his worries behind and embrace the love and forgiveness waiting for him inside.

With a gentle hand on his brother's shoulder, Calvin urged Biscuit forward. He could sense his inner turmoil and wanted to offer some comfort. "Remember, you're always welcome here," he said reassuringly. Biscuit felt a shaky breath escape his lips as he finally managed to summon a weak smile, grateful for the support of his brother. With a nod from Calvin, Biscuit followed him into the warm embrace of the Steele home. The familiar sights and smells enveloped him, chasing away some of the shadows clouding his mind. "Thanks, Cal," he murmured gratefully as he crossed the threshold. The warmth of the house seemed to seep into his very bones, offering solace from the cold and harsh world outside. With its profound healing power, the Steele home was a sanctuary for his troubled soul, where wounds could be mended and hearts could be restored.

As he stepped into the room, Biscuit was immediately struck by the warm and loving atmosphere that enveloped him. He couldn't help but compare it to the emptiness in his heart for too long. Now, as he stood before Calvin and his family, he knew that he had to make amends - not just for them, but also for himself. "Let's catch up, my friend," Calvin said gently, leading Biscuit toward the cozy living room. The soft glow of candlelight and the comforting home scent filled the air. "We've got a lot to talk about." Biscuit nodded, barely able to speak as he followed Calvin into the room, feeling a sense of warmth and belonging for the first time in a long while.

As the mouth-watering scent of freshly popped popcorn wafted through the air, Biscuit's eyes followed the source to Lena, who busied herself in the kitchen. She was a vision of warmth and love, her nurturing nature evident in every movement. The soft hum of a gospel tune escaped her lips as she stirred the kernels around in the pan, her face a picture of contentment. "Hey there, Biscuit!" Lena called out, her brown eyes sparkling with genuine happiness at his presence. "Do you want some popcorn too?" Biscuit shifted uncomfortably on his feet, not wanting to impose on the family's hospitality. He glanced around the room, taking in the well-worn furniture and the numerous framed photographs adorning the walls – each telling a story of the life they shared and the love that bound them together. In Lena's actions, he felt the family's genuine care and warmth, a love that made him feel welcomed and truly a part of their family.

"Uh, it does smell good," he admitted, noting how his stomach growled in agreement. It had been a while since he had a home-cooked meal or shared food with friends. "Ha, that means he wants some, too!" Junior and Ryder chimed in almost simultaneously, their voices filled with the innocent joy only youth could bring. Laughter filled the room as Lena made more popcorn for everyone to share, the sound wrapping around Biscuit like a warm embrace.

As he gingerly sat on the slightly worn couch, Biscuit couldn't help but envy the Steele family. They had something precious that he had lost sight of – the ability to find joy in the simplest things and share it with others. Even though times were tough, they still held onto their faith and each other, weathering the storms that life threw at them. "Here you go, Biscuit. I hope you like it," Lena said, handing him a generous bowl of popcorn. The warmth of her smile made him feel like he truly belonged, even if just for a moment. "Thank you, Lena," he replied, his voice thick with emotion. He hoped she couldn't see the tears threatening to spill from his eyes – tears born from gratitude and regret.

As they all settled in to enjoy their popcorn and each other's company, Biscuit realized that while the road to redemption would be long and arduous, every small gesture of kindness and understanding would be a beacon of light, guiding him back home. Biscuit took a moment to absorb the scene before him: Lena's hands dusted with popcorn salt, Junior and Ryder playfully fighting over a throw pillow, and Carmen intently focused on her math problems. It was like looking at a Norman Rockwell painting brought to life - everything he once had and now yearned for.

"Who's the little cutie doing homework with Junior and Ryder?" Biscuit asked Calvin, nodding towards Carmen. The laughter from earlier still lingered in the air, blending with the scent of buttery popcorn. Calvin followed his gaze and smiled. "That's their friend Carmen from school. They all like hanging out together; it's cool with us since it's here. Plus, her father is usually busy, and she's an only child." "Seems like a smart girl," Biscuit said, observing Carmen print her answers in neat, precise handwriting. He couldn't help but feel a sense of pride for the Steele family – they were making a difference in this young girl's life, just as they were trying to do for him.

As the evening wore on, they finished watching a TV show. The lively banter that accompanied the program slowly faded, replaced by the gentle lull of sleep. Junior, Ryder, and Carmen had all fallen asleep, their heads resting on each other's shoulders. The occasional soft snore punctuated their peaceful slumber, the sound adding to the room's warmth.

Biscuit glanced at Calvin and Lena, who were also beginning to show signs of fatigue. The weight of their daily struggles seemed to settle on their shoulders, yet they still managed to emanate love and strength. Just as he was about to suggest it was time for him to leave, another knock at the door startled them all. "Who could that be at this hour?" Lena whispered, her brow furrowed in concern. "Let me get it," Biscuit said, sensing the fatigue in the room. He rose to his feet and approached the door with caution, his heart pounding like a wild drumbeat in his chest. "Stay alert, Biscuit," he thought as he gripped the doorknob, praying that whoever was on the other side wouldn't trouble this precious family.

"Who is it?" Biscuit asked cautiously, his voice muffled by the closed door. The person on the other side replied in a similarly muffled tone, "It's Carmen's father." Carmen's eyes flew open at the recognition of her father's voice. She hastily scrambled to gather her belongings, her movements a whirlwind of urgency. Biscuit could sense the tension in Carmen, which started to rise as he turned the doorknob. The door creaked open, revealing Lenny – the drug dealer hunting Biscuit down – standing before him. Biscuit's heart lurched in his chest, and he fought to keep his expression neutral. Lenny assessed the situation with a predator's gaze, his eyes darting between Biscuit and the others in the room.

"Hey," Lenny spoke softly to Carmen, his voice a warm caress against her skin as she gathered her belongings. "Take all the time you need, baby girl." His words held a gentle strength, but an underlying hardness made Biscuit's skin crawl. With a forced smile, Lenny reached out a hand to Biscuit, introducing himself with a firm grip. "I'm Lenny, and you?" Biscuit couldn't help but wipe his damp palms on his pants before taking Lenny's hand, trying to keep his nerves in check as he replied, "I'm Biscuit." Lenny raised an eyebrow and said, "You might want to dry your hands off more. They're still quite moist. And are these your lovely children?"

Biscuit's gaze flickered between Junior and Ryder's peacefully sleeping and the storm brewing inside him. His chest felt tight, and his mind raced with conflicting emotions as he struggled to find the right words. With each passing moment in Lenny's presence, Biscuit felt threatened to unravel the fragile peace he had found with the Steele family tonight. "Uh, no, they're Calvin's kids," Biscuit finally replied, nodding towards Calvin and Lena, who stood nearby, watching the interaction with concern etched on their faces. "I'm just a friend." "Ah, I see," Lenny said, his piercing eyes lingering on Biscuit for a moment longer.

Calvin stepped forward, his posture exuding strength and pride. The warmth of their home and their love was palpable, standing in stark contrast to the unease from Lenny's presence. "Those are our children," Calvin announced, his voice steady and robust. "I'm Calvin, and that's my wife, Lena. We love having your daughter over." He turned to glance apologetically at Lenny before adding with a genuine smile, "Sorry we didn't hear your car horn earlier."

Lenny waved off the apology with a dismissive flick, his fingers long and thin like spider legs. His eyes narrowed as they locked onto Biscuit, their corners crinkling slightly as his lips twisted into a grin that sent shivers down his spine. The aura around him felt dark and intense, like a brewing storm. "It's about time I got a chance to meet this fine family," Lenny drawled in a low, gravelly voice, the words dripping with thinly veiled malice. "I told Carmen the other day I wanted to see what was happening here." Biscuit struggled to maintain eye contact, feeling trapped beneath the weight of Lenny's gaze. He wondered if Calvin could sense the danger lurking behind those narrowed eyes.

"Okay, I'm ready to go, Daddy," Carmen said quietly, her voice small and timid compared to Lenny's booming presence. Her face was confused as she stood beside her father, clutching her books tightly in her arms as if they were shields. The innocence in her voice tugged at Biscuit's heartstrings, fueling his determination to protect her and the Steeles from harm. His heart raced, a sense of vulnerability creeping over him. "Nice to meet you all," Lenny said with a false sense of deference, extending his hand for everyone to shake one last time – lingering a moment longer on Biscuit's as he added, "You still need that towel."

Biscuit swallowed hard, forcing a weak smile as Lenny released his grip. Then, turning to Calvin with an almost unnatural charm, Lenny warmly shook his hand. "You're a good man, and thanks for everything you guys do for Carmen." As he spoke, something was unsettling about how Lenny's gaze swept over the group with intense scrutiny, as if he were searching for any sign of weakness or vulnerability he could exploit. The hairs on the back of Biscuit's neck stood up as he watched Lenny walk away, leaving a lingering sense of unease in his wake.

As the door creaked shut behind Lenny and Carmen, Biscuit's thoughts were consumed by the danger he had unknowingly brought into his friends' cozy home. The weight of guilt pressed down on him as he tried to devise a plan to make things right, but the path forward seemed dark and uncertain. Shadows danced along the walls, casting ominous shapes in the dimly lit room. Biscuit couldn't shake the feeling that something could jump out from the shadows at any moment and attack. He desperately hoped to find a way to fix his mistake before it was too late.

The door closing reverberated through the room, sending shivers down Biscuit's spine. He couldn't shake off the feeling that Lenny had more on his mind than pleasantries. His instincts were screaming at him, warning of danger lurking beneath the surface of their seemingly innocent meeting. "Stay alert, y'all," Biscuit whispered as he watched Lenny and Carmen reach the parked car. The evening air was cool, but it did little to alleviate the burning sensation in the pit of his stomach. It felt like a blazing fire raging within him, fueled by uncertainty and unease.

Biscuit's voice trembled as he called over his shoulder, his hands fidgeting nervously. "Hey, Lena, can I get some water? I'm feelin' a bit parched." Lena's comforting reply did little to ease the uneasiness clawing at Biscuit's insides. She quickly fetched a glass of water for him, her eyes reflecting concern and understanding as she handed it over. Biscuit mumbled a quick thanks before gulping down the cool liquid in one long gulp, hoping to steady himself. His gaze remained fixed on the window, watching Lenny and Carmen enter the car and prepare to drive off. As they pulled away, Biscuit knew that he had to stay vigilant for the sake of his friends and their family. The weight of responsibility settled heavily onto his shoulders as he braced himself for what was to come.

Biscuit's heart raced like a caged animal as the car pulled away from the curb. His eyes burned holes into Lenny's back, tracking every movement with a mix of fear and determination. When Lenny's gaze met his through the rearview mirror, Biscuit felt like he had been punched in the gut. The intensity of Lenny's stare was suffocating, leaving him gasping for air. Suddenly, Lenny raised a hand and slowly molded it into the shape of a gun, pointing directly at Biscuit. A frigid chill shot down his spine, a stark reminder of the high-stakes game he had recklessly stumbled into. He couldn't shake the image of his friends and their families being caught in the crossfire of his mistakes, a weight that threatened to crush him with guilt and regret.

"Damn," Biscuit whispered as his heart raced as he watched Lenny's car speed away, leaving behind dust and tension. He couldn't shake the feeling that something needed to be fixed, but he wasn't sure how. His hand was still clenched around the empty glass, a physical manifestation of his inner turmoil. As he gazed into the night, he felt a sense of duty towards Calvin, Lena, and their children - he had to make things right for them, no matter the consequences. But with each passing moment, it seemed like time was slipping away from him.

The silence that followed Lenny's departure only amplified Biscuit's racing thoughts and pounding heartbeat. Calvin's voice suddenly cut through the tension, jarring Biscuit back to reality. "Are you okay, Biscuit?" he asked, genuine concern etched on his face. Biscuit smiled, not wanting to burden his friend with the truth. "Yeah, just a long day," he replied unconvincingly. The weight of his lie hung heavy in his throat as he realized that this was far from over. "I should probably head home now. Work tomorrow." The words tasted bitter on his tongue as he turned to leave, unsure of what the next day would bring.

Lena, who had been watching the exchange with curiosity and concern, nodded in understanding. "You're always welcome here, Biscuit. Take care of yourself." "Thanks," he mumbled, feeling the weight of guilt settle on his shoulders as he turned towards the door. The warm, loving atmosphere of the Steele home beckoned him to stay, but he knew he couldn't risk putting them in any more danger.

As he stepped outside, the cool Chicago night air wrapped around him like a damp blanket, chilling him to the bone. He glanced back at the house, taking in the soft glow of the lights spilling from the windows – a beacon of hope amidst the darkness threatening to consume him. I can't let anything happen to them, he thought desperately, his heart heavy with worry. But what am I supposed to do now?

His mind raced with possibilities, each one more terrifying than the last. Should he go to the police and tell them everything? Or would that only put his friends in greater danger? As he walked down the dimly lit street, his footsteps echoing in the stillness, Biscuit couldn't help but feel like a pawn in a deadly chess game – and he was running out of moves.

"Lord help me," he whispered silently, begging for guidance. "I just want to keep them safe." The wind howled around him, carrying his words away into the night. With a heavy sigh, Biscuit climbed into his car, the cold metal of the door handle biting into his skin as if to remind him of the harsh reality he now faced. "Godspeed, my friend," he murmured, starting the engine and pulling away from the curb. As the Steele family's home disappeared from view, Biscuit knew that he would do whatever it took to protect them – no matter the cost. And with that determination fueling him, he set off into the night, uncertain of what lay ahead but resolved to face it head-on for the sake of his friends, their family, and his redemption.

CHAPTER 29

The thick, foggy morning air clung like a damp, heavy curtain to the bus windows. Biscuit gripped the worn steering wheel with both hands as he navigated the familiar street of Pulaski Road. The steady hum of the engine offered a comforting melody as he drove, his gaze flickering nervously from side to side in search of any sign of Lenny. But the sidewalks were empty, save for a few early risers to work or school. "Morning, Biscuit!" called out Mrs. Thompson, her voice cracking slightly with age. She shuffled up the steps, clutching her battered purse and bulging shopping bag tightly. "How's your day goin'?"

"Can't complain, Mrs. T," Biscuit replied with a forced smile, his mind still preoccupied with his fruitless search for Lenny. He needed to shake off his unease and focus on the people who depended on him daily. After all, bus operating was his job - shuttling folks to and fro, ensuring they arrived at their destinations safely and on time. Biscuit glanced at the rearview mirror, watching the usual passengers enter their familiar seats. "Hey there, Biscuit!" greeted Mr. Jenkins, a burly man in his mid-forties with a pleasant grin plastered across his face. He slapped a few coins into the fare box with a loud clang. "You got any good stories for us today?" The lively chatter of the passengers filled the bus as Biscuit eased back onto his route of Pulaski Road and ventured into the bustling cityscape ahead.

Biscuit chuckled, a twinkle in his eye as he remembered the tall tales he'd spin on slow days to keep the passengers entertained. "Not today, Mr. J. Just tryin' to steer clear of trouble, ya know?" His hands gripped the steering wheel tightly with anxiety. "Trouble?" Mr. Jenkins raised an eyebrow, concern flickering across his weathered face. A cloud of worry seemed to hang over him like a shroud. "You ain't caught up in somethin', are ya?" The question hung heavily in the air, echoing through Biscuit's mind and stirring up memories he'd rather forget. "Nah, nothin' like that," Biscuit assured him, forcing a lighthearted laugh that felt hollow in his chest. His mind wandered to Lenny and the tangled web they were both trapped in, a knot of fear forming in his stomach.

"Alright then," Mr. Jenkins said, still eyeing him with concern. "You take care of yourself, Biscuit." "Will do, Mr. J," Biscuit nodded, offering another tight-lipped smile. As the bus continued down Pulaski Road, Biscuit tried to focus on the steady hum of the engine and the chatter of his passengers. But his mind was restless, plagued by thoughts of Lenny. There had to be a way out, a path to redemption. But where to begin? "Next stop, Pulaski and Madison!" Biscuit called out, his voice wavering slightly. He couldn't let fear control him; he had to keep moving forward, one step at a time.

The loud, rumbling engine of Biscuit's bus echoed through the west side of Chicago as it chugged toward its final stop. The faint voices and whispers of conversation from his passengers mingled with the distant laughter and shouts of children playing in the streets, creating a brief moment of serenity amidst the chaos that swirled inside him. As the bus neared its last destination, Biscuit glanced in his rearview mirror and noticed a few men seated at the back. He cleared his throat, projecting his voice with authority. "Gentlemen, we've reached the end of the line. You'll need to exit now. The bus will change direction in approximately 15 minutes." His words were met with grumbles and protests, but Biscuit remained firm as he pulled up to the curb and opened the doors for them to depart into the city streets.

One of the men, who introduced himself as Turk, approached the front of the bus and sat nearby. His dark, piercing eyes bore into Biscuit like daggers as he asked casually, "So, do you have the bag? That's all we want to know." The air around Biscuit seemed to grow heavier, making it difficult for him to take a deep breath. He could feel the weight of Turk's gaze bearing down on him. Stammering nervously, he replied, "I-I don't have it yet. I need a little more time." He glanced at Turk, silently pleading for understanding. But Turk's expression remained cold and unrelenting. Leaning in close, his low voice dripped with menace. "Time is running out, Biscuit." The words hung like a noose tightening around Biscuit's neck, filled with an ominous sense of danger and urgency.

Biscuit's heart pounded against his chest, a rapid drumbeat of fear and uncertainty. His mind raced through a thousand different scenarios, searching for a way to fix this mess and protect Calvin and his family. But the weight of the situation pressed down on him like a ton of bricks, suffocating any glimmer of hope. "Please," Biscuit pleaded, desperation seeping into every word. "Just give me a little more time. I promise I'll make things right." The air in the bus grew thick with tension as Turk studied Biscuit, his dark eyes unyielding. Every muscle in Biscuit's body tensed, waiting for Turk's response. Then, with a nod so slight it was almost invisible, Turk stood up and motioned for the other men to follow him to the back of the bus. Biscuit's breath caught in his throat as he watched them move, unsure of their subsequent actions.

Biscuit released a shaky breath, relief washing over him like a wave crashing against the shore. He'd bought some precious time but couldn't afford to waste a single second of it. Whatever it took, he vowed to set things right – not just for himself but for Calvin and his family. They deserved far better than being caught in his mistakes' dangerous crossfire. As the bus sputtered back to life, Biscuit focused on the winding road ahead, every stop bringing him one step closer to redemption or ruin.

The steering wheel shook beneath Biscuit's trembling fingers, sweat beading on his forehead as Turk's unreadable gaze lingered in the bus's rearview mirror. The silence within the vehicle seemed to stretch out endlessly, each passing moment feeling like an eternity. Finally, Turk gave a slow nod, and relief washed over Biscuit. But it did little to quiet the storm of emotions raging inside him.

"Fine," Turk muttered with a cold detachment that sent shivers down Biscuit's spine. "But don't think we'll be so understanding next time." Biscuit could only whisper a grateful "thank you," barely audible above the engine's hum. There was no turning back now – too much was at stake for him to falter or fail again.

Turk's intense gaze burned into Biscuit's back as he sat behind the bus's steering wheel. Biscuit's heart raced as he closed his eyes, desperately praying for a way out of this precarious situation. The rumbling engine beneath him roared to life, its reassuring hum offering a slight sense of stability amidst the chaos. "Dear Lord, please show me a way out," Biscuit pleaded in his mind as he gripped the steering wheel with determination. With a deep breath, he bravely steered the bus back onto the bustling streets of Chicago, determined to find a solution to their dilemma.

The passengers shuffled in and out, their faces a blur to Biscuit as he struggled to focus on anything other than the looming danger lurking just beyond the bus doors. His heart pounded in his chest, knowing that he couldn't outrun his past for much longer. Every person who boarded the bus seemed like a possible threat, a reminder of the mistakes and wrongdoings that had led him here. "Calvin... I'm so sorry, man," he thought, guilt gnawing at the edges of his mind like a persistent rat. He had always prided himself on being a loyal friend, but now, when it mattered most, he felt he was failing everyone he cared about. His mistakes hung heavy on his shoulders, making them ache with regret.

With each stop, the weight of his choices grew heavier on Biscuit's shoulders. The burden weighed down on him like a sack of bricks dragging behind him as he trudged forward. He could feel the weight pressing against his chest, making it hard to breathe. But he was determined to make things right – no matter the cost. As the bus rumbled down Pulaski Road, Biscuit closed his eyes and prayed silently to the Lord above. "Promise me you'll take care of them," he whispered, feeling tears prick at his eyes. "Please, don't let my mistakes hurt Calvin or his family." The sound of traffic and chatter outside provided a slight distraction from the heavy thoughts weighing on Biscuit's mind. Each passing car and person seemed to blur together in his mind as he focused on his prayers, seeking guidance and forgiveness for his choices.

As the streetlights flickered on above him, casting their orange glow across the darkening city, Biscuit knew in his heart that he had to face whatever consequences lay ahead. The hum of the empty bus filled Biscuit's ears, providing an eerie soundtrack to the scene unfolding before him. The dim overhead lights cast long shadows across the worn linoleum floor, heightening Biscuit's sense of unease.

"Look, Turk," he stammered, his voice barely audible above the engine's low rumble. "Whenever I get the bag, I only give it to Lenny, period."

Turk's laughter boomed through the bus, bouncing off the metal walls and amplifying the sound tenfold. But his eyes had no humor; they were cold, dark, and unyielding. "Can't y'all see? I ain't got no choice," Biscuit thought, his hands shaking on the steering wheel. "I gotta protect Calvin and his family – even if it means my life." "If you want to play the game that way, Biscuit," Turk said, a wicked grin spreading across his face, "you must be willing to live or die with the results."

Biscuit could feel the sweat beads forming on his fore-head, trickling down his face like tiny rivers of fear. He wiped them away, leaving a damp smear on his skin. "I heard you were a little moist," Turk smirked, his gaze never leaving Biscuit's face. With a nod, he motioned for the rest of his crew to follow him toward the exit. "Lord, help me," Biscuit prayed silently, clutching the steering wheel until his knuckles popped. "Give me strength to stand up to these men – and to make things right again."

Before stepping off the bus, Turk turned back to face Biscuit one last time. "I'll deliver this one message, but if you see me again, there will be no talking. Do we under-stand each other?" Biscuit swallowed hard, the lump in his throat making breathing difficult. He nodded once, feeling the weight of Turk's words settle heavily on his shoulders. "Understood," he whispered, his voice barely audible above the engine's steady hum. "I understand."

As the bus doors hissed closed behind Turk and his crew, Biscuit allowed himself a moment of silence to gather his thoughts. The bus was empty now – save for the ghosts of his past mistakes, which seemed to linger like a heavy fog. "Calvin... I won't let you down again," he vowed, his grip tightening on the steering wheel as the bus lurched back into motion. "No matter what it takes." And with that, Biscuit steered the bus into the darkness, determined to face whatever lay ahead – for himself and for those he loved.

As promised, the sun crept above the horizon the following day, bathing the city in a golden glow. Long shadows stretched across the sidewalk, and the faint hum of traffic rose as people commenced their daily routines. The air was fantastic, with a hint of dew clinging to the leaves of the trees lining the street. Biscuit sat on the cold concrete steps outside Pam's law firm, his bus driver uniform rumpled and weary from the previous day's work. He rubbed his hands together for warmth, eyes scanning the street for any sign of Pam.

A sudden clicking echoed through the empty streets, growing louder and more rhythmic as it approached. Biscuit looked up just in time to see Pam round the corner, her hair pulled back into a neat bun and her face obscured by oversized sunglasses. She walked purposefully, her heels striking the pavement like a metronome and her leather briefcase swinging at her side. "Morning, Pam," Biscuit called out hesitantly, unsure if she would appreciate his presence at such an early hour.

Pam stopped in her tracks and peered over the rim of her sunglasses, surprise etched across her face. "Biscuit? What are you doing here?" she asked, her voice both curious and concerned. "Waiting for you," he replied, his voice heavy with exhaustion. He rose from the steps, feeling a stiffness in his joints from sitting in one place for too long. "How long have you been sitting here?" Pam asked, stepping closer and studying his haggard appearance.

"Ever since I got off work yesterday," Biscuit admitted, averting his gaze. "I want to try and fix this situation, and with your brilliance, we can figure something out." Pam sighed, her initial shock giving way to compassion. She could see the desperation in Biscuit's eyes, the worry lines etched deep into his face. She knew he wouldn't have come to her if it wasn't serious, and she couldn't turn her back on him now. "Alright," she said finally, unlocking the front door to the law firm. "We'll talk inside."

As they entered the dimly lit office, Biscuit felt a momentary relief. At least he had taken the first step towards fixing his mistakes. And with Pam by his side, there was a glimmer of hope that things might work out.

Pam eyed Biscuit's unkempt appearance, her hand disappearing into the depths of her purse. She emerged with a stick of gum and handed it to him. "Chew this, and let's fix that first and foremost," she said, her eyes twinkling with a hint of amusement. "Thanks," Biscuit mumbled, unwrapping the gum and popping it into his mouth. The minty flavor refreshed his parched tongue, a small comfort amidst the chaos he found himself in. He could sense Pam's genuine concern for him, and it steeled his resolve to come clean about the situation with the drug dealer's bag.

The faint scent of old leather and yesterday's coffee hung in the air as Pam closed the door to her office behind them—warm sunlight filtered through the blinds, casting tiger-like stripes across the room. Biscuit's fingers drummed nervously on his thighs, leaving temporary indentations on the worn fabric of his bus driver uniform. He glanced around at the framed diplomas and awards that adorned the walls, reminders of the brilliance and dedication that had earned Pam her place as one of Chicago's most respected attorneys.

Biscuit's hands twitched nervously, his fingers fiddling with an empty gum wrapper as he began to speak. "Alright, so here's the thing," he started, his voice shaky and uncertain. "You know, my ex-Willow. She got mixed up in something bad, and now Calvin and his family are caught in the crossfire." Pam could see the worry etched on Biscuit's face and urged him to continue, her voice soft but firm. As he began to repeat the same story as he had at the restaurant, Pam hoped for something new. But she could sense a new urgency in Biscuit's demeanor. He felt Pam gave him a sense of comfort, and with a deep breath, he continued. "Willow left this bag in my car. I didn't know what was inside, but it turned out it wasn't anything good. Calvin and his family are in danger because of my mistake." The weight of guilt pressed down on Biscuit as he spoke, his voice trembling with emotion. Yet, despite his fear and regret, seeing the fire and determination in Pam's eyes gave him a glimmer of hope for a solution to his problems.

Pam's determined expression shone like a ray of sunlight as she sat behind her desk, ready to tackle the mess before her. Her eyes were sharp and focused, her brow furrowed with determination. "Alright, Biscuit," she said firmly, "I'll do everything I can to help you fix this mess. But you have to promise me one thing." Biscuit could feel the weight of her words hanging in the air, and he braced himself for what she would ask. "Anything," he replied without hesitation, his voice rough and sincere. Pam took a deep breath before continuing, her tone serious and unwavering. "From now on, you stay out of trouble. No more getting involved with people like Lenny and Willow. You owe it to yourself, and you owe it to Calvin and his family." Her words were filled with both concern and a stern sense of responsibility. Biscuit knew she was right; he needed to change his ways to make amends for his mistakes. He nodded solemnly, grateful to have found an ally in this mess. "You're right, Pam," he said quietly, his gaze dropping to the floor. "I swear I'll do better." Pam leaned forward on her desk, her concerned expression softening as she spoke again. "Look, Biscuit, I want to help you."

As Biscuit's eyes met Pam's, she couldn't help but notice a newfound determination and resolve. It was a look she hadn't seen since their childhood days. His jaw was set firmly, and every facial muscle tensed with sincerity. "More than anything, Pam," Biscuit's voice rang out strong and unwavering. She could feel the weight of his words, knowing they came from the deepest parts of his heart. This was a different Biscuit, a man ready to take control of his life and make amends for his past.

"Calvin and his family have the best lawyer they could ever have. The only problem is me, so I have to do my part. I just needed someone as smart as you to hear me out." Pam studied him momentarily, her eyes searching his face for any hint of doubt or deception. But all she found was the raw, unwavering determination of a man who finally decided to take control of his destiny. With a nod, she placed her hand on the stack of legal documents before her, her understanding and support unwavering.

"Alright," she said softly, her fingers brushing against the crisp pages. "Let's get to work." Pam's eyes lingered on Biscuit's face, taking in the desperation and conviction that shone from the depths of his tired eyes. She could see the weight of his mistakes resting on his shoulders, threatening to crush him if he didn't find a way to make things right.

"Alright, Biscuit," Pam said softly, rising from her chair. The soft rustle of her skirt filled the room as she walked around her desk, maintaining eye contact with him. The air between them seemed to crackle with an energy that spoke of their childhood bond, now renewed by their shared determination. They were in this together, a united front against the challenges ahead.

"...But don't get any funny ideas, okay?" Pam said, stopping before him, her voice gentle and laced with care. "Let me hug you." Biscuit's eyebrows shot up in surprise, but he didn't protest. As Pam's arms encircled him, he felt the warmth of her embrace seep into his bones, providing a flicker of excitement and hope. He closed his eyes and leaned into the hug, feeling the strength of her slender form against his own.

"Wow, you feel so good," Biscuit murmured into her shoulder, his heart racing with newfound confidence. Her perfume, a delicate mix of jasmine and vanilla, filled his senses and made him feel much more alive than he had in years.

Pam chuckled and playfully pushed him away, a smirk dancing on her lips as she met his gaze. "I told you, no funny ideas." "Who said anything funny?" Biscuit replied, his eyes shining with sincerity. "I'm as serious as I've ever been." As they stood there, the air between them heavy with unspoken words and lingering promises, Biscuit felt a surge of hope. He knew they would find a way to fix this mess together. And for the first time in a long while, he embraced the hope that danced within his heart.

"Good," Pam said, her warm smile illuminating the dimly lit office. "Now go and do what you need to do. We'll get through this together." "Thank you, Pam," Biscuit replied, his voice thick with gratitude. He rose from the worn leather chair, feeling the weight of his bus driver's uniform as it clung to him like a second skin. "Take care of yourself, alright?" she added, concern furrowing her brow. "Of course," Biscuit assured her, nodding with determination.

As he turned to leave, the sunlight filtering through the blinds cast a lattice of golden beams on the polished wooden floor. The soft hum of the city outside beckoned him, reminding him of the urgency of the task ahead. "Hey, Pam?" Biscuit paused, his hand resting on the brass doorknob. "I won't let you down."

Pam's eyes met his, the glimmer of hope within them mingling with something more - an unspoken understanding that bound them together in their shared purpose. "I know you won't," she said gently. With one last nod, Biscuit stepped out of the office and into the bustling world beyond. The door shut behind him, sealing away the sanctuary he had found within Pam's presence. As he descended the stone steps leading to the sidewalk, his heart felt lighter than it had been in a long time.

The streets of Chicago teemed with life, people bustling about their daily routines. The scent of fresh bread wafted from a nearby bakery, mingling with the heady aroma of gasoline and the distant clamor of construction. Biscuit took a deep breath, steeling himself for what lay ahead.

"Alright," Biscuit muttered, his thoughts racing as he navigated the crowded streets.

He could feel the lingering warmth of Pam's embrace, a reminder of the strength he knew they would share in their fight to right the wrongs that threatened to derail the lives of those they held dear. She believed in him, and it was up to Biscuit to prove himself worthy of that trust.

"Time to make things right," he whispered, his stride purposeful as he disappeared into the city crowd, determined to face whatever challenges lay ahead.

CHAPTER 30

A warm, golden light filtered through the parted curtains of Calvin Steele's bedroom, casting a soft glow on the walls. He sat on the edge of his bed, his hands clasped tightly together as if in prayer. The looming court date felt like a storm cloud hanging over his mind, weighing down his thoughts like an anchor. Despite his efforts to remain hopeful, the uncertainty gnawed at him relentlessly, leaving a bitter taste in his mouth and a knot in his stomach. The room was filled with tense energy, as if it, too, could sense the weight of what lay ahead for Calvin.

With a soft creak, the door swung open, and Lena glided into the room, her presence offering immediate solace to his troubled heart. She was dressed in a pastel-colored house dress, the light fabric swaying with each graceful step. Her dark hair was pulled back into a neat bun, emphasizing her warm brown eyes filled with love and concern. A gentle smile graced her lips as she crossed the room, the delicate scent of lavender trailing behind her. She settled beside her husband on the bed, her hand reaching out to gently caress his shoulder. The room seemed to brighten with her presence, and he couldn't help but feel a sense of peace wash over him in her company.

With a soft, soothing murmur, Lena spoke to Calvin, her voice like a gentle stream flowing over smooth stones. "Calvin," she said, her eyes filled with love and pride, "I just wanted you to know how truly proud I am of you. You have been our rock, our pillar of strength through all our trials." Calvin's heart swelled with emotion at her words, and he reached for the worn Bible that always rested atop their bedside table. Its leather cover was cracked with age, but its pages held the wisdom and guidance he sought in times of need.

As he opened it, the familiar scent of old paper and ink filled his senses, bringing comfort and calm. He held the book before them like a shield against their troubles. "God will always be with us, Lena," he declared confidently. "So, who should we fear?" The room seemed to fill with a warm, golden light as they both took solace in the unshakeable faith that bound them together.

Lena's deep brown eyes sparkled with pride and warmth as she gazed at her beloved husband. Her lips curved into a tender smile, and she gently kissed his forehead. "No one," she whispered, her voice filled with conviction and adoration. "We have each other, and we have our faith. That's all we need." As they sat together on the soft couch, the morning sun began to rise, its golden rays stretching out to illuminate every corner of the room.

The shadows that had clung to the walls retreated, leaving only brightness and warmth in their wake. At that moment, Calvin felt a renewed sense of courage and hope to wash over him. With Lena by his side and their family's unwavering love and support, he knew he could face any challenge ahead. Their home was filled with an undeniable feeling of peace and contentment, like a cozy oasis in a chaotic world.

Lena stood at the stove, the soft melody of a hymn escaping her lips as she expertly flipped another piece of French toast in the skillet. The sweet aroma of cinnamon and vanilla hung in the air, like a warm hug that enveloped Calvin as he entered the room. His eyes immediately sought Lena's form, admiring how her hair fell in gentle waves around her face and how she moved with grace and ease. "Morning," he greeted, his voice still husky from sleep. He leaned against the counter, content to watch as Lena coated each slice of bread in the rich egg mixture before placing it carefully into the skillet. "Good morning," Lena replied radiantly, her hazel eyes sparkling with warmth and love. "I thought I'd make your favorite today." "French toast?" Calvin's grin widened at the mention of his favorite breakfast dish, and he couldn't help but feel grateful for Lena's thoughtfulness. The familiar scent of cinnamon and vanilla helped ease some of the tension in his chest, reminding him that no matter their challenges, he always had Lena by his side to make things better.

The sweet sound of Lena's laughter filled the room, her eyes sparkling with love and affection as she gazed at Calvin. "That's my job, isn't it?" she teased playfully. She skillfully arranged slices of perfectly cooked French toast on a plate and handed it to Calvin, who eagerly accepted it with a smile. "Now sit down and eat before it gets cold," she instructed, gesturing towards the cozy breakfast table set for the family. As he took his seat, Calvin couldn't help but feel a sense of peace and contentment wash over him as he savored each delicious bite. He glanced up at Lena, who was preparing plates for their two children, Junior and Ryder. There was a quiet moment between them, a tender understanding of the challenges they would soon face together as a family. "Thank you," Calvin murmured sincerely, his gratitude evident in his tone. "Always," Lena whispered back, her soft gaze meeting his with unwavering love and support.

Junior's heart raced as he fidgeted nervously, his fingers clenching and unclenching. He looked up at his parents with pleading eyes, knowing what he was about to ask was important. "Mom, Dad, before we go to the prayer service, I must do something. It's crucial," Junior said, his voice trembling slightly with anxiety. Calvin and Lena exchanged puzzled glances, but seeing the determination and sincerity in their son's eyes, they nodded their agreement. "Of course, son. Just make it quick. We don't want to keep the congregation waiting," Calvin said in his deep voice, trying to hide his nerves for Junior's sake.

Junior breathed a sigh of relief as he replied, "Thank you. It shouldn't take too long." Relief washed over him like an incredible wave, soothing his nerves and doubts. With quick steps, he entered the dining room, his heart drumming a steady rhythm in his chest. His mind raced with thoughts of what lay ahead - conversations, laughter, and memories that would linger long after the night had ended. He pulled out the fine China, saved for special occasions, each plate gleaming with intricate designs and delicate edges. Silverware glinted in the soft light, carefully arranged next to crystal glasses that shimmered with every movement. These were all symbols of love and respect in their household, and Junior couldn't help but feel proud of what he was about to do.

His family watched in silent curiosity as he meticulously set the table, their expressions mixing confusion and anticipation. But Junior was focused on one person in particular - his father, who stood in the doorway with a furrowed brow. Their eyes locked and held briefly before Junior finally spoke, his voice steady and clear. "See, Dad, I'm preparing a place for you," he said, gesturing to the seat at the head of the table. "That's what Jesus did for us, and I want to do it for you." A sense of peace washed over him as he spoke these words, knowing that this small act of service was just a glimpse of his immense love for his father. But he couldn't end there, not when there was still so much to say. "And this won't be your last supper," he added, determination shining. Many more meals would be shared around this table, with stories to tell and moments to cherish. And Junior couldn't wait for all that was yet to come.

The room fell into a peaceful stillness, the only sound being the steady ticking of the grandfather clock in the hallway. Calvin's eyes welled up with tears as he gazed at his son, overwhelmed by the depth of love and devotion in this simple gesture. Lena's hand flew to her heart, her eyes glistening with unshed tears. "Junior," Calvin choked out, his voice thick with emotion. "This means more to me than you could imagine." Junior's face lit up in a shy smile as he spoke softly, "Grandma Rose always told us about Jesus' unwavering love and sacrifice. I just wanted to show you that I understand and appreciate everything you do for our family." His words hung in the air, filled with sincerity and gratitude. The room seemed to glow with warmth and love, enveloping them all in its embrace.

Lena's arms enveloped her son in a warm, secure embrace that could chase away fear or doubt. She held him tight, feeling his small frame pressed against her own, and whispered words of love and pride into his ear. They stood together, golden rays casting a warm glow over their faces. The Steele family shared a profound bond in that moment - strengthened by their unwavering faith, unconditional love, and resilience from facing life's challenges together. Time seemed to stand still as they basked in the beauty of their bond, which would carry them through any storm coming their way.

Later that morning, the Steele family filed into their local church, seeking solace and support from their close-knit community. The scent of freshly cut grass and blooming flowers filled the air, adding serenity to the already peaceful morning. As they looked around the church, familiar faces smiled warmly at them, offering words of comfort and support. The congregation settled into their seats, the murmurs of conversation filling the peaceful sanctuary. All eyes turned to the Pastor as he stood at the pulpit, commanding attention. His deep voice echoed through the hall as he began to speak.

"Today, we gather not only to worship and give thanks but also to pray for one of our own," he said solemnly. "Our dear brother, Calvin Steele, is facing a difficult trial. But we know our Lord is our refuge and strength, and He will provide for those who trust Him." The church erupted in murmurs of agreement and encouragement as hands clapped Calvin's shoulders, offering their support. "Let us bow our heads in prayer," the Pastor continued, his voice steady and robust. "Heavenly Father, we ask that You be with Calvin during this challenging time. We humbly request Your strength, wisdom, and courage to guide him through whatever may come. Protect his family and grant them peace during these uncertain days ahead." The room fell into a reverent silence as all bowed their heads in prayer, seeking guidance and comfort from above.

As the congregation continued with bowed their heads and lifted their voices in prayer, Calvin could feel the weight of their love and faith surrounding him. He closed his eyes and let the soothing hum of their united prayers wash over him like a gentle wave on a shore. The fear that had gripped his heart began to dissipate, replaced by a newfound sense of hope and determination. "Thank you, Lord," he whispered, his words carried away by the rustle of pages turning and the soft murmur of voices. He could almost feel the warm touch of God's hand on his shoulder as he spoke.

The sanctuary was now quiet, the echoes of prayer and hymns still lingering. Calvin knelt at the altar, his head bowed as he poured his heart into God. The stained-glass windows cast a soft, kaleidoscopic light over him, each color representing a different facet of faith and love. The light danced on the wooden pews and polished floors, creating a serene atmosphere within the holy space. "Lord," he whispered, "I know this trial is just another test You've placed before me. But I ask that You watch over my family and everyone else struggling even more than I am." His words hung in the air momentarily before joining the prayers that filled the room.

His voice was barely a whisper, yet it held within its timbre the weight of his deepest fears, fervent hopes, and unyielding love for those gathered around him. His hands grasped the altar's edge with desperate insistence as if trying to find purchase in the unknown. Lena stood nearby, her eyes fixed on Calvin with pride and concern. Junior and Ryder flanked her, expressions mirroring their mother's unwavering support. Rose appeared by their side, her countenance etched with wisdom and an unshakeable faith. She motioned for the Pastor to join them, beckoning with a serene grace that seemed to radiate from within her very being.

Rose's voice was soft yet authoritative as she turned to the Pastor. "Pastor, would you please pray over Calvin?" The Pastor nodded, his kind eyes filled with understanding and compassion as he approached Calvin's kneeling figure. His hands stretched out in a gesture of blessing, radiating warmth and strength.

"Calvin, my son," the Pastor began, his voice gentle yet powerful. "We are all here to support you in every way we can." He touched Calvin's shoulder, a silent comfort that spoke volumes. "The Lord is always by your side, guiding you through life's storms."

"Thank you, Pastor," Calvin replied, lifting his head to meet the Pastor's gaze. At that moment, he felt a sense of peace, like a warm embrace from above.

"May the Lord continue to strengthen and protect you, Calvin," the Pastor prayed, his voice carrying the weight of years of experience and faith. "May His grace and mercy envelop you and your family during these trying times."

Calvin felt tears prickle at the corner of his eyes as he listened to the heartfelt words, knowing that they were not just for him but for his entire family.

"Thank you, Pastor," Calvin whispered, his voice choked with emotion. The congregation had gathered around him, their faces a tapestry of love and support. In that moment, he could feel their collective strength coursing through him, bolstering his resolve to face the challenges ahead.

With closed eyes and a heart full of gratitude, Calvin prayed silently to God. "Lord," he whispered, "thank you for this community that has become my family. Thank you for Your unwavering presence in our lives. With You by our side, we can overcome anything." As the Pastor finished his prayer, the congregation murmured their amens, their voices filling the sanctuary with love and faith. Calvin felt a surge of gratitude and determination, knowing that he was not alone in this trial. With his family's love and his community's unwavering support, he was ready to face whatever lay ahead.

CHAPTER 31

Biscuit's breath caught in his throat as he peered through the diner's fogged-up window, his eyes fixated on Lenny sitting in a booth with a woman and a young girl. But to Biscuit's surprise, this was not Willow - the woman had long, chestnut hair cascading down her back, and her laughter filled the air like music. With a deep breath, Biscuit pushed open the door and was hit with a warm blast of air as he walked inside. The familiar smell of coffee and freshly baked bread greeted him, along with the sound of dishes rattling in the kitchen. "Hey, Lenny," Biscuit said cautiously, trying to hide his shock as he approached their table. The small bell above the door tinkled cheerfully, but the mood at the table suddenly became tense.

Lenny's deep voice cut through the quiet chatter of the small, cozy diner. "Ah, Biscuit," he said, sipping his steaming coffee. "Let me introduce you to Nicki, Carmen's mother." Nicki smiled warmly and extended her hand towards Biscuit, who briefly shook it before turning toward Lenny. His face was solemn as he leaned in close. "Hey, little lady," Biscuit said with a small smile, his gaze shifting to Carmen. She blushed and returned the smile shyly before focusing on her plate of fluffy pancakes. The aroma of maple syrup filled the air, making Biscuit's stomach growl. "Can we, uh, talk in private for a second?" Biscuit asked Lenny urgently, his tone low and urgent. Lenny nodded understandingly and slid out of the booth. "Nicki, excuse us for a moment," he said, leading Biscuit to a quieter corner of the diner.

The two men made their way to the far end of the rustic diner, the clinking of silverware and hushed conversations fading into the background. Biscuit leaned against the peeling wall, gripping his hair in frustration as he tried to collect his thoughts.

"Look, Lenny," Biscuit began, his words tumbling out in a desperate rush. "I gotta apologize from the bottom of my heart. I had no clue Willow would set me up like that, and I didn't know she was dealing with you until it was too late." Lenny regarded him with narrowed eyes and lips pressed together in a thin line as he listened intently.

"That woman played both of us, man," Biscuit continued, his voice cracking with emotion. "She used me, and I never meant to drag you into this mess." "Damn," Lenny muttered, rubbing his temples as if trying to ease a headache. "I knew something was off about her. But it's done now." Biscuit could see the storm of emotions brewing in Lenny's eyes – anger at being manipulated, confusion over Willow's true motives, and perhaps even a hint of relief at finally understanding the situation.

Carmen's eyes shone like polished jewels as she approached Lenny and Biscuit, her innocent curiosity radiating from every pore. With a gentle tug of Lenny's sleeve, she spoke in a soft voice that was tinged with longing, "Daddy, can we attend church today? I want to pray for Junior and Ryder's father, Mr. Steele, so he doesn't go to jail." Lenny couldn't resist the pleading look on his daughter's face and found himself wrestling with his thoughts. He knew attending church would mean facing the people who were a part of what had caused so much pain for their families, but he also didn't want to deny Carmen's heartfelt request.

After a moment of deep contemplation, he finally relented. "Okay, sweetheart. Give me a few minutes, and we'll go." Carmen's radiant smile lit up as she skipped away, leaving Lenny and Biscuit in a profound silence. "Even your daughter loves them because they're great people," Biscuit remarked, watching with admiration as Carmen returned to Nicki's side. The warmth of love and forgiveness filled the air, making it seem like even the birds were singing hymns of hope and redemption.

Lenny's steps reverberated in the charged silence as he approached Biscuit, his jaw tightly clenched and his voice a low, intense murmur. The palpable tension between them crackled in the air, thick and heavy like an impending storm. "Whatever happens," Lenny's words were sharp and pointed, "it better not affect me and my people." Biscuit hesitated, trying to decipher the weight of Lenny's words and the gravity of his situation. He could see the unwavering determination in Lenny's eyes, a sign that he wouldn't back down easily. "So, what are we going to do?" Biscuit finally asked, breaking the tense silence. Lenny's reply was cold and final. "There's no 'we,'" he stated, his tone icy and resolute. "I'm going to take my daughter to this church," he gestured towards the nearby building with a clenched fist, "which she has her heart set on doing today." With that, Lenny turned and walked away, leaving Biscuit alone to ponder their conversation and what it meant for them. As he stood there in the moment's stillness, Biscuit couldn't help but feel a sense of foreboding settled over him like a dark shroud.

As the congregation exited the church, each person basked in the radiant beauty from above with renewed hope and strength. Amidst the sea of faces, Carmen's eyes locked onto Calvin's familiar figure, and she made a bee-line towards him. "Mr. Steele!" she called out, her voice ringing with youthful enthusiasm. "Can I hug you too?" Calvin looked around and saw Lenny and Nicki watching from a distance. Their approving gazes met his, giving him a sense of comfort and support. Grateful for their presence, Calvin smiled warmly at Carmen, his smile a beacon of kindness in the crowd. "Thank you, sweetheart." He bent down to embrace her, feeling the warmth and innocence of her petite body envelop him. Junior joined the hug moments later with his innocent smile, adding to their pure joy and love.

As the tender moment unfolded, Rose leaned closer to Ryder and whispered. She couldn't help but feel a sense of nostalgia as she watched the interaction between the two young children. "Is that the little girl from school?" she asked, her voice filled with a warm admiration that echoed through the air, her admiration palpable.

Ryder nodded, her eyes shining with admiration as well. "Yeah, that's Carmen," she confirmed. The scene in front of them reminded her of her parents' love story, which had also started at church – a place where love, faith, and hope all came together.

Rose continued with a wistful smile. "You know, this is how your parents started, too. They met at church just like this." She gestured towards the group of children playing together.

Ryder looked at her parents and then at Carmen, Lenny, and Nicki. She could see the threads of forgiveness and understanding beginning to weave through these broken relationships, guided by the power of love and faith. The air was thick with a sense of hope and possibility.

At that moment, Ryder couldn't help but believe things would turn out alright for everyone involved. Love honestly had a way of healing even the most broken of bonds.

A gentle breeze rustled through the leaves of the towering oak tree, its branches swaying like dancers in a slow waltz. The stone steps leading up to the courthouse were bathed in dappled sunlight, casting scattered shadows on the ground. Calvin Steele couldn't help but feel the weight of the situation bearing down on him as he adjusted his tie for what felt like the hundredth time.

He looked over at his family standing beside him - Lena, a pillar of strength with her head held high; Rose, her unwavering faith shining through her bright eyes; Junior, trying to hold back his tears and look brave for his father; and Ryder, always fiercely protective no matter the circumstance.

"Are you ready?" Calvin asked, his voice wavering slightly. "Ready as we'll ever be," Lena replied with a determined nod. Rose squeezed Calvin's hand tightly, silently channeling her love and support, a testament to their unwavering determination.

The congregation from their church followed closely behind them, a sea of familiar faces offering prayers and words of encouragement. Pam emerged from the crowd as they approached the courthouse's imposing front doors, her confident stride cutting through the tense atmosphere like a knife. "Calvin, Lena, don't you worry," she said, her voice firm and reassuring. "I know it's a lot to go through, but hang in there. We're going to fight this thing together." Their unity was powerful, binding them together in this challenging time.

"Thank you, Pam," Calvin replied, his heart swelling with gratitude for their tenacious lawyer who had become more than just a legal advocate but a true friend and ally during this difficult time.

Just then, Biscuit appeared, his usually cheerful face marred with deep lines of concern. His movements were quick and urgent as he closed the distance between himself, Calvin, and Lena. Without hesitation, he pulled them both into a tight embrace, squeezing them like a lifeline. "I'm so sorry, Cal," he whispered, his voice heavy with remorse. "I never wanted any of this to happen." "It's okay," Calvin replied, trying to mask the unease gnawing at his heart. The familiar feeling of uncertainty settled over him like a dark cloud, threatening to consume him entirely.

Pam's eyes rested on Biscuit, her face a mask of indecipherable emotions. Calvin sensed the need for secrecy and quickly ushered her to the side, whispering something in her ear. Pam's eyebrows shot up in surprise, a hint of uncertainty flickering across her features before she composed herself and gave Calvin a look that said, "I'll reserve judgment for now." With a determined click of her heels against the hard concrete, she strode towards the looming courthouse doors, beckoning Calvin and his family to follow her into the unknown world. Their footsteps echoed through the empty halls, adding to the tension and anticipation hanging in the air.

With trembling hearts and united spirits, "Lord, please guide us through this," Rose prayed quietly, Junior echoing her sentiments as they approached the towering courthouse. Ryder felt a surge of determination as she squeezed her fists tight, mentally bracing herself for future battles. Hand in hand, they entered the grand building, fortified by the unwavering support of their loved ones, their unshakable faith, and their tight-knit community. With every step, they drew strength from each other and the knowledge that they were not alone in this daunting journey. Together, they would face whatever lay ahead with unwavering courage and resilience.

Calvin took a deep breath and sank onto the unforgiving wooden bench in the courtroom. His heart was pounding so hard it felt like it might burst out of his chest at any moment. He looked around, frantically searching for the familiar faces of his family amidst the sea of strangers. The harsh fluorescent lights beat down on him, making his skin feel clammy and uncomfortable.

He gripped the edge of the bench tightly, trying to steady himself physically and emotionally. With a quiet plea to the heavens for strength, he closed his eyes and took a few deep breaths. When he opened them again, the world seemed to be spinning uncontrollably around him, everything a blur except for the comforting presence of his family. The muted murmur of hushed conversations blended into an incomprehensible hum in Calvin's ears.

His body tensed as he waited for his name, each second feeling like an eternity. But then he caught sight of Biscuit, sitting near the front of the courtroom with a look of unwavering support on their face. Their eyes met briefly, and Calvin drew strength from that connection. With renewed determination, he straightened his back and lifted his chin, ready to face whatever challenges ahead with courage and dignity, inspiring those around him with his unwavering resolve.

Just then, Willow glided silently into the room, her presence as delicate and elusive as a shadow cast over the proceedings. She chose a seat in the corner, far from the watchful eyes of the Steeles, almost blending into the shadows herself. Biscuit's gaze flickered towards her, his expression darkening with suspicion. But she seemed unaware of his piercing stare – or perhaps she didn't care. Nicki sat with her daughter Carmen, their faces etched with worry and concern for the Steele family's future. Like two statues carved out of stone, they held each other for support in this moment of uncertainty and fear, unaware of the enigmatic figure in their midst.

Pam's gentle voice cut through the heavy haze that clouded Calvin's mind like a beacon of light in the darkness. Concern filled her eyes as she gazed at him, taking in the beads of sweat that dotted his forehead and the faint tremble in his hands. "Calvin, would you like some water?" Her words were soft and soothing, offering a lifeline amid chaos. "Yes, please," he managed to say through parched lips. Pam reached for a plastic cup, filling it with cool water from a nearby pitcher. The crisp scent of lemons drifted up as she handed the cup to Calvin, who held it with trembling hands. He took a slow, deliberate sip, savoring the refreshing taste as it quenched his dry throat.

As the cool water continued to trickle down his parched throat, Calvin's whispered, "Thank you, Pam," was filled with layers of gratitude, not only for the life-saving liquid but for the unwavering support of his family, who stood by him like a beacon of hope in this stormy sea. Soft and loving, Pam's voice responded, "Calvin, you know we're always here for you." Her words brought tears to his eyes and a lump to his throat. The love and reassurance in her voice were like a soothing balm to his troubled soul, comforting him in this time of uncertainty.

As he looked into the loving eyes of his family, Calvin felt a renewed sense of determination. They were his anchor, his rock amid this tumultuous journey. He may have been afraid, but these were the people who mattered most – and for them, he would face whatever challenges lay ahead with courage and faith.

The dull hum of anticipation hung heavily in the courtroom as Calvin Steele sat stiffly on the hard wooden bench. He could feel the weight of each beat of his heart reverberating throughout his chest, a constant reminder of what was at stake today. The atmosphere was tense and uncertain as if fate had turned up the volume at this pivotal moment. The low murmurings of conversations and shuffling papers seemed to fill the room, overwhelming Calvin's senses as he braced himself for what was to come.

The heavy, wooden door to the judge's chambers groaned as it eased open on its hinges. With a sense of anticipation and unease, Calvin held his breath as the judge made her grand entrance. Her black robe flowed behind her, imbuing her with an air of power and authority. As she settled into her chair at the front of the room, the lawyers approached the bench with measured steps and solemn and determined expressions. "Order in the court!" boomed the bailiff, demanding attention from all present. The once bustling room now fell silent, every eye fixed on the legal proceedings unfolding before them.

Calvin felt a cold sweat slowly trickle down his brow as he stared at the daunting jury box. Rows of individual chairs, each facing him with stern judgment and impartiality, would soon be filled by strangers who knew nothing about him or what he meant to this community. His heart raced with anxiety as he wondered whether they would see beyond the charges brought against him to the man he indeed was - a loving husband, devoted father, and dedicated city bus driver. Would they see the years of hard work and sacrifice he had put into serving his community, or would they only see a faceless defendant? The weight of it all pressed down on Calvin's shoulders as he waited for the proceedings to begin.

As the courtroom began to fill with people, Calvin's eyes scanned the faces of his neighbors on the hard benches. Some he recognized from the neighborhood, others were strangers to him. But they were all here for him, their eyes filled with compassion and concern. Would the jury see that love and support, or would it even matter? Calvin's gaze shifted to where Lena sat with Rose, their hands clasped together tightly. The warm glow of their inter-twined fingers symbolized their unbreakable bond.

Lena's eyes met his, a mixture of fear and unwaver-ing faith shining within them. He knew she was pray-ing for him; her strong connection to Jesus had always been a guiding light during challenging times. Next to her, Rose remained stoic and steady, her years of experience providing her with a quiet resilience that matched her sharp wit. "Your Honor," the prosecutor began, breaking through the heavy silence, "the state is prepared to present its case." The judge's voice echoed throughout the room as he replied solemnly, "Very well."

As the trial began, Calvin closed his eyes briefly, savoring the warmth and strength of God's presence in the courtroom. He could feel it surrounding him and his family like a protective embrace, filling him with peace and determination. With one last glance at Lena and Rose, their unwavering love and unshakable faith shining from their eyes, he steeled himself to face whatever lay ahead. The judge's gavel fell with a resounding thud, breaking the hushed murmurs in the room as all eyes turned to Calvin - the lone defendant standing tall amidst a sea of doubt and accusation. But he was not alone - for in that moment, he knew God was with him every step of the way, guiding him towards justice and redemption.

The atmosphere in the courtroom was charged with anticipation, the air thick with tension. Every person in the room seemed to be holding their breath as they waited for the trial to begin. Calvin Steele sat rigidly in his seat, his dark eyes fixed on the prosecutor across the room. The man was known for being sharp and formidable, and today was no exception. He was impeccably dressed and exuded confidence as he surveyed the room like a hawk.

"Impressive as always, Mr. Steele," the prosecutor addressed Calvin directly. "But I feel your charm won't get you very far in this case." Calvin's heart pounded as he mentally prepared to face this man who could potentially ruin his life.

"Will the prosecution please call their first witness?" the judge's voice boomed through the chamber, signaling the start of the trial.

"Your Honor, I would like to call Officer Harrison to the stand," the prosecutor announced confidently. Calvin couldn't help but feel a twinge of fear at the sight of the police officer taking his place on the stand. This was the very man who found the drugs in his car – the reason he was sitting here today, facing serious charges. For a fleeting moment, Calvin wondered if Pam, his family friend and lawyer, could outwit such a formidable opponent.

"Officer Harrison, can you please describe the events of the night in question?" asked the prosecutor, his tone clinical and calculated. "Of course," Officer Harrison replied, recounting every detail of that fateful night when he approached Mr. Steele's vehicle during a routine checkpoint. Calvin's gaze drifted over to Biscuit as he spoke, seated nervously in the gallery. Biscuit's eyes held a glimmer of hope and worry for Calvin and their entire family, who depended on him.

"Thank you, Officer Harrison," said the prosecutor. "No further questions."

"Your witness, Defense," he announced, gesturing to Pam. She rose from her seat, her posture straight and confident, her face a picture of stoic calmness. As she began questioning Officer Harrison, Calvin couldn't help but feel pride swell within his heart, marveling at how poised and professional Pam was in her approach. Even Biscuit, who usually struggled to sit still during trials, seemed impressed; he leaned forward in his seat, his eyes glued to Pam's every move. "Officer Harrison," Pam began in a firm voice, her words carrying weight and authority, "were any fingerprints taken from the bag or the drugs in question?"

The officer hesitated momentarily, his brow furrowing as he searched his memory. "I can't recall if anyone took them, ma'am," he finally replied. "Our main priority was securing the scene." Pam nodded slowly, seemingly unfazed by the answer. "Interesting," she said thoughtfully. "So, since you secured the scene, my client wouldn't have had access to the bag or the drugs after they were removed from his vehicle, correct?" Officer Harrison shifted uncomfortably in his seat before reluctantly admitting, "Uh, no, ma'am." Pam smiled politely at him before returning to her seat with an air of confidence and authority.

Calvin let out a trembling breath, his heart beating frantically in his chest as he caught Biscuit's eye. In that shared moment, they were both filled with a glimmer of hope, a sliver of possibility that they could win this fight.

The rhythmic tapping of the gavel reverberated through the tense courtroom, each wooden thud a reminder of the finality that awaited Calvin Steele. The air was thick with anticipation and anxiety, the tension almost palpable. The judge, an older woman with salt-and-pepper hair, peered down at the Defense with stern eyes. "Are you ready to proceed with your case?" she asked, her voice firm and unyielding.

Pam, Calvin's attorney, glanced at her client with a mixture of sympathy and determination. She could see the fear in his eyes and the deep lines etched into his face from sleepless nights spent praying for his family's safety. "Your Honor," she said confidently, "I request a ten-minute recess to confer with my client."

"Very well," the judge replied, granting the request without hesitation. As the courtroom emptied for the brief respite, Biscuit couldn't shake off the knot of concern tightening in his chest. He knew how much was at stake in this trial, which weighed heavily on him. Hoping to clear his head, he stepped into the bustling hallway, where hushed conversations and nervous chatter filled the air.

Biscuit's footsteps echoed in the empty hall as he was making his way back to the courtroom. The tension in his shoulders was palpable, and he couldn't shake off the impending doom over him. Turning a corner, he spotted Lenny leaning against the wall, his eyes fixed on the floor. Noticing Biscuit, Lenny straightened up, pulling a crumpled envelope from his pocket. "I don't do courtrooms, Biscuit," he admitted, his voice low and gravelly. "It's not good for my line of work. But for Carmen, I'll do this one thing, this time, for you and your people."

Biscuit couldn't help but feel grateful for Lenny's willingness to help despite the risks involved. Taking the envelope from Lenny, Biscuit hesitated before opening it. What could be so important that it required Lenny's involvement?

Lenny sighed, shaking his head at Biscuit's curiosity. "You sometimes ask too many questions, Biscuit," he remarked with a hint of amusement. "But in this case, it's better if you don't know. Your guys' attorney will know what to do with whatever is in the envelope."

Feeling relieved and intrigued by Lenny's words, Biscuit clutched the envelope tightly and headed back into the courtroom. He knew whatever was inside would be crucial to their cause and trusted Pam to make the right decisions.

As Pam stood poised to continue her Defense, Biscuit approached with purpose, an envelope in his hand. He leaned in close, the warmth of his breath tickling her ear as he whispered, "Lenny said you'd know what to do with this."

Pam's eyes widened in surprise as she carefully opened the envelope. The faint scent of vanilla wafted out, mixed with a hint of musky cologne. A smile tugged at the corners of her mouth as she pulled out the contents – new evidence that could not just sway but completely alter the trial's outcome. The significance of this evidence was not lost on her, and a surge of hope and determination flooded her veins, replacing the previous sense of defeat. The fate of Calvin Steele now hung in the balance, and Pam was ready to tip the scales in their favor.

CHAPTER 32

The hushed whispers and shuffling of feet filled the courtroom, creating a palpable sense of anticipation. Calvin Steele sat at the defendant's table, his hands folded in prayer as he sought strength from his unwavering faith. The weight of this trial felt heavier than any he had faced before. Lena, Junior, and Ryder stood tall and resolute in the gallery, offering silent support to their loved ones as they anxiously watched the proceedings. Biscuit lingered at the back of the room, his brow furrowed with worry and regret. He knew his past choices had led them all to this pivotal moment, and he could only hope for a favorable outcome. The tension in the room was so thick it was almost suffocating, each breath filled with the weight of the impending verdict.

"Order in the court!" The booming voice of the bailiff echoed through the courtroom, silencing the murmurs and shuffling of feet. The Judge reentered the room with a commanding presence, her eyes scanning the tense faces before her. The weight of the situation was palpable in the air. "Defense, are you ready to proceed?" she asked, her voice firm yet laced with empathy. Pam, Calvin's attorney, hesitated for a moment before standing. Her face held a hint of worry as she addressed the Judge. "Your Honor, may we approach the bench?" "Very well," the Judge consented, gesturing for Pam and the prosecution to come forward. They stepped closer, their shoes tapping against the polished courtroom floor together in unison.

As they gathered around the bench, Pam felt the weight of Calvin's future on her shoulders. Her heart raced as she prepared to present new evidence crucial to her client's defense. The courtroom was silent, except for the steady beat of her pulse and the shuffling of papers around her.

"Your Honor, the Prosecution," she began, her voice resolute despite the tremor in her hands. She met Calvin's gaze, finding strength in his unwavering faith and determination.

"I have just received some new evidence vital to my client's defense," Pam continued, holding a manila envelope tightly. She could feel everyone in the room's eyes on her, waiting with bated breath for what she would reveal next.

"Since there wasn't enough time for proper discovery, I request that this evidence be presented to the court and the prosecution immediately," Pam stated boldly. Her heart pounded even harder in her chest as she awaited the reactions of both parties.

"Furthermore," she added, her confidence growing with each passing moment, "I ask that this evidence be submitted to the court as part of my client's defense." The Judge raised an eyebrow, clearly intrigued by Pam's sudden revelation. The prosecution exchanged uneasy glances, their ironclad case now threatened by this unexpected turn of events.

After a tense deliberation, the Judge finally spoke up. "Very well," she announced, her voice measured but curious. "I will allow this new evidence in the case." Pam exhaled deeply, relieved to have been granted this last opportunity to save Calvin from a lifetime of unjust consequences.

Pam nodded gratefully, her heart racing with anticipation as she breathed deeply. She knew the information she would reveal could change Calvin's life forever. Her gaze flickered back to the Steele family, who sat huddled together in the courtroom, their faces filled with desperation and hope. With a determined nod, Pam turned to face the Judge, her voice trembling slightly. "Thank you, Your Honor," she said, trying to convey the unwavering conviction in her words. This was it – the moment of truth. The responsibility for Calvin and his family hung heavy on her shoulders, but she refused to let them down.

The tension in the courtroom was palpable as Pam argued her evidence to the Judge. Every eye was trained on the honorable figure sitting on the bench, carefully examining each piece of evidence. Pam adjusted her glasses nervously before meeting the piercing stare of the prosecution team seated across from her. She knew they were feeling the pressure, too. "Does the prosecution have a rebuttal for this new evidence?" the Judge's stern voice cut through the silence like a knife.

The lead prosecutor shifted uncomfortably in his seat before rising to speak. "Your Honor," he began, frustration lacing his words, "we simply want to know where this information is coming from." Pam stood tall and confident, her shoulders squared as she responded. "It was provided to the court by a concerned citizen, Your Honor," she stated firmly, never once breaking eye contact with the

Judge. "And I believe it will be enough to raise reasonable doubt in our case." The entire room held its breath as they waited for the Judge's decision, which could drastically alter Calvin's fate and finally bring justice to the Steele family.

A low murmur rippled through the grand gallery, echoing off the ornate marble columns and high vaulted ceilings. The Judge, dressed in a regal black robe with a white lace collar, raised a hand for silence. Her piercing blue eyes scanned the document before her, causing her dark brows to furrow in deep contemplation. Calvin sat nervously behind the defense table, his fingers clenching and unclenching into tight fists. His heart raced with hope and fear as he awaited the verdict.

He thought of his mother, Rose, a devout woman who often prayed fervently in church every Sunday. Her unwavering faith had always been a guiding light for their family. Could this decision change everything for them?

As the Judge pored over the evidence, Pam, Calvin's lawyer, turned slightly towards him with a reassuring smile and said, "I've got you." Her determination to fight for him and his family gave Calvin a glimmer of hope. But as Pam's gaze swept across the room, her eyes caught onto a figure sitting in the back row of the gallery – Willow. Just seeing her sent an icy chill down Pam's spine, but she couldn't let fear overcome her. She took a deep breath and addressed the Judge with confidence.

"Your Honor," Pam began, her voice steady but the unease in her stomach palpable as she addressed the Judge. "I must bring to the court's attention that Willow, a crucial figure in this case, is currently present in the courtroom." The Judge's expression remained inscrutable as she peered over her glasses at Willow, who met her gaze with an unreadable look. The tension in the room thickened like molasses in the air. Calvin could feel his heart pounding in his chest, knowing Willow's presence could mean trouble for their case. But he had to trust Pam and her unwavering dedication. With bated breath, he waited for the Judge's next move, praying that justice would prevail for him and his family.

The Judge leaned forward on her bench, deliberating over her decision like a weighty burden on her shoulders. Her eyes narrowed, and she spoke in a low, almost secretive tone that only those closest to her could hear. "Bailiff," she said, addressing the security officer. "Please escort Ms. Willow out of the courtroom until further notice." As Willow was led out, the weight of uncertainty lifted from Calvin's shoulders, and he gave himself a small sigh of relief. He knew they were one step closer to achieving justice for his family.

The bailiff, an imposing figure with broad shoulders and a stern expression, surveyed the courtroom before striding purposefully towards Willow. She sat near the back, her eyes wide with shock as she realized what was happening. She had only come to observe from a safe distance, never imagining that she would become the center of attention. "Wha-what's going on?" she stammered, her voice barely audible over the murmurs rippling through the room. "Ma'am, you'll need to come with me," the bailiff said firmly, his hand resting on her arm as if ready to enforce the order.

Willow's mind raced, her thoughts spinning in confusion and fear. Had they discovered her role in all of this? Was her carefully constructed façade beginning to crumble under scrutiny? She looked over at Pam, who stood resolute and unyielding before the Judge, and then at Calvin, whose face betrayed hope and dread.

"Your Honor," she began, her voice trembling with a desperation she couldn't quite conceal. "I don't understand why I'm being removed from the courtroom. I ain't done nothing wrong." "Miss," the Judge said sharply, her tone leaving no room for argument. "We will discuss your presence here after thoroughly reviewing some new evidence brought to my attention." The atmosphere in the courtroom shifted as all eyes turned towards Willow, their gazes filled with curiosity and suspicion.

With a sharp nod, the bailiff motioned for the now visibly shaken Willow to follow him out of the courtroom. Her eyes remained locked on Calvin as she passed by, filled with an unsettling mix of anger and fear. The door closed behind them with a resounding thud, leaving an uneasy silence. Every beat of Calvin's heart felt like a thunderous pounding against his ribcage, his thoughts racing as he struggled to process what had just transpired. He knew Willow was capable of great deceit, but something about her reaction made him question if there was more to this than met the eye. Could Pam's new evidence be enough to turn the tide in their favor? Or would Willow again find a way to manipulate the situation, as she always seemed to do? As he watched Pam confidently return to her position at the defense table, Calvin couldn't help but feel a flicker of hope ignite within him like a small flame in the darkness.

Calvin's heart thundered in his chest as he leaned closer to Pam. The tension in the courtroom was thick enough to cut with a knife. His palms were slick with sweat, and he could feel every pair of eyes in the room trained on them. "Pam, what's happening?" he whispered urgently, barely able to hear his voice over the steady hum of conversation echoing off the walls.

But it was as if every person present had stopped breathing, waiting with bated breath for Pam's next move. She turned to Calvin with a determined look, focused on this crucial moment. She had poured her heart and soul into defending him, fighting tirelessly to prove his innocence.

"Give me a minute," she replied softly before turning back to face the front of the courtroom. The air seemed to thicken with anticipation as she stood up from her seat, her heels clicking like a metronome on the polished floor. It was like the sound of a sad and somber song, marking each beat of this monumental moment.

The Judge's gravelly voice cut through the silence like a sharp blade. "Is the defense ready to proceed?" she asked, her tone serious and unyielding. With all eyes now on Pam, she returned their gaze with unwavering determination and confidence. "Your Honor," she began, her voice strong and sure, "we would like to motion for dismissal of all charges against my client, Mr. Calvin Steele."

The words hung in the air like a single note on a grand piano, reverberating through the otherwise silent room. Calvin felt his chest tighten and his breath catch in his throat as he awaited the Judge's response. He gripped his chair's smooth, polished armrests until his knuckles hurt. This moment could change everything for him and his family - their entire future rested on this decision.

As Pam, their lawyer, continued to plead their case with unwavering conviction, Calvin's heart thudded painfully in his chest. He looked around the room, taking in the faces of those present—would they believe in his innocence? Would they see past the false evidence presented by the prosecution? His family's fate hung in the balance; all he could do was hope that justice would prevail.

"Your Honor," Pam repeated, her voice steady despite the moment's gravity, "we move for dismissal."

A hush fell over the courtroom at Pam's words, everyone leaning forward in their seats with bated breath. Whispers of hope rippled through the gallery as people held each other for support. Calvin felt Lena's hand reach for his own, their fingers intertwining in a silent gesture of love and solidarity. "Order," the Judge commanded, immediately silencing any murmurs growing louder. The tension in the room was palpable as all eyes turned towards the Judge, waiting for the final decision to determine their future.

Pam stood tall before the Judge, her voice like a steady stream as she began, "Your Honor, this new evidence – accepted by the court with open minds – reveals that no fingerprint can be attributed to my client on any of the items presented. With this discovery, we are confident that the prosecution will uncover another suspect's prints on the bag and its contents." The tension in the courtroom was palpable. Calvin could feel it pressing against his chest like a weight. His heart beat rapidly, mimicking the clock on the wall. Every second counted – his family's future hanging precariously in the balance of Pam's words and the Judge's decision. "Furthermore," Pam pressed on, her unwavering gaze fixed on the Judge, "we firmly believe that this other suspect played a significant role in the crime for which Mr. Steele stands accused today. Therefore, we respectfully request a dismissal of all charges against him." The gravity of Pam's words filled the room, leaving an almost tangible impact on those present.

The atmosphere in the courtroom was thick with anticipation as Pam took her seat. The hushed whispers and shuffling of feet echoed through the space, creating an almost tangible tension. Calvin's eyes scanned the sea of onlookers, finally settling on Lena, who sat behind him. Her expression was a mix of nerves and hope. Her glistening eyes reflected the overwhelming emotion of the moment.

Junior and Ryder sat quietly beside her, their young faces serious and focused. They, too, were waiting for the Judge's response, their future hanging in the balance.

Pam's voice cut through the silence, confident and unwavering despite the gravity of the situation. "Your Honor," she repeated firmly, "we move for dismissal."

Calvin closed his eyes briefly, allowing himself to imagine a life free from the cloud of uncertainty that had loomed over his family for so long. He visualized Rose, her unyielding belief in his innocence, and the way she had always led them to church on Sundays, instilling the importance of a solid spiritual foundation. A silent prayer escaped his lips, begging for justice to prevail.

As he opened his eyes and returned to the present moment, Calvin could see hope in the faces of his loved ones and those who had come to support him. No matter the outcome, he knew their love and faith would be their guiding light.

The Judge was an imposing figure, her stern expression adding to the weight of the situation. She turned her gaze to the prosecution as they shuffled through their papers. The sound of Calvin's heart beating filled his ears, each thump like a ticking clock counting down to the moment that would define his future.

"Does the prosecution have any rebuttal to the defense's motion for dismissal?" The Judge's authoritative tone reverberated through the courtroom, silencing all in attendance. Calvin's gaze shifted to the prosecutor, who seemed to be carefully considering his next move. The atmosphere was tense, with the Steele family holding their breath as they awaited the prosecutor's response.

The prosecutor stood confidently, but his voice had a hint of unease as he addressed the court. His eyes swept over the room, briefly landing on Calvin and his family before returning to the Judge. The Steele family leaned forward in anticipation, trying to decipher the legal jargon being used.

"Your Honor," the prosecutor began, his voice steady but tinged with uncertainty, "if this case is dismissed, we request that it be done so with prejudice in case we find fingerprints or other evidence linking Mr. Steele to the bag or drugs." Junior and Ryder exchanged confused looks, struggling to understand the implications of what was being said. The tension grew as everyone held their breath, waiting for the Judge's decision.

The Judge nodded thoughtfully, stroking her chin as she considered the prosecution's request. Calvin's mind raced, his heart pounding in his chest as he prayed for a favorable outcome while bracing himself for the possibility of disappointment.

"Very well," the Judge said, her voice carrying weight and authority. She leaned back in her chair, her dark robes swishing around her like waves in an ocean of justice. "I have carefully weighed the arguments presented by both parties. In light of the compelling new evidence brought forward by the defense, I am left with no choice but to dismiss the case against Mr. Calvin Steele." A sense of relief washed over Calvin like a cool stream on a hot day.

However," she continued sternly, "should further investigation reveal fingerprints belonging to Mr. Steele on the items mentioned above, the state may refile the charges." The room fell silent as the weight of those words settled upon them. Calvin's hands trembled slightly as he reflected on how narrowly he had escaped a fate he did not deserve.

"Thank you, Your Honor," Pam's voice trembled with gratitude as she turned to the Judge, her eyes wet with tears of relief. The courtroom erupted in a symphony of whispers and gasps, family members embracing one another while friends clapped each other on the back in celebration. "Order!" the Judge called out sharply, hushing the room. Her gavel struck the bench with a resounding crack, signaling the end of the trial.

Calvin felt a weight lift from his shoulders as Lena threw her arms around him, pressing her face into his chest. He closed his eyes briefly, savoring the warmth and comfort of his family's love and the knowledge that they would face whatever challenges lay ahead together. The air was thick with emotion and the scent of stale coffee from hours of testimony. It was a moment he would never forget, a turning point in their lives that marked a new beginning after a while of turmoil and uncertainty.

Calvin's heart swelled with overwhelming gratitude and relief as Lena rushed towards him, her eyes glistening with tears of joy. He opened his arms, pulling her into a warm, loving embrace. Their combined emotions mingled, creating an unbreakable bond. The courtroom buzzed with excitement and chatter, but it felt like they were the only two people.

Lena's soft voice broke through the chaos, whispering words of thankfulness into Calvin's ear. Her delicate touch sent shivers down his spine, reminding him of their unwavering love. As he held onto her tightly, Calvin couldn't help but blink back tears of pure happiness.

His forehead pressed against hers. He took a deep breath and let out a content sigh. The familiar scent of her perfume surrounded them, reminding him of all the good times they had shared. Their love had been a guiding light during this dark time, giving them strength to persevere through every challenge.

Watching from a distance, their loyal companion, Biscuit, cleared his throat before approaching the couple. With genuine sincerity in his eyes, he spoke up to express his gratitude to God for answering their prayers. His heartfelt words echoed throughout the courtroom, a testament to the power of faith and the mercy of the Lord.

Pam turned to Biscuit, her own eyes glistening with unshed tears. For a brief moment, they shared a silent understanding, an acknowledgment of the tumultuous journey they had been on together, even in this short amount of time. Their emotions hung heavy as they moved towards each other, drawn together by an inexplicable pull. In one fluid motion, they embraced each other tightly, seeking solace and comfort in each other's arms.

"Thank you, Pam," Biscuit murmured into her hair, his voice thick with gratitude. "You fought for Calvin when the odds were stacked against him."

"Thank you, Biscuit, for standing by him," Pam replied, her voice equally choked with emotion. They pulled back slightly, their faces only inches apart, as they gazed into each other's eyes. Time seemed to stand still as they were lost in the moment's intensity. And then, without warning, they leaned in and shared a tender kiss—a pure expression of their deep connection and unspoken feelings.

As they broke away, cheeks flushed with surprise and something more profound, Pam spoke up again. "Let's celebrate with everyone," she said softly yet determinedly. Biscuit nodded in agreement, and hand in hand, they made their way toward the rest of their gathered friends and family. Each step forward felt like another milestone reached - a testament to the strength of their bond and the love that had blossomed between them amidst chaos and uncertainty.

As they merged with the circle of their supportive group, Calvin's gaze swept across their faces, his heart swelling with gratitude for everyone who had stood by his side through this long and challenging journey. Despite their trials and tribulations, the unbreakable bonds of love and faith that united them would always carry them through. "Let's go home," he whispered to Lena, his grip on her hand tightening gently as they walked. Together, they wove through the jubilant crowd, filled with joyous laughter. But amidst all the revelry, Pam and Biscuit couldn't resist sneaking glances at each other, their shared kiss still fresh in their minds like a promise of what was yet to come.

CHAPTER 33

The sound of unrestrained laughter and pure joy filled the air outside the small red-brick church. Calvin Steele stood at the center of a bustling crowd, surrounded by family, friends, and fellow church members who had come to celebrate their victory. The scent of crispy fried chicken and mouthwatering homemade pies wafted through the warm summer air, enticing everyone's taste buds. Conversations buzzed around him, punctuated by hearty laughter that echoed off the nearby buildings.

"Alright, everyone!" Pastor Williams' voice boomed over the chatter, his hands clapping loudly to gain the crowd's attention. "Let us all gather around Calvin and his family to give thanks for everything God has done and will continue to do for them." The birds in the surrounding trees began singing as if on cue, adding their melody to the jubilant atmosphere.

The congregation closed around the Steeles, forming a protective circle with their clasped hands. They stood with heads bowed low as if in reverence to God. Calvin felt the warmth of his mother Rose's hand on his shoulder, her faith and love radiating to him like a beacon of hope. He glanced at his wife Lena, her eyes shimmering with unshed tears, and squeezed her hand gently, offering a silent reassurance.

"Dear Lord," Pastor Williams began, his deep, melodic voice resonating through the gathering. The sound seemed to fill the space between them, enveloping everyone in its comforting embrace. "We thank You for Your divine intervention today, for Your unwavering protection over this loving and devoted family." As he spoke, his words seemed to carry a weight of sincerity and gratitude that spread through the crowd like wildfire. "We ask that You continue to guide and bless them on their journey, and may they be a shining example of hope and inspiration for all who know them." The congregants murmured their agreement, nodding solemnly as the pastor finished his prayer. "Amen," they said in unison, their voices rising together in a chorus of heartfelt appreciation.

As the prayer circle disbanded, people returned to their conversations and activities with renewed vigor. The sound of friendly chatter filled the air as card games resumed on folding tables, surrounded by a sea of brightly colored lawn chairs. Children darted around playing tag, their joyful giggles echoing off the church walls. Calvin's heart swelled with happiness as he watched them play, knowing they were safe and loved in this community.

"Hey, smells like Brother James fired up his grill!" someone exclaimed, pointing toward the church parking lot. Sure enough, the scent of sizzling burgers and hot dogs wafted into the church, drawing more than a few hungry attendees in its direction. The tantalizing aroma mingled with the sweet fragrance of freshly cut grass and blooming flowers, creating a sensory overload for those gathered.

"Calvin, why don't you and Lena grab yourselves something to eat?" Rose suggested, her eyes crinkling with the warmth of her smile. "You both deserve a bite after everything you've been through." "Thanks, Mama," Calvin replied gratefully, giving her a quick hug before guiding Lena toward the enticing aroma. They went through the bustling crowd hand-in-hand, feeling grateful and blessed to be surrounded by such love and support.

As they reached the food tent, Calvin couldn't help but feel that God had lifted a weight off his shoulders. This celebration wasn't just for him but for everyone who had stood by their side – their family, friends, and the community that had shown them unwavering support. His heart overflowed with gratitude as he looked around at all the smiling faces, knowing they were all connected by something much bigger than themselves – faith and love for one another.

Arm in arm, they joined the snaking line for food, their stomachs rumbling in anticipation. While they waited, Calvin took a moment to look around and drink in the sight of their beloved friends and family, gathered together and enjoying each other's company. The air was filled with snippets of conversations and laughter, mingled with the enticing aromas of savory dishes and sweet treats. A warm sense of gratitude and contentment enveloped Calvin as he silently prayed to God for this blessed gathering. Despite the long journey ahead, he knew that with faith and love, they would navigate it together.

"Here's to new beginnings, Lena," he whispered, gently squeezing her hand as they moved forward in the line. The sun hung low in the sky, casting a golden glow over the scene and highlighting the joy on everyone's faces. Calvin felt truly blessed as the last rays of sunlight danced on his skin.

Meanwhile, Pam was drawn to the makeshift refreshment table, her mouthwatering at the sight of homemade delicacies and refreshing drinks. She excused herself from Calvin's relatives and approached the table, grateful for quiet moments amidst the lively church crowd. As she sipped on a cool glass of lemonade, she couldn't help but smile as she watched loved ones catching up and making new memories together. This was what life was all about - surrounded by those we hold dear, cherishing every moment together.

As she reached out to grab another cold drink, a familiar hand beat her to it. With calloused fingers that spoke of hard work and determination, Biscuit offered the chilled can to Pam with a crooked grin. "Thought you might need this one," he said, his voice low and playful like a secret shared between friends. "It's been a long, hot day in the courtroom, and you might want to cool off." Pam took the can, feeling the condensation drip down her hand as she looked at Biscuit with renewed admiration. His unwavering support for Calvin throughout the trial was evident in his actions. "Thanks, Biscuit," she replied, her voice soft but genuine.

With her drink in hand, Pam began to make her way back towards the bustling center of the crowd. Her hips swayed subtly with each step, drawing admiring glances from those around her. Biscuit followed close behind, a broad smile on his face though his eyes betrayed his uncertainty. It was endearing to see him this way – chasing after her like an eager puppy. "Is that all the heat you experienced today?" Pam asked, a teasing lilt in her melodic voice. Biscuit scratched his head, searching for the right words to match her playful tone. "Well, you know," he began, stumbling over his words before finding his footing. "It was quite the day."

Pam took a long sip of her drink, relishing the refreshing taste as it cooled her throat. As she brought the can down, she caught Biscuit's gaze and noticed how his eyes seemed to linger on her, almost like he saw her in a different light. A strange flutter stirred in her chest that she hadn't anticipated. "Quite the day indeed," she murmured, her thoughts drifting momentarily to the tender moments they had shared during the trial. But now was not the time for such thoughts – there was a celebration to be had, and they were both there to support Calvin and his family.

Determined, Pam gestured towards the heart of the gathering and gave Biscuit a warm smile. "Come on," she said, excited at being surrounded by loved ones and good food. As they strolled back into the festivities, Pam basked in the lively atmosphere—laughter and chatter filled the air, mingling with the delicious aroma of grilled meats and savory sides. At that moment, everything felt perfect, like all was right in their little corner of the world.

As they approached the bustling crowd, Biscuit's heart raced, and his palms began to sweat. He took a deep breath, steeling himself for what he was about to do. With determination in his eyes, he stepped in front of Pam, blocking her path. His voice wavered slightly as he spoke, but his words were sincere. "I just drank about three cans," he confessed, struggling to control the rush of emotions inside him, "and I haven't cooled off yet because you have probably changed my temperature forever." A charged silence hung between them, thick with longing and unspoken desires. Pam's gaze softened as she met his intense stare, unable to resist his words' charm fully. A hint of a smile played at the corner of her lips, betraying her tough exterior. "I told you, no funny ideas," she warned playfully, trying to hide the sudden flutter in her chest at Biscuit's confession.

Biscuit's expression turned serious as he responded, "Hey, what happened in that courtroom wasn't a joke to me. It was one of the most overwhelming and unexpected moments I've experienced." The weight of his words hung in the air, echoing off the outside of the church walls. The sounds of laughter and music seemed distant, as if they had been transported to their private world. Pam released a soft sigh and found herself sitting on a nearby bench, her gaze drifting towards the lively celebration inside.

She couldn't help but think about how she had never felt this way before, not even when she looked at Calvin and Lena. "I don't even know why it happened," she admitted softly, her voice barely audible over the distant merriment, "but I must admit, I did like it." Biscuit's face lit up with happiness and confusion as he joined her on the bench, leaning forward with his elbows resting on his knees. "This might sound crazy," he began earnestly, looking into her eyes intently, "but do you believe in love at first kiss? Not just love at first sight... because we did go to high school together." The question hung between them, full of hope and wonder.

Pam tilted her head thoughtfully, curls cascading over her shoulder as she mused, "True, but that was in high school. I think I just saw you now." She glanced over at him, her piercing brown eyes searching for something deeper within him. Biscuit met her gaze confidently, his heart thumping wildly in his chest. The warmth of her touch lingered on his skin as he leaned in closer to her. "Well, let me repeat: do you believe in love at first sight? Because I see you now."

As the festive sounds of the celebration faded into the background, time seemed to stand still as their eyes locked.

At that moment, it was as if the world had disappeared, and there were only two of them. Something profound had shifted between them, whether love or something else entirely; only time would tell. But for now, they were content to sit together, side by side, lost in each other's gaze as the world continued.

Biscuit allowed his gaze to wander around the crowded room, taking in the faces of friends and family as they laughed and chatted. The comforting hum of their voices served as a backdrop to the intimate conversation he had just shared with Pam. But soon enough, she pulled him from his reverie with a gentle touch on his arm.

"Hey, Biscuit," she said, looking at him with such intensity that it sent shivers down his spine. Her bright green eyes seemed to bore into his soul, unraveling his thoughts and emotions without effort. "Are you planning on coming back to the house with us once we leave?"

Without hesitation, Biscuit answered, feeling warmth at the thought. He couldn't help but smile, feeling something akin to hope sprouting within him. "Absolutely."

Pam nodded, her expression softening as she gazed at him. Her eyes flickered towards Calvin and Lena, who stood nearby, surrounded by well-wishers congratulating them on winning the case. "Good," Pam said, her voice low and filled with meaning. "Let's talk more about... this... after we leave their home."

As Pam turned to walk away, Biscuit couldn't help but watch her, his eyes tracing every subtle movement of her body. The curve of her neck mesmerized him, and he could feel the heat rising in his cheeks as he took in the way her curls brushed against her shoulders. The smell of grilled food wafted in from the parking lot, enticing his senses and mixing with the lingering scent of Pam's perfume that still hung in the air.

"Alright," he agreed, his voice barely audible over the joyful clamor of the celebration. Pam glanced back at him over her shoulder, a knowing smile on her lips. Something deep inside Biscuit stirred, a long-dormant part of him coming to life under her gaze. He couldn't believe it - after all these years of searching for something real, could he have found it in this unexpected place?

Biscuit took a deep breath, trying to steady himself as emotions flooded his chest. He knew now was not the time to get lost in thoughts of what might be; he needed to stay grounded in the present and focus on current events. But a part of him couldn't help but wonder about the possibilities ahead with Pam by his side. He would savor this moment and let himself dream of what could come next.

He would bask in his friends and family's warmth and love, grateful for their unwavering support. As he walked through the jubilant crowd, Biscuit felt as light as a feather, his heart brimming with joy and hope. He knew that when discussing things with Pam, he would do so with an open heart and a willingness to embrace whatever the future might hold. The air was filled with laughter and music, creating a festive atmosphere that seemed to swirl around him like a comforting embrace. Biscuit couldn't help but feel that this was just the beginning of something beautiful and wondrous.

CHAPTER 34

The stark, frigid holding cell emanated an overwhelming sense of desolation, mirroring the emotions swirling within Willow. She huddled on the hard metal bench, trembling with fear and regret.

The dim light flickered above her, casting eerie shadows across her face as she stared blankly at the grimy floor. Memories of the men she had entangled over the years flooded her mind, each a reminder of the power and control she once held.

But now, all she could feel was a deep sense of remorse. Her once cunning smile and innocent demeanor were no longer enough to protect her from the consequences of her actions. "Was it worth it?" she whispered to herself, the sound barely audible amidst the hum of the fluorescent lights.

Willow's bright eyes, now dull and lifeless, slowly surveyed her surroundings. The chipped paint on the walls and the lingering stench of despair in the air served as a constant reminder that this was not another game she could manipulate her way out of.

The stakes were higher this time, and the outcome was far grimmer. Lost in these bleak thoughts, she barely noticed as the heavy steel door creaked open, revealing a stoic-faced officer standing in its frame. He motioned for her to stand and follow him, signaling yet another turn in Willow's fate.

Willow's voice was light and hopeful as she asked, "Did someone finally pay my bail?" The officer's reply was cold and emotionless, crushing any glimmer of optimism that had momentarily surfaced. As they walked down the narrow hallway lined with cells filled with other forlorn faces, Willow's head fell, feeling the weight of her actions in every step. Her wrists, shackled together by heavy chains, added to the heaviness in her heart.

The distant memories of laughter and camaraderie during her past games with men now felt like a lifetime away, replaced by the harsh reality of her current situation. "I've pushed my luck too far this time," she thought to herself as she reluctantly followed the officer deeper into the bowels of the county jail. The interview room was sterile and cold, the fluorescent lights casting a sickly hue over everything.

Willow sat on the hard metal chair, her hands chafing against the handcuffs that bound her to the table. She shifted uncomfortably, trying to find some relief from the discomfort. Suddenly, the door creaked open, and a tall figure entered, looming over her like a shadow in the dimly lit room.

Willow's voice cracked with desperation as she yelled, "Can I go home?" The words escaped her lips in a rush despite the fear and uncertainty in her chest. The detective's deep, gravelly voice responded calmly and collectedly as if he were used to dealing with panicked suspects.

"Before we continue, allow me to read you your rights," he said, pulling a small card from his breast pocket. Willow's eyes widened as he recited the familiar phrases. She had never thought she would be on the receiving end of them.

Her heart pounded in her ears as she asked, "Am I going to jail for real?" She searched the detective's face for any hint of leniency but found none. He was a stern man, someone who didn't tolerate nonsense or games.

"Everything here is for real," he replied, meeting her gaze without wavering. His eyes seemed to see right through her facade, and Willow felt a shiver run down her spine. This was not a man she could charm or manipulate.

Tears welled up in her eyes and blurred her vision as the reality of her situation finally sank in. She had always been able to talk her way out of trouble, but this time felt different. This time, she was trapped by her own cunning and recklessness.

"Look, I know I've made some mistakes," Willow whispered, her voice barely audible as she looked up at the detective with pleading eyes. "But I can change. I really can." The detective's expression remained stoic as he continued reciting her rights, his words cold and emotionless.

"Save it for the judge," he interjected, cutting off her desperate pleas. Willow's tears fell freely now, cascading down her cheeks steadily. "Please... just let me go," she begged, her voice trembling with fear and regret. "I swear, I'll leave town and never come back."

"Sorry," the detective replied, his tone firm but not unkind. You'll have to face the consequences of your actions, just like everyone else." His words hung heavy, a final verdict on Willow's fate.

As the detective concluded reading her rights, Willow's sobs grew louder and more desperate. They echoed through the cold, empty room like a haunting melody, a constant reminder of the price she must pay for playing games with other people's lives. She knew that these tears would continue to haunt her long after she left the confines of the county jail, a painful reminder of the consequences of her choices.

The Steele family home, a quaint brick house adorned with vibrant red geraniums, greeted Calvin, Lena, Rose, Ryder, and Junior with open arms as they stepped onto the front porch. The sweet scent of freshly baked biscuits wafted.

Pam and Biscuit followed closely behind, their infectious laughter blending with the symphony of cicadas in the background. The cozy atmosphere of the home felt like a warm hug, inviting them to come in and make themselves at home.

"Come on, kiddo," Junior whispered to Ryder, motioning for her to help him in the kitchen. They disappeared down the hallway while listening to the living room, filled with animated conversation about the day's court victory.

Calvin sank into the plush cushions of his favorite armchair, allowing himself to relax fully for perhaps the first time in weeks. His eyes swept around the room, taking in the familiar faces of his family and friends who had gathered around him. A sense of overwhelming gratitude filled his heart, brought on by the outpouring of love and support he had received during his recent struggles.

With a slight tremble, he spoke up, "I barely had time to eat today, you know?" He couldn't help but smile as he looked at each person, wanting to spend every precious moment thanking them for their unwavering support and prayers.

And to Pam, his heart swelled with pride and admiration, "Your hard work and dedication paid off. That prosecutor always had me on edge, but you never faltered."

Pam's smile lit up her entire face, the corners of her eyes crinkling with unshed tears. "I just want to thank all of you for trusting and believing in me. We've been friends since high school, and I truly believe the world is a better place because of people like you." She glanced at Biscuit briefly, her cheeks flushing a delicate shade of pink. Calvin, Lena, and Rose caught the fleeting exchange, their smiles mirroring Pam's joy.

"Isn't she wonderful?" Biscuit crooned softly, his deep baritone voice reverberating through the room. Each word he spoke carried its melody, intertwining with the soft music playing in the background. The love and admiration in his eyes were unmistakable, shining like stars in the night sky.

As the family basked in the warmth of their bond, Calvin couldn't help but reflect on the journey that led them here. There had been trials and heartaches, but they remained steadfast in their love for one another. He knew that whatever obstacles lay ahead, he would face them with the strength and support of his family by his side.

"Alright now, what's going on in here?" Rose asked playfully, her eyes darting between Pam and Biscuit. Her laughter filled the room, a blend of amusement and curiosity. "I haven't heard Biscuit sing like that since he was a teenager."

Biscuit rubbed the back of his neck, trying to deflect the attention with a casual shrug. "Aw, come on now, Rose. You know, I just felt inspired by the moment." He flashed a crooked grin as Pam blushed, turning away from everyone and busying herself with adjusting a picture frame on the wall.

"Can't blame a man for wanting to share a little joy, can you?" Biscuit added, hoping to shift the focus to the day's triumphs. But his eyes lingered on Pam, betraying the deeper emotions beneath his lighthearted demeanor.

Just then, Junior stepped into the room, his hands still damp from helping Ryder in the kitchen. "Uh, Daddy? Can you please step into the dining room for a moment?"

Calvin nodded and followed Junior toward the dining room, curious but trusting his son's intentions. The others exchanged glances, sensing that something special was about to unfold.

As they walked, Calvin couldn't help but wonder what Junior had planned. The warmth and love that filled their home today were palpable, and he couldn't shake the feeling that God's hand was guiding them through every step of this journey.

He knew that whatever awaited him in the dining room would be yet another reminder of the incredible love and support that surrounded him.

As they all stepped into the dining room, a warm glow from the chandelier above bathed the table in a gentle light. Calvin's eyes widened at the sight before him: Junior and Ryder had taken great care to prepare an elaborate feast using the leftovers from the church celebration, arranging it all on the family's cherished fine china.

Ryder stood by Calvin's chair, her eyes shining with pride as she held it out for him. Calvin took a moment to take it all in – the love and effort his children had poured into this surprise, the smiles on everyone's faces, and the feeling of belonging that enveloped him like a warm embrace.

His heart swelled with gratitude, and he knew their family bond would remain unbreakable no matter what trials life threw at them.

"Take a seat, Daddy," Ryder urged gently. Calvin obliged, sitting in his chair. He looked around at the faces of those he held most dear, feeling a surge of emotion inside him.

"Thank you, Junior, Ryder," he said, his voice thick with emotion. "This... this means more than you know."

Junior smiled broadly, his eyes sparkling with love and admiration for his father. "We have prepared a place for you, Daddy, because this is your home, just like Jesus does for us. I told you haven't had your last supper yet." He paused, then added softly, "Welcome home, Daddy."

Love overwhelmed the room and filled the moment's weight, and each person present was acutely aware of the love that bound them together. Calvin reached for a forkful of mashed potatoes, the comforting aroma permeating the air as he lifted it to his lips. The flavors melded together on his tongue as he took that first bite – a symphony of warmth, familiarity, and love.

"Thank you, Lord," he whispered, his eyes glistening with unshed tears. He looked around at each member of their close-knit family circle, forever imprinting this moment onto his heart.

"Thank you for my family."

The clink of fine china and the murmur of soft laughter filled the dining room as the family gathered around the table. The golden glow from the chandelier above cast a warm light, illuminating the smiles on their faces.

Biscuit couldn't help but steal glances at Pam, her cheeks flushed with happiness. He knew it was now or never - he had to tell her how he felt. As he moved closer to her, his heart pounded like the heavy bass line of a soulful love song.

"Hey, Pam," Biscuit whispered, making her turn towards him. "I just wanted to say that this right here... is what I want for us."

Pam's eyes widened slightly, a mix of surprise and curiosity flickering. "What do you mean, Biscuit?" She asked gently, leaning in closer to hear him over the cheerful sounds of the gathering.

"Look, I ain't perfect," Biscuit continued, his voice barely audible. "Hell, I'm not even whole. But when I'm with you, I feel complete. You're my other half, and we can make it work."

As realization dawned on Pam, her gaze softened, and she reached for Biscuit's hand, holding it with an affectionate squeeze. Their fingers intertwined, their connection was electric, and Biscuit couldn't contain his joy.

"I'm in love!" Biscuit's voice rang out with an exuberant shout, the pure joy and love in his heart overflowing. This family had shown him more grace and mercy than he ever thought possible, opening his eyes to God's grace and mercy. He looked around at everyone gathered here, overwhelmed with gratitude and love for them all.

"I want to thank every one of you," he said, his voice shaky with emotion. "From my heart, I am grateful for your kindness." A wide smile spread across his face as he added, "And I love everyone here! Let's celebrate this beautiful moment with a supper together." The warmth of their love surrounded him like a warm embrace, filling him with a sense of belonging and contentment.

Laughter and whoops of delight echoed through the room as everyone embraced one another in a series of hugs. Tears glistened in the eyes of some, while others wore wide, beaming smiles.

Standing back from the flurry of affection, Rose gazed up towards the heavens. Her heart swelled with love, gratitude, and an overwhelming sense of belonging.

"Lord," she whispered, her voice thick with emotion. "This right here is what it's all about – love."

As the family gathered around the table, their bond stronger than ever, they shared a meal that was as nourishing for their souls as it was for their bodies.

The tantalizing aroma of the food filled the air, reminding them of the love and laughter they were about to share. Each dish's story was passed down through generations and woven into every bite. As they savored each mouthful, they couldn't help but feel grateful for everything they had at that moment - a warm home, a loving family, and an abundance of delicious food. It was a simple yet meaning-ful reminder that they had everything they needed at the table.

The End

EPILOGUE

The evening air was crisp as the laughter and warmth from the Steele family's home spilled into the night. Biscuit and Pam walked side by side, their breaths visible in the cool air. The stillness of the night enveloped them; even the rustling trees seemed to hold their breath. Their footsteps crunched on the gravel driveway, each step a reminder of the time ticking away.

"Beautiful night, isn't it?" Biscuit finally said, breaking the silence.

"It is," Pam agreed, eyes scanning the vast sky filled with stars. She took a deep breath, appreciating the serenity around them.

"Hey, I wanted to ask you something," Biscuit began hesitantly, rubbing the back of his neck. His voice held a subtle tension that hinted at the importance of what he was about to say.

"Sure, what's up?" Pam asked, her curiosity piqued.

"Would you consider attending the Bible study with me tomorrow night?" Biscuit blurted out. He held his breath, waiting for her response.

Pam looked at him, surprised by the unexpected suggestion. Her eyes searched his face, trying to decipher his intentions. "I've been thinking about it, actually," she admitted. It would make my mother happy."

The contrast between the tranquil setting and the newfound tension in their conversation gave the evening a dramatic touch, leaving them intrigued about what lay ahead. Biscuit smiled at Pam, his eyes filled with warmth and sincerity. They had reached her car, and he walked over to the driver's side door, opening it for her.

"Go on, then," he said gently. "Just look around – God has been good to us."

Pam smiled back at him, touched by his words. "He is a good God," she agreed.

Biscuit held her gaze, letting the moment linger. "Yes, He is," he whispered. They embraced, their hearts swelling with gratitude and hope.

As Pam got into her car and drove away, Biscuit stood there momentarily, watching her taillights fade into the distance. The night sky stretched out infinitely above him, a vast canvas painted with possibilities. As the stars twinkled overhead, Biscuit felt the first stirrings of a new chapter in his life beginning to unfold.

Biscuit stood alone on the sidewalk, bathed in the soft glow of a flickering streetlight. He gazed up at the moonlit sky, the vast expanse above him reminding him of his insignificance. With a heavy heart, he decided to walk for a while, needing the solitude to process everything that had happened in his life.

As he wandered the quiet streets, Biscuit's thoughts swirled like autumn leaves caught in a gust of wind. Now and then, tears welled up in his eyes, spilling down his cheeks and splashing onto the pavement below. The weight of his past mistakes was a burden he could no longer bear alone.

Finally, Biscuit sat at a bus stop, watching several buses pass him. One bus pulled up, its door creaking open, and the driver recognized Biscuit from their shared station. "Hey, man, you alright?" the driver asked, genuine concern etched on his face.

"Y-yeah, I'm fine," Biscuit stammered, wiping away his tears with the back of his hand. "Just needed some time to think, you know?"

"Alright, if you say so." The bus driver hesitated for a moment before nodding. "Well, hop on if you want—if just for the sake of the ride."

"Thanks, "Biscuit muttered, climbing aboard and sitting near the back of the bus. The familiar engine hum and gentle rocking motion provided a small comfort, but it wasn't enough to erase the turmoil within him.

Eventually, the bus stopped outside the church where they had gathered earlier that day. Biscuit stepped off the bus, grateful to be alone with his thoughts again. As he walked through the empty parking lot, the echoes of laughter and love that had filled the air just hours before seemed to wrap around him like a warm embrace.

"God, what's happening to me?" Biscuit whispered to himself, his heart swelling with hope and uncertainty. He could feel something stirring within him, a transformation he couldn't quite understand—but one he desperately needed.

Reaching his car, Biscuit slid into the driver's seat and rested his head on the steering wheel. With a shaky breath, he lifted his eyes to the heavens and prayed for the first time in years. "God," he murmured, his voice cracking with emotion. I'm so sorry for everything."

As the words tumbled from his lips, Biscuit felt like a dam had burst within him. All the pain, regret, and sorrow he had been carrying for so long came pouring out, leaving him raw and vulnerable. But amidst the flood of emotions, there was also a quiet undercurrent of hope—a sense that, perhaps, a new beginning was on the horizon.

Biscuit drove through the streets of Chicago. The weight of his past mistakes seemed to be gradually lifting from his shoulders, replaced by a sense of clarity and new-found purpose. As he maneuvered through the familiar neighborhoods, Biscuit couldn't help but marvel at the transformation he felt taking place within him.

"Yesterday, I didn't know if I could ever change, "Biscuit thought, gripping the steering wheel tighter. But now, maybe there is hope for me yet."

The following morning, Biscuit woke up with a determination he hadn't felt in years. Before he could even brush his teeth, he found himself drawn to the black book hidden in a drawer—a reminder of the many women he had wronged in his life.

"Enough is enough," Biscuit muttered under his breath, feeling a surge of resolve. He began tearing out pages, each symbolizing another piece of his tarnished past. Some pages were more challenging to rip than others, memories of relationships that still held a lingering sting. Setting those aside on the table, he resolved to deal with them later.

After brushing his teeth and splashing cold water on his face, Biscuit returned to the task. He stared at the remaining pages, hesitating for a moment before finally tearing them to shreds, just as he had done with the rest. The sound of ripping paper echoed through the empty room, punctuating the finality of his decision.

"God, give me strength," Biscuit whispered, his hands shaking slightly as he let the pieces fall into the wastebasket.

With every torn page, he felt like he was shedding more of the baggage that had weighed him down for so long. As the last remnants of his black book were destroyed, Biscuit could feel a sense of lightness settling into his heart.

"Maybe I can be the man I was meant to be," he thought, the faintest hint of a smile playing at the corners of his mouth. "For my friends, the Steele family... and myself."

This newfound determination would guide Biscuit as he faced the challenges ahead—a journey of redemption that would change his life and touch the lives of those around him.

Biscuit stood in front of the bathroom mirror, tears and water dripping from his face, making it hard to distinguish between them. His eyes held a sense of determination that hadn't been there before. "I fully trust you, God," he said quietly, the words feeling both foreign and familiar on his lips.

Later that day, Biscuit found himself walking into a nice jewelry store on the west side of Chicago. The bell above the door chimed softly, announcing his arrival. The glittering rows of rings seemed to stretch on forever, making his heart race with anxiety.

"Can I help you find something?" asked the saleswoman, her voice warm and welcoming.

"Uh, yeah. I'm looking for a ring," Biscuit replied, trying to sound more confident than he felt.

"An engagement ring, perhaps?" she asked, a knowing smile on her lips.

Biscuit nodded, fighting the urge to wipe his sweaty palms on his pants. "What's the price range for these?"

The saleswoman led him to a display case filled with beautiful engagement rings. She began listing prices, and with each number, Biscuit felt his heart pounding harder. Despite the anxiety, he couldn't help but think that this was the right thing to do—a way to show his commitment to Pam and the journey he had begun.

"Take your time," the saleswoman said gently, sensing his hesitation. I'll be here if you have any questions."

"Thank you," Biscuit replied, his voice barely above a whisper.

As he gazed at the rows of shining diamonds, Biscuit couldn't help but think about the Steele family and how they had welcomed him with open arms. He thought about Pam and how her eyes lit up when she smiled. Finally, he thought about the man he was becoming—ready to face his past mistakes and build a better future.

"Lord, I'm putting my trust in you," Biscuit murmured as he reached for a particularly stunning ring, its modest price tag a small comfort. He would find a way to make it work, just as he was finding a way to rebuild his life one step at a time.

The afternoon sun cast a golden glow over the bustling streets of Chicago's West Side. Cars honked, people shouted, and the savory aroma of Italian beef drifted through the air as Biscuit walked into the cozy eatery that he and Calvin had frequented for years. The familiar white checkered tablecloths and vintage photographs on the walls welcomed him like an old friend.

"Hey, Biscuit! You made it!" Calvin called out from a corner booth, his smile warm and inviting. Biscuit slid into the seat across from him, feeling the weight of the ring in his pocket like a secret treasure.

"Man, I'm Starving," Biscuit said, picking up a napkin to wipe the sweat from his brow. "You already ordered?"

"Of course," Calvin replied with a chuckle."You know I can't resist these Italian beef sandwiches."

As if on cue, the waitress arrived with two towering sandwiches, their juices dripping onto the plates below. Biscuit's mouth watered at the sight, and without wasting any time, they both dug in, letting the flavorful juices run down their arms as they enjoyed every bite.

"Calvin, I've been meaning to ask you something," Biscuit started, pausing between bites of his sandwich. How did you know Lena was the one? And how is it living with a wife?"

Calvin almost choked on his food, his eyes widening in surprise. He took a moment to compose himself before responding. "Biscuit, I never thought I'd hear you ask about marriage," he said, his voice filled with genuine curiosity."But answering your question was simple forme. It has nothing to do with Lena being gorgeous or how to live with a wife. God led me to someone's spirit that I can't live without, and together, no man can put us where God is taking us. When that happens, that's your wife."

Biscuit stared at his friend momentarily, processing the depth of his words. A mixture of anxiety and hope bubbled inside him like the fizz of a soda pop. "I think I've found someone like that, too," he admitted quietly, his heart pounding.

"Really?"Calvin asked, his face lighting up with excitement. "Who's the lucky lady?"

"Promise you won't laugh?" Biscuit said nervously, wiping the juices from his hands with a napkin. "It's Pam. You know, Ruth's daughter."

"Man, that's amazing!" Calvin exclaimed, clapping his friend on the shoulder. You two would be great together. But remember, it's about more than love—it's about walking this journey hand in hand with God leading the way."

Biscuit nodded, feeling the weight of responsibility that came with such a commitment. As they continued to share their meal, laughter, and stories, he couldn't help but feel grateful for the friendship and support he had found in the Steele family. Each day, he grew stronger in faith and love, ready to embrace the path ahead.

The sun dipped low in the sky, casting a warm golden glow over the church's brick facade as Bible study attendees began to arrive. Biscuit sat in his car, drumming his fingers on the steering wheel, his heart pounding with anticipation. He glanced down at the small velvet box resting beside him, the ring nestled inside shimmering like a promise.

"Alright," he whispered to himself, taking a deep breath. "Tonight's the night. I'm ready."

As Biscuit watched more familiar faces of the congregation gather, exchanging hugs and greetings, he felt a stirring within him—a desire for change, growth, and something more substantial than the life he had been living.

"Look at that," he murmured, noticing Pam and Ruth making their way toward the entrance, laughter and affection radiating between them. The sight of Pam stirred something deep within Biscuit, an unshakable feeling that she was the one God had chosen for him.

"Okay, okay," he said, gathering his courage. He picked up the ring box, tucking it securely into his coat pocket, and stepped out of the car.

"Evening, ladies," Biscuit called out, striding toward Pam and Ruth. Pam looked up, her eyes brightening with surprise and delight.

"Hey there, Biscuit!" Ruth greeted him warmly, pulling him into a brief hug. Pam told me about the beautiful dinner you shared the other night."

"Ah, yes, it was lovely," Biscuit replied, smiling at Pam. Her chocolate cheeks flushed with color, and he couldn't help but feel a surge of pride, knowing he had contributed to creating such a special memory for her.

"Y'all heading into Bible study?" Biscuit asked, trying to keep his voice casual despite the nerves twisting in his gut."Mind if I join you?"

"Of course not!" Ruth replied, gesturing for him to walk with them. "The more, the merrier."

As they approached the church doors, Biscuit couldn't help but think back to his earlier conversation with Calvin. He had asked about knowing when someone was"the one" and how it felt to live with a wife. Now, as he walked beside Pam, he realized that he, too, had found someone whose spirit connected with him in a way he had never experienced before.

"Lord," he prayed silently, his heart swelling with hope and determination. Guide me and give me the strength to be the man Pam deserves, the man you want me to be."

With each step toward the church, Biscuit felt more confident than ever about his future, his decision, and the love blossoming between him and Pam. As they entered the building together, he knew that this night would be one to remember—a turning point in both their lives.

Pam and Ruth'slaughter filled the evening air like sweet music, causing Biscuit to smile even wider. "That's right," he chuckled, rubbing the back of his neck."No food here is tonight. I came here for something else entirely."

"Then you're in the right place," Ruth said warmly, her eyes twinkling with kindness. She patted Biscuit's arm and guided them toward the sanctuary entrance. As they stepped inside, Biscuit felt a mixture of excitement and anxiety course through him.

The sanctuary energized as everyone settled into their seats, waiting for the Pastor to begin. Biscuit fidgeted, his fingers tapping in an erratic rhythm on his knee as he scanned the room, a myriad of thoughts racing through his mind. 'I'm doing this,' he thought. For the first time, my heart is truly open.'

When the Pastor Finally entered, the atmosphere shifted. The room fell silent, and all eyes were on him. But before the man could even utter a word, Biscuit stood up, his voice clear and strong: "Pastor, can I be baptized today?"

Murmurs rippled through the congregation as shock gave way to praise. The Pastor's eyes widened in surprise, but a warm smile spread."Biscuit," he said, walking toward him, "I am pleased to hear that you have decided to get baptized and want to do it today."

"Is it okay with everyone here?" Biscuit asked, his voice wavering slightly. "I'd like to do it right now."

As the Pastor Looked around the room, a chorus of affirmations rose, echoing off the walls."Yes, do it right now!" the people declared, their voices united in support and encouragement.

Feeling a swell of gratitude, Biscuit nodded, his heart pounding. 'I'm ready, Lord,' he thought. Guide me and make me whole.

The Pastor's Voice echoed through the sanctuary like a gentle breeze, carrying the weight of years. "Well, the people have spoken. Biscuit, if you want to do it now, follow me to the pool." The congregation began to sing hymns, their voices harmonizing and filling the air with unity and love as they approached the baptismal pool.

Standing at the water's edge, Biscuit couldn't help but feel the enormity of what he was about to do. His heart raced, and his palms were clammy with anticipation. He looked around, seeing the familiar faces of those who had prayed for him over the years and couldn't hold back his emotions any longer.

"Pastor," he said, his voice cracking, "can I speak first?"

The Pastor smiled gently, nodding. "Of course, Biscuit. That is how this goes, with your confession that you accept Jesus as your savior. The floor is yours."

Taking a deep breath, Biscuit turned to face the congregation. He could see Calvin and LenaSteele, their eyes filled with hope and compassion. Junior and Ryder stood by their parents, their young faces open and expectant.

"Thank you all for being here," Biscuit began, struggling to keep his voice steady. "I... I realize it's time for me to be responsible for the messes I've created in my past, the ones others always had to clean up. I've hurt the ones I love and those who love me." His gaze lingered on the Steele family, feeling the weight of his words. "I want to apologize to you all, especially the Steeles. I ask for your forgiveness, and thank you for your grace and mercy on me."

As if responding to an unspoken cue, the congregation spoke in unison: "We forgive you, Biscuit."

The Pastor stepped forward, his eyes compassionate. "Remember, Biscuit, grace comes from God. Even when you see it on people's faces, it comes from Him. Some people, at times, may not have a pleasant look on their faces. Just remember grace comes from God."

Biscuit nodded, taking in the Pastor's words, feeling a newfound purpose and determination. With God's grace and the forgiveness of those he cared about, he was ready to face the future and put his past behind him. All that remained was the cleansing waters of baptism, a symbol of rebirth that would mark the beginning of his new life.

"Grace," the Pastor continued, his voice gentle but firm, "is God's redemption at Christ's expense. Do you understand?"

Biscuit wiped the tears from his face, nodding as he took in the profound words. The church fell silent, the moment's weight hanging heavy in the air.

"By your confession that Jesus is your Lord and Savior, Pastor declared, "I now baptize you in the name of the Father, the Son, and the Holy Spirit."He gently guided Biscuit beneath the water's surface, a symbolic cleansing of his sins and his past.

As Biscuit emerged from the water, the congregation erupted in joyous celebration. Blinking away the droplets running down his face, Pam was the first person he sought out. Her eyes shone with pride and happiness as she met his gaze.

"Could you please get the box in my coat pocket?"Biscuit began, his voice shaking.

Looking shocked, Pam glanced at her mother before she reached into his coat to retrieve the small box. As Biscuit approached Pam, still dripping wet from his baptism, he couldn't help but feel his heart race with anticipation.

Dropping to one knee before her, he opened the box to reveal the ring inside. "Pam," he said, his voice filled with love and hope, "will you marry me?"

Pam seemed unable to speak for a moment, her emotions overwhelming her. Then, with tears in her eyes, she nodded and whispered, "Yes."

The entire congregation gathered around them, showering them with love and congratulations. Biscuit could feel their warmth and support, a powerful reminder that despite his past mistakes, he had found redemption and forgiveness through God's grace.

As he stood hand in hand with Pam and surrounded by friends and family, Biscuit knew this was only the beginning. A new chapter in his life had just begun, filled with love, faith, and the promise of a brighter future.

The End

***Recipe for Giving Grace**
Ingredients:*

- *1 cup of Empathy*
- *two tablespoons of Patience*
- *A dash of Humility*
- *one teaspoon of Forgiveness*
- *A handful of Understanding*
- *A sprinkle of Kindness*
- *An open heart*
- *A generous portion of Time*

***Instructions:**

Prepare Your Mindset: Set aside any judgments or preconceived notions. Clear your mind of negativity and open it to seeing things from another's perspective.*

***Combine Empathy and Patience:** In a large mixing bowl, gently blend 1 cup of Empathy with two tablespoons of Patience. Empathy will allow you to feel what others are feeling, while Patience will help you give them the Time and space they need.*

***Add a Dash of Humility:** Stir in a dash of Humility, remembering that none of us are perfect. This will help you to lower your defenses and accept others as they are.*

Mix in Forgiveness: *Carefully fold in 1 teaspoon of Forgiveness. It can be challenging to let go of hurt, but Forgiveness is a critical ingredient in Grace. Mix until well combined.*

Incorporate Understanding: *Gradually add a handful of Understanding, taking the Time to listen to and comprehend the perspectives and experiences of others.*

Season with Kindness: *Sprinkle generously with Kindness. A kind word or action can go a long way in showing someone you care and that they are valued.*

Open Your Heart: *Ensure your heart is open and receptive, ready to give and receive love and Grace without reservation.*

Let It Simmer: *Allow the mixture to sit and simmer over Time. Grace often needs Time to develop fully, so be patient and consistent in your efforts.*

Serve with Love: *Serve your Grace with a generous portion of Time. The more time you invest in others, the more Grace you can give. Share freely and abundantly.*

Yield:

An endless supply of Grace is enough to nurture and transform relationships, one person at a time.

Enjoy the profound and rewarding experience of giving Grace, and watch as it spreads, enriching the lives of everyone it touches.